edge of glory

a romance

rachel spangler

Bywater BOOKS

Ann Arbor
2017

Bywater Books

Print ISBN: 978-1-61294-109-7

Bywater Books First Edition: October 2017

Printed in the United States of America on acid-free paper.

Cover designer: Ann McMan, TreeHouse Studio

Back cover photo credit: Will Banks

Bywater Books
PO Box 3671
Ann Arbor MI 48106-3671
www.bywaterbooks.com

For Susie: This one goes to eleven,
which of course is all your fault.

Prologue

March 16, 2016
St. Moritz, Switzerland

"The last skier of the day is our current World Cup leader, Elise Brandeis," a male commentator said somewhere behind her. She couldn't tell if someone had a TV or radio in one of the official tents, or if perhaps one of the techs was watching online.

"It's certainly her race to lose," a female voice added. "The young American has been a force to be reckoned with all season long, and she owned this course in practice all week."

"She's certainly been a cut above the rest all week, throwing down faster times with each run, but we've seen her blow a lead before."

Elise closed her eyes and pulled on her helmet. She didn't need to hear any more. She didn't need anyone to give voice to the refrain that haunted her every start, her every turn, her every crouch for years.

"Conditions are growing worser," Paolo said close to her ear, his thick Argentinean accent always more pronounced when he got amped up. "You saw the rut on Helga's run."

She nodded solemnly. She'd seen the number five skier in the world take a back-cracking bounce out of turn four before she'd managed to right herself. Helga would likely spend some quality time with the Swiss team chiropractor in the week ahead, but she'd still managed to finish with a decent time.

"Every person who hits that spot packs it down more harder," Paolo said.

She nodded again and rocked back and forth on her skis in the ruts the women before her had made while sliding up to the starting gate.

"You go just a little around it and get the same time."

"To the inside," she muttered.

"No, Elise." He drew out her name to sound like, Eeee-Lease. "Outside. You're so far ahead in practice. Four inches in one turn won't hurt you. You stay safe. You don't bounce. You win."

"It's getting softer," she said, no longer referring to the spot he'd isolated, but the entire mountainside. The full afternoon sun made for the beautiful pictures that filled Austrian travel brochures, but it also slowed down the snow, and by extension her skis. Her stomach clenched. She'd rather ski a sheet of ice than slush. Competitors and teammates alike called her the ice queen for several reasons, and only a few of them had to do with her personality.

"Outside, Elise," Paolo reiterated. "One hair outside. Tiny."

The start referee motioned her forward, and she slid her skis between the starting posts. The only thing between her and the course now was a start wire that would snap back the moment she pressed against it. Placing her poles carefully over the line, she fixed her grip. The first of her three pulse warnings blared.

Beep. Breathe in, breathe out, rock back.

Beep. Breathe in, breathe out, crouch.

Beep. Explode.

She jumped, pushing off with her knees and poles as she angled forward as far as she could and let gravity catch hold. One pump, she pushed off again with her poles. Two pumps, she pushed with her right leg as the wind began to whistle. Three pumps, a push with the left leg, and she lowered her head. She'd been over this course so many times she could've seen the line she wanted even in the dark. Poles up now, she pushed once more with each leg before ducking into a tuck. Butt down, spine curved, chin up, she leaned into the first curve. Roaring around

2

the bend, she took flight for several yards. She held her form, not moving so much as a finger while her skis cut through the air above the snow.

Angling her body toward the second turn, she remained low and slid her right leg wide. She held steady, both skis slicing across the snow, until her sharp edges did their job and held her on a perfect pitch into turn two. She heard nothing but the whir of the wind and the rush of her own breath cresting through her head.

Shifting her body weight out of the curve and onto the flat, she aligned herself for a small jump. She set her form as the snow dropped out from under her, and once again she shot through the air in a textbook tuck. Her poles molded along the curves of her crouch, and she felt as if the wind didn't even recognize her presence as she flowed weightlessly over the course.

Landing effortlessly, one flick of her eyes across the snow confirmed she'd set up exactly the way she wanted to for turn three, but her skis chattered through the flat as they cut across the ruts made by previous skiers. Her breath broke rhythm as she processed the development. One tenth of a second lost, she figured as she smoothed back into her favored line for turn three, but the prime position couldn't shake the whispers. *Two tenths.*

Pulling her chest lower, she led with her chin, jaw set. She tried to hold her pose through the wide arc of the turn, but between the little drop-off on the outside and the softening snow, one of her skis bit off more than she wanted to chew, and her shoulder rolled back. Suddenly the wind was no longer her ally. The brunt of Old Man Winter's wrath landed a lancing blow to her open chest. She had to rise a full inch or two out of her crouch to hold.

Time. Precious seconds whirred past as she righted her body once more. How much time had she lost now? Half a second? More? The refrain beat like a drum. *Two tenths. Zero point two.* Each breath wheezed the painful reminder. She could've done more. She had to do more.

At nearly seventy miles an hour now, she felt turn four coming even before she saw the flag. The mountain had a natural fall line, one she'd ridden to record-splitting times in practice, one she could no longer count on. Onto the straightaway, onto her angle, onto her edges as she leaned toward the turn. In the full sun, she caught the glint of the ridge Paolo'd warned of. She couldn't hit it. She couldn't afford another tenth of a second. She couldn't afford the six inches on the outside.

Two tenths.

Zero point two.

Bending her right knee all the way to her sternum, she cut hard against the snow, against the wind, against centrifugal force to the inside. Every muscle tightened as she tried to bend Earth and time to her will. The mountain moved beneath her as if tilting to accommodate her desire, and she cleared the ridge to the inside.

Then, before the sigh of relief could kiss her lips, the snow gave way. A slight slip, a sliver of a second, and the sharp, silver edge bit into the bright red polycarbonate of the gate marking the edge of the course. The faintest of brushes, the lightest touch at seventy miles an hour, a nick was more than enough.

Her left ski continued to hurtle forward as the right one caught. The combined effect sent her body spinning in a barrel roll. Vaguely aware of hurtling through the air, she didn't grasp the full impact of her error until her body bounced. The first impact knocked all the air from her lungs. The second knocked her knee into a back bend.

Her scream died along with her hopes of a world championship. Fighting desperately for air, she sucked in a gasp that ripped through her throat, bringing with it an icy inhale of snow. Still she spun downward across the mountain. Choking on pain and cold, she hit the first fence. A blur of orange shrouded her progress but didn't impinge on her momentum enough to keep her from skittering across on her back and into the second row of neon netting.

The spinning stopped as the pulsing stabs of pain took over. The knife to her knee radiated anguish as the suffocating weight of fence and failure pressed down on her chest, making it impossible to breathe. Icy hands of panic gripped her throat. Voices cried out. Distant footsteps crunched across the snow. Bright light cut through shadows overhead. Her senses faltered as raw pain superseded them all. First the sounds faded. Then the cold gave way to numbness. Finally her vision tinged orange, then gray, then black, and she submitted to nothingness.

Chapter One

July 7, 2017
Lake Henry Olympic Training Center,
Lake Henry, New York

Corey laughed as she pumped the skateboard over the section of rollers and into Nate Walsh's path. She cut him off and mounted the twelve-foot wall in front of her in one fluid arc before reversing course and bobbing back over the set of three small, rolling hills. She tucked a tight line around a high-banked corner in the track, then stayed low as she arced up another short wall. She had the lead, and she'd take it all the way to the top, but on the last run of the day she didn't intend to stop there. Instead of kicking to a halt when she reached the peak, she clutched the middle of her board and exploded through her knees to send her whole body arching, not only over the wall, but also the safety rail. Tapping the metal with the tail of the board for style points, she then curled into a neat little ball and front flipped into a pit of blue foam blocks.

As she lay sprawled on her back, chest rising and falling rapidly, she gave a mock salute to acknowledge the smattering of applause.

"You're such a show-off." Nate leaned on the rail and smiled down at her.

She smiled at the steel rafters above and relaxed back into the foam blocks, the scent of sweat and Lysol filling her nostrils. "It's one of the many things you love about working out with me."

"Working out?" a female voice called from somewhere behind them. "Looked more like screwing off."

Corey flopped onto her stomach and crawled over the blocks to the edge of the pit. "I nailed the rollers. I worked my knees, my calves, and my quads."

"And the acrobatics? Last I checked, they don't award style points for Boardercross."

Corey hauled herself onto the sidewall and hopped up to her feet. "It's called 'air awareness.' It's an essential skill in my line of work."

"Hi, Holly," Nate called.

"Hi, Nato." Holly switched her tone to something more coy. "Did you miss me?"

"Always." He tipped his board back down the wall, but instead of running through the course, he turned hard and rolled onto the mats before hopping off next to them.

"The LaCroix sisters are back together. Training season must be heating up."

"It's July. A lot of things are heating up," Corey said, a hint of frustration in her voice.

"Overland training makes her grumpy," Nate explained.

"Why do you think I went out of town for four weeks?" Holly asked. "I should've stayed gone longer."

"No," Corey said, coming out of her pout. "I'll be in a good mood even when it's hot. I missed you."

Holly smiled sweetly and wrapped her in a hug. "I missed you, too."

She rested her chin on her sister's shoulder and sighed. The team was back together again in a place she loved. All was right with the world.

The doors to the gym swung open, and a camera crew poured in. Long boom mics and bright lights extended overhead as a reporter tried to walk casually beside a young brunette in gray cargo shorts and a bright blue racerback tank.

"We're here at the Lake Henry Olympic Training Center with Nicole Prince to get a little peek inside the world of an Olympic snowboard hopeful. Can you tell us about this room?

"This is one of my favorite rooms in the whole facility," Nikki said as she began to walk them through the various stations.

"Apparently the new blood has arrived as well," Holly said dryly. "What's she like without the cameras on her?"

"Bouncy," Nate said dryly.

"What is she, like seventeen?" Holly asked.

"Barely," Nate said.

Holly slapped him in the stomach. "Don't sound so disappointed. You can use the year before she's legal to work off your beer gut."

"Not even tempted," Nate said. "She's a poodle. I'm more of a golden retriever sort of guy."

Corey winced. Nate didn't have much of a way with women, or words for that matter. Holly didn't seem pleased with the comparison, so she jumped in before they could escalate. "You're more the dog in this scenario, Nate. Besides, The Kid's not bad."

They all turned to watch the teenager turn a few flips and twists on a massive trampoline as she explained her methods. "These exercises aren't pure play. They help with air awareness."

"See?" Corey said. "Air awareness is a real thing."

"Hey, are you Corey LaCroix?" The man wore khakis and a red polo as if he'd escaped from a day job at Target.

She straightened her shoulders. "I am."

"Would you mind giving us a few quotes on camera about Nikki? We're featuring her as the future of the sport, and it'd be great to get some perspective from a veteran like you. Sort of a passing of the torch, you know."

Corey forced a smile. "Sure. Yeah. Happy to."

"Great, let me pull a camera over." Mr. Target-polo ran off.

Both Nate and Holly stared at her, embarrassment crossing their features. Nate spoke first. "Passing the torch, Core?"

"You should've told him to shove the stupid feature and do one on a legit Olympian," Holly piled on.

"It's no big deal. I don't have to be a jackass to beat her. Besides, she can do all the interviews she wants. Interviews don't get you points in the standings."

"They don't hurt with sponsors," Holly said.

"I'm not concerned about those, either. This isn't my sponsor season, or my interview season, or my torch-passing season." The newly familiar urgency built in her chest. "I'm here to ride."

"Hey, Corey, stand here." Mr. Target-uniform grabbed her bicep and spun her around so they could get Nikki continuing to bounce on the trampoline behind her. A white light shone hot on her face, and she had to squint until her eyes adjusted. It'd been awhile since she'd faced the cameras, and she felt a lot more rusty in this area than she did on a board.

"What do you think of the new crop of American snowboarders coming up?"

"The American prospects are amazing. Our boarders are faster, stronger, and younger than they've ever been." Corey rolled her head back all the way until she caught sight of Nikki high above them. "They're springy, too."

"And what do you make of their chances at the Olympics this winter?"

"It's an unpredictable sport, but we've put the world on notice." She tried not to put too much emphasis on the "we." "Boardercross has always been a North American stronghold, but we're not resting on our keisters here. We're working out year-round. I mean, look at Tigger up there. She's like a regular Rocky Balboa in moon boots. Probably strikes fear into the hearts of the fiercest competitors."

The camera guy smirked, and she felt the little thrill that always accompanied positive reinforcement. "The sky's the limit, or, well, in this case the ceiling is probably the limit, but you get my drift. The Kid is going up in the world. I expect her to set the bar high."

How much longer could she go on with her tongue planted firmly in her cheek? She could make big air puns all day long.

"And what about you?" He cut her off before she even got halfway through her material. "Ever consider coming out of retirement?"

She tried not to let her jovial camera expression fade, but the muscles in her shoulders tightened. "Actually, I haven't retired. Shocking, I know, at the ripe old age of thirty, but I'm still on the tour, Chad."

"I'm Mike," the interviewer corrected with a twinge of irritation. Nate snickered in the background.

"Sorry, Mike. Any more questions?"

"Do you see this season as sort of your farewell tour?"

This time her jaw did twitch. She felt it, and knew the camera probably caught it, too. The cameras caught everything, so she went ahead and took a second to compose herself. Staring past Target Mike and his lights and all the trappings of fickle fame, she noticed a woman slow to a stop outside the large plate glass windows dividing the gym from the lobby.

She had long, blond hair falling down past her shoulders and eyes such an icy shade of blue they appeared almost translucent from a distance. Something about those eyes sent a chill down her spine. She felt as if she could see right through them, and even more as if they could see through her.

"Uh, Corey?" Target Mike asked.

"Yeah, sorry, what?" she asked, not looking away from the woman.

"Who's that?" he asked in his non-interview tone.

"I don't know."

"It's Elise Brandeis," the cameraman said almost reverently.

"Oh." Mike arched up on his toes as the excitement overtook him. "Let's see if we can get an interview."

He headed for the door, and then almost as an afterthought called out, "Thanks, Corey."

"Wow." Nate laughed. "Shows how you rate. Nice job with calling him the wrong name, though."

"And Tigger? I think you gave the poodle a new nickname," Holly added.

She heard them but didn't respond. Instead she watched a shadow pass over the woman's face as she saw the cameras coming. She wrinkled her brow, lifted her chin, and strode purposefully away. The view from the back wasn't bad either. Her black yoga pants and thin gray T-shirt highlighted a highly honed physical form, but Corey had seen more than her share of athletic bodies. None of them ever came with a set of eyes like those apparently belonging to Elise Brandeis.

"Who is she?"

"Who?" Nate and Holly asked in unison.

She turned back to face them, trying to shake the trance she'd felt while trapped in the woman's gaze. "Elise Brandeis, who is she?"

Holly rolled her eyes. "She's a world champion skier. She was like the biggest thing in winter sports a couple years ago."

"Was?"

"She wrecked. Spectacularly. Do you live under a rock?"

"You know I don't follow skiing like you do."

"I'm sure I mentioned it," Holly said, then shook her head. "I guess I should've shown you a picture."

"Even I've heard of her," Nate said. "She was in Sochi."

"Forgive me. I was a little busy in Sochi."

Both of them smirked.

"I didn't mean it that way. I had my own events. I didn't have time to watch skiers, but if she's been around so long, why haven't I seen her here before?"

"She's too big a deal to train with mere mortals, or at least she used to be," Holly explained. "She had all the major sponsors, but I guess she lost them after the crash."

"She's only deigned to appear here in order to secure funding on her way back to the top?" Nate asked, disdain in his usually easygoing voice.

"Yeah. I wouldn't expect her to hang around for long."

"Did you see her expression? Icy. Even if she does stick around, I doubt she'd lower herself enough to engage a bunch of board bums like us."

"At least she won't be around long enough to steal any more of your thunder, Corey," Holly said. "Then again, maybe it's good she interrupted that train wreck of an interview."

Corey didn't care nearly as much about the stupid, insulting interview as she did the queasiness she felt at the thought of not getting any time with Elise. "Surely she'll be here for little while though, right?"

Nate laughed and punched her shoulder. "'Cause a little while is all you need, right?"

"No. I meant I . . ." She didn't know what she meant.

"You like a challenge," Holly offered.

"Maybe."

"I suggest you focus on the challenge of the upcoming season," Holly said, "or you're going to get a lot more questions about retirement."

Her stomach tightened another uncomfortable notch, but she dug deep and pulled out the smile she usually felt when pushed. "Let them ask. Doesn't change the fact that they're going to have to scrape me off the side of the mountain someday. I'm not retiring. I'm here to race."

"Are you sure this is a good idea?" Elise asked as she stood in the doorway of dorm room twenty-five.

"What's wrong now?" Paolo asked, sounding even more exhausted than she felt.

Elise lifted her arm in one sweeping motion trying to encompass the whole room, which wasn't hard since the whole room consisted of only 150 square feet.

"It's a dorm room," Paolo said drolly. "Be thankful you have one for yourself."

"I expected something more state of the art."

"You saw the gyms. The equipment is the best, the trainers are the best, the doctors are the best."

"The dorms are not the best," Elise finished for him. The bed seemed narrow under a plain white comforter, not a queen as she'd grown used to, probably not even a full double, and the single dresser didn't appear big enough to hold her summer training clothes, much less her bulky winter gear. Add in a small table, not even the size of most hotel desks, with two wooden chairs, and tour over.

"Also you have your own bathroom," Paolo said excitedly. "No sharing with strangers."

"Why do you keep mentioning this sharing with strangers thing as if you almost expected it?" she asked suspiciously.

"No need to worry about something that might not happen." He waved her off. "Why don't you get settled, and we'll go to the cafeteria."

"Cafeteria," she repeated with a groan.

"You went to boarding school. Shouldn't you be used to this setup?"

"An elite boarding school, not a juvenile detention center. When you pay $70,000 a year, sharing bathrooms with strangers isn't common."

"When *your parents* pay $70,000 a year," Paolo corrected.

The barb stuck under her skin, and her face flamed. He was right, of course. Both the comment and the tone in which she'd delivered it reflected a part of her she wasn't proud of. She took a deep breath and tried again. "I don't have enough money left to keep us in the lap of luxury, but I read online there's a lovely little inn by the lake. We could both be more comfortable without going overboard. They have cabins and homemade blueberry muffins in the morning and no cafeteria."

"Do they have a weight room?"

"Maybe."

"Do they have a masseuse?"

"You don't know; they might."

"Do they have an ice tub and a nutritionist?"

"No." She tried not to sound pouty, but she failed.

"Do they have Olympic ski team officials there to watch you work out? People with the power to nominate you for a spot on the team? Or vote you into the Olympics in less than seven months?"

"No," she said forcefully, then softened her tone once more. "You're right. I'm here to train. I can do this. I will make these Olympics. I'll do whatever I have to do."

He smiled sympathetically. "I know. And I know change is hard for you, but you've come a long way already."

"Not far enough." She shrugged off the frustration that had followed her for a year and tossed her suitcase onto the bed. "Give me ten minutes, and I'll meet you in the cafeteria."

"You can have as much time as you need. They serve dinner all night."

"No. I'm tired of waiting around. If people need to see me get back to work, we'll do a nice public dinner followed by an even more public evening workout. Then I'll report to the trainers for an eval."

He opened his mouth, then paused and nodded. "Okay. Back to work."

He shut the door behind him, and she entered her private bathroom. She splashed some cold water on her face as she muttered. "Back to work."

She'd never left work. Not since the minute she'd woken up in a Swiss hospital. Every single step of this journey had been work. And pain. So much pain. At least she'd have less of that here than she'd had in the rehab clinic. She'd grown used to a certain amount of discomfort, and she'd overcome all of it. Surely the Lake Henry Olympic Training Center wouldn't be the thing to break her.

Chapter Two

"Ah, my favorite restaurant," Holly said, in a voice similar to the one she used when talking to a man she intended to brush off. Holly had perfected the "let 'em down easy" routine.

"Does it feel like your first day back at school?" Nate teased. "What if the cool kids don't want you to sit with them?"

"What do you mean?" Corey asked. "Holly always was the cool kid."

"That's right," Holly said. "And if I let you sit with me, people will think you're cool, too."

Corey shook her head as she grabbed a plain white plate and got into line at the main chef station. Holly veered off toward the salad bar, and Nate made a beeline for the panini press. Typical.

As she waited behind a group of men's hockey players, she scanned the cafeteria. There wasn't a huge crowd in July. Athletes came and went year-round, but mostly for short training sessions or camps. She was one of only a handful of Olympians who called Lake Henry home. Most of the other boarders chose to train at the Park City Olympic Center, but she didn't see any need to move halfway across the country when she had everything she needed in her own back yard. She spent an undue amount of time with archers, skaters, and any number of high school and college groups, but with this being a Winter

Olympics year, most of the big names would pass through at some point. She kept her eyes open for kindred spirits.

She inched up in line as the hockey heads began to find their seats. The smells of sweat and baked chicken lingered in their wake.

"Big crew tonight, Mac?" she asked her favorite cook.

"Not too bad. The hockey heads, your crew, and the young boarder who chatters all the time."

"Tigger's already been in? Probably still has a curfew."

He grinned as he slid a chicken sandwich with an extra slice of cheese onto her plate, but he wouldn't join in the reindeer games, and she respected him for it. "Oh, and the new skier's here."

She glanced up at him quickly, then out across the cafeteria. "Where?"

"She and her coach are at the long table around the corner."

Corey had to fight from craning her neck. "Cool."

His grin widened as he scooped on a large helping of steamed vegetables, but all he said as he slid her plate back was, "Enjoy your meal."

"Thanks." Corey headed back to the middle of the cafeteria.

Holly was already there waiting for Nate's panini to finish. "Usual spot?"

"Actually, remember how you were talking about this being like the first day of school?"

"What, you mean two minutes ago? No, I forgot already."

"Right, well I know you're senile and all, but there are some new kids over there." She tried to act casual as she nodded to the area Mac had indicated. "Maybe we should go welcome them or, you know, haze them. Either way's cool."

Holly glanced over her shoulder, her grin slow as she shook her head. "You're seriously gonna go there?"

Corey shrugged. "Trying to be friendly. You don't have to come with."

"Oh, I wouldn't miss this for the world," Holly said as Nate joined them. "Come on, Nato, let's go watch Core get burned."

"I'm so in," Nate agreed gleefully.

16

Corey ignored them as she carried her plate over to the table Elise shared with her trainer. "Hey, mind if we join you?"

Elise glanced up, her icy eyes even more startling up close. Corey froze as Elise flicked her gaze quickly over her. She didn't dare get any closer until given permission, something Elise obviously didn't intend to offer. "Actually, we're in the middle of something."

"Something that can wait," the trainer said, rising and extending his hand. "I'm Paolo Diaz. Please join us, Ms. LaCroix."

She welcomed the warmth of being recognized after the chill from Elise. Shaking off the cold breeze, she claimed the seat next to Elise. An opening was an opening; she didn't need a big one. Flashing her most winning smile, she added, "Everyone calls me Corey."

"And you're Nate Walsh," Paolo said. "I saw a video of your weight training regimen last year. I'd love to talk to you sometime about exercises that transfer stress from the lower body to the core."

"Sure, man." Nate plopped down next to him.

"And . . ." Holly cleared her throat, "I'm the big sister, not that either of these two would make polite introductions. You can call me Holly, or you could ignore me."

"She's kidding," Corey said.

"You can't ignore her," Nate added.

"Why would you want to?" Paolo asked, giving her a completely different once-over than the one Elise used. It was the reaction Corey was used to having directed at her, but maybe that ran in the gene pool, because Holly never had any trouble in the appreciative appraisal department, either. They both had the same golden hair and eyes, but Holly had their mother's build, taller, thinner, while Corey favored their father's muscle tone and strong jawline. Women and men usually knew instinctually which sister would be more receptive to their attention.

"Please, Holly, come sit by me and tell me a little bit about your amazing hometown."

Paolo clearly knew enough about them to realize they could be useful. Elise showed none of the same awareness or interest.

She cut her plain chicken breast into tiny bites and chewed slowly.

"So, how long are you in for?" Corey asked.

"Excuse me?" Elise asked, not looking up from the steamed asparagus she'd begun to slice into evenly measured pieces.

"The Olympic Training Center. I've never seen you here before, so I figured you must be visiting for a camp. How long does it run?"

Elise searched her eyes for a second before turning back to her food. "As long as it takes."

"As long as what takes?"

"Everything," Elise said coolly.

She glanced at Nate, who smothered a grin behind his panini.

Not much of a conversationalist, Corey noted, and bit off about a quarter of her sandwich at once.

Elise ate more deliberately, meticulously, but she didn't waste any time either. She speared one small piece of chicken, then one equally proportioned bite of asparagus, and put them both in her mouth at the same time. While she chewed, she'd start the spearing process over. Her repetitive movements had an efficiency Corey found almost hypnotizing.

"You're here for the duration of overland season, then?" Corey asked once again, flashing a smile she hoped showed her to be jovial even in the face of adversity.

Elise halted the tiny bite parade only long enough to say, "If need be."

Shut down again. The answers weren't rude exactly, but not friendly either. She should've bowed out. She'd made a genuine attempt to be nice, and Elise clearly didn't appreciate the gesture. Maybe Holly'd been right and the skier was a massive snob, but something wouldn't let her walk away yet. Maybe she liked the challenge of cracking the icy resolve, maybe she was bored with the usual fare, or maybe something in those eyes held her captive. She didn't consider herself overly superstitious, but she trusted her gut, and it gave a disconcerting little twitch every time Elise hit her with that translucent stare.

"I hear we had a near miss in Sochi."

Elise shook her head, and her shoulders dropped in sadness or maybe exasperation, but she didn't look up this time, and her voice sounded drained. "Nice. Real nice."

"What?" Corey glanced around in time to see Holly grimace. "What did I say? I thought we were both in Sochi?"

"You were both in Sochi. I think you meant you may have even crossed paths without knowing it. Right?" Holly clearly tried to cover for whatever mistake Corey had made.

"Of course. That's what I meant. We nearly crossed paths in Sochi."

"Are you kidding me?" Elise mumbled.

"You'll have to forgive Elise." Paolo sounded slightly embarrassed. "She's jet-lagged."

"Oh?" Holly picked up the slack. "Where did you guys come in from?"

"Park City."

"Were you working out there?" Corey tried addressing Elise again.

"It was work related."

"Medical Center?" Nate asked.

"Orthopedic imaging," Paolo answered for her, which won him one of the sharp glares Elise shared liberally. "She doesn't like to talk about it."

"Fair enough." Corey bit her sandwich down another quarter. She didn't much care for injury talk, either. Some boarders thought it bad luck. She didn't believe in jinxes, but what was the point of dwelling on the depressing aspects of the sport when there was so much to love? "What's next on the agenda? Medical? Massage? A scotch on the rocks? We could help point you in the right direction."

Elise finished her last perfectly balanced bite and dabbed her mouth with a paper napkin. "I'm sure we'll find our own way around, thank you."

"Actually, we'd better turn in early tonight," Paolo said, even though he didn't seem happy about it. "But maybe tomorrow if you guys have time in between training sessions, you could show us around?"

"Sure thing," Corey said, trying to end the evening on a hopeful note. "We'll be in the weight room first thing tomorrow morning, then yoga at eleven o'clock."

"Sounds like a good schedule for a first day out, don't you think, Elise?"

"We need to check in with some people before we make those decisions," Elise said matter-of-factly.

"Maybe Corey could offer a few insights in that department, too," Paolo said pointedly.

Elise gave a noncommittal nod and rose gracefully, but before she could walk away, Paolo added, "You don't win two Olympic medals without learning a few things about the USSA, right Corey?"

Elise froze. Her back and shoulders went rigid as she turned her head slowly from Paolo to Corey, her cold eyes bright with an emotion Corey couldn't quite place. Confusion? Suspicion? Envy? Or maybe just a spark of life that hadn't been there a moment earlier. The effect warmed Corey through to the point she forgot she'd been asked a question until Nate kicked her under the table.

"Huh?" she asked with a little jerk. "What?"

Paolo grinned and Holly snickered. "You know a thing or two about the USSA?"

"Yep, it stands for 'United States Ski and Snowboard Association,' right? But wait, that's too many 's' words."

"Brilliant." Elise shook her head. "There's my cue to call it a night."

Then she turned and left.

Paolo appeared torn between politeness and the need to go after her. In the end, loyalty won out, but as he hurried off, he called, "Sorry, we've had a long day. We will find you tomorrow when everyone is less sleepier."

They watched them, all a bit in shock from the abrupt departure. Finally Corey asked, "Was it something I said?"

Nate laughed, then dropped the remainder of his panini to his plate, and made a crashing sound.

"'Too many s-words,'" Holly repeated. "That's going to go down as one of your all-time great quotes."

"I don't know what you're talking about. I thought things went well."

"Oh yeah, from an entertainment standpoint," Nate said.

"She'll be back," Corey said.

Holly shook her head. "She thinks you dissed her hard with the near-miss comment."

"Why?"

"She missed the podium in Sochi by like a sliver of a second . . . twice."

Her chest tightened, but she flashed another bravado-laced smile. "Almost four years ago. Who even remembers stuff like that?"

"I remember it," Holly said. "I'm pretty sure she still does. And I'm also pretty sure she kind of hates you now."

"No one hates me. I'm freaking adorable. You watch, she'll be back."

"Dude," Nate sighed. "It's so over."

"You're wrong. She likes me." She grinned and stuffed the rest of her sandwich into her mouth while they both laughed. Okay, maybe 'like' wasn't the right word, but something had shifted in Elise for a few seconds. This wasn't over. She didn't know what it was, or why, but she recognized the spark of something powerful in those translucent eyes, and for whatever reason, the spark had been pointed at her.

When it came to Elise Brandeis, she was just getting started.

"Two medals." Elise mumbled as she rocked a steady rhythm on the elliptical machine. A bronze and a gold. She picked up her speed another notch. "Freakin' snowboarders."

"Pace," Paolo called from across the room. He probably hadn't even looked up from the weight machines he'd been inspecting the whole time. He could tell from the sound if she was working too hard too soon. She'd been cleared to return to a full training regimen two days ago, but he wanted to ease her back in. She found the caution frustrating. It wasn't as if she'd spent the last year sitting on the couch with her leg up. They'd begun rehabbing less than twenty-four hours after her last surgery, but she couldn't say so to him. He knew. He'd been there. He'd been the only one. She reined in her motions once more.

"I thought you'd be in a better mood after going to bed early," he called.

She grunted.

"You did go to sleep early, yes?"

"Early enough."

"You don't like the bed here?"

"It's fine." She'd actually found the bed much more comfortable than expected. Despite the smaller size, the mattress was high quality and couldn't be blamed for keeping her awake. No, that honor went to Corey LaCroix and her goofy smile. Though maybe if she had two Olympic medals and a couple of world championships in her pocket, she'd smile all the time, too. Then again, if she'd chosen a sport like snowboarding instead of the more technical discipline of Alpine skiing, she would probably have some medals by now.

"What were you researching this time?" Paolo walked over and checked the screen tracking her heart rate, blood pressure, and oxygen levels.

"Just going over some video," she said noncommittally.

"Videos of you?"

"No, some random competitions."

"Snowboarding competitions, maybe?"

Her rhythm faltered, only for a second, but he caught it.

"Do you have a tracker on my computer?"

He laughed softly. "I don't have to spy. You have mumbled 'freakin' snowboarders' three times since you started your run."

This was one of many reasons she didn't play poker despite Paolo's constant invitations to do so.

"Corey left an impression last night, no?"

"I didn't even know who she was."

"She's a freakin' snowboarder," he said with a grin, "one with two Olympic medals and a pocket full of world championships."

"In snowboarding," Elise qualified.

"Do you think that makes her lesser than any world-class athlete?"

She did, which probably made her a snob, which she hated, but it didn't change the way she felt. The sports couldn't be compared. Corey wasn't even a freestyle or half-pipe snowboarder. Boardercross was a cross between BMX and a mountainside bar fight. She'd met a few boarders over the years, and they always reminded her of pot-smoking skateboarders in teen movies. They said things like "dude," and "bro," and "wicked" or "sick," or some other term du jour for people crashing into each other. She'd admit the sport required a certain set of talents, but none of them had anything in common with her skill set. She imagined Corey spent as much time working on her keg stands as she did working out.

"She can help us here, Elise," Paolo said seriously. "This is her hometown. She knows everyone. She grew up with these trainers, these doctors, these officials. They like her."

"And they don't like me."

"I didn't say that."

"You didn't have to. I know I've never gotten any votes for Miss Congeniality. I'm not here to win a popularity contest. I'm a serious athlete."

"Corey proves you can be likable and win. You can have friends *and* world championships."

The comment stung, but she didn't break her stride.

"Besides," Paolo continued, "if you're serious about getting back on the team, you'll take any edge you can get, and Corey knows this facility like her own playground."

"I bet she treats it like a playground, too."

He laughed. "Probably, but a little bit of play wouldn't hurt you right now, either. You've had less appealing playmates."

The comment finally broke her focus completely, and she slowed enough to give him a disapproving stare.

"The glare doesn't work on me anymore. I'm the only person who's not afraid of you."

True, but she didn't have to agree with everything he said, and her personal life was the place where she usually took her stand. She fought for her privacy with a tenacity almost on par with her fight for a world championship. She wouldn't risk her reputation for anyone, especially for the likes of Corey LaCroix. "She's not my type."

"Uh-huh," Paolo said, barely hiding a grin behind his clipboard.

She slowed all the way to a stop and grabbed a towel to mop the sweat off her neck. She didn't like whatever he'd insinuated. She'd never let a personal relationship get in the way of her goals, and the times she had allowed herself any sort of personal release, she'd always chosen like-minded women. Classy women. Driven women. Women with similar levels of tact and discretion. Perhaps she could be physically attracted to Corey's golden quality, from her amber and honey hair to her hazel eyes that hinted at a mischievousness she lacked in her own life. If she were the type of woman who had extra time, or was prone to flings or misadventures, she might have to worry about distractions.

Annoyance mixed with something unsettling deep in her stomach as her mind wandered to more specific images of exactly what those distractions might entail. She'd never come anywhere near the level of distraction someone like Corey could present, and she didn't intend to start now.

Shaking her head, she hopped off the elliptical. She wouldn't even go there in her mind. "I'll do whatever I have to do to get back on the team. If that means making nice with locals and snowboarders, then I will, but it's all a means to the same end."

"Okay." Paolo relented. "Whatever you say."

"I say it's time to get back to work."

Corey broke into a massive grin as she swung wide the door to the yoga studio. There, rolling out an electric blue mat, in all her stretchy-pants glory, was Elise Brandeis, and damned if she didn't have some junk in her trunk. In her regular clothes she'd appeared lithe and fit, but the curve-hugging getup revealed thighs so muscular they could probably crack a walnut . . . or someone's neck.

"Whoa," Nate said from behind her, alerting Elise to their presence.

"What?" Holly asked, craning her neck around them both to get a better view as Elise straightened up and glanced over her shoulder. Her polite smile twitched into something tighter as she recognized them. Corey's grin never faltered, though. How could it in the face of such good fortune?

"Move along, dirtbags." Holly shoved Corey more fully into the room. "Good morning, Elise."

"Hello, Holly? Right?"

Holly nodded, giving no indication how she felt about Elise remembering her name, then her voice dropped into the more personal register that made Corey marvel. "Hi, Paolo."

Paolo? Corey hadn't even noticed his presence in the room.

"Hi, Holly." He beamed at her. "I've been hoping we'd run into you all again."

"Really?" Corey asked, recovering from the spike in hormones Elise's backside had caused. "When I didn't see you for almost a week, I thought you guys might be avoiding us."

"Never," Paolo said cheerfully and scooted his mat over to make space for them.

Holly took the opening between him and Elise, but Corey never set up in the front row even when the view from the back wasn't as appealing as today.

She grabbed one of the community mats from a wall rack and unfurled it behind Elise. "What about you, Ms. Brandeis? Had you been hoping to run into me again?"

Elise raised one arm above her head before catching the elbow in her other hand and pulling it down behind her as she seemed to ponder the question. "I can't say as I'd given the prospect much thought."

Nate fake-coughed to cover his mumbled, "Burn."

Corey had felt worse, though. "I'll assume you're pleasantly surprised."

A few more people she didn't recognize filtered in as she flopped onto her back and tried to simultaneously inventory her aching muscles while watching Elise stretch. She did an admirable job of conveying disinterest, but every time the door opened, her eyes flicked up as she did a quick scan of the new arrivals. Was she expecting someone? Hoping for a specific mat buddy? Or did she merely keep her guard up at all times?

The instructor started up some soothing music and assumed his place in front of them.

"Morning, Mikael," Corey called. "How's the new baby?"

"She's not a fan of sleeping," he said, even as he smiled widely.

"Good. Maybe you'll doze during class and we'll get the day off."

"When have you ever needed a day off?"

She tried not to frown at the question. When had she started hoping for days off? "You're right. I was trying to go easy on Nate. You know he's getting kind of old."

Nate didn't argue, but Mikael laughed. "I doubt it. Maybe you should come over and babysit some time."

"Sure, next time your wife is at one of those bigwig USSA meetings, I'll come over and we'll teach the baby a few tricks." She'd only been making conversation, but she caught Paolo and Elise exchange an indecipherable expression. What had she said? Something about babysitting? No, something about the USSA. The topic tripped triggers for those two.

The door swung open once more, and a few adolescents strolled in. Elise did her quick scan, her expression neutral except for a brief furrow of her brow.

"They're archers," Corey whispered as the teens moved to the opposite corner of the studio. "Juniors. Three years out from their first Olympic bid."

Elise nodded once as if letting the info sink in.

"They're here for a two-week camp. Quiet bunch, always travel in packs. For fifteen-year-olds, they're strung pretty tight." She waited a couple of beats before adding, "Get it? Strung tight? They're archers."

Elise kept her gaze pinned to the front of her mat, but the corners of her mouth twitched up.

"Yeah." Corey grinned. "You see what I did there."

"All right, everybody." Mikael called their attention to the front of the room. "Let's start the class in child's pose. Feet together, knees apart, settle your body into the open space."

Corey popped onto all fours, then eased back. Her right knee creaked audibly as she lowered herself down.

"Extend those arms, but clear your shoulders away from your ears. Feel the stretch through your back."

She felt the stretch all right, and not just in her back, but also her arms, her shoulders, even her tailbone. She didn't even remember busting her ass recently.

"Now pushing up into downward-facing dog," Mikael continued in his soothing voice. "Pedal out your feet. Do some knee bends. Feel those hamstrings lengthening."

Corey blew out a heavy exhale and flexed all the appropriate muscles, trying not to groan as a couple of them protested the shift. She only intended to check her arm positioning in the forward mirrors, but when she lifted her head, she caught a full-screen, high-def panoramic of Elise's ass in the air. The view offered the best pain relief she'd ever experienced, as in—pain? What pain?

"Lowering down into plank, hands shoulder-width apart. Keep your neck neutral."

Corey obeyed every cue except the neutral part. She couldn't remain neutral about anything with Elise's body, long and strong, directly ahead of her. Damn. Aside from Holly's earlier assessment of her dirtbaggery, she didn't often ogle women to the extent she seemed to have fixated on Elise. She'd done yoga for years, and while she'd given the occasional nod of respect to a fellow practitioner, no twinge of arousal had lasted for more than a second, and certainly not on this level.

"On your next exhale, bring yourself to low plank, then transition into up dog."

Corey barely noticed the muscles in her abs screaming as she arched her back in a c-curve. The new pose gave her an unobstructed view of Elise's full form. Her muscled shoulders rippled in the exposed cutout of her racerback T. Her blond ponytail fanned out across her back, which flowed in a graceful line down to her spectacular ass, where Corey paused only momentarily to entertain thoughts of bouncing quarters before visually tracing the lines of her powerful legs all the way down over the beautifully smooth curve of her calf muscle.

"Once again pushing up, find your downward dog, trying to settle those heels a little lower this time."

Corey allowed herself another breath to watch in awe as Elise made the transition fluidly.

"Lord, have mercy," she mumbled, causing Elise to shoot her a look between her legs.

She quickly popped up and faced the back wall, relieved she could at least summon some modicum of embarrassment at getting caught staring. What about this woman turned her into a puddle of ineptitude? It wasn't like she was some reclusive computer geek with braces and acne. She generally did pretty well with women. Though she hadn't tested her skills in a while. Maybe she was out of practice.

"Either hop or step your feet to your hands now."

Everyone in the room hopped. Olympians hopped. It was an unwritten rule, but it didn't go without notice that some of them did so more gracefully than others. Elise landed like a cat, without ever making a sound, while Paolo and Nate managed with a grunt and a thud. Corey hoped she fell somewhere in the middle, or that the guys made enough noise to drown out her own.

"Landing in a forward fold, nod your head, then shake your head," Mikael intoned melodically. "Stretch out the remaining tension in your neck."

It would take more than a few nods to release the tension building in her now, but she tried anyway. The weight of her skull pulled her down, torquing a tight muscle between her shoulder blades. She gritted her teeth and breathed through her nose until the sharp pulling sensation lessened.

"Now rising up slowly one vertebrae at a time, chin last, roll your shoulders back, and prepare yourself to ease into chair pose," Mikael said. "Corey, I know this is your favorite, so we'll do an extra long one."

"Thanks, Core," someone called, receiving a mix of laughter and grumbling.

"I've got a bit of a history with this pose," she whispered to Elise, who didn't turn around. She bent her knees over ankles, straightened her back, and eased down as if searching for a tiny chair, one she'd never find. Her dreams would be haunted by the pain of the stupid, nonexistent chair.

"I tend to give the hard poses nicknames." She waited a few seconds as the burn spread through her thighs and hoped Elise would bite. When she didn't, Corey tried the more direct approach. "Don't you want to know what this one's called?"

"Not really," Elise whispered, causing Corey to smile. A negative response was better than no response at all.

"Come on, you're not even a little curious?" Now her knees trembled, and she glanced at the clock, pretending she wanted to see how long Elise would last, and not because she was silently begging Mikael to cue a different pose. As her abs contracted and shook, she had to either find a more pleasant distraction or succumb to the pain. "I'm only thinking of you, you know? You're going to lie awake at night, still aching from this pose, and be sad you don't know what to call it in order to accurately describe its level of torture."

"Fine," Elise finally whispered in a tone laced with resignation. "What do you call chair pose?"

"Pig fucker."

Elise lost her balance and rose almost to standing before shooting Corey a glare that didn't quite reach the freeze-ray level

29

she'd employed in the cafeteria. Her brow furrowed, but she didn't quite frown. "I can't believe you said that."

"I know. It's perfect, right?" Corey said, holding her chair a little easier now.

Elise shook her head as if she couldn't think of any way to respond.

"You can use it any time you want. You don't even have to credit me. Wait till you find out what I like to call boat pose."

"I can't even imagine," Elise said coolly. "Do you come to this class every day?"

Corey beamed. "Never miss it."

"Okay," Mikael cut in. "Grab a sip of water."

Everyone let out a collective sigh of relief. Corey straightened and reached for her water bottle, trying to act nonchalant instead of guzzling. Had yoga hurt this much last off-season? She didn't think so. And yet the disbelief still written all over Elise's face reminded her it hadn't been nearly as entertaining either.

"All right, now we're warmed up. Let's go back to the mat," Mikael called out. "We're going to do a nice long core-strengthening flow. Get ready to engage those abs."

Corey tried to stifle a wince at the prospect of engaging her abs any more than she already had. Could Elise provide her with enough motivation to make it through the next half hour? She didn't know which prospect should worry her more, the fact that she needed a distraction to get through a regular workout or that she may have actually found the woman who could offer her that. Oh well, women or workouts, the solution to being out of practice was to get more practice, and as it turned out she happened to be in the right place to get plenty of both.

Chapter Three

"I want you to be nice today," Paolo said, as they wound their way through the halls of the training center.

Elise rolled her eyes.

"Promise?"

"Fine. I promise."

"Honest," Paolo said. "She's good at what she does. And she's funny."

Elise didn't have to ask who. Paolo had spent the last week extolling the virtues of Corey LaCroix. He could probably be the president of her fan club by this point, though he seemed even more enthralled by Holly. Come to think of it, he'd spent time hanging out with Nate as well, though you could hardly become close with only one of them. When it came to the LaCroix entourage, you rarely saw any one of them break away from the pack. They ate together, they worked out together, and they started pickup basketball games in the gym, always three on three. Hell, they apparently even had rotating poker nights in one of the common rooms. Paolo had been their most recent victim, nearly losing his shirt to the trio last night. She'd even wondered if today's joint workout session was part of some bet he lost.

"If you gave her a chance, you'd be impressed."

"I'm sure she's a riot around a poker table, but gym time is serious business."

"Which is why we need some outside opinions to make sure we're making the most of our workouts."

"That's what I pay you for," Elise said as she pushed open the door to the gym area.

"Right, you pay me to give you the edge. You have to trust me to do my job, which includes listening to me when I tell you to work with different people."

Elise shrugged grudgingly. "I walked right into that one, didn't I?"

"Yes, and thank you. Now try to smile."

"I said I'd be polite. I didn't say I'd smile. Smiling is Corey's thing."

"Smiling isn't one person's thing. Everyone should smile occasionally."

"I do smile occasionally, but come on, she's like constantly grinning. I don't trust someone who's constantly happy. No one's happy all the time. It's got to be fake."

Paolo put a hand on her shoulder. "Elise, stop."

She halted her progress to give him the full attention his tone demanded.

"Think about what you just said."

She opened her mouth, but he cut her off.

"Don't respond. Think about what you just said about happiness, because it says a lot more about you than it does about Corey."

Her heart thudded dully in her chest as she paused to let his point sink in. Did she believe happiness wasn't a real option? Surely not. She'd worked hard to get back to a place where she could be content with her progress, with her accomplishment. But with her life? She couldn't imagine ever being happy during a training session, or in a cafeteria, or bantering during hard yoga classes. She tried to summon some feeling to the contrary but found the task surprisingly hard. When was the last time she'd loved a mundane moment? Before the crash? Before Sochi? More than four years ago?

She hung her head. "Okay."

"Okay?" Paolo asked, wrapping an arm around her slumped shoulders.

"I know I've said it before, but I mean it this time. I'll try to give her a chance today."

"Give you a chance, too? To have fun, to smile, and maybe you'll learn something useful none of the other skiers know yet."

She stifled an eye roll and said, "I suppose stranger things have happened."

"Stranger things than what?" Corey asked, coming around the corner with Nate close behind her.

Elise and Paolo exchanged a look of "You want to field that one?" but neither one of them had to say a thing before Corey laughed. "It's okay. I often come around the corner to find people talking about me. I have that effect on people for all sorts of reasons."

Paolo chuckled nervously, but Elise smiled along with Corey. She might not enjoy much about her, but she did appreciate her ability to forge on under seemingly any awkward circumstance. Then again, Elise suspected she'd had plenty of practice with that particular skill. Still, she'd promised to try to embrace whatever the snowboarder had to offer, so she extended the olive branch. "I hear you're going to try to teach an old dog new tricks today. Thank you for taking the time to work with us."

Corey and Nate couldn't keep their eyebrows from shooting up in unison at the pleasant greeting, but neither one of them seemed to harbor any resentment for her previously cool demeanor.

"Yeah," Nate said, "we're going to run through our usual mid-overland routine. Muscle building, polymetrics, core."

"Sounds about right. Shall we get started?"

"Are you warm?" Corey asked. "I already did my cardio for the morning."

"Yeah, I swam."

"Nice." Corey gave her a nod of approval. "I was on the bike today."

"Low-impact endurance training," she noted, as much to herself as to the others. "I know it well."

"She's spent plenty of her rehab time pedaling various machines," Paolo added.

"Exactly," Nate said. "We need them to build endurance and leg

33

strength, but neither one of them needs to be jarring their knees at this stage of the season."

Corey shot him a glare that mirrored what Elise felt at being reminded she wasn't as young or fit as she used to be.

Paolo didn't have any problem with the assessment though. "We're to the point where we need to build back the explosive leg power, glutes, hamstrings. She was known for making great starts."

"I've got the perfect setup," Nate said. "Ready to go?"

She and Corey both nodded, but Paolo hesitated. "Aren't we going to wait for Holly?"

This time she and Corey got to exchange the amused expressions. She liked the way Corey's hazel eyes widened playfully as the grin lifted her cheeks.

"Not one for subtlety, is he?" Elise asked.

Corey shrugged. "Maybe that's why we've hit it off."

Her smile widened. "Now that you mention it . . ."

"Holly's got a meeting with some sponsors this morning," Nate finally explained. "Not that Corey could care less about sponsors, but I stay out of the business end . . . and the sister end."

Paolo seemed mildly disappointed, but he didn't argue with the conclusion, leaving Elise to ponder the LaCroix team dynamics as they made their way between weight machines and past various sporting apparatus. Everyone seemed to know their roles but her. Not that she needed to know, but she did feel a little twitch of curiosity. As an only child with hands-off parents, she'd never given any consideration to working with a family member. Then again, Paolo had been more like family than any of her blood relatives over the last few years. Had she missed out by not forming stronger relationships with other members of her team?

"Okay, Corey, tie up," Nate said, as they stopped in front of a contraption Elise had never seen before. The equipment consisted of several metal bars and levers. Some were stacked with weights. Others appeared tethered to a thick, leather, back-support style belt.

Corey didn't seem confused by the arrangement at all, though. She stepped quickly into the open circle of the belt and hoisted it up to her waist before snugging it into place. Once she got everything secured, Elise could see how the belt connected to the weighted arms via a series of straps. When she stood up fully, the straps lifted the weights. When she crouched down again, they lowered.

"Perfect," Paolo muttered, circling the whole ensemble and rubbing the dark stubble on his chin. "Knee-centric without any sudden jarring contact."

Elise saw the potential, too. Corey was essentially using the same muscles Elise would need to punch through an explosive start and doing so without the impact that exercises like box jumps inflicted. "You engage the hamstrings and the glutes like you do with leg presses, but you're upright instead of recumbent."

Corey glanced over her shoulder with her ever-present smile. "It transfers the weight pressure to your core. The leg presses waste all those little stabilizers, plus we don't go down a mountain on our asses . . . hopefully, right?"

She had a point. Not brilliant, but her comment spoke to a little more consideration than Elise would've expected. "How high up does it trigger?"

"Everything below my pecs. Here, come around and watch," Corey said, grabbing her gray T-shirt by the back of her neck and pulling it off with one rough motion. Underneath she wore only a navy blue sport bra. Elise blinked a few times. Seeing women working out in sport bras or even bikini tops wasn't exceptionally rare, but she hadn't expected Corey to be quite so open with her body. Then again, why wouldn't she feel comfortable displaying a body like hers? Her stomach was flat and firm, the subtle C-curve of obliques etched along her side even while she crouched with the weights in neutral position.

Elise adjusted her position on autopilot, either because she was too stunned not to obey the command, or because she actually wanted a better view for her own personal reasons.

"Watch this time when I push up," Corey said, straightening

her legs quickly enough to pop a few inches off the ground before the weights exerted their resistance. Still, Corey locked herself into position, body trembling slightly as she held the pose. "I feel it in my obliques, my transverse abdominis, my rectus abdominis, the total package. Can you see everything contract?"

She nodded, unable to speak as she did, indeed, see every muscle of Corey's abs tighten. Obviously she knew all the terms Corey used when describing them, but somehow seeing such a perfect, real-life model rendered the technical terms unnecessary. Elise could've traced lines with her fingers like a textbook diagram if the idea wasn't completely inappropriate. But damn, she worked as hard as any skier, and she'd never had abs like those. Not before the accident, not at the last Olympics, not even when she'd been a teenager. Abs like those existed only on body builders and in action films.

"Let go, Core," Nate finally said, and Corey obeyed, letting her legs go slack as the weights clattered to the floor.

"Fantastico!" Paolo applauded.

"She's not supposed to hold it," Nate grumbled protectively. "It's polymetrics. If you use this method, you need to focus on speed and blowing up out of the low stance. Quick up, quick down."

"Did you hear him, Elise?"

"Huh?" She tore her gaze away from Corey's abs and found everyone watching her expectantly with varying degrees of confusion and amusement. She felt her face flush. "I'm sorry. I was thinking through the benefits of this method."

Paolo did a sorry job of hiding his silly grin, but Nate and Corey didn't seem to notice her lapse in concentration.

"Your turn, then." Corey unbuttoned the belt and let it drop to the floor.

Elise almost winced at the sound, or maybe at the prospect of Corey disrobing any further in front of her. "No, actually, I'd rather see your full circuit before I start anything."

"Sure, but a lot of it's pretty standard from here. We do weight training to build mass."

Elise nodded. "Heavier equals faster."

"As long as it's heavy from muscle, not heavy from fried chicken," Nate cut in.

Corey elbowed him in the ribs. "You don't know that for sure. I think we need to see more of the research replicated before we rule out the chicken diet. The pizza diet showed great potential as well in clinical trials."

"Your eating pizza for sixty days in a row doesn't amount to a clinical trial."

"And yet, I won four of five races in that time period." Corey turned back to Elise. "I also had a personal best at Squaw Valley on pure pizza."

"You're joking, right?" Elise asked.

"I wish she were," Nate said. "She takes coaching better than almost anyone. Nutritional advice, not so much."

"I can't even . . . sixty days in a row? What's wrong with—" She cut the criticism off, but just barely. "That's a unique process for an athlete."

"I'm a unique athlete." Corey laughed. "Hey, that reminds me; we also do some cool gate training and balance board training. Do you need either of those?"

"Skiers use different starting gates than snowboarders," Paolo said, "but I'd love to see the balance workout."

Elise sighed, thankful for the redirect, but not fully over the pizza diet concept. One second Corey showed off an incredible physique and talked about her transverse abdominis training, and then she bragged about eating like a pothead. And yet, still winning apparently. She didn't know how many snowboarders entered a boardercross event, but she didn't delude herself into thinking competition wasn't steep at the professional level of anything. Then again, if one could win four out of five races on only cheese and pepperoni, something didn't add up. Corey at least sparked her interest enough to make her want to find the missing variable. "Yes, let's see the balance technique."

Corey and Nate once again seemed surprised by the comment, but Paolo spoke first. "Seriously?"

"Yes," she said almost defensively. "I haven't been on the snow for over a year. I spent six months basically on my backside. If I'm going to be competitive in a few months, I can't only do the same exercises my competitors do during overland season. I have to do more. I have to do better. I have to try everything, or I don't get another chance for four years." Panic rose in her voice, and she tried to tamp it down as she added, "Or maybe never."

They all stared at her, wide-eyed.

"All right," Corey finally said. "Saddle up, sister."

She practically jogged through the weight room with Elise striding purposefully behind her and the men straggling.

"Check this," Corey said, swinging open the door to a smaller room with a few monitors and a low black box in the center of the floor. There were a couple of balance training aids in one corner, but otherwise the space was sparse. "Grab a balance ball. I'll show you the hardest stabilizing exercise I do. It's wicked."

"Wicked," Elise repeated in her best impression of Corey's laid-back inflection, which earned her a warning look from Paolo. "Right, well, I've worked with Bosu balls during my rehab."

"Yeah?" Corey's grin once again turned mischievous. "Let's see what you got. You know, for bench-setting purposes."

Bench setting, her ass. She heard the challenge there, and she liked it. She hadn't had nearly enough direct competition lately. She grabbed the Bosu, half exercise ball and half balance board, and flipped the flat surface to rest against the linoleum floor with the blue rounded side facing up. She stepped steadily onto the rubberized surface. Her glutes engaged immediately; then she tucked into a squat with her elbows pinned tight against her side as if she were holding ski poles. She pedaled her heels slightly, getting a solid seat, then rose up to a chair position. Closing her eyes and quieting her mind, she found her center and felt her core temperature drop instead of rise. The sounds of weights dropping and heavy treadmill footfalls faded, replaced by the low whistle of a mountain wind. She took deep cleansing breaths through her nose as the course appeared before her. Sinking into her weight, she leaned her right shoulder toward the turn and lifted her left leg off the ball in a perfectly executed skater squat. She hovered, balanced at a forty-five-degree angle on one foot and a curved surface, her body weight perfectly united with gravity. She could almost feel the metal edge of her ski slice through the snow.

Corey's low whistle sounded an alarm clock on her pleasant dream. "Damn, that's graceful."

"Yeah," Nate agreed. "You got nothing serene in your bag, buddy."

With her concentration broken, Elise rose as steadily as she could and hopped off the ball, her only comfort coming from the fact that the slight lateral impact didn't cause her knee any noticeable pain. Her shoulders, on the other hand, knotted from frustration once again. She wanted to be on the slopes so bad, the need made her chest hurt. Instead she was getting whistled at by some snowboarder who couldn't decide whether or not she wanted to be an Olympian or a competitive eater.

"What you're doing there is working, right?" Corey asked, then plowed on before she could even register the question. "It's super pretty."

"Super pretty?"

"The ballet. It's nice, but if I did the quiet eyes-closed-one-leg thing, I'd get killed."

"Maybe you should re-evaluate your life choices."

"Maybe." Corey refused to bite back. "But then again, maybe you should, too."

"Excuse me?"

"I'm not the trainer. You got two of them right here, but going out on a limb, I'll bet things are going to be a little rougher for you this season. You're going to be working muscles you haven't had to use in a long time. Things won't feel as smooth. You'll have to fight harder against the little tweaks and twinges."

"I'm plenty familiar with fighting, thank you."

"Hear her out," Paolo suggested, once again settling into fan boy mode.

"I'm just saying you can't expect things not to be a little tippy out there, especially in the early races."

She didn't even try to fight the eye roll now. "A little tippy? Is that your clinical definition?"

"I said I'm not a trainer, but you said you wanted a leg up, something new, something a level higher than what the rest of the pack is doing. I can start with the same premise you're using in your exercises and crank it up to eleven."

"Forgive me if I don't follow your lead. You admit you know virtually nothing about my sport, and you're not even a trainer in yours."

"No, but I am, and she's right." Nate came to her defense. "We've used this technique for a couple of years now in snowboarding, but I've never seen the skiers take things quite as far as we do."

"I'm listening," Paolo said before Elise could respond.

"Here." Nate grabbed the Bosu ball and flipped it onto the metal box, round side down. "This is a vibrating plate, it's like those shaky foot massagers at the mall, but times ten. Hop on, Corey."

Corey grabbed two ten-pound hand weights and did as instructed. She found her balance quickly, one foot behind the other, in snowboard stance. Knees bent, weights out front, she blew out a deep breath and nodded to Nate. "Let 'er rip."

The plate began to vibrate on a low frequency, but Nate didn't wait long to crank it up. Soon Corey's whole body shook from the vibrations below. Even her cheeks jiggled. She wasn't smiling now. Her eyes narrowed, and her jaw pulled tight in concentration. She tucked low, her legs and abs contracting in a myriad of ways to maintain her balance. Elise's temperature spiked once again. Corey's body functioned like a mechanical work of art as she held steady, but now she'd added an intense focus to the mix. The entire shape of her face changed as her focus shifted from the things around her to something only she could see. Elise recognized the change, but what did it mean for someone like Corey? Had she mentally transported to some race course that haunted her dreams or symbolized her hopes?

"Give me what you've got," Corey said through tight lips, her voice wavering from the vibration affecting even her vocal cords.

Then unexpectedly, Nate reared back and kicked the balance board beneath her. Corey winced and tipped back on her heels but stayed in her tuck. The second blow Nate landed sent her onto her toes, but she didn't break form until the third kick. When Nate assaulted the rounded part of Corey's leaning, shaking tower, she practically hopped into the air, raising the weights all the way over her head in the process.

Elise gasped and reached out instinctively to catch her fall, but Corey only sank right back into place on the board. Nate didn't give up though. Angling behind her, he kicked again, causing another jump and another reflexive wince from Elise. She felt the bounce in her own core as she watch the amazing body before her twist and contort itself back into position.

Another sharp kick to the board reverberated off the walls of the now too-small room, and something inside her cracked. "All right. Fine. I get it. Turn it off."

Everyone jerked their heads toward her in surprise, but she didn't care. "I'm done here. This isn't a real thing."

"Elise," Paolo whispered embarrassedly as Nate turned off the vibrating plate and Corey hopped to the floor.

"I'm sorry Paolo, but this isn't a workout. It's a frat party, or a practical joke. It's not Olympic training."

"Actually," Corey said, annoyance now breaking through her usually laid-back tone. "It mimics coming across the rough surfaces pretty well, especially at the finish line where you've got multiple riders bumping and rubbing elbows."

"No one rubs my elbows across the finish line," Elise cut back. She didn't know why the sight of Nate kicking Corey had made her irate, and she didn't care to examine any further at the moment. She merely wanted to get out of this circus tent. "I'm a serious athlete."

"Oh, well, that's the crux of it all, isn't it?" Corey asked. "You're a serious athlete there in your ivory tower while the rest of us common folk are the riffraff."

"I didn't say that."

"You didn't have to. Believe it or not, we're not imbeciles.

We're every bit as dedicated and highly trained as you are," Corey said calmly, "and actually I think we're training harder than you are right now."

"I highly doubt that."

"Care to hop on the board and find out?"

"Training differently doesn't mean training harder. Our skill sets are completely different."

"And yet you judged mine as inferior without even thinking about what I do."

"I know what you do. I've seen the videos. It's BMX meets WrestleMania on snow."

Corey laughed, and the sounded grated on her nerves. "I like that description. Can I use it?"

Why did she find everything so damned amusing? Elise shouldn't let the cavalier attitude irk her. It only proved Corey wasn't capable of taking the work seriously.

"Does it scare you?" Corey asked.

"What?"

"Does it scare you? What I do for a living? The unpredictability, the pressure of someone breathing down your neck, the thought of someone else being able to take away everything you've worked so hard for?"

"Save me your armchair sports psychology," she snapped, even as her chest constricted.

"It doesn't require an advanced degree to see you like control. And my sport doesn't offer that option. It's gritty. It's unreliable. It's riding an edge. It's staring your competition in the eye. It's a powder keg of close quarters, steep grade, and speed."

"Speed? You don't think I can handle speed? I go down steeper grades than you do, and I hit upwards of seventy miles an hour."

"Cool story." Corey shrugged, studiously unimpressed. "Does anyone kick you while you're at it?"

"I'd like to see them try."

Corey gestured to the balance board. "Hop on, sister."

"Whoa, whoa." Paolo stepped between them. "No kicking. Nada."

"She started it," Elise said before she realized how childish she sounded. "I mean, she asked me to try something, and you said I should listen to her today."

"And I stand by my request," Paolo said, rubbing his chin. "This exercise actually has a lot of potential for you, but I also see why it isn't common among skiers."

"Because it's insane?" Elise asked.

"No." He sounded exasperated. "The kicking doesn't mimic what a skier experiences on the slopes."

"Exactly, that's what I said. Completely different skill set."

"Not completely," Paolo corrected. "The vibration and the balance ball combined will likely work well to stimulate many of the core and balance muscles we need. And Corey's right, we need to work on recovery strategies. You're not in the shape you're used to. You can't assume smooth transitions anymore."

Her stomach tightened, but she didn't argue. Nothing about her life had been smooth for a long time.

"I'd like to see you try your skate-leg squats on the vibrating plate, then move up to the ball and the vibration together."

"I can show you how to calibrate the vibration to simulate different conditions," Nate said calmly. "We can also use the heart rate monitors and oxygen masks to measure responses at simulated altitudes."

Paolo nodded. "Yes. We can adapt this nicely."

Elise sighed heavily. She'd lost again. Lost her temper, lost the argument, and lost a chunk of self-respect in the process. Something else for Corey to lord over her.

Only Corey didn't seem smug as she leaned against the wall and watched the trainers fiddle with various remotes and wires. She'd merely gone back to her usual relaxed expression, slight smile, eyes kind, one hand jammed casually into the pocket of her athletic shorts. A thin sheen of sweat glistened across her bare shoulders and torso, and Elise had to turn away to keep from getting sucked into studying her again.

"Am I going to do this today, or is this show and tell?" she asked.

43

"I need to learn a little more," Paolo said, still inspecting the machines. "Why don't you and Corey go through a couple of weight circuits while you wait."

"Works for me," Corey said, pushing off the wall.

Elise followed her out the door before saying, "Thanks for the tour."

"You're welcome, but don't you want us to spot each other through the weights?"

"I'm good, thanks." The last thing she wanted was to have to stand over Corey while she flexed and stretched. She needed to get away, to regain her focus, and to remember what she came here to do. "You can do your thing, and I'll do mine."

Corey shrugged. "Sure, but I'll be across the gym. If you need help, just call out for me."

"Right." She nodded and bit her tongue to keep from saying something crass. She didn't anticipate calling out for Corey anytime soon. Not in the gym, and not anywhere else.

"All right, dude." Nate flipped some switches on the heart rate monitors next to Corey's stationary bike. "You're at five miles."

"Don't turn it off," Corey said, continuing to pedal. "I've got another one in me."

"You already swam this morning," Nate said as if Corey could have somehow forgotten the mile she'd covered in the pool earlier in the day. "I thought you'd want some time in the skate park by now."

"I'll get there, but I haven't been pushing myself hard enough on cardio lately."

"What did she say?" Holly slowed her treadmill.

"I'm not sure," Nate said. "Sounded like she said she wants to do more cardio, but I must've heard wrong."

"Cardio? That doesn't make any sense. She probably said she wants a beer to go."

"Or some crunchy tacos?"

"Or more time to party, yo?" Holly suggested.

"Are you finished?" Corey asked.

"Oh, she's cranky too." Holly turned her treadmill off completely.

"Extra cardio will do that to you," Nate said.

"Maybe you've got a fever." Holly reached up and put a hand on her forehead, then wrinkled her nose and wiped her palm on the towel hanging off Corey's handlebars. "You're certainly sweaty."

"I'm not cranky. I don't have a fever. I'm sweaty because I'm working out, which is my job."

"Whoa." Nate cast a worried glance at Holly. "It's her job? Did you know she had a job?"

Holly shrugged. "She doesn't look employable to me. She's a mess."

Nate laughed. "And she smells bad."

Corey wiped her face with the sleeve of her T-shirt, which happened to feature a T-Rex on a snowboard. "Go ahead, yuk it up, but it's already the end of July, and I'm the one who has to face a mountain in a month."

Nate frowned. "You have to? Or you get to?"

"Yeah."

Holly's eyes narrowed. "That wasn't a yes-or-no question."

"It's both." Corey picked up her speed, ignoring the burn in her thighs. "I get to race, but I have to stay competitive in order to keep racing."

Nate and Holly both glanced across the gym, to where Tigger was running full speed on a whirring treadmill without breaking a sweat. Corey rolled her eyes. "Exactly."

"What?" Holly asked.

"You both looked at the Tigger."

"No," they said in unison, then laughed nervously.

"You did. I know she's on the treadmill, and I don't care." She wasn't freaking out about Nikki. She didn't care if the kid spent hours upon hours in here without breaking a sweat. Corey didn't care if Tigger never needed a turn on the massage table or even mussed her ponytail on the trampoline.

"Okay then, if it's not Tigger, who is it?" Nate asked.

"It's not like there's anyone else vying for your spot on the team," Holly said. "I know you didn't finish as high as you wanted to last year, but you're the top American woman. You say the word, and I could find you ten new sponsors today."

"It's not about that." She heard the frustration in her voice, and she didn't like it, but she couldn't explain it either. "It's not about other snowboarders at all."

"What else is there?" Holly asked.

"Skiers," Nate answered before Corey could even ponder the question.

"Skiers?"

"Skier," he corrected. "Tall, blond, smoking hot, and yet cold as ice."

"No," she offered up, as a pathetic defense.

"Elise tore into her pretty hard last week," Nate explained to Holly.

"When? Why?" Holly immediately sprang into big sister mode. "What did she say?"

"Nothing." She rose up off the seat of the bike throwing her body weight into a standing pedal.

"Some bullshit about Corey not being a serious athlete."

"Pretty sure Corey could kick her candy ass."

"Pretty sure that argument isn't helpful," Corey said through gritted teeth.

"Slow down, Core," Nate commanded. "You're at seven miles."

"I'm fine."

"I don't think so," Nate said. "You're pressing. You have been all week. I thought you were bored with overland, but if Elise got under your skin—"

"She didn't," Corey snapped. "I don't care what she thinks about boardercross, or me for that matter."

"Then why are you killing yourself right now?"

Corey pedaled steadily, legs pumping, muscles screaming, but they couldn't drown out the questions both external and internal. Why did it matter? Why did she care? Elise? Tigger? The sponsors? The tour? The Olympics?

Had something changed?

46

Nate was right. She'd been restless, bored, pressing all week, but did it tie back to Elise? It would be easy to blame her. Some woman had spun her head around. It wasn't too far-fetched, and yet she'd never in her life worked this hard to impress a woman or to prove her wrong. Elise was a snob. A smart, hot-tempered, stacked, and sexy snob, but Corey could appreciate her fine physical features without listening to a word she said. Hell, she'd done that with pretty much every woman she'd ever hooked up with. The idea of biking her ass off to score some woman who wouldn't give her the time of day wasn't her style.

"Have you ever known me to bust my butt over a woman?"

"No," Nate said.

"But," Holly added, "I've never known you to go extra miles on an exercise bike when you could be on a skateboard either."

Fair point.

Something didn't add up, but she couldn't explain to them what she couldn't understand herself. She couldn't imagine some angry outburst by Elise could bug her for a week. Everyone had bad days. Everyone shot off their mouth from time to time. She'd actually liked to see a little fire out of Elise. She preferred her hot under the collar rather than frozen solid, but it didn't mean she gave any weight to her opinions. Elise thought she was a joke. She didn't think she was working hard enough. She didn't think she deserved to be taken seriously. She'd heard it all before. Didn't mean anything . . . unless she was right.

"Nine miles, Core," Nate said, the warning in his voice growing stronger. "This is no longer a cooldown. I can't train you if you won't level with me."

"All I know is I'm not done yet," she finally said. "Maybe it's someone chasing me, maybe it's something I'm chasing, but it doesn't feel that way to me. It just feels like I'm not done."

Neither one of them said anything, and the weight of their combined concern settled on her shoulders. She'd never cared about anyone else's opinions of her or her work. All that mattered was what she believed. Which, of course, meant if Elise's comments had upset her, they'd struck a chord. Somehow that prospect was even more disturbing than the thought of her breaking character to get laid.

She sat back down and slowed her speed, trying to bring her heart rate down, but she suspected her elevated pulse couldn't be completely attributed to her exertion.

Nate glanced at the monitors and frowned. Had he noticed the same thing?

"I'll bring it down easy," she offered, trying to ease their minds even if hers continued to spin. She released a few slow breaths and tried to think logically as her endorphin levels subsided. She'd swum a mile easily, done a full weights workout, spent an hour on polymetrics, put in time on the gate simulators, and then ridden ten miles at a healthy clip, all before noon.

"Come on, guys," she said. "I'm fine. I'm mentally ready to hit the slopes, and I want to make sure my body is ready to keep up. That's what we're here for, right?"

"Yeah." Nate sounded unconvinced.

Holly at least managed to smile as she tousled her hair. "Sure, sweat bucket. As long as you mean it."

"I do." She punctuated the statement with a smile. "No one's in my head but me, okay?"

Nate finally chuckled. "Then your head must be a pretty scary place."

She grinned and hopped off the bike, refusing to let her trembling muscles break her bravado, but she couldn't find either the strength or inclination to argue with him.

Chapter Four

The training room was cool, dark, and quiet this time of night, a direct contrast to every other part of the Lake Henry Olympic Training Center. Elise relished the solitude, leaving most of the lights off and staying clear of the TV. Silence wasn't easy to come by this weekend. Both the men's and the women's US hockey teams were on site for big qualifying matches, or games, or whatever hockey contests were called. Curlers were in the house, too, along with their Canadian counterparts. The cafeteria overflowed, yoga class had gotten crowded, and for the first time since arriving in upstate New York a month ago, she'd had to wait for a turn on some of the weight machines. Never mind it was only the beginning of August. Never mind that heat and humidity assaulted her every time she stepped outside. Never mind that, even now at nine o'clock, the sunlight hadn't fully faded from the mountain-cropped horizon. The scent, the taste, the buzz of the winter Olympics hung heavy in the air.

Elise avoided it all—the crowds, the camaraderie, and the cameras. She told herself she didn't want any distractions, and she didn't. She'd worked hard and made too much progress to let up now. She was still weeks behind her competition, and she couldn't afford to slow down long enough to even take in the excitement building around her. That's why she'd stayed in tonight when everyone else had headed down the road to the hockey arena. She had the facility to herself for the first time in days, and she intended to use the time productively.

She sat on a bench near a bank of lockers and stripped off her shoes and socks, checking carefully for signs of blisters. So far so good. The shirt hit the floor next, and she grimaced as she lowered her arms, taking stock of the aches in her shoulders and the slight pinch under her right scapula. Still, aches and minor pains were part of training. She'd certainly had worse. Then again, if she had enough pain to drive her to the training room on a Friday night in August, how would she feel after a race in February?

"No," she mumbled, shaking her head and stripping off her navy track pants to reveal a set of black boy-short swim bottoms. She tried not to inspect the scars on her right knee, as they always made her a little nauseated, but she couldn't avoid pressing her index fingers to the swollen tissue around them. She also made note of a few new bruises along her calf and ankle. Where had those come from? Her ski boots during the start gate simulations? Her tumble off the balance board yesterday? Or maybe when she'd slipped on the climbing wall the day before? Panic rose in her chest at the realization that any one bruise could signal a deeper problem. Which exercise would be the one to reveal her as unfit? Paolo had her cross training harder and in more varied forms than ever before. A few bumps and bruises should probably be expected, right?

"Right," she answered her own question aloud as she walked over to a tub large enough to border on the size of a small pool. Totally normal to need to sneak into a training center after her own trainer had called it a night. It wasn't as though she intended to do anything against the rules. Cold baths were standard operating procedure for athletes trying to minimize swelling or cut down on rebound time. Of course, most of them weren't also trying to prove themselves on a tightrope of pain and expectations.

She climbed the steps to the cold pool and sat on the shellacked wood railing, hesitating only because she didn't relish the thought of dropping into the fifty-five degree water, and not because she probably shouldn't be in here alone. God, what if she shouldn't be here at all? What if she'd made a mistake in not telling Paolo how sore she felt? What if she needed rest or massage or something else? No, she knew her body well enough to make these decisions for herself. If she'd told Paolo she needed an ice bath he would've arranged it for her. She'd merely cut out the middleman to let him enjoy a night out with friends. The logic was sound, but the rationale didn't stop her from jumping when the door to the training room swung open and someone flipped on a bank of overhead lights.

She steadied herself on the edge of the pool once more, then braced herself to confront her company, excuses already spinning through her brain. If it was a trainer, she'd say Paolo'd approved the treatment and plead her case to him later. If the person was another athlete, she'd act natural. Worst of all would be a USSA official, but she could always try to spin it as though she'd felt so good earlier she'd done an extra workout and say a cold bath was standard procedure after increasing her load. They probably wouldn't believe her. They'd doubted her all along, which was why she'd rather face just about anyone else right now.

"Oh, hey, sorry. Elise?" the words all spilled out of Corey in the instant she stepped into view, and then she laughed loudly. "Shit, you scared me."

Scared wasn't exactly the right word for what Elise felt at Corey's presence. More like a mix between relief and annoyance. She supposed having her walk in would be better than being caught by an official, at least in the long run, but she also suspected there'd be no getting rid of her now.

"Good evening, Corey." She wondered if her voice managed to sound as cool as the water below.

"Whatcha doing?"

"I'm getting ready for a cold bath."

Corey ambled over and leaned against the side rail, her interest seemingly engaged now. "Why?"

"Because it's good practice."

"Practice for what? Iditarod? Polar Bear Plunge?"

She rolled her eyes and deadpanned, "A good practice for rejuvenating muscles. You see, it reduces swelling and constricts blood

51

vessels. Then when you warm up, blood rushes back in, flushing out waste to speed healing."

"Uh, yeah . . . I'm pretty clear on that. But why are you using the cold bath right now. Alone. On a Friday night," Corey asked, concern finally filtering through her normally playful tone.

"It's a standard part of my recovery." The comment wasn't a total lie. She and Paolo spent plenty of time using various cold therapies.

"If it's a normal part of your workout, why didn't you do it earlier with Paolo?"

She clenched her jaw and then released it, trying to sound as calm as possible. "I gave him the night off."

Corey nodded and smiled. "So you really do think I'm stupid, huh?"

"Excuse me?"

"All your comments the other day about me being a joke weren't just you losing your temper or lashing out in frustration. You view me as some sort of village idiot."

"Corey, I . . . I'm . . . I don't know what you're talking about."

"Oh, come on. It's only the two of us here now. Why not cut the crap, because I can handle anger. I can withstand the cold shoulder and the snotty comments, but I'm not a fan of playing games."

"I'm not playing games."

"You're slipping into a cold pool with the lights off, after hours, and without the supervision of a trainer. None of those things point to a night off, but more than that, I've spent a lot of time with Paolo over the last few weeks, and I know him well enough to call bullshit on his behalf. If he knew you were here, he'd be here, too."

Elise hung her head. "Fine, Paolo doesn't know I'm here."

"Great. If you'd led with that, I would've told you I have zero shits to give about your sneaking around on your trainer. Do you think I call Nate every time I have a cheat day and eat twelve tacos?"

"I don't even know what to say. Twelve tacos?"

Corey shook her head. "I'm a snowboarder. We're rule benders.

I'm not going to narc on you, but don't lie to me. If you want me to shut my trap and move along, say so."

"You'd really walk away if I told you to?"

Corey frowned but said, "Yeah. I would."

"And you wouldn't run to your posse and tell them what a bitch I was?"

"No. I might not love bitchy Elise, but I respected you more when you were yelling instead of lying."

Her stomach churned at the statement. She'd been either a bitch or a liar, and still Corey wouldn't turn against her. Even though she'd been nothing but awful, while Paolo had become a friend, Corey would still cover for her. "Why protect me? Why even speak to me, much less honor my wish to keep this quiet?"

Corey shrugged. "Your body, your business."

She laughed. "My body has been a lot of people's business for a long time."

"Yeah," Corey sighed. "I guess we've all been there."

The sudden wistfulness in her tone made Elise wonder if maybe she had underestimated her seriousness. Corey's hazel eyes certainly carried more understanding than she'd ever given her credit for. Maybe that's what gave her the nudge to continue with an explanation she would've normally withheld. "I've got a lot of people betting against me. Even Paolo has moments of doubt. He's got gray hairs popping up in the stupid three-day beard he keeps trying to grow, and I know I put them there. I see the new wrinkles on his forehead, and I know each one represents a "What if" he won't say. 'What if we push too hard? What if I reinjure myself? What if we're not ready in time? What if I never get back to where I was? What if—?'"

"Hey," Corey whispered. "You gotta stop. You have to breathe."

She hadn't even noticed her breath had grown shallow and her heart rate accelerated.

"You're going to make yourself crazy with those what ifs. And you can't obsess about Paolo's worries either. He's a big boy. He made his choices. He could've bolted. It sounds like plenty of others did."

She winced. "Yeah, plenty of them did."

"Well, fuck 'em," Corey said forcefully. "Fuck every one of them and the skis they slid in on. Did you want a bunch of freeloaders and good-time Charlies riding the Elise Brandeis bandwagon?"

"Um, I think the answer to that question is 'no.'"

"Damn right." Corey slapped her open palm on the side of pool. "No love for the haters."

"Some of those so-called haters are sponsors. Some of them work for the USSA. If they caught me in here right now, they wouldn't be as easygoing as you."

"They don't own you," Corey said, her cheeks flushing pink. "They don't own your name. They don't own your body. Get in the pool."

"What?"

"That's what you came here for, right? It's your right. You're an Olympian, damn it. This is your facility. You don't have to sneak around. You're doing nothing wrong."

"Do you really believe that?"

Corey's momentum faltered. "Well, maybe you should talk to Paolo. He cares about you, but you don't owe anyone else anything."

She smiled. "I almost believe you."

"Almost?" Corey laughed. "That was a good speech. You're a tough crowd."

"Yeah, not to detract from your rousing pep talk, but it's still going to be me alone in the pool."

"Oh, I see. We've reached a money-where-my-mouth-is moment." Corey kicked off her tennis shoes and peeled off her socks.

"What?"

"Move over." Corey whipped off her shirt, leaving her in only a black sports bra and a pair of basketball shorts. "I'm coming in."

"You're crazy." Elise laughed. "You don't have to do this."

"I can't be outdone by you in the rebel department. I'd lose all my credibility as the resident rabble-rouser."

Elise shook her head, but she couldn't argue with the logic. Well, maybe she could've argued, but with laughter in the air and Corey's beautiful body exposed and so close, she simply didn't want to.

※ ※ ※

"Holy shit balls, mother of frozen tundra, damn, hell, icy ass fucktrumpet." Corey let fly every curse that sprang to mind as she splashed down into the frigid water.

"Wow, you have an extensive vocabulary," Elise said, an amusement in her voice Corey had never heard before.

"You haven't even heard the beginning of it," Corey said through gritted teeth. "How long do we stay in here?"

"Let's just do ten minutes," Elise said, easing into the water much more gracefully and with only a slight grimace.

"Oh sure, only ten minutes. How long did those people on the Titanic last?"

"It's not that bad, you big baby."

"You're right. It's not bad at all, until it hits your who-ha."

"Did you call your female anatomy a who-ha?"

"Yes, yes I did." Corey pouted. "As you pointed out, I have an extensive vocabulary, but when that body part is submerged in ice water, it definitely feels like a who-ha."

Elise rolled her eyes, but this time the expression seemed more playful than annoyed as the corners of her mouth also curled up. She had a pretty mouth when she wasn't scowling. Corey much preferred even the little smile to the anguish she'd seen flash across those beautiful features moments earlier. Something inside her had twisted painfully when Elise had talked about all the people who'd abandoned her when she'd gotten hurt. At least her own exile had been self-imposed. She couldn't stand to think of the bewilderment Elise must've felt when she'd woken up in the hospital to realize her fair-weather friends had all moved on to the next big thing.

She started to shiver, either from the cold or from the direction her mind had wandered. "How long have we been in here now?"

"About thirty seconds," Elise said evenly.

"Are you sure? Are you counting?"

"No."

"Then how do you know?" Corey spun around in the water. "Where's the clock."

Elise sighed. "Hold still. I'll set the stop watch on my Fitbit if you promise to stop squirming."

"Won't squirming make me warmer?"

"First of all," Elise said, pushing a few buttons on her watch and folding her arms neatly across the side of the pool, "you're in a cold bath to get cold, or at least to make your muscles cold."

"*You're* in a cold bath to make your muscles cold. I'm in the cold bath because I'm a rebel without a cause."

"Regardless of your cause or lack of one, squirming will make you colder. The water you're warming with your body temperature will swish away and be replaced by fresher, colder water."

"You're like super smart about these things, huh?" Corey asked, trying to mimic Elise's stance by folding her arms on the rail and holding her lower body completely still. The water came to her chest, chilling everything below with little pinpricks of cold. Holding still wasn't ever her strong suit, and doing so under this much discomfort would only make the task harder, but if Elise could hang tough, she could, too. "I bet you study a lot."

"I've studied a lot of various therapies, yes." Elise's voice turned almost as cold as the water below.

"Hmm," Corey made the noncommittal noise, unsure of what land mine she'd triggered, and worried there might be some more in the area.

"Hmm, what?"

"Hmm, nothing. Hmm, I'm hungry and cold."

"Now who's bullshitting?"

Corey laughed. "Good call. You tensed up. I wondered if I said something wrong inadvertently. You don't know me well, but I actually do that a lot."

"What, inadvertently say the wrong thing?"

"Shocking, I know, what with me being so smooth all the time."

"Yeah, you could knock me over with a feather. After you told me what you call chair pose, I thought to myself, 'Corey sure has a way with words.'"

"I get that a lot, actually. I'm pretty likable." She played up the jovial shtick even though she understood Elise hadn't meant it as a compliment. She was smiling, which mattered more than the words she chose.

"I've noticed you do have a following around here. I'm actually surprised you're not down at the hockey arena tonight. I expected you and your entourage to be in the thick of all the excitement."

"Yeah, well, Holly is there, maybe on a date with Paolo actually, or hanging out, but I, well"—she let out a low whistle—"I may or may not have been a little too likable to one of Team USA's goalies two years ago."

Elise raised her eyebrows. "Too likable?"

"She was here for a week. We had some fun, maybe too much fun. What was supposed to offer a little light entertainment turned into a stage five clinger situation."

"Stage five clinger." Elise shook her head. "There you go with your brilliant use of language again."

"I could've said she turned into a crazy stalker."

"I guess everything's relative," Elise admitted. "Do you run into her often?"

"You wouldn't think so, because hockey and snowboarding don't have much in common, but they play here several times a year for national events, and since I live nearby, it's harder to hide. She kind of slept over at my place. Hindsight's 20/20 on that one."

"Wait, 'your place,' as in a house with a real kitchen and non-dorm-style beds?"

Corey nodded, then rested her chin atop her folded arms. The water wasn't so bad since her lower extremities had gone numb. "Yeah, a log cabin in the woods. Why?"

"Why in God's name are you here?" Elise practically yelled.

"I told you. Stage five clinger knows where I live. I have to sneak in the training room while she's not around, then make sure she's headed back here before I make my break for home tonight."

"I don't mean tonight. I mean all the time. You're never not here. You eat in the cafeteria every night. You hang out in the break rooms. Why?"

She'd never given the question much thought. "Why not?"

"Because dorms and cafeterias and break rooms are for people who can't have the comforts of home. They're a sad reminder of everything you miss while you're away."

"Do other people really think of this place as somewhere they have to go?" she asked.

"Yes," Elise said emphatically.

"That's funny," Corey said, though the thought actually made her sad. "I've always felt blessed to be here. It's an Olympic training facility. Hundreds, if not thousands, of athletes would kill to have an opportunity like this, and it's right in my backyard."

"But the food?"

"The food is free, made by someone else, cleaned up by someone else, and especially suited to athletes' diets."

"But surely you've got more comfortable furniture at your house than the breakroom couches."

"Yeah," she admitted, "but the breakrooms are filled with interesting people. Athletes and trainers and officials come from all over to study all kinds of different things. If you engage them, you hear the best stories and learn the coolest things. In my house, it's just me."

Elise turned to face her fully now, her blue eyes filled with curiosity instead of their usual frost, but before she could say anything, the timer on her watch began to beep.

Corey nearly cursed the sound. Ten minutes ago she wouldn't have thought it possible to want anything more than she wanted out of the water, but now she would've gladly withstood the discomfort another minute or two to hear what Elise would've said. Instead, she watched Elise straighten her arms and haul her beautiful body onto the railing. The water ran in rivulets down her cold, tightened muscles. Funny, Corey didn't feel cold at all anymore.

"You survived, champ," she said, shaking out her limbs. "You had your first of many ice baths?"

Corey shuddered and climbed out as well. "Yeah, we'll see."

"I don't know how you live without them."

"I know, right?" Corey said sarcastically, "I lived thirty years without purposely freezing my nipples off until I met you."

Elise's eyes flickered to Corey's chest, and she saw it. Just a little movement, but enough to make it clear the ice woman had a little heat in her veins after all. Corey didn't even try to hide her grin as Elise carried on in her professional tone.

"You'll notice a difference tomorrow. Especially as we age, it's important to maximize the rebound process."

Images of Tigger and reporters flashed through her mind. "Age?"

"I may be twenty-five, but I've already pushed my body harder than most people do in an entire life. Don't tell me your joints have had an easy quarter century."

She didn't point out she actually had five solid years of heavy competition on Elise. She didn't even want to think about the exponential rate at which her body had deteriorated in that time. She certainly wouldn't admit she'd come in to snag an extra packet of bio-freeze.

"Trust me. You'll notice less soreness tomorrow."

"What makes you think I had soreness to begin with?" Corey asked, trying to keep the defensiveness from her voice. She started for the stairs, saying, "I got in there for you, remember?"

Instead of laughing or shooting back in the same tone, Elise stopped her with a soft hand on her arm. "There's nothing wrong with being a little sore sometimes. You're an elite athlete in the middle of training for the Olympics. Aches and even minor pains are expected."

Corey sighed as the tension slipped from shoulders she'd barely realized were knotted. "An elite athlete? Not a joke?"

Elise looked away. "Corey, I said some things, and I'm not sure why, but—"

"But nothing." Corey shrugged as she settled back on the ledge to let some feeling return to her legs. "I've been competing my whole life. I know what other athletes think of boardercross. You're not the first person to say those things. Hell, it wasn't even an Olympic sport when I got started."

"Really?" Elise asked.

"Sure, it's not like your gig. We're the new kids on the mountain. I never got into the sport with an end game in mind. We didn't even get invited to the party until I was eighteen."

"You trained for years before that, though, right?"

"Oh sure, I've been rubbing elbows with the boys since I was eleven. The tours and championships and the USSA, they're all Johnny-come-lately."

"But what about all your success? I don't follow snowboarding, but people around here seem impressed with your accomplishments. Surely you had a hand in cultivating the sport into what it is today."

She shrugged off the compliment and the weight of responsibility accompanying it. "I got lucky to be in the right place at the right time. I peaked with the sport. There was no precedent to chase. I didn't even understand what I was getting into in Turin in 2006. The Olympics came into my world more than I came into theirs."

"And yet you *medaled*," Elise said in the way that she might whisper the name of a lost lover.

"Yeah, I had a blast. The most fun I'd ever had until that point."

"Fun," Elise repeated, as though the word sounded foreign. "I bet the sponsors came pouring in."

"Oh sure," Corey admitted, her shoulders tensing again, and this time she couldn't blame the cold. "I did the press junkets, all the morning shows, and the late night shows, too. Even I got sick of me on TV. I'm sure you did, too."

"Actually, I don't remember seeing you on TV ever."

"Ouch. Way to knock me down a peg."

Elise laughed. "To be fair, I was fourteen and at boarding school. I didn't watch much TV, and when I did, I focused on obscure ski races, not daytime talk shows."

"Fourteen?" Corey made a show of putting some space between them. "I didn't know I've been half naked with a minor all this time."

"I was fourteen eleven years ago," Elise corrected. "I'm not jail-bait anymore."

"No, now you're the Ice Princess."

"Ah, you've heard the rumors?" Elise asked, her facial expression returning to a studiously neutral position. "I don't apologize for my focus or my demeanor. I'm here to ski, not rush a sorority."

"Rumors?" Corey teased. "What? You mean that wasn't an original nickname?"

Elise didn't smile, but her shoulders relaxed. "Original? I've heard it every season since I won my first race at age ten. My skiing, my eyes, my . . . stoicism."

"Stoicism," she repeated. Not the word she would've chosen, but it fit. "When you were ten? I've never even heard of a stoic ten-year-old, much less met one."

"I wasn't some sort of childhood robot. I had fun, too," she said. "But I had more fun when I won. I've never understood what's so hard to get about that? People always said, 'go out there and have fun,' but given the choice between winning a race and coming in last, don't you think it's more fun to come across the finish line first?"

"Sure," she said, almost dreamy with the memories of seeing her board slide in ahead of all the others. "All the tensions fade away, but the adrenaline is still pumping. It's the best high in the world."

"If I'm supposed to have fun, and winning is the most fun part of my job, why should people act like wanting to win is some sin?"

"Sound logic," she agreed, amused and a little surprised no one had ever laid out the argument so concisely for her. "That's why you're sneaking into the trainers' room on a Friday night? You're doing it all for the fun?"

Elise scoffed. "Yeah, that's my excuse. I'm taking cold baths to prepare myself to have more fun than the USSA thinks I'm capable of having on a bum knee."

"Damn right. We do squats for the fun. We deadlift for the fun. We drink chalky protein shakes for the fun."

"You do chair sits for the fun?" Elise nudged her playfully.

"Yes. From now on, 'fun' will be our code word for everything we do to get to the kicking-all-the-ass part."

Elise did finally crack a smile. "No one will know but us."

Corey's chest expanded, a lightness pressing at her ribs until they almost ached. "An unsupervised cold bath and a secret code word. We're becoming real partners in crime tonight. What would people think if they heard we'd spent time together without wanting to kill each other?"

Elise didn't respond, but she continued to smile as she rose and headed for the stairs.

"What? Do you disagree? Most of the people we know, and pretty much every one we don't, would be shocked to find us hanging out."

"Probably," Elise finally admitted, grabbing herself a towel and tossing another to Corey. "But I did sort of want to kill you when you first came in."

"Okay, well, if we're being fair, I might've been a little torqued off when you tried to lie to me, but now we've gone at least fifteen minutes without any murderous fantasies, right?"

"Oh, at least. I'm sure our trainers would consider this session a real breakthrough, not that either of our trainers can ever know."

Corey hopped down and stole one more glance at Elise's phenomenal form before she wrapped herself in a towel. "It'll be another one of the secrets we get to share."

Chapter Five

"Explode up, Elise," Paolo commanded. "More harder, not the toes, the whole leg."

She squatted down, gritted her teeth and tried to jump three feet off the ground. She probably could have, too, if not for the added weight Paolo'd piled on today.

"More harder," he called enthusiastically, and she crashed back down to a squat, the weights crashing loudly on either side of her.

"More harder," she muttered. "More harder. Why don't you get a whip and shout, 'mush, mush'?"

"Don't tempt me," he said. "Go again."

She braced herself for the fire that would race through her quads, but she didn't back off. Setting her jaw once more, she pushed up with all the brute force her body could muster, certain this time both feet would leave the ground, only to be disappointed when she barely made it onto her toes before getting yanked down again.

"She's phoning this one in, Paolo," Corey called as she ambled across the gym and slapped him on the back. "You going to let her off easy almost two weeks into August?"

"Easy?" Elise snapped as she tried to stand up. She liked to tower over Corey, but she couldn't with the weights anchoring her down.

"It's not a real workout until you get off the ground."

"Would you like to come a little closer and say that?"

"What? You couldn't hear me from here?" Corey laughed. "I could talk louder for you."

"You can get loud and obnoxious at the same time? Shocker."

"Sassy. I like it."

"Get a little closer, see how much you like it," Elise said.

"All right." Corey tossed a water bottle to Paolo and dropped her sweaty towel to the floor. "I'll climb into the ring."

"Corey," Paolo warned, "it's not wise to poke the bear."

She'd have to punish Paolo for the bear comment later. Right now any predatory instincts she had were focused solely on Corey, who'd wandered dangerously close to being within arms reach. Elise eyed her like a cat ready to pounce. Today Corey wore bright blue track shorts and matching tennis shoes. She'd topped off the outfit with a tight fitting T-shirt featuring a picture of a snow-boarder on a ski lift and a caption reading, "Do you even lift, bro?" Corey's golden mane hung almost to her shoulders, but the few sweat-soaked strands sticking to her forehead and neck suggested she'd already put in a strenuous workout of her own.

"You can't get it up, huh?" Corey joked. "I've been known to help a woman or two out of that predicament."

Elise's cheeks flamed, but she only shook her head as Corey edged closer, then moved in a circle behind the stabilizer bar Elise had her hands on. One more step, and she'd be able to grab her by the scruff of her silly little T-shirt. She wasn't sure what she'd do from there, but Corey wouldn't make another smart-ass remark so quickly next time. But instead of coming closer, Corey started to climb. First, she hopped from the floor to a nearby weight-lifting bench. Then she scrambled onto the weight-lifting apparatus closest to Elise.

Several people stopped their workouts to watch Corey monkey into position. She was nimble and strong. Elise would grant her that. Corey swung one leg and then the other around to the front of the equipment. She now balanced three feet above ground, braced between two metal uprights with her feet on two of the pegs normally used to hold weights.

"Oh for fuck's sake," Nate called from across the gym. "Get down, Corey. You'll break a leg."

"I'm fine. She's not going to jump this high," Corey teased.

The comment cut through Elise's confusion and caused her annoyance to boil over once again, only this time she had an audience to contend with. Nearly a week had passed since their covert cold bath, and she'd grown used to seeing Corey across the gym or in yoga class without feeling the grating sensation usually associated with fingernails on a chalkboard. On her more generous days, they'd even managed to make polite conversation in short doses. Paolo had been angling for a group outing with the LaCroix crew that weekend, and she'd almost relented, her only concerns focused more on the distraction from the training schedule rather than a general dislike of her present company. And yet, all her goodwill evaporated as Corey stretched out an arm above her like a chimp swinging between trees and said, "Hey, Elise, gimme a high five."

She stood as much as she could under the weighted belt, but even without stretching out her arm, she could tell Corey's hand hovered about an inch out of reach. She'd have to jump higher than she had yet been able to, which of course Corey knew as well. Hell, the whole gym probably knew. If the other athletes hadn't watched her workout earlier, they were certainly watching now. Everyone for rows around them stopped to see their local celebrity play the part of lion tamer. Elise didn't appreciate being cast in the role of lion.

Of course, she could refuse the part. She could tell Corey to fuck right off. Corey seemed to respond to that kind of language. If she delivered the message in the icy tone she'd worked hard to cultivate, she could freeze her dangling from her perch. Then again, she didn't want Corey frozen on her perch. She wanted to make her fall. She wanted to jump up there, drag her down and shake her senseless.

She ran her hands over her sweat-beaded face and blew out a heavy breath before meeting her eyes once more.

Corey smiled down at her, all golden and charming and oh so

cocky. Her hazel eyes flashed with mischief. "Come on, E. Don't leave me hanging."

"You're going to regret this," Elise warned.

"Nah, I've made a lot of regrettable decisions with women, but I feel pretty good about this one."

"Fine," Elise mumbled. Go ahead and doubt. Corey wouldn't be the first or the last person to do so. Every detractor only laid another log on the fire burning inside her. The higher the flame grew, the more it fueled her desire to prove them wrong.

Settling deep in the crouch, knees bent, back straight, she coiled every muscle in her lower body, then without even a countdown or a word of warning she exploded into the air. Her arms and legs straightened in unison. Both her feet cleared the ground, but she wasn't worried about her feet. All her attention focused tightly on the end of her outstretched fingers as they rocketed toward Corey's hand. Not only did they reach their target, she overshot Corey's palm and wrapped around her wrist as the weights took hold.

When gravity and cast-iron conspired against her, she refused to relinquish her prize, and holding tight to Corey, dragged her down from her self-selected throne.

A cheer went up from the onlookers, but she barely heard them. All her focus remained on reeling Corey in. Still grasping her wrist like a winning lottery ticket, once Corey's feet landed catlike on the padded gym floor, Elise did some pouncing of her own. She caught hold of her other arm and pulled her forward as close as the bars and restraints would allow. Then cupping the back of Corey's neck, she doubled her over the handrail.

"Uncle, Uncle," Corey cried, laughter shaking her shoulders, but Elise had no mercy to offer. All the endorphins of the challenge and ensuing victory still coursed through her, and she had to burn them somehow. Taking Corey into an awkward headlock, she knuckled the top of her scalp and rubbed aggressively, twisting the amber mane as she did.

"Noogies?" Corey laughed heartily. "I never pegged you for a noogie woman."

"Yeah, well"—Elise worked hard to keep from smiling—"I'd rather strangle you, but people are watching."

"All right, all right. You made your point."

"No, I'm still making it." She rubbed some more. "I don't like being teased."

"But you responded," Corey protested, though she did little to try to squirm away.

"She's right," Paolo cut in. "Go easy on her. She got you off the ground."

Elise stopped as the comment sank in. She'd gotten off the ground. Weights and all. To grab Corey's whole wrist, she'd had to jump almost two inches higher than the best she'd been able to muster on her own. Despite all the grit and work and burning muscles and doubling her efforts or adjusting her stance, stupid Corey with her games and her annoying court-jester antics had pushed her to a personal best.

She released Corey and quietly started to unbuckle her restraint belt. "Let's call it a day on this one."

"Yes," said Paolo almost gleefully. "You're done here. How do your legs feel?"

Letting the belt fall to the floor, she took a couple of uninhibited knee bends to confirm what she already suspected. "No pain."

Paolo looked from her to Corey, who wore her usual excessive grin. "It might be time to try another joint workout. I can live with the bickering better if you two can produce these results together."

She shook her head. "No. This wasn't a shared workout. We didn't produce anything together. We aren't training buddies. That's not what any of this was about."

"No," Corey said, still giggling. "It was about the fun."

Elise bit the inside of her cheek to keep from smiling. She didn't want to give away her pleasure at having Corey recognize how much she enjoyed the allusion to ass-kicking. "No, that wasn't even about fun. It was me teaching you not to doubt me."

Corey stilled her laughter as her expression grew serious. Then leaning close, she clasped Elise on the shoulder, looked her straight in the eye, and whispered, "I never did."

⁂

Corey stepped gingerly through the office wing of the training center complex trying not to garner the attention of anyone working behind some of the open office doors. She didn't normally come over this way, but upstate New York was experiencing a rare one-hundred-degree day.

"Thanks global warming," she muttered, as she turned another corner, trying to cool down inconspicuously. She should've been walking on the indoor track, but the gym was packed with all the outdoor athletes who'd moved inside due to the heat, and the old air conditioning units could barely keep up with the weather, much less all the added sweaty bodies. This side of the compound smelled better, too, like clean paper instead of perspiration.

Besides, these hallways wound around forever and were deliciously cool. Who could blame her for choosing an unconventional venue for her half-mile wind-down? Even Nate hadn't argued. Maybe he shared her eagerness to get the hell out of the gym and into a cold shower. He also had a meeting with Holly. Something about sponsors for Team USA. She didn't pay attention because she didn't care about billboards or names painted on the side of table jumps. As long as no one tried to paint a McDonald's logo on her board, she'd rather stay out of the conversation.

She appreciated the officials and race organizers and travel agents and fundraisers. Without them, she'd probably work 9-to-5 at the Lake Henry sporting goods store and teach snowboarding to local kids on the weekend. While she could do worse, she wouldn't trade her current life for anything. Racing was all she'd ever wanted to do. As long as the people here didn't interfere with her work on the slopes, she'd intrude on their domain only long enough to steal ten minutes worth of their air conditioning and carpeted hallways.

"Dammit, Don." A familiar voice cut through the subdued sounds of keyboard typing and copy machines. "She's going to be ready before the Olympics."

"But will she be ready in time to qualify for the Olympics?"

"She'll *be* qualified. She'll be more better qualified than anyone to win you a gold."

Paolo. No missing that accent. Corey slowed drastically.

"I'll admit when I reviewed her initial X-rays, I thought she might be done for good," the other voice—Don, apparently—said. "But I no longer doubt she'll come back and compete eventually, but questions remain about when and at what level."

"Will you fund her?"

"Of course," Don said, and Corey let out a sigh of relief.

"She can start the season on the B Team," Don continued.

"The B Team?" Paolo exploded again. "She's an Olympian. She's a world champion. She was number one in the world when she went down."

"You don't have to give me her résumé. I've known her since her first year in high school. I've always done right by her."

"Have you, Don?" Paolo asked in a way that made the hair on Corey's arms stand up.

"I've always treated her like a daughter. I've met her parents. I know how they get. I've always made the extra effort to let her know we cared about her. Hell, she even spent two Christmases with my family."

"Did she get an invitation last Christmas?" Paolo asked pointedly. "Did you visit her in the hospital? Did you ever call to check on her rehab progress?"

"I got updates from the team doctors."

"Did you ever once personally check on the woman you say you treated like a daughter?"

Her stomach churned as the silence stretched on. She knew the answer. She'd heard it in Elise's voice when she mentioned all the people who didn't believe in her anymore.

"Okay, Paolo," Don finally continued, his voice tight and tired. "I know you want to make me the bad guy, but I'm running an Olympic team here. I have at least twenty other skiers who want a spot on this team, and every one of them has a story. Every one of them has potential to be a star."

"She's already a star," Paolo said.

"She *was* a star, and I hope she will be again someday soon, but is it fair to ask everyone else to put their dreams on hold because she *might* make a highly unlikely comeback?" The question was clearly rhetorical because he didn't wait for an answer. "I can't bank my career and the career of everyone else on your word that she'll be ready in time."

"Will you consider her for a discretionary pick?"

Corey rubbed her face as she considered what a nightmare that would be. Discretionary picks were not democratic. They didn't depend on hard-and-fast criteria like World Cup standings. They were made by a committee of suits and coaches in back rooms shrouded in what-ifs and might-bes. It wasn't that she didn't think they had their place, or Elise didn't deserve one, but they never came without controversy. Could someone like Elise stand up to that kind of doubt? Or would it only compound the panic Corey had seen on her face in the cold bath?

"I'll give her the same consideration I give every other athlete," Don finally said. "But I have to caution you against trying to put too much emphasis on past performance. With her injury, she might never be who she was, and just because she's on track now—"

"She's ahead of the track," Paolo cut in.

"I'm not going to argue that point, but I can't hold up the future because of her past."

Corey clenched her fists as tightly as her stomach had been clenched through this entire conversation. She could barely contain the protectiveness welling up inside of her now. She knew little about knee injuries but a lot about passion and competitive drive, and Elise had plenty to go around. If she'd already come so far so much faster than the doctors expected, it seemed stupid to bet against her finishing the job. She deserved every ounce of support and confidence Team USA could show her.

"Have you stopped to wonder if you might be pushing her right off the Olympic podium?" Paolo asked.

Don sighed heavily. "We're going around in circles, and it's time for both of us to get back to work. Unless you have any new information for me, I'll see you in Argentina."

Paolo stepped out of the doorway and Corey scrambled around the corner to keep from being caught eavesdropping, but he was too busy firing his final shots to see her. "She gave you everything she's had since she was kid, Don. Maybe she won't make the team, and if she doesn't earn her spot, that's on me and her, but if you don't give her every fucking opportunity to do so, that's on you."

Corey raised her fist in silent solidarity as Paolo slammed the door behind him and thankfully stormed off in the other direction. She stood in the once-again quiet hallway with her back to the wall and her eyes toward the bright florescent lights. She took deep calming breaths as she tried to kill the desire to stomp into Don's office and do a little yelling of her own. She had no points to add to Paolo's and much less right to make them on Elise's behalf. Hell, she barely knew the woman. And yet her urge to run to her rescue, to kick down the door, and to shake some sense into a man she'd also never met screamed so loudly inside her head she could barely think straight.

Did she really care about Elise? Did she even know her well enough to make that call? Hadn't Don made a few good points himself? He'd at least asked some reasonable questions. Maybe that's what bothered her most of all. Don had landed a few blows of his own. Snow sports were grueling and dangerous and competitive and taxing. If the mountains didn't break you down, the next generation was bound to pass you on the turns. Where did loyalty belong in the equation?

She didn't know the answer. She didn't even like knowing the questions. She lifted her hand to massage a tight muscle where her neck met her shoulder and take inventory of her own body.

So much for cooling off. She flexed a slight cramp near her left ankle. Was it just her or did winding down take more time than it used to? No, she quickly banished that thought. She'd merely tensed up while eavesdropping on a heated conversation.

71

This is why she stayed out of the business end of the building. She didn't want any part in any of these conversations. She didn't like the questions asked here, and she definitely didn't want to wonder if those questions needed to be asked about her.

"Corey and crew are gate-training this afternoon," Paolo said casually, as she joined him outside the locker room.

"And?" She tried to sound neutral. She'd had a great massage, and she didn't want to risk tensing up again after a trainer had worked so hard to undo the damage of her most recent increase in core workouts.

"I thought maybe, since we're done for the day," he glanced at his watch with contrived nonchalance, "and it's not time for dinner yet, you might want to stop in and say hi."

"You thought *I* might want to say hi to Corey? Or you thought *you* might like to say hi to Holly."

He grinned sheepishly. "We could do both at the same time."

"I'm sure we could, but I think one of us wants to more than the other."

"I think it's easier for one of us to admit what we want."

She shook her head. Why did Paolo always have to push things one step further than she was comfortable with? "I might have given in if not for that comment."

"What? Why do you keep pretending like you hate her?"

"I never said I hated her," Elise said, then grimaced when she remembered a few conversations where she might have purposely tried to convey the message without using those exact words.

"But you're pretending you don't like her."

She flipped her hair over her shoulder and turned to face the plate glass window overlooking a gym filled with glorified toys and foam pits. "I'm not. We've made our peace."

"She's gotten you to try new things and push harder than your previous records, and we both know you push pretty hard on your own."

"Let's not overstate things. She pushed buttons. A few of them happened to be the right ones."

"If anyone else pushed the same buttons, you would've shut down. If I climbed a weight machine and told you to jump, you would've threatened to fire me."

She laughed lightly. "I might have actually fired you."

"And yet you smiled at the memory of Corey doing the same thing. And it's not the first time. She made you smile in yoga class yesterday, during boat pose, or whatever she called it."

"The 'honey-I'm-home' pose," Elise said with a smile. "I don't deny she's funny. But I can't let the class clown cause me to lose focus."

"You didn't think she was such a joke when you were on the balance board today."

"No." Elise agreed quickly. "The exercise turned out to be a stellar addition to our regimen. And I didn't mean to imply she wasn't a serious athlete."

"Didn't you?"

"I honestly didn't. Not anymore." That night in the cold pool she'd seen reflections of the same doubts she faced flash across Corey's eyes, and she'd hated being the one to spark them. Then again, she'd also seen her abs. No, nothing internal or external suggested Corey was anything less than a serious contender. She turned to face him again so he could see her sincerity. "I only used the term 'clown' to describe her sense of humor, which I'll admit I've learned to appreciate."

"But?"

"I'm tired, and I'm focused, and I'm busy. I'm five months away from being named to an Olympic contingent. I don't have time to make new friends."

He looked past her into the gym and frowned.

"What?"

"Hmm?" he asked.

"You looked away when I mentioned the Olympic team."

"No." He shook his head. "I got distracted."

She briefly considered pressing him for more details, but a

small part of her didn't want to know where his mind had gone.

"There's always time for friends," he said, pulling the conversation back to more comfortable topics.

"That's never been my experience."

"Because you've never picked the right kind of friends."

So much for comfortable topics. "You think Corey and company are different from the others?"

Paolo smiled and nodded over her shoulder. She turned to watch Corey ride a snowboard down a fiberglass ramp. Knees bent, eyes forward, feet strapped to her board, she executed a textbook start, but instead of sliding to a stop at the base of the ramp, she reached out, caught Nate by the scruff of his T-shirt, and dragged him into the foam pit with her. As she lay atop a pile of foam blocks, she threw back her head, and her shoulders shook with laughter Elise could feel even if she couldn't hear.

"What do you think?" Paolo asked, bumping her shoulder with his own. "Does she seem like anyone you usually hang out with?"

She shook her head and sighed. "Fine, we can go say hello."

Paolo slapped her on the back, his smile bright before he turned and speed-walked down the stairs into the gym. She followed him slightly less enthusiastically. He had a point about her track record with so-called friends. She had people she enjoyed talking to occasionally and people she compared notes with. She exchanged Christmas cards with a few women from school. For a while, before the accident, she had people she traveled with, people she often dined with, people she thought she could trust to help her out in a pinch. She hadn't heard from any of those people in quite a while. Watching Holly pull Nate out of the foam pit before turning to offer a hand to Corey, Elise knew for certain these weren't the same kind of people. Their circle would go unbroken no matter what favor or misfortune the fates heaped on them. She felt much less sure of whether or not she could ever fit in a circle of that nature.

And, even though she'd grown to appreciate Corey's sense of humor, she didn't share it. She wasn't jovial or even-keeled. She didn't relax easily. Playfulness didn't come naturally to her. She'd always banked on her success to win her the connections she needed, but Corey had enough success on her own. What could a woman like Elise possibly offer them to garner their acceptance?

"Hey, Easy E," Corey called. "How'd your workout go today?"

"Easy E?" she asked.

"Yeah," Corey said with a grin. "Easy, 'cause you must be going easy on your workouts since you're already in your non-sweaty clothes at three o'clock."

"Are you kidding me?" she sputtered.

"Yeah," Corey laughed. "I'm joshing. I saw you in the gym at 7:45 this morning. Looked like you were having some fun."

"Tons of fun," Elise said seriously. "So I won't expect to hear that nickname again."

"Oh, the nickname sticks, E," Corey said, obviously undeterred by her business face, "but from now on you should know the 'easy' part is because you're easy on the eyes."

Paolo laughed nervously. "See, a compliment? She's nice. I can't imagine why you didn't want to come down here and talk to her."

Everyone else laughed along with him. Everyone but her. She didn't find the joke particularly funny. She didn't find it unpleasant either. She'd been told her whole life she was beautiful, or rather that she'd be beautiful if only she'd smile more. She never knew how to respond to those comments. They always came with an expectation at best and a sense of entitlement at worst. Corey's comment carried neither, just a simple, joyful statement of fact.

"Hey, whatcha doin' Friday night?" Corey asked, bending down to unlatch her board.

"Studying video."

Corey made the sound of a game show buzzer. "Oh, I'm sorry, wrong answer."

"We've got the video room reserved from seven to nine. Friday night is definitely study night."

"I'm going to have to check my calendar," Corey pulled out

her phone and tapped the screen a few times before turning it around to show Elise. "You're mistaken. Says right here, Friday night is cheat night."

She checked the screen, and sure enough Corey had marked cheat night in bright red letters for the space between eight p.m. and midnight. "Looks like we have conflicting schedules."

"Looks like you should try to reserve the video room for Thursday night, then name your poison, and I'll be sure to have it on hand on Friday." Then looking over her shoulder, she said, "Malbec for you, Paolo?"

He eyed Elise hopefully, as though he were a small boy and Corey had just asked him if he wanted a puppy.

"Friday's video night," she said, with a little less force.

"We could get the room Thursday. I checked."

"You already checked?" She planted a fist on each hip and tapped the toe of her sneaker against the gym mat. "This isn't a casual drop-in at all, is it?"

"Whoops," Corey said. "Misplayed that one, dude."

Holly and Nate apparently found something interesting on the ceiling and Corey backed away.

"Oh, I get it," Elise said. "I'm being ambushed."

"It's for your own good, honey," Paolo said. "You haven't taken a day off since we got here. And we'll be on the snow in two weeks. You won't get one then."

"I'm wrestling my body back into shape."

"And you're doing a marvelous job, if you ask me," Corey cut in.

"But you can't let your body think you're going to run it right into an early grave," Paolo said seriously. "Cheat days are used by a lot of programs to keep you from plateauing in your progress."

"Sorry, Paolo," she said. "I'm not buying what you're selling. You want a night off to drink wine with Holly."

"Well"—he turned to smile at Holly, who returned the expression—"can you blame me? She's really pretty."

Elise finally cracked a smile. "At least you're being honest now."

"So, points for honesty?" Corey asked hopefully.

Elise turned from one expectant face to another. She supposed a cheat day wouldn't be the end of the world. And she could do her video work on Thursday. She wouldn't lose the work time outright. Who was she trying to kid? She could logic all she wanted, but she'd only be justifying her real motive of wanting to see what it felt like to be part of a fun group for once. "All right. Friday is cheat night."

They all cheered.

"Thanks," Paolo whispered as he hugged her. "I owe you one."

"Yeah, you do," she said with a smile that made it clear they both knew that wasn't at all the case. He'd been much more than a coach to her the last few years, and even now she suspected the deal he'd struck had been made on her behalf as much as his.

Chapter Six

Corey surveyed the rented room at the Lake Henry Inn. Dark wood floors and natural light combined for a soothing effect. Along one wall stood a fully stocked bar, and on the opposite was a long buffet table loaded with foods not traditionally served at the training centers. Overstuffed chairs and leather sofas scattered about and clustered together offered ample seating, and the music was upbeat enough to keep the mood lively without drowning out conversation. On the far side of the space, two sets of French doors led to a small balcony overlooking Lake Henry, and between them stood a large stone fireplace, which might get put to use after sunset for the sole purpose of roasting marshmallows. The setup wasn't ostentatious. The room could probably hold thirty people at most, and Corey had no intention of maxing out its capacity tonight. She'd thrown her fair share of star-studded blowout bashes over the years, but these days she favored the casual company of a chosen few. This venue offered a little privacy, a little comfort, and a lot of ambiance.

She glanced up as another handful of people walked in. She smiled and waved to Mikael the yoga instructor and his wife, then waited patiently while the doorman she'd hired to work as part security, part coat check relieved them of their cell phones and pointed them to the bar.

"Keeping an eye on the door?" Holly asked as she sidled up next to her, glass of red wine in hand.

"I'm the host. I have to be hostessy."

"That's what you kept me on the payroll for, to handle the glad-handing."

"Naw, you're off the clock tonight. No official business happening here. We don't get many cheat nights, and there will be even fewer in the months to come. You should make the most of your night off, too."

"Oh, I plan to," Holly said with a sly smile. "But I don't mind mixing business with pleasure."

"You do it exceedingly well." Corey threw an arm around her shoulder. "And that's why I pay you the big bucks. You get the work done without cutting into my fun."

"I'm glad you think so. I used to worry you'd cut me loose as soon as you turned eighteen and didn't need a chaperone anymore."

She laughed, "Yeah well, I still needed someone to drive Mom and Dad's old minivan while I slept in between races."

"The baby blue beast." Holly joined in the laughter. "With the peeling fake wood on the side, like something out of a seventies porn flick."

"Sometimes we used it that way, too."

Holly raised her eyebrow. "Maybe *you* did."

"Oh come on. You never made use of the shaggin' wagon with Nato?"

"What?" Nate asked, joining them.

"Nothing," Holly said quickly. "We were talking about the good ol' days of being board bums before Corey made the tour."

A huge smile stretched his cheeks. "Good times. Who would've thought back then that we'd get to stand here now?"

"Or have first-class tickets to New Zealand for training in two weeks."

"No shit," Corey said. "Remember when we drove cross-country to get to Aspen the first time and we slept in the back of the van?"

"And you still won gold," Nate reminded her. "Me, not so much."

"Yeah, but didn't it feel like life couldn't get any bigger?"

He tousled her hair. "Why the stroll down memory lane?"

She shrugged, not knowing the answer. She'd never wanted those days to end, but she was glad to have the best parts of them with her all these years later.

"She's killing time until you-know-who arrives."

"Who?" Nate and Corey asked in unison, then exchanged a look of confusion and a joint shrug before turning back to her.

"There." Holly nodded toward the front door as Paolo walked in.

"She's waiting for Paolo?" Nate asked. "He's more your type than Core's."

"He is," Holly said with an exasperated sigh, "which is why I'm lucky Corey's every bit as interested in Elise."

"Am not," she said even as her heart gave a little jump at the sight of her coming into view.

Both Holly and Nate laughed.

"Whatever you have to tell yourself, honey." Holly gave her a little shove toward the door. "But go tell it over there long enough to give me some alone time with Paolo, okay?"

Corey frowned slightly, but she knew better than to disobey. She didn't like the implication that she'd been waiting for Elise's arrival, but she was happy to see her. She hadn't fully shaken the protective instincts she'd felt while eavesdropping last week, and she'd be lying to herself if she said she hadn't enjoyed their last few encounters.

"Hi guys," she said, meeting them at the door, where the doorman had requested their phones. Paolo handed his over easily. Elise seemed suspicious.

"I'm going to tag it with your name, Ms. Brandeis, and if you get any calls I'll let you know."

Elise's elegant brow furrowed. "If I keep it, I'll know when I get a phone call."

"It's for privacy," Corey cut in. "It's cheat night. There's beer on tap and cigars on the patio. There's a good chance a poker game might break out, and while I don't expect any truly illicit behavior, I want everyone to relax without fear of someone filming a YouTube video featuring Team USA stuffing their faces full of wings and betting the house on a pair of deuces."

"I appreciate the idea behind the gesture, but I'm an athlete. I'm the one with everything to lose and nothing to gain. Do you think I'm the type to post a cell phone video online?"

"If I made an exception for you, how could you trust me not to make them for everyone?"

"Does he have your phone?"

"Mine and Nate's and Holly's, too."

"How egalitarian of you." Elise sounded mildly impressed.

"It's a good idea," Paolo said. "Thanks for thinking of it, Corey."

"To be honest, I wish I'd thought of it a few years ago, but once bitten, twice shy." Then turning to Elise, she added, "Trust me, okay? Also, don't ever google my name combined with the words 'hot tub' or 'women's bobsled team.'"

Elise's blue eyes widened. "Are you kidding? I never know if you're kidding."

Corey held out her hand. "Hand over the phone, and let's hope you forget the question by the time you get it back, shall we?"

Elise made her wait a few more seconds, hand extended, eyes pleading, before she relented and passed the phone over. "I suppose it's not a bad policy. I have enough to deal with without some amateur paparazzo."

Corey slid the phone over to the doorman and nodded toward the bar. "Now with that out of the way, why don't we find you a nice martini?"

Corey threaded her way through clusters of people and between a few chairs to the bar as Elise followed closely behind.

"Actually, I'm pretty picky about my martinis. I don't usually drink the stuff they keep behind the bar at small hotels."

"Are you suggesting you're a liquor snob?" Corey flashed her a smile, and then before waiting for a response signaled the bartender. "I'd like a dry martini, up. Please use the Plymouth for this one."

Elise pushed close enough to lean on the bar and examine the bottle as the young bartender poured. He set the martini glass delicately before Elise, who warily lifted it to her perfectly poised mouth. Corey held her breath watching her sip. She closed her eyes, the corners of her lips twitched up, and Corey exhaled.

Victory.

The pride filling her chest might have made her wonder again about Holly's earlier comment if Elise hadn't once again fixed her with her blue gaze.

"Well-played." She lifted the glass in salute. "And well-researched. I assume you don't have Plymouth on hand at all times."

"Paolo may have dropped a hint or two. Holly has some Malbec in store for him."

"Again, nicely done." She sounded pleasantly surprised. "You're a thoughtful hostess."

"We don't get to go off-track often. When we do, I want everyone to make the most of the opportunity."

"You want everyone to be as happy as you are," Elise said matter-of-factly.

"I guess so. Or I at least want to give everyone the opportunity."

"A noble pursuit. Most people of your success level would expect to have their wishes catered to rather than catering to the wishes of other people."

"Been there. Done that. Believe it or not, it's not nearly as satisfying. What's the point of having it all if you can't share it?"

Elise let her eyes drift slowly around the room before settling back on Corey more intently. "I find it hard to believe someone like you would lack for people to share things with."

She held her gaze before saying, "Having people around to drink my gin and eat my food isn't the same as having people to share the important things with. It's entirely possible to be in the middle of a crowd and still be completely alone."

"Corey," Elise whispered, and for the first time, the sound of her own name twisted in her chest as the two of them hung suspended in that moment with nothing and no one else around.

What had made her say something so heavy, so personal, and what had Elise heard in the comment that had frozen even the woman who normally sped over ice? Did she know the feeling? Did she fight it? She seemed more like the type to embrace the prospect of standing on the mountaintop alone. Then again, maybe she'd cultivated that mindset out of necessity. The thought bothered her more than any of the others preceding it. She couldn't handle the idea of anyone hurting her.

"Anyway, this is cheat night, not a therapy session."

Elise blinked and her smile returned, but only to its polite position. "Right. Cheat night. You have a much more well-developed concept of that than I do."

"Basically you start with all the things you normally have to say no to during training, and instead you say yes to them."

"Sounds simple."

"It can be, or when done right, it can be an art form."

"Do tell."

"Some people go all in on their big kahuna. They eat the entire pizza or down the whole six pack."

"Or eat twelve tacos?" Elise teased.

"Right. Rookie mistake," Corey said, inordinately pleased Elise remembered the comment and felt relaxed enough to joke with her.

"But then you're stuffed and bloated and feel like you consumed lead. You only satisfied one craving when you had a million different fantasies running through your dreams all month."

"And now you have to wait another month before you get to fulfill the others."

"Exactly," Corey said. "You're a quick learner."

"You paint a vivid picture for me."

"I could draw you a legit diagram, but it'd be easier to stroll along the buffet."

Elise followed closely behind as Corey headed to the far end of a long row of tables pushed up against the wall.

"Wow," Elise said as she surveyed the spread. "I've been doing cheat days all wrong for my whole life."

"I'm not about to tell a woman her business, but yeah you probably have," Corey said. "But don't get carried away now. It's not about quantity. You don't want to gorge yourself and feel terrible."

"I feel you're going to impart some of your hard-won wisdom on how to avoid that."

"Like I said before, I share with my friends." She paused to see if Elise balked at being called a friend. Instead she sipped from her martini glass and waited for Corey to continue. Pleased by the acceptance of the new label, she pushed on. "When we're training, we have our goals for healthy eating, and they are different for every athlete, but we all know what we need a lot of."

"Lean meats, proteins, whole grains, calcium, vitamins A, C, and D."

"Right, things like carbs are a mixed bag based on what we've done and what we have to do," Corey added. "But we also have similar lists of what we shouldn't have."

"Booze, fat, bad carbs, refined sugars."

"You see where I'm going here, right?"

"I do see connections between the list and what's on the tables."

"And what's in your hand." Corey nodded to the gin. "That's your base layer. But aside from not wanting a massive hangover tomorrow, I suggest limiting yourself to one or two of those all night because you don't want to fill up. Both lessons I learned in Sochi, by the way."

"Right. It's shocking we didn't run into each other while there."

Corey caught the sarcasm of the dig and smiled. Elise's droll comments probably put a lot of people off, but she didn't mind having her chops busted by beautiful women. She preferred sass to sycophants any day, another lesson she'd started to learn in Russia. "Anywho, the same premise applies to the food. Variety and moderation."

"But aren't cheat days all about gluttony?"

"They are, but we're professionals here, not 17-year-olds on prom night. You can't blow your wad in the first fifteen minutes."

"Seriously, your way with words, have you ever considered a career in poetry?"

"You never know, maybe I'll write a self-help book when I retire." The last word stuck to the roof of her mouth a little bit, but she didn't want to dwell there. "You can be my first follower."

"Please, lead the way."

"If we call the alcohol level one, then this table represents level two, high-fat foods. As you can see, we've got bacon cheese-burgers, pepperoni pizzas, French fries, buffalo wings, nachos, and so on, but do you notice anything unique about the setup?"

"They're all mini servings."

"Ding ding, we have a winner. Sliders, small plates, pizza cut in squares instead of wedges, get your fix without filling up."

Elise strolled down the line. Same with the bad carbs and sugars. Mini bagels, donut holes, personal cups of chicken Alfredo, cake balls, and kid-size candy bars.

"When I said a little something for everybody, I meant literally little bits."

"Indeed you did. I'm impressed. When you first mentioned this event, I sort of expected a drunken bacchanal, not anything well-planned or tastefully executed."

Corey handed her a small lunch plate. "Here's another pro tip. Use smaller plates. Make a first pass, sit down and enjoy it, then come back for another round or two. Don't shovel it in. Savor."

Elise accepted the plate and started down the line, picking up a slider and a small cup of pasta.

"And when you're locked and loaded for round one, I've got an Adirondack chair on the back deck with your name on it."

"One? Does that mean you aren't going to join in the revelry with me?"

She scanned the room once more, trying to hide her pleasure at the invitation. She should probably circulate and say hi to a few more people, but as much as she wanted her guests to be comfortable, this was her night off, too. She'd purposely kept the list of attendees small and low maintenance so she could relax. Plus Elise might need that concept demonstrated for her. She didn't seem to have much practice settling into the moment. Who was she kidding trying to make excuses? She was going to spend the better part of her evening by Elise's side, not because she needed to, but because she wanted to.

Elise hadn't checked her watch a single time all night. Before arriving at the inn, she'd told Paolo she planned to stay only for an hour, but judging by the way dark blue had begun to overtake the last hints of orange along the Adirondacks' uneven horizon, she'd overstayed her self-imposed limit. Still she made no move to extract herself from the chair her body had molded itself to. She'd probably entered a food coma, or a sugar crash, but she didn't care. Much to her surprise, she felt full and relaxed instead of stuffed and guilt ridden, and it must've shown.

"You look better than I've seen you in years," Paolo said as he leaned against the porch rail opposite her.

"Uh, thanks?" Elise said. "I won't even get mad about the backhanded aspect of that compliment, because I actually feel pretty good, too."

"Didn't I tell you Corey could teach you a thing or two outside the gym as well?"

"Did you?"

He laughed and raised his glass of red wine. "I think I did, though at the moment I can't remember when."

She smiled, and sipped from her second martini. She'd followed Corey's advice on the drink front as well and nursed her first one for over an hour, then chased it with a bottle of water. It wasn't the way she'd been raised, but then again, she didn't put a great deal of stock in the way she'd been raised. Corey certainly knew more about taking time off than any role model she'd had throughout her childhood. In her current state, she didn't mind admitting Corey knew a great many things she didn't. She wasn't sure how important those things were in the grand scheme, but they'd proven helpful tonight. She intended to say so, but as she turned to the chair beside her, she noticed Corey's attention focused not on her, or even on the scenery. She stared at a young woman who'd emerged from the French doors.

"Corey," she called, "this is awesome! Thank you for including me. I've always heard stories about your cheat nights being epic, but I didn't think I'd ever get invited."

"Me either," Holly said under her breath.

"Whoa, Tigger," Corey said, standing up and extending her hand. "It's no big deal, just a little get-together."

Instead of taking her hand, the girl threw her arms around Corey's shoulders and squeezed. Elise raised her eyebrow over the rim of her martini glass. Despite Corey's innuendo about her past indiscretions she wouldn't have pegged her as a cradle robber.

"You finding everything your heart, or at least stomach, desires in there?" Corey asked.

"You know I can't drink, but I'm going to hit the buffet hard," the girl said. "Also, someone said something about s'mores, right?"

"Sure thing." Corey stepped back. "If the fire's not already going, I can get one started for you."

"You can do that? Like now? I want a s'more and you can make it happen?"

"When you set the bar that low, I actually have a chance of meeting expectations." Corey laughed.

"Awesome." The girl bounced off.

"What in all the fucks, dude?" Nate whispered.

Corey threw a chagrined smile over her shoulder as she followed more slowly. "Go Team USA, right?"

"Who was that?" Elise asked when they were both out of earshot.

"Nikki Prince."

Elise shook her head. "Sorry, but again, who is she?"

Paolo raised both his palms to his forehead. "Do you never pay attention to anything other than skiing?"

"What? Is she like a pop star or something?"

"Pretty much," Nate said. "She's the next big thing in boarder-cross. The media loves her. Doesn't hurt that she's young and cute and bubbly."

"But can she race?" Elise asked.

"That's the million dollar question," Holly said. "She rocked the junior circuit pretty hard for the last two seasons. All the coaches and sponsors claim she's the future face of the sport, but she and Corey have yet to face each other. She's only seventeen."

"Wait a second. She's a teenager who's never faced a pro-level competition and they've already crowned her the future of Team USA?"

"They've done the math." Nate said the word "math" as if it were unsavory. "Corey's not getting any younger, but none of their other prospects have eclipsed her in productivity or popularity."

"That speaks highly of Corey. You think they'd do everything they could to keep her happy instead of focusing on a possible replacement."

"You'd think." Nate drank from a bottle of Saranac beer. "But the younger athletes are easier to mold."

"Corey could make things a little easier on herself on that front," Holly said wearily.

"She made it pretty damn easy on them for a long time," Nate shot back with enough force to make Elise wonder what she'd stepped into.

"I'm not saying she should go back. I'm enjoying this version of Corey much more than the one I managed three years ago, but there's a middle ground between selling your soul to a multinational corporation and 'drink water.'"

"I agree, but if we focus on winning again, we won't have to worry about making those kinds of compromises quite so often."

"I'm sorry." Elise cut in, still confused. "What do you mean by 'drink water' or 'selling your soul'?"

"Guys," Corey said in a tone made up of equal parts embarrassment and annoyance as she stepped back onto the patio. "It's cheat night. I leave for like five minutes and you start a corporate takeover?"

"The topic came up in conversation," Holly deflected.

"I started it, apparently," Elise said, still not sure what exactly "it" was. "I don't follow snowboarding much—"

"And by that you mean not even a little bit."

"Right, not at all, but I was only trying to get caught up on your underage guest in there, and somehow we ended up talking about water, though I now think water might be a code word for something else."

"It is," Corey said matter-of-factly as she settled back into the Adirondack chair next to her.

"You seem fond of those," Elise enjoyed the little quirk of a smile Corey tried to hide behind her mug of hot chocolate.

"This one isn't as, shall I say 'fun,' as others you might've heard about. It's not even a code so much as a movement."

"A movement?" she asked, amused. "What, like civil rights?"

"Maybe not that lofty, but progressive. The 'drink water' movement is pushback against over-corporatization of a sport that should belong to athletes and fans," Corey explained.

"How so?"

"When I got started in boardercross racing, we all competed because we loved to. We raced for fun or pride or because we wanted to push the limits. We were outlaws on most slopes. We cut courses between trees and on the backsides of mountains. Even when the tours got running, we were sponsored by board makers or ski resorts. One of my first pro races was funded by two chiropractors and an orthopedic surgeon."

"Fitting," Elise said, not sure where Corey was going, but captivated by the passion in her voice. She'd seen a more serious side to her the night in the trainers room, but she hadn't seen this kind of spark in her before. Now her hazel eyes shone like the stars popping out in the sky overhead.

"We found the connection hilarious, but it still made sense. We rode boards, at ski resorts, and we broke a lot of bones. The sponsors reflected the sport. Then we got bigger. The events got bigger. The crowds got bigger. All of a sudden we were Olympians, and grandmas knew my name. Then people wanted to buy my name."

"You mean they wanted to sponsor you?"

"Yeah, but not like give me money. They wanted me to use their products and to convince other people to use them, too."

"Pretty standard for advertising."

"I did what they wanted . . . for years. But it wasn't only boards and gear and stuff I actually liked. Soon it became cereal and fast food and the Air Force," she scoffed. "'Cause nothing says military recruits like a bunch of board bums with long hair wearing baggy pants, cutting school to crash into each other."

"I can see where there'd be a little bit of a disconnect."

"Yeah. I thought they were stupid, because none of the kids following us around were ever going to join the military and wear uniforms and buzz their hair. I didn't mind because what did I care about how the government wasted their money on advertising? Then I got a deal with a big soda company."

"Corey, that's excellent," Elise gushed. A deal with a company of such mass appeal was the holy grail of sponsorship. She'd been there. Her comeback was still being financed by those residuals long after the ad campaigns ended and the sponsors stopped calling.

"I thought so, too, but after a while these kids started acting like what I said mattered. I had young girls chugging soft drinks on the slopes and acting like they were bosses 'cause they drank what I drank on the posters. And I'm not talking about a can of Coke at the end of a long day. I mean the hyped-up energy drinks that have enough caffeine to kill a cow and so much sugar you practically have to chew them."

"She's talking about Rush." Holly interrupted her story.

"Wait, isn't Rush made by Pepsi? Pepsi is a Fortune 100 gig." Her brain spun trying to do the math on an endorsement of that magnitude.

"Yeah, but it tasted like ass."

"I'd be able to swig castor oil right from the bottle if Pepsi told me to."

"Oh, I did," Corey said. "At least at the photo shoots or the big events, but the kids were all hopped up on the stuff all the time, like speed. And it didn't make them better or faster. It made them slower and weaker and probably dumber, too. I couldn't imagine why any aspiring athlete would put such utter crap in their bodies, so I finally asked a young boarder. "What makes you think you can win a championship with that stuff running through your veins?"

"What did she say?" Elise asked.

"This fourteen-year-old girl stared up at me, no joke, and said, "Because you do.""

Elise's stomach ached, but she couldn't look away from Corey's clenched jaw and faraway stare.

"I finally got it. The Air Force wasn't stupid. Pepsi wasn't stupid. McDonald's wasn't stupid." She shook her head. "I was."

She couldn't decide if she found Corey's conclusion to be admirable or crazy. Probably both. "You walked away from Pepsi?"

"She didn't just walk," Holly said. "She twirled hard and flipped 'em the bird on the way out."

"I was sick of people who didn't know us, people who'd never been on a board acting like they owned us. No one owns me. I wiped all the stickers off my board and replaced them with one big clean white catchphrase that simply says, "Drink water.""

"I remember that," Nikki said, startling them all. No one seemed to have noticed her rejoining them.

Elise suspected everyone else was wondering how much she'd heard. Holly and Nate didn't seem to be fans, or even to trust her particularly. They both clammed up and looked anywhere but at her.

Corey didn't wear her usual smile, but she was gentle. "Oh yeah? Well now there's a big fish left in the sea for you. You can thank me later. Someday you'll probably get the same offer."

"I already did," Nikki said, resting her back against the deck railing in a clear ploy to try to act casual. She appeared impossibly young, her brunette hair pulled back in a simple headband and her jeans slung low enough to reveal a sliver of flat stomach below the hem of her long T-shirt. "They called right after I turned pro a few months ago. I turned them down."

The comment turned every head on the deck. Only the crickets and the muted sound of conversations from inside filled the silence stretching between them. No one knew what to say. Elise

91

wanted to shake her, or ask if all snowboarders were morons or some sort of moralistic communists. Maybe they took too many hits to the head. Instead, she stared from her to Corey with the same slack-jawed expression as everyone else, wondering when someone would offer some sort of reasonable explanation.

Nikki cracked first, her youth showing through once again as she rushed to fill the void. "I, um, I had a poster of you on my bedroom wall when I was seven years old. And later my parents let me stay up late to watch you race in Vancouver when you won the gold. I had this jersey I cut to match like the bibs you wore in races, and when I started competing I couldn't have sponsors because, well, you know the rules, but I scrawled "drink water" on the tail of my board in silver Sharpie."

Corey opened her mouth, then shut it as the kid spilled her heart out, fan-girling for her childhood hero.

Nikki must've realized she'd lost her cool and quickly tried to rein it back in. "I mean, I followed your career all the way up. I tried to race like you did and train like you did. When Pepsi called, it seemed only logical to answer them like you did."

"Logical?" Elise squeaked.

"Yeah." She shrugged without actually portraying an ounce of carelessness. "It's the first time I felt like a real athlete, you know, 'cause when you turn down money like that on principle, you can make a statement, right?"

Everyone continued to stare at her, Elise included. This kid, a literal teenager, turned down life-changing money because Corey said to drink water. What sort of bizarre world had she entered where people made financial and career decisions based on the model of a woman who referred to a yoga chair pose as "pig fucker"?

Corey must've sensed the absurdity of it all as well because she burst out laughing. Not her normal chuckle of amusement, or even the giggle fit she usually got when someone accidently used a double entendre, but deep, rolling laughter that shook her whole body and washed over everyone within a half-mile radius. Several people from inside stuck their heads out to see what was so funny, and Elise couldn't have found the words to answer even if they'd asked.

"I'm sorry. I'm sorry," Corey said, between gasps for air. "I'm not laughing at you. You're a total boss. I had no idea. Really, it's just, did you say you had a picture of me on your wall when you were seven years old?"

Nikki nodded, embarrassment coloring her cheeks enough to be seen even in the dim light spilling out through the French doors.

"Holy fuck," Corey said, laughter still ringing through her voice. "I've never felt as old as I do right now."

"You're not that old, Core," Nate said calmly. "She's really young."

"About as young as I was when she started watching me race," Corey said. Then she turned to Elise, her eyes growing serious. "Is thirty old?"

"No," everyone else on the deck said in unison, even Nikki.

But Elise only smiled, her heart feeling tight in her chest. She understood the real question in Corey's eyes. She'd seen it in the mirror plenty of times. She'd felt the panic that accompanied the math when no matter how you worked the equation you couldn't make it say you had more races ahead of you than behind. She finally sighed and said, "They don't know what we do, do they, Core?"

Her grin returned, more genuine this time. "No. I guess not."

"You want to tell the kid, or should I?" Elise asked.

"She won't understand. Would you have if someone had told you?"

Elise shrugged. "Probably not. I'm sure people tried, but I didn't get the message until I woke up in a hospital."

"You still learned a few years ahead of me. I'm not sure I got it until right now."

"Are they drunk?" Paolo whispered to no one in particular.

"I'm freaked out they're getting along. I liked it better when they were being witty assholes to each other," Holly said.

"Tell me what?" Nikki asked.

Corey shook off the haze that had settled over them and smiled brightly once more. "Don't blink, Tigger."

The girl, did, in fact, blink several times, then looked from one person to another as if hoping for an explanation. "What, like during a race?"

Elise shook her head. "Not ever."

Chapter Seven

"Someone put a bee in those tight britches of yours?" Corey asked as she straddled the exercise bike next to Elise and allowed herself a few seconds to watch her powerful thigh muscles ripple while they worked. Her core temperature rose a few degrees before she even had a chance do any exercise of her own.

"Nope, it's leg day," Elise answered without breaking pace.

"Every day is leg day." Corey fiddled with the resistance nobs on her bike to distract herself from the surge of attraction.

"Not Friday," Elise said, a wistfulness in her voice Corey had never heard before. "Friday was cheat day."

"Ah, cheat day. I remember thee well."

"'Cause it was only two days ago," Holly called from the treadmill. "Stop yapping and start pedaling."

"Ouch," Elise said, glancing over her shoulder. "When did she get bossy?"

"The day I was born and she wasn't the youngest anymore."

Elise smiled, not a full-blown, toothy smile, but not the tight-lipped line Corey had seen in their early encounters. She'd seen the new expression enough lately not to be shocked anymore, but not often enough to expect it.

"Do you remember in school when the teacher would have to leave the room and she'd always put one kid in charge, the one who was strict, even stricter than her?"

"Yes. I suspect you weren't often selected for that job."

"No, I wasn't, but I get to relive the experience every time Nate has a meeting because he always asks Holly to run me through my warm-ups."

"Ah, I get it now. Give her an inch, and she makes you run a mile."

Corey laughed outright. "Was that a joke? Oh my God, Elise Brandeis made a joke."

"I make jokes all the time," Elise said. "I just keep them inside my head."

"You don't want to share the joy?"

"I like to think my mere presence brings enough joy to go around. No need to overload anyone."

"Well, that's true," Corey said with mock seriousness as she began to do some light pedaling. "I've often thought you radiate joy. Sometimes it's distracting when I'm trying to work out."

"Or stalling," Holly said, powering down her treadmill. "Do I need to separate you two?"

"Maybe you should," Corey said. "Elise is pulling me off task with her joke cracking."

"Yeah, she's a regular class clown," Holly said. "I'm sure she had that written on her report cards all the time."

"Don't mind her," Corey said and then stage whispered, "she's grumpy because Paolo's not here."

"I'm not grumpy. Don't tell him that. He's probably in the same meeting as Nate. Everyone wants to check in before we all leave town next week."

"He's meeting the USSA?" Corey asked. "Oh yeah, US Ski *and* Snowboard. I forget we have the same bosses."

"If by bosses you mean the same governing organization, then yes," Elise said.

"Huh?" Corey frowned and picked up her pace.

"What?" Elise asked.

"She's thinking," Holly explained. "She always pedals harder when she's confused. It's like the wheel on the stationary bike makes the hamster wheel in her head spin faster, too."

"Maybe if we hooked her up to one of those kinetic generators and gave her some algebra problems, she could power the whole training complex," Elise suggested.

"Wow," Holly said, "two jokes in ten minutes."

"Don't you think it's weird?" Corey asked.

"That I made two jokes?"

"No, aside from the fact that you have a sense of humor, isn't it weird to think about us answering to the same organizations. USSA or FIS, doesn't matter, national or international, they always put skiers and snowboarders together, whether we want to or not."

"Most of the time we don't want to," Elise said. "No offense."

"None taken. Snowboarders complain about it more than the skiers do."

"We pretend you guys don't exist," Elise said breezily, as she continued to power through her warm-up without breaking a sweat.

Corey, on the other hand, was already feeling the burn in her legs. Maybe she was pedaling too hard, too soon, but a little voice whispered maybe she hadn't fully recovered from yesterday's workout yet. She tried to drown out that voice by verbalizing her stream of consciousness. "Our collective personalities couldn't be more different, right? You guys are uptight, type A, snobs."

"Right." Elise's voice dripped with sarcasm. "And you guys are immature, reckless burnouts."

Corey laughed. "It's abundantly clear why we fought the powers that be swooping in and lumping us all together."

"We?"

"Yeah, you forget I'm old apparently. I was there at the beginning when this unholy alliance was formed. A bunch of snowboarders talked about boycotting the Olympics all together because we don't like being bossed around by people who've never been on a snowboard in their life. That's why they call Boardercross 'Snowboard X' in the Olympics. We wouldn't let them have the trademark. They don't know us or what we care about. They're a bunch of dudes in suits making us go to meetings and putting a bunch of rules on us that don't even make sense," Corey explained. "Also, we worried they might try to make us wear some tight little spandex body suits."

"What? You mean like the ones I wear?"

"Exactly those," Corey said, then grinned as she thought of Elise's long, athletic body in such an outfit.

"Yeah, I can't imagine why world-class racers would want to wear something aerodynamic."

"Aside from style and self-respect, no reason. But this right here, what we're doing now, showcases the differences perfectly, right?"

"Style over substance?" Elise got her dig in. "Probably sums it up pretty well."

"And don't forget elitism," Corey said.

Elise rolled her eyes but didn't argue.

"Still, we both strap boards to our feet and fly down mountains at breakneck paces. We have some common ground."

"Yes, if you mean literal physical terrain. They're both covered in snow and angle downhill."

"And speed," Corey added. "We're all trying get across the finish line faster than everyone else in the field."

Elise nodded. "Similar objectives. Are you working around to a point of some sort?"

"Maybe." She shrugged. Why had she followed this tangent down the rabbit hole? It didn't take a brain surgeon to point out commonalities between ski and snowboard racers, but to what end? Their worlds didn't generally intersect. She and Elise had never crossed paths before, and once Elise got back on track, they wouldn't likely do so again with any regularity. Maybe that felt odd given how they'd only recently made peace with each other. So much buildup, only to fizzle out as they transitioned back into their separate disciplines. Perhaps she only felt pensive about the transition ahead.

It always seemed odd to start packing snow pants and boots during the hottest month of the year, but the time had come for everyone to turn toward the southern hemisphere. She never thought very far ahead, but the pull of the next race always drew her forward. Usually she relished any chance to get back on snow, as well as the opportunity to hit the slopes months before anyone in the US could. Laid-back attitude or not, she lived to compete. She'd worked hard to get ready. Hell, between chasing Elise and getting pushed by Tigger, she'd trained harder than ever. By every measure she should be chomping at the bit to board her flight to New Zealand and leave all the emotional baggage filling the Olympic training center behind. Why was she spending her bike time trying to force connections that didn't exist?

"Hey guys," a chipper voice called from across the room.

All three of them turned to see Nikki jogging toward them. "You're such good role models. I slept in this morning 'cause my coaching team had a USSA meeting. I heard some of the Olympic Committee people are there, too. Won't it be cool if we're all together again like this at the Olympics? Elise, I googled you and I know you're a long shot for making the team this year, but you can do it. You're working hard every day, and you're super fierce. I bet you make it for sure, and maybe we can all walk in together at the opening ceremonies."

"Whoa, easy there, Bounce-A-Roo." Corey hopped off the bike as Elise's face turned beet red. "Slow your roll."

"Oh no!" The kid's eyes went wide. "Did I say something wrong? Are we not supposed to talk about the Olympics? Is that a jinx?"

"No, no." Corey threw an arm around her shoulder and angled her away from Elise. "We have a ton of work to do before then."

"Work?" Nikki nodded with as much seriousness as her exuberant face could convey. "Right. It's a job. I didn't mean to imply we could just go the Olympics. We might not make the team. You'll make the team, of course, but I never have before, and—"

"Don't stress out about the teams yet," Corey said, more for Elise's benefit than the kid's. Nikki would make the team, and while she suspected Elise would, too, one of them faced a steeper climb. She didn't want to draw any attention to the contrast. "Where're you heading to train?"

"Patagonia, with the development team. Isn't that awesome? Patagonia, like the coats."

Corey chuckled. She was kind of amusing, or at least she would be if she wasn't a threat to kick her ass this season.

"My mom is coming, too," Nikki continued. "We're going to travel together this year because I'm still underage, and she worries about boys even though I'm way too busy for a boyfriend, but I told her you travel with your sister and always have, and she thought that was a great idea to help you stay out of trouble."

Holly almost choked on the water she'd just swigged. Coughing loudly, she wheezed a few times before saying, "Sorry, sorry, something went down the wrong pipe."

Corey shook her head. Wrong pipe, her ass. Holly had likely suffered from a flash of memories of all the trouble they'd gotten into when they'd started touring together. Traveling with a sister wasn't anything like traveling with a mom, unless of course Nikki's mom had a thing for older men and tequila, but she didn't say so. "Sounds boss."

"Have you been there?" Nikki asked.

"Argentina? Yeah. Awhile ago. I did some team training camps there between Vancouver and Sochi, but the last few years we've done our own thing in New Zealand. Patagonia's nice though."

"Nice?" Paolo bellowed from the doorway to the cardio room. "Patagonia? It's heaven on earth."

"Nikki," Elise said. "You remember Paolo from Friday night? He happens to be from Bariloche, Argentina. If you're training at Cerro Catedral, you'll be on his home mountain."

"If you're a friend of Corey's, you're welcome on more than the mountain," Paolo said in grand fashion. "My family has a wine bar near the base of the mountain. They serve the finest cheese imported from Spain, and my mother makes bread daily. My father prefers fútbol to snowboarding, but I will make introductions, and you will dine there any time."

"Wait. You guys will be there, too?"

"Eventually," Elise sighed. "We've got to go back to Park City first."

Corey's chest tightened. There wasn't any snow in Utah this time of year, which meant Elise likely had more medical appointments before she could resume skiing.

Nikki clearly missed the allusion though. Her eyes sparkled. "I'm excited we're going to have friends there." She threw her arms around Paolo's neck. "Thank you."

"Friends," Holly repeated. "Friends with Paolo, and wine, and Patagonia. Peachy."

Corey edged closer to her as Nikki continued to hug Paolo. How many women could Nikki manage to torque off in a few minutes? Corey simply didn't have enough body mass to get between them all.

"Anywho," she tried to redirect in a loud, singsong voice. "How about those Red Sox? I'm ninety percent certain it's still baseball season."

Holly and Elise stared at her like she'd shoved her whole foot in her mouth.

"Not helpful, Core," Holly said, under her breath.

Elise nodded to Nikki, who continued to hug Paolo.

Corey opened her mouth as if she intended to say something, then closed it into a tight line and shook her head slowly. When had she become Tigger's handler? And when did it become her job to babysit Paolo, too? She couldn't help that they'd all be training in the same location. Okay, maybe she'd introduced them, but it's not like she knew where Paolo lived or where the kid would start her snow workouts. If anything, they should thank her. They could all work out together off slope or share notes. Elise would still have a snowboarding connection to steal exercises from or relax with when she got too high strung. Maybe they could trade barbs or hang out in a cold pool together.

Her stomach felt like it'd dropped over the edge of the biggest hill on a roller coaster. Was that the emotion causing the schmoopy expression on Holly's face? The frowny one with the furrowed brow? Oh God, did she feel the way for Elise that Holly felt for Paolo? Is that why she'd been digging for a stupid snowboard and skier kumbaya moment earlier? Now she'd found one, only it didn't include her. And while it did include Elise, she didn't seem thrilled by the prospect. In fact, her clenched jaw and the sheen of ice in her eyes made her seem more tense than Corey had seen her in weeks. But what could she do?

She couldn't travel back in time and uninvite Nikki to the cheat day party. Hell, if she could've done so, she would have, right after her seven-year-old-poster comments, but none of them could have a do-over. The only option on the table was moving forward. Unfortunately, Elise and Nikki would progress to the same spot from here, and there wasn't a damn thing she could do about it.

Nikki finally unwrapped herself from Paolo, who appeared a little shell-shocked as he rubbed the stubble on his chin and glanced sheepishly at everyone but Holly. Still, he didn't seem any worse for the experience. The same might not hold true after Holly got ahold of him.

"And Elise," Nikki bubbled, stepping up as if she intended to hug her, too.

Elise braced herself for the impact, arms pinned against her side, but as visions of the embrace flickered through Corey's mind, she blurted out, "Wait."

Everyone turned to stare at her.

"Wait, what?" Nate said, coming into the room. "What did I miss?"

"Um." Corey rocked from one side to the other, shifting her weight as if trying to find her balance on her board. "I was thinking about things."

"Things?" Nate asked. "Did you give yourself a headache?"

"Maybe. Or maybe I'm about to give Holly a headache, but I mean . . . oh fuck, let's go to Argentina."

"What?" everyone asked at varying decibel levels.

"I've been there before," Corey said with a shrug. "They have mountains and snow. Works for me."

Everyone stared at her like she'd sprouted a second head, but only Tigger had the wherewithal, or lack of social understanding, to ask the obvious question: "Didn't you already make reservations and tell the USSA and everybody you were going to New Zealand?"

"Yeah, but plans change."

"Can you do that so close to departure?"

"Uh, yeah. I mean, sure." She turned to Holly and Nate. "Right?"

Nate ran his hand through his hair and sighed heavily. Holly simply shook her head.

"We'll figure it out," Corey said, her confidence wavering. "Other Americans will be training there. We're not going to have to build our own course. And it's not a big switch or anything training-wise."

"It's kind of a big switch," Paolo said.

"New Zealand and Argentina aren't far apart."

Holly slapped her palm to her forehead. "Core, come on."

"What?" she asked. "They're both south."

"They're two different continents," Elise said hesitantly, as if she still wasn't sure the entire conversation wasn't an elaborate joke.

"Right, but in the southern hemisphere, where it's snowy this time of year. Same concept."

"They're literally on opposite sides of the globe, dude," Nate said. "Even I know that."

"Okay, well, Argentina's closer, right?"

"Relatively speaking," Holly said as if choosing her words carefully. "But you chose New Zealand six months ago. I made all the reservations. We have a cabin rented. We've scheduled training sessions and slope time. We've got a team of techs lined up. You've told other boarders to expect you."

"There'll be trainers and techs in Argentina, too," she reasoned even as the sinking feeling in the pit of her stomach multiplied. She hadn't thought this through. She shouldn't have shot off her mouth. Why dig herself in deeper? Still, the more she talked, the more she convinced herself. "And the youth development program will be there. You know, go team USA."

"Okay," Holly said. "I'll make it happen. It won't be easy, but

Nate and I will make this happen if it's important to you, but we deserve to know why."

She shrugged. "Like I said, Argentina has everything we need, and it's closer, and we'll know people there."

"Yeah, and all of those things were also true six months ago, and a year ago, and two years ago, but you've trained in New Zealand for the past three seasons. Why in all the fucks do you need a change *right now*."

"The last few seasons sucked, okay?" Corey blurted out.

Holly blinked, "What?"

She couldn't believe what she was saying, but everything poured out anyway. "My ranking dropped every year for three years. I know we like to pretend we don't notice or act like we don't care about rankings. They're totally tools of the establishment, but you can't call it a coincidence when I fall three years in a row."

"Hey," Nate clasped his hand on the back of her shoulder. "How about we go somewhere else?"

"Why?" Corey asked, then laughed. "You don't want to argue in front of the kid? Or you want to ask me if this is about hanging out with Elise?"

"Is it?" Elise asked.

"Yeah," Corey said, then amended her knee-jerk reaction. "Maybe. But not in the way he thinks."

She then turned to Nikki. "And don't you get any ideas about my career being over."

She shook her head frantically. "I wouldn't."

"Good. Because it's not. I'm not phoning in this season. I'm not trying to chase tail halfway across the globe, either, and I'm not pinning my problems on our training habits, but what I've always done isn't working anymore. Maybe we should shake things up."

"And you can't shake things up in New Zealand?"

"I'm sure I could, but we'd have to start from scratch, on our own, and why? The two people pushing me the hardest right now are headed to Argentina. There's an inherent challenge there. Why not accept?"

Nate and Holly exchanged a look of concern, while Paolo, Elise, and Nikki all awkwardly refused to make eye contact. It reminded her of those times in middle school when one kid did something to accidently embarrass themselves and everyone else tried to pretend it wasn't a big deal but were totally going to talk about nothing else for the rest of the week. Middle school sucked. She shouldn't have to relive those moments at thirty years old with two Olympic medals and a handful of world championships in her pocket.

"I've never pulled rank before, but at the end of the day I'm the one on the board, and I think Argentina offers the best chance for me to get better right now."

"You're right," Nate said quickly and patted her on the back. "You gotta do you, Core. Let's wreck some shit."

Holly laughed. "You're going to owe me many massages and margaritas for the work I'll have to do to make this happen, but okay. I'll make it work."

Corey blew out a heavy breath as the tension fell from her shoulders and excitement rushed in to fill the void. "All right, Argentina it is."

"Well, Ms. Brandeis. I won't say I'm not surprised with your progress. A year ago, the idea of clearing you to ski competitively before at the start of summer snow season seemed laughable."

"Thanks for your vote of confidence," Elise said drolly, garnering a warning glance from Paolo.

"My prognosis had nothing to do with my opinion of you as a competitor. Obviously you're in top shape, with an admirable drive . . . " The doctor went on, and Elise tuned out the platitudes, instead focusing on the way his wiry, gray eyebrows danced up and down as his facial expression fluctuated. She'd heard this speech before. Pretty much every milestone she achieved got met with surprise, admiration, and the inevitable warnings that all her progress could still get blown to bits with one wrong move.

"As you can see on the latest X-Ray. . ." He flipped off the overhead light and indicated the illuminated projection on his wall. "The break has healed nicely. You can barely see a seam there where the fracture molded back together. However, there will always be some weakness associated with the bond."

She did her best not to appear outwardly bored. She didn't tap her toe impatiently or drum her fingers on the faux mahogany finish of his office chair. She had to play nice with the man who would ultimately report to the USSA coaching team, but she refused to dwell on the possibility, or even probability, of reinjury.

She wasn't reckless. She hadn't overextended herself. She followed the training plan even when it hurt, even when it drove her crazy, even when she wanted to do much more. She didn't intend to abandon course this far in.

"But you have to concern yourself with more than the bone. You've been off your skis for a long time. During recovery, your muscles atrophied significantly. Tendons tightened, and in some cases actually shortened."

"I haven't been inactive," she defended. "I've run a near full overland training course. I'm not frail or flabby."

"Of course you're not," he said, in the patronizing tone one uses to affirm a potty training toddler that she is indeed quite grown up. "You've done an admirable job of simulating the conditions your muscles and joints will be subjected to on the slopes. And we've come a long way in athletic rehabilitation procedures over the last decade. You're living proof of the possibilities open to us now. However, no matter how many simulations we run, there's no way to adequately predict every variable a real mountain will pose."

She nodded placidly. Did Mr. White Lab Coat and Loafers honestly think he had something new to tell her about what she'd face when she got back on a steep sheet of ice? She didn't need a psychologist, a pep talk, or a safety lecture. She needed medical clearance to resume training on snow, and it irked her to no end that she had to sit through condescending small talk in order to get the green light.

She did appreciate the hard-working doctors and nurses who'd helped her along the way. She understood she couldn't be where she was without significant medical advances and millions of people's shared knowledge. But no one could crawl inside her skin and assess how strong or steady or confident she felt. She was a grown woman with an above-average physical awareness and a strong belief that her body was her own damn business, both figurative and literally. She should have the final say, not some men in offices who had never, and would never, click into her ski boots.

She smiled slightly as she realized that she'd heard Corey say almost the same thing about sponsors and governing organizations. Had part of the snowboarder mentality begun to wear off on her, or had they shared a bit of that cavalier attitude all along? Her smile grew a little wider as she remembered the two of them together in the cold tub and their pursuit of fun on their own terms. Maybe they did have more in common than she'd initially wanted to believe. Was that the point Corey had been trying to make when talking about how skiers and snowboarders always got lumped together, despite not caring for each other? Had that connection factored into her decision to make a last-minute about-face on training in New Zealand?

She still couldn't unpack all the emotions swirling within her every time she thought about Corey being in Argentina, not right now while she sat, still and quiet, in a doctor's office half a world away. She couldn't begin to process through the decision or how seemingly fast Corey had made it. Her anal-retentive side shuddered at the idea of throwing a long-held training plan out the window without weeks, if not months, of research and deliberation. She also got a little queasy when she considered the prospect of Corey making a decision of that magnitude based in any way on her.

"With that said . . ." The doctor's tone shifted to one sounding like a conclusion, pulling her attention once again to the situation at hand. "I don't see any reason why we should keep your rehab off the slopes."

"I'm cleared to ski?" she said, perhaps a bit too loudly, but she wanted to make herself heard over the rapid beating of her own heart.

"You're cleared to ease back in under the watchful eye of your trainer. You're *not* cleared to compete yet," he stressed. "I also recommend more regular check-ins with the USSA medical team in Argentina."

"I've always made myself available for medical check-ins."

He nodded. "You've been a model patient, but your biggest challenges are still ahead."

She bristled inwardly at the comment, but kept her mouth tightly shut.

"You need to be abundantly careful. You'll be working muscles you haven't tested in a long time, and not only in your knee. Don't try to regain your Olympic standing during your first week, or you'll end up back here."

"And we wouldn't want that, now would we, doc?" She'd intended to sound playful, but she hadn't quite mastered the tone she heard from Corey all the time.

"It's not that I don't love to see you," the doctor explained carefully. "But I know you'd rather be on the go than in an office, and it's my job to help you get back to what you do best."

"I appreciate the sentiment," Elise said as she rose and headed for the door.

"Thank you for everything," Paolo added. "You'll fax over your report? We'd like to leave for Argentina tomorrow."

"It'll be on the desk of every ski team official before your flight lands. I'm sure you'll have a whole team of friends eagerly awaiting your arrival."

Elise smiled more brightly as she walked out the door.

Friends.

A month ago she would've rolled her eyes at the idea. By her former standards, she wouldn't see any friends in Argentina, but she would see Corey. Corey, who annoyed her. Corey, who made inappropriate jokes. Corey, who wouldn't leave her alone even when given the cold shoulder and an icy glare. Corey, who butted into any conversation or workout whether invited or not. Corey, who brought with her a complex entourage of family and friends and teenage tag-alongs who made her laugh even when she didn't want to. Corey, who continued to surprise her with her unexpected thoughtfulness or sincerity or passion or her rock hard abs.

"What?" Paolo asked as they exited the building into the bright mountain air.

"What?"

"You're smiling."

"It's a beautiful day. I got a good report from the doctor. I'm going to be on the snow in forty-eight hours. Isn't that enough to smile about?"

"For most people, yes. For you, not usually. Every other doctor's appointment has left you with this grim sort of glint in your eye, more like a tiger stalking prey."

"There's nothing wrong with a killer instinct."

"Debatable, but today you didn't even argue with the doctor when he mentioned going slow and checking in. Normally I have to threaten to sedate you in those meetings. You seemed a million miles away in some happy place," he said, then his smile widened. "You're also blushing."

"I am not."

"You are. You're thinking about Corey." He laughed. "Your cheeks are getting more redder and more redder."

"It's hot. It's August. The sun is out."

"You're happy. Stop right there. I want to memorize this picture of what happy Elise looks like. I've never met her before."

The little joke hit her square in the chest. "Never?"

His face softened immediately. "You're always thinking about what comes next, and in your mind what comes next is always a race, or a test, or another chance to prove yourself. You have so much focus, and I wouldn't change you, because it makes you a champion."

"But?"

"But, I want you to be happy, too. I can teach you to race, to turn, to train. I've tried to teach patience and balance and perspective, but I can't teach you to be happy. I didn't think anyone could teach you that, but Corey's come a long way."

"You're overstating her influence and her importance," Elise said coolly. "Besides, you're my coach. It's your job to help me win, nothing else."

"Right, as your coach I have no opinion on your social life, but as your friend, I think she's good for you. I like to see you two together."

"We're not *together*," Elise said quickly. "I find her amusing in limited doses. She certainly offers alternative perspectives from the people I'm used to, but please don't read too much into anything. If anything, you're projecting your own happiness about seeing Holly onto me."

"Nice with the redirect, but I can admit I like Holly. She's funny and smart and very attractive. I like spending time with her, and I know Corey made her life a little more harder by changing plans, but I'm glad she did. I'm not giving up my job or getting down on one knee, but I'm happy to get more time with her."

Elise's stomach tightened at the simple statement of emotion. "Good for you." She didn't feel the same way about Corey. She simply didn't. Maybe she felt something she didn't care to examine too deeply. Maybe it was a feeling she hadn't felt in a long time, or ever, but what did that even mean in the face of a return to the slopes?

"You can't do it, can you?" he asked, throwing his arm around her shoulder. "You can't admit that something makes you happy without there being an end goal to it?"

She sighed and pushed him away. "I'm happy I'm cleared to ski. That's going to have to be good enough for you."

He laughed and shook his head. "Okay, good enough . . . for now."

Chapter Eight

September 5, 2016
Bariloche, Argentina

Corey glanced at her watch as discreetly as possible.

"I saw that," Holly said, seemingly without ever looking up from her magazine.

"I'm checking to see how long I have to wait until I get dinner."

"You're checking to see how long before Elise gets here."

Corey snorted. "You don't know me."

"No. I just had to rearrange our entire fall training and travel schedule in a week so you could train near the woman, but I know nothing about what you're feeling."

"When are you going to let go of the whole I-messed-up-your-schedule thing?"

"When you and Elise name your first-born child after me . . . maybe."

"You know the idea of anything happening between me and Elise is insane, right?"

"About as insane as us being in Argentina right now."

Corey shook her fist in the air. "Everywhere I turn, I walk right into that."

"Fine, I resolve to mention the gross debt you owe me only five times a day from here on out."

"Generous of you."

"Yeah, well, now that I finished the soul-crushing amount of extra work, I'll admit Argentina has a few perks."

"Like Argentinian trainers whose parents own wine bars?"

Holly smiled a dreamy little smile.

"And now you don't have to wonder if he's sharing his evenings with Tigger while you're halfway across the world."

"I don't worry he'd do anything with Tigger," Holly said. "He's not the type, and the more she hangs around, the less I think she is either. But it would be hard to know he was spending his evenings with anyone else when I could've been here."

She sat forward and eyed her sister. There was a softness to her expression and her tone Corey wasn't used to hearing. "So, this thing with Paolo is really a thing?"

Holly lifted a shoulder with pretend indifference, but the flush in her cheeks gave her away.

"Wow. I knew you guys had some fun together, and he's nice and well kept, and I suppose handsome if you like the tall, dark, and rugged thing he's working."

"I do," Holly said. "I really do."

"So, does he feel the same way?"

"We haven't had 'the talk' yet. I mean, it seemed silly because we thought we'd be on different continents. And even now, our little joint training trip is a massive anomaly. You bought us another month, maybe six weeks if we all linger, and we'll work most of the time."

"We'll still see each other sometimes on the tour."

"How often do we cross paths with skiers? Our competition schedules don't line up at all."

Her stomach tightened. "Surely we've got to get close a few times. I mean how many snowy mountain ranges are there in the world? Three?"

Holly sighed. "Sometimes I wish you'd had a super hot geography teacher at some point in school so you could've learned a couple things."

"Is that your way of saying there's more than three big, snowy mountain ranges?"

Holly smiled and shook her head. "Never mind. We stole some more time. We might as well enjoy the month. It'll be over before we know it. I don't want to bog us down in labels and heavy discussions."

Corey didn't know what to do with the sadness in Holly's tone. Of the four LaCroix girls, they'd always been the two to share a wanderlust that went well beyond the next race or the next stop on the tour. Holly always looked forward to the next challenge no matter what the stakes, even with men—especially with men— and now she was worried about the prospect of having to move on five weeks before she actually had to do so.

The uneasy feeling Corey'd had right before she made the call to come to Argentina settled over her again, like searching for something in a dark room, and knowing there's a table leg some- where waiting for you to stub your little toe on.

"They're here." Holly hopped up and dropped her magazine in Corey's lap. "How do I look? Is my hair okay?"

"You're perfect."

Holly grinned. "I am pretty fabulous, aren't I?"

"Always." Corey laughed as the old Holly bounced back to life and headed breezily toward the glass doors as Paolo pushed through.

"*Hola*," he called with a wide smile, then dropped his bag and clasped both hands on her shoulders and kissed her on each cheek twice. Then holding her at arms length they beamed at one another before kissing on the mouth. Corey's chest con- stricted. She'd watched Holly with a lot of boys, and then a handful of men, and she'd seen plenty of them moon over her, but she'd never seen Holly return the expression. The experience made her feel happy and lonely all at once, but before she could begin to understand why, Elise pushed through the door behind them.

Her jeans hugged her slammin' hips and muscular thighs per- fectly, and she'd topped them off with a long-sleeved gray sweater underneath a black down vest. The style was comfortably sexy, but her dark sunglasses added a touch of chic. The ensemble suited her personality more than the gym clothes Corey had grown used to seeing her in. Well put together, but multi-layered.

Elise raised the sunglasses to rest atop her blond hair and shook back a few locks that had fallen down across the fronts of her shoulders. She paused in the doorway only long enough to notice Holly and Paulo's total entrancement with each other before stepping past them. She seemed headed for the front desk when her gaze fell on Corey. Her beautiful lips curved up in a tired smile Corey couldn't help but mirror as the two of them got caught in the same schmoopy haze that had trapped Paolo and Holly, only without the kissing.

"Hi," Corey finally said.

"Hi."

Corey nodded to the leather lobby chair next to her. "Seat's open."

Elise nodded as if she wanted to accept the invitation but wasn't sure she should. "I should probably get checked in, but Paolo has our reservations."

"Then you should definitely kick back for a bit. I suspect the lovebirds might need a few minutes."

Elise glanced back over her shoulder at them, then lowered herself into the chair. "I suppose it's better if we let them get it out of their systems before we have to start training."

Corey wondered if Holly would ever get Paolo out of her system, or if the feelings would actually get stronger as their stay went on. But saying so might constitute a betrayal of sisterly trust. Instead she said, "I've already started training."

"Oh sure, rub it in that I'm a week behind," Elise said, "or a year and a week behind."

"You're here now." Corey tried not to let her dwell on what she'd missed. The time for mourning those losses had passed, and allowing them to linger once she got on the slopes might be dangerous. "I assume you got the all clear to ski again, or you wouldn't have made the long-ass flight down here."

"Oh my God, the ten hours from Atlanta to Buenos Aires was bad enough, but the two extra hours on a puddle jumper to

Bariloche felt mean-spirited after . . ." She eyed Corey more seriously. "Who told you I hadn't been cleared to ski?"

"No one had to tell me. I've been on the tour for twelve years. I know the orthopedic specialists are in Park City, and I've known you long enough to realize you would've been the first one down here if you'd had the green light."

"Does everyone know?"

Corey shrugged. "I don't think anyone else cares. Believe it or not, most people don't sit around pondering the life and times of the great Elise Brandeis."

She scoffed. "I think my life inspires a lot of pondering."

Corey smiled, glad to have induced a little sass. "Maybe a little pondering, but what do you care if people know you had a doctor's appointment? You got the go ahead. That's what counts."

"I guess I don't like the idea of my competitors knowing how close we cut things. I want them to worry I'm already back in top form. I hate giving them a boost of confidence from knowing I'm not up to their level."

"Yet," Corey amended, "you'll get there, and it'll be all that much sweeter when you do. Everyone loves a come-from-behind win. Imagine the stories the networks will run on you during the Olympics. Bob Costas and Mary Carrillo will visit you at the gym, and you can cry on TV."

"All right," Elise stood up and turned to go. "I'm going to go check in now that you've apparently checked out of the reality hotel."

Corey caught her hand and gave her a little squeeze. "It'll happen, Elise. You're going to be Team USA's comeback kid. I know you don't love the idea of being anything other than a front-runner, but you're going to excel at this role as much as you did the other one. And the sponsors will eat that shit up."

Elise looked down at her, fingers locked, blue eyes bright, and an expression Corey had never seen crossed her beautiful features. Something softer, more introspective, but without the sharp edge of her usual defenses.

"Corey," Paolo bellowed. "*Amiga, bienvenidos* to Argentina."

Elise's smile returned to its more polite state, but she gave her hand a little squeeze before pulling away. "Yes, welcome. We're all in for an interesting season."

Corey grinned broadly as she sat back and folded her arms behind her head. "Interesting." Yeah, she could work with that.

"If you try to start me on the children's tow rope, I swear by all things holy, I'll push you off the side of this mountain."

Paolo laughed. "As if I didn't know that already, but we're not going to start at the top, either."

"That's where the rest of the team is today," Elise said. Few other skiers were out at seven a.m., much less the children who would likely populate this particular area later in the day.

"Which is why we're down here," Paolo explained. "We don't need an audience, and you don't need to prove anything to anyone."

"Apparently I need to prove to you I can still ski a trail bigger than this one. What's it even called?" She craned her neck to read the bright green Cerro Catedral trail sign. "ABC? Are you kidding me?"

"Actually, this is ABC *Norte*," Paolo explained calmly. "We're only going to ski this half. ABC South is harder."

"Where's that one?"

"It starts up higher."

"And where are we in relation to the nearest steep cliff?" Elise asked.

"The one you want to push me off of?"

"Precisely."

"I'll show you as soon as you show me you can handle the beginner's terrain."

She ground her teeth together and stared up at the stunning views all around her. Snow-covered mountains rose up in the southern skies. Crisp air numbed her nose with each inhale and transformed into a small translucent cloud as it left through her slightly parted lips. The cold tingled the back of her neck, invigorating her in a way she hadn't felt in over a year as long-dormant muscles twitched with yearning to spring to life once more.

"Please, Paolo," she pleaded. "I've waited so long, and we've already lost two days here to techs and paperwork and worthless meetings."

"Don't lose another day to complaining," Paolo said, exasperation growing thick in his voice. "Put your helmet on."

She obeyed, tucking a few stray strands of hair behind her ear, then snugged up the ponytail holder at the base of her neck before pulling the helmet down completely. "I imagined this moment a thousand times a day during my rehab, but I never imagined it quite like this."

He smiled kindly. "I know, but if I'd told you you'd have to start on the bunny slope, you wouldn't have worked so hard."

She nodded, trying not to remember the excruciating pain in the early days after her surgery. He had a point.

"Don't go back there now," he whispered, then pointed down the gentle slope. "Go forward."

Done arguing, she angled her skis downhill, then closing her eyes, took a long, slow breath. This might not be the moment she'd envisioned, but it was closer than anything she'd yet to experience on the long road back. Butterflies fluttered in her stomach a second before she leaned her body ever so slightly. Her skis started to slide. Such a little movement at first, but her heart jumped inside her chest. A gentle push with her pole extended the glide. Gravity took hold, pulling her more softly than before, but even the subtle tug felt like a call toward home.

Opening her eyes now, her vision narrowed, closing out the skiers and the peaks around her. She saw only smooth snow and a slight grade. Easy skiing had never been her favorite, but now she relished the cut of her skis through the groomed trail. So effortless, so beautifully harmonious. She couldn't remember the last time she'd felt so at ease.

Shifting her hips a fraction of an inch, she slid right, then pedaling the balance of her weight back to center, her line straightened again. She tried the same move on the other side and thrilled as she eased left. Weightless after a year of pain and the pressure of every physical and emotional burden, she once again moved as freely as a bird in the sky.

Then it ended. She straightened slightly and slowed to a stop at the base of a ski lift, and her chest constricted at the sense of loss akin to the sun burning through the most beautiful dream.

Paolo pulled up beside her, his smile pressing his cheeks against the earflaps of his helmet. "Yes?"

She nodded, unable to speak for the emotion clogging her throat.

"You moved like an angel riding over a bank of clouds," he exclaimed, his chest puffed out with pride.

The sentiment made her uncomfortable, and the emotion behind it even more so. She was not an angel. She couldn't view this mountain as heaven, or even a cathedral, as its name implied. She'd merely angled downhill for less than a quarter mile. A slope of that nature didn't even constitute a warm-up. She had work to do, so much it scared her, and she couldn't allow herself to grow accustomed to pleasure under the prospect of the pain one false move could bring.

"No more wasting time," she said brusquely, hoping the frustration in her voice covered the deeper emotions she didn't want to convey. "Let's move up."

Paolo's broad shoulders fell. "Never happy in the moment, Elise?"

She bristled at the comment. "I'll be happy when I stand on the podium with the medal around my neck."

"I hope so," he said genuinely, but the sincerity of the sentiment did little to hide his doubt.

For some reason tears stung her eyes. She tried to blink them away, but when they continued to come, she lowered her ski goggles and turned toward the lift. Anger burned like a hot rock in her stomach.

Damn him. Why did he have to make such a big deal out of the silly little baby slope? She didn't have the time or the energy for frivolity or sentimentality. And why all the concern about intrinsic happiness now? Had he been mushy when she'd struggled in the hospital? Had he gotten flowery when she sweat in the gym or tried to freeze her muscles back into submission under icy waters? Why did one moment of joy matter amid all the other grueling tasks? Nothing mattered but the podium, and she couldn't get there from the middle of the mountain or the middle of the pack. There could be no rest, no joy, until she pushed to the top.

She shook her head as she eased into position beside him on the lift. Maybe he'd gotten a little misty the first time she'd stood after the surgery. And she had perhaps noticed a small crack in his voice the first time she'd walked without a cane, but an "angel riding over a bank of clouds"? She wouldn't settle for being a pretty sight, and since when did he get so damn sappy?

Holly.

She didn't say the name aloud, but she knew the answer instinctively. He was falling in love with her. Poor guy. And for what? To be disappointed in a few months when the bottom fell out? It would be a sad story if it weren't an Olympic year, but it was, which meant this little romance also posed a career-altering distraction. She needed to deal with the problem before the situation got truly out of hand.

"You know I'm happy for you and Holly, right?" she asked. "I like her. A lot. She's fun, and she's sassy, and she knows her stuff. Honestly, sometimes I've wondered if Corey could even manage to dress herself without Holly."

"You underestimate Corey," Paolo said.

"Maybe, but she thought Argentina and New Zealand were next-door neighbors."

Paolo laughed.

"But Holly stepped in and handled everything. I don't even know what goes into arrangements of that magnitude, but I assume she must've performed miracles to get them all here and practicing on time."

"We're almost to the top of the lift," Paolo pointed out. "You'd better get to the 'but' part of this conversation."

"I don't want her to become a distraction," Elise blurted out.

Paolo sat quietly as they neared the top of the lift, then skied silently down the ramp, this time veering farther right before stopping at the top of a slightly longer slope. "Do you think my spending time with Holly has taken my attention way from your training?"

"No," Elise said quickly. "I didn't mean your time. Paolo, you've been more dedicated to me than any coach could be expected to be. I know you had other offers. I know you could've found other clients or stayed with the team. Hell, you could've even taken a few vacations, and I wouldn't have thought less of you."

"Then where does your fear of distraction come from?"

"You just seem a little softer lately. You're not pushing me as hard."

He smiled again. "And you think Holly has made me more weaker?"

"You haven't exactly been a hard-ass lately," she said. "Not that I want you to treat me like a slave or anything."

"Oh yes, the Argentineans often use blond-haired, blue-eyed, white women from prep schools to do their manual labor."

She laughed. "Well-played, but you know what I mean, right?"

"I do," he said, dropping a big open palm on the top of her helmet and giving her head a soft shake. "But you're wrong to worry. Holly makes me more stronger. She makes the work joyful again. Think about Corey in the gym with you. Do you not work harder when she's pushing you?"

She didn't like the quick jump from Holly to Corey. The relationships were completely different. "I don't know if I work harder or better."

"You do," he said plainly.

"She annoys me. She makes me angry. If I pedal faster or lift higher, it's to prove her wrong."

"But you smile when you do. She makes you more better than you are on your own. You have a long way to go, *amiga*. You will fall. You will have bad days. You will lose to people you should beat."

Her shoulders knotted with stress, and she opened her mouth to protest, but he cut her off.

"The anger won't sustain you, not at the pace we must set in order to catch up. Only joy can."

"How did this become about me? I only meant to talk about you and Holly."

"The two are related. Holly makes me happy. I need to find ways to make you happy. Holly has a sister."

"Stop," she said quickly. "This conversation did not go how I intended."

He shook his head, but his dark eyes still danced with amusement. "The best ones never do."

"I'm leaving now." She scooted her skis until they pointed downhill once more.

"Not so fast," he said.

"What else do you have to say? And it better be coaching, because if you mention Corey again, I'm going to find a steep cliff myself."

He grinned. "That *was* coaching advice. Don't ski too fast. But it's nice to know the mention of Corey can get you worked up. The knowledge will be useful later."

"Shut up," she grumbled and leaned into the slope, but her burning face didn't feel the cold this time.

"Hot damn," Nate said as Corey scraped the heel edge of her board across the snow to stop. "You slayed the start, dude."

Corey flexed her biceps. "Do you want to kiss the pythons?"

"Give 'em here." Nate grabbed her arm and made a dramatic smooching sound. "But it's not only your arms, you're using some seriously explosive power between your hips and thighs."

Pulling off her goggles and resting them atop her head, she said, "While I appreciate the sentiment, you cannot kiss anything between my hips or thighs."

He gave her a shove. "Go over there."

She slid a couple of feet to the side of the course, then plopped down on her butt. She unclipped the ankle and toe straps on her right foot, then relaxed back on the snow as Tigger slid into one of the starting gates high above her. She had a center chute between two Canadians, a veteran Corey had raced for years and a newcomer she'd yet to meet. A bevy of coaches shouted instructions while they all worked on their positioning.

"Get back up there," Nate said. "You're not done for the day."

"I wanna watch the kid."

"You want to sit on your keister and catch your breath."

"Maybe," she admitted, "but I haven't gotten to see her much out there. The team has her on a tight leash."

"She's seventeen," Nate said, turning to face the gates as well. "She's barely housebroken. They can't let her roam around the mountain freely. She might get lost or run off."

"We roamed freely, and look how we turned out."

"Exactly." Nate laughed. "And now you know what they are trying to avoid in the next generation."

"Good point, but we sure had some good times, didn't we?"

He turned. "You sound like you think they're over."

Had she? She hadn't meant to. When had she started thinking of her wild days in the past tense? Sure, she'd made some conscious choices to surround herself with better people, and maybe not be quite as reckless off the slopes as she had in the past, but she still had plenty of adventures ahead. Didn't she? The gate above her sprang open with a loud metal clang, and the racers shot out. Both the Canadians jumped hard and fast over the edge and cut toward the first jump, leaving Tigger nearly sideways behind them.

Corey raised her eyebrows at Nate.

"What?"

"She got boxed out."

"Not my circus, not my monkey."

"But she's kind of our friend," Corey said.

"Something you decided on your own," Nate pointed out.

"I didn't mean to. It just happened. I only invited her to one party to be nice, because she's Team USA."

"You keep saying 'team,' but I thought we're all about being individuals and doing our own thing. Aren't you Ms. I Hate Uniforms? Ms. Don't Tell Me What To Do? Ms. 'Drink Water'?"

She grinned. "You summed up my whole life."

"We've met."

"Yeah, but you forgot the part where we're not assholes. We do this for the love and thrills."

"And to score chicks," he added.

"Mostly for the chicks, but also not being assholes."

"Fine," Nate said, then called to Tigger, who was bent over unstrapping the board. "Hey, kid."

"Yeah?" Her smile had grown grim, but not completely vanished.

"Hike the start with Corey, okay?"

"Uh, really?" She brightened. "Can I do that?"

"It's easier to ask forgiveness than to ask permission," Corey said, hauling herself to her feet.

"And as Corey reminds me," Nate said, "you're on the same team."

"We are!" Nikki said, seemingly over her burn-out moments before. "Okay."

They kicked their boards off completely and carried them up the steep incline back to the starting gate with Nate close behind. As they reached the top, another group came flying out of the gate, two Brazilians and two Brits, judging by their bibs. After training in New Zealand for years, Corey had lost track of all the people who trained in Argentina. She sort of liked the fresh crop. Most of them had crossed paths at various tour events over the last few seasons, but the training camps offered real chances to interact for prolonged periods, and even with the language barriers, she still got a pretty good sense for who someone was as a racer by how they worked in close quarters with others on the same patch of track over and over and over.

Another set of racers edged into the gates, this time all men, most of them recognizable to Corey. Five of them this time, promising more congestion on the first dip toward the turn.

"You know who Nate Holland is?" Corey asked.

"Uh, yeah." Nikki said, leaving the obvious 'duh' unspoken.

"He's, like, 36 years old, but he's still hanging strong with these guys half his age."

Nikki stared at her, clearly confused. "Okay, and?"

"And nothing," Corey said. "I only wanted someone else to note that fact. But he's not the Nate you should focus on right now. The Nate huffing and puffing up the hill behind you is going to break down your start."

"Right," Nate said. "Watch these guys here. You've got the same positioning, but you lacked the fluidity."

The men got into position with their arms gripped tightly on the little handlebars sticking out from each side of their chute, then slid back with their boards until their arms extended and their backs were level and flat.

"Riders ready," came the call. "Attention."

Then the barricades dropped and they sprang forward. Jostling for position, they didn't stop at the top of the turn but kept right on going farther down the course.

"What they did there wasn't any different technically from what you're doing," Nate explained. "Your starting form is good, but you run through each and every step as if you're trying to get them off a list. Like they're separate little boxes and you're ticking them as fast as you can, but you can't check three things faster than one."

"Nate." Another coach walked over. "How's it going?"

"Good, Chad."

"I'm Matt."

"Right," Nate said in a way that made Corey snicker.

"What's up?" Matt asked.

"Going through a little starting-gate practice."

"Cool," he said, then nodded to Corey. "Nice work out there."

"Thanks," she said.

"All right, Nikki." Matt motioned for her to follow him. "I want you to come back to the tech tent real quick."

"Actually, Corey invited me to hike the start with her a couple times."

He frowned, then made a show of checking his watch: a bullshit move. He didn't have a time schedule to follow.

"Two runs," Corey said.

"Normally," he shrugged, "I'd be all for it, but the youth camp directors . . ."

She let the silence hang long enough to make him feel awkward. "She's got a chance to work with the pros. Isn't that who she'll face when she makes the tour this year?"

He nodded thoughtfully. "It's just, we're working a tight program these days. It's not like it used to be."

"Back in ancient times?" She laughed. "I'll make you a deal. You give us two runs, and if you don't see improvement by the second time, I'll come over and practice with your kids, your way, for two whole days."

"And if she does show some magical improvement?"

"Then you let her spend some more time running with the big dogs."

"I assume by 'big dogs,' you mean you and Nate?"

"Anyone else out there have three world championships and two Olympic medals?"

He gave her a grudging nod of respect, and she felt a little relief to find her accomplishments still carried some weight, even if she hated having to play on the past to make a point.

"Deal?" she asked.

He folded his arms across his chest and lifted a shoulder. "Two runs."

"Come on," Corey said to Nikki as they slid into position once again, between the two Canadians.

"I can't believe you talked back to him," Nikki said, wonder heavy in her young voice. "I've never talked back to a coach."

"We'll deal with that later. Now listen to Nate."

"Like I said, your arms, your chest, your hips, your board, they are not separate starting mechanisms. You have to use them as one. With a slingshot you don't think of the front part of the band and back part of the band as moving separately. You wouldn't tug on one side, then the other. The tension has to be even throughout, and the release has to be simultaneous."

"But I always run through the steps in my head. First I set my arms, then I lower my head."

"Don't," Nate said. "You're a snowboarder. Your muscles know that even if your brain doesn't. You could assume the position in your sleep. Do it now."

"Riders ready," called the gatekeeper. "Attention."

They popped low, and the barricade fell. Corey jerked her arms and her board jumped over the ledge. Her vision focused as the shot of adrenaline hit her veins. Her knees stayed bent as she pressed her toes toward the turn and then pumped up with her legs and hips to power over a little incline in her way. Once on the downside, she skidded to a stop, the veteran Canadian at her back, followed closely by Nikki and then the young Canadian.

"Better," Nate called, coming down the side to meet them on their way back up. When he got closer he said, "But you should've beaten the big maple leaf there. Why did you let her cut in on you?"

"Oh, well, I didn't want to hit her. Maybe in a real race, but we're practicing."

"She's practicing cutting you off," Corey said bluntly.

"What?" Nikki asked.

"Sorry, Tigger." Corey slapped her on the back. "We all love you, but we also want to beat you. And while we're all working the same section of course, we aren't all working on the same fundamentals. You're working on getting out of the gate smoothly, but those Canadians are working on getting in front of you."

"And if they can do it with consistency here, you'd better believe they'll feel better about doing it to you in the Olympics," Nate added. "What's more, they're hoping you'll believe it, too."

"They're in my head?"

"Not if you kick them out," Corey said. "Hold your line. You've got as much right to be there as they do."

"But they're going to hit me."

"They might." She shrugged. "You've been hit before. You'll get hit again. That's part of the game, but they know as well as you do that friction slows them down. No one wants to go slower when headed into an incline and a turn."

Another set of racers went down behind them, and Nate glanced over his shoulder as the Canadians hiked up to the top of the hill once more. "You've got one more shot."

"To prove Matt wrong? Then I can practice with you?" Nikki asked.

"Forget Matt. You're not racing Matt. It's not Matt's neck on the line."

"It's not mine, either," Corey put in, wanting to stop any sense of obligation the kid felt to her. "You're being challenged by another boarder, three of them. If that isn't enough to motivate you, you don't belong out here with us."

Nikki squared her shoulders. Corey turned her back and headed uphill, so Nikki wouldn't see the grin on her face. She'd seen the spark in her eyes, the one that already told her how this would end, but she didn't want to spoil the surprise for the kid.

Back at the top, they got their middle slots once more, and as expected the Canadians flanked them to the outside. She pulled down her goggles and with a slight turn of her head gave Nikki a subtle nod. One corner of the kid's mouth quirked up, but she quickly lowered and grasped the handles.

This time when the gates fell and the board exploded forward, Corey didn't have to look back to see how Tigger finished. Instead she could clearly see her holding fast and firm in her periphery as both Canadians fell away behind them. They approached the incline neck and neck, shoulders squared and faces focused dead ahead until Corey threw her board sideways and ground to a stop.

There was no finish line, and Corey tried not to feel too grateful for not having to think about which one of them would've crossed it first. Tigger, on the other hand, only had to worry about reining in her enthusiasm. She stood right in the middle of the course beaming like she'd won gold.

127

"Get out of the way," Corey said, scooting past her to the side of the course.

"Oh yeah. Right." Nikki followed until they could both sit down and snap out of their bindings without the fear of being run over.

"Totally boss," Nate said, half jogging, half skidding across the snow to them. "You guys were flawless side by side. Like freaking Batman and Robin shooting out of the Batcave."

Nikki's smile pushed her goggles up into her helmet. Corey's grin felt more subdued.

"All right," Matt called, coming down to meet them at more leisurely pace. "I'm impressed."

"I can train with them?" Nikki asked hopefully.

"It doesn't work that way," he explained. "I represent the USSA. Nate is Corey's private trainer. She pays him. He works for her, not Team USA."

"Oh." Nikki's shoulders fell, and she turned first to Nate, then Corey. "Sorry, I didn't mean to barge in on a private lesson. I thought we were all on the same team."

"It's not really a team sport," Nate explained, sounding a little embarrassed. "It's every boarder for herself on the way down."

"Right. I get it. I just . . . well, Corey mentioned running with the big dogs . . ."

Corey sighed. She hadn't thought the comment through. She'd only been trying to get Matt-the-tool off the kid's back. She didn't mean she wanted the responsibility of carrying the weight herself. Still, Tigger seemed so damn sweet and innocent standing there, her eyes wide enough to read clearly even with her goggles on. Gah, she didn't want a kid hanging around all season, especially one who'd almost beat her out of the gate moments before.

"Besides," Matt finally stepped into the awkward silence, "Corey's at a different stage in her career. You'll be working on different things."

The comment wasn't false. It wasn't even a shitty dig on the surface, but it made the hair on Corey's arms stand up. She was at the end of her career, and Nikki's was only beginning. Today, the kid had fought to keep up with her, but it might not be long

128

before their roles reversed. She could either shy away from that challenge or meet it. She looked to Nate, the unspoken question passing between them.

He frowned, then shrugged, then nodded grudgingly.

"You know," Corey said. "I think you're right. She's going to need different lessons, but it might be good for her to see both sides, you know? The youth side and the veteran side."

"What are you proposing?"

"I don't know," she said honestly. "She's got to work with you, but maybe sometimes we could get together, too."

"We'd each keep our autonomy but coordinate a few targeted workouts a week?" Matt asked.

He'd produced the plan a little too quickly for her comfort level. She'd been thinking of something more informal, like when they happened to sync up they'd go with it, but she supposed that wasn't anything different than what she'd done today. If she wanted to push herself, she should probably do more than depend on happenstance. "Yeah, sure. I'll tell Holly to get in touch."

"Sounds good," Matt said, then motioned for Nikki to follow him.

Instead she threw her arms around Corey's neck and squeezed tightly. "Thanks, Corey. We're going to have such fun!"

Corey chuckled. "Fun. Yeah. That's what I'm here for."

Chapter Nine

"What would you do if I went into a tuck right now and shot off down the mountain at top speed?" Elise asked

Paolo's face went ashen. "One of us would die."

She rolled her eyes.

"You'd probably break your neck, or I'd have a heart attack. Or you could break your neck, and then I'd have a heart attack. Then we're both dead."

"Or I could make it down in one beautiful piece, and you could follow me at a leisurely pace, and we'd meet at the bottom."

"Then I'd kill you, and you're still dead, but I go to prison."

"It's been over a week," she said flatly.

"Over a year off, to over a week of working our way up the mountain. I don't think the ratio is unreasonable."

"What if I die of boredom?"

"What if I die from your nagging?"

Elise's mouth fell open, but he only laughed. "You're trying to pick me apart like a vulture at a carcass, but I'm made of metal. I didn't come this far to have you throw everything away now."

She sighed. "I know you've invested so much time in me, but don't you ever worry it's been too much time? Like we're running out?"

His eyes softened, and he laid a hand on her shoulder. "I know watching the other skiers race every day hurts your pride as much as the surgery hurt your knee."

She swallowed a ball of emotion in her throat and looked away. From this high up, she could see much more of the mountain range. She preferred the view.

Paulo pointed along the line of the ski lift. "Can you see the first chair from here?"

She shook her head.

"We were all the way down there a week ago, so far down you can't see the point where you were then. Think about how far you came before even that."

She understood his point.

"This whole journey you've wanted to go fast, but you need to realize you're already speeding. Speeding through the recovery, speeding through your workouts, speeding up the mountain. Every minute, every task is fast now, but one."

"Which one?"

"We need to start sliding the course slowly, and we need to do it more than once."

Paolo knew their program as well as she did, and even in her most frustrated moments, she trusted him. He was right about her pride, too. It was the only thing still hurting, and not reason enough to go against him. This late in the day, no one else would be around to see her scoot, inch by inch, over the terrain they flew across.

She'd had little interaction with the other skiers since arriving. She couldn't stand seeing them come in from the mountain every afternoon sweaty, disheveled, and smiling smugly. She hadn't been close with many of them even before her accident, but she'd had her fair share of admirers. They respected her enough to want to keep her close. During training sessions past, she might not have responded to many of the invitations for drinks or dinner, but they'd come anyway. And no matter how many times she turned down social graces, the others never failed to show up when she hit the snow. Two years ago they would've all gathered to watch her runs, trying to glean some insight or advantage.

Then again, two years ago they would've all been on the same slope to begin with. Now she didn't even inspire curiosity in the other skiers. None of them had even made the trip down mountain to sneak a peak at her new training rituals.

She didn't know what made her feel worse: knowing no one cared to watch her now, or knowing that, even when they had clung close behind her, they'd never truly done so out of admiration or friendship, but rather out of competitive drive and perhaps a bit of professional jealousy. Even if she did make it to the highest peak once more, literally and metaphorically, the crowds would likely return, but only for the same reasons. The thought made her shudder.

"Where did you just go?" Paolo asked.

"Nowhere important."

"Any time your mind isn't on this slope, it's important," he said seriously, then added, "Your muscles won't react as quickly as they used to. Your brain has to make up the difference."

Her jaw twitched, but not with the urge to argue anymore. She'd skied enough on the lower half of the terrain to know he was right. She might have the strength, but she didn't have the muscle memory anymore. "Let's go."

He paused as if he expected another smart remark, but when none came, he nodded resolutely. "We'll work on the starting gate later. For now, we start at the first flag."

She followed him at what felt like a snail's pace, but dedicated herself to making as many mental notes as possible. Fall lines, inclines, hairpins, and cross winds—she set to memorizing them the way a child repeats multiplication tables. Turn by turn, flat to flat, flag to flag, they worked their way down for over two miles. By the time they neared the bottom, her calves screamed, not from exertion, but from the work required to restrain their natural desire to let loose. Once they reached the second to last flag, Paolo turned to her with a weary grin. "Straight shot from here. You tuck and fly."

"I thought I wasn't allowed to fly."

"Well . . ." He finally shrugged. "I have to let you spread your wings sometime. Besides, I don't want to disappoint your adoring fans."

Her cheeks burned. "Thanks for that."

"What?"

"Reminding me there's no use hurrying because no one's waiting at the bottom?"

"Isn't there?" he asked, clearly trying to restrain a grin as he nodded downhill.

Elise peered toward the finish line and, with a little focus, could make out someone standing near the fence. She couldn't discern any distinguishing features from this distance. The observer wore the same sort of clothes and helmet favored by almost everyone else they passed on the lifts, but they also had a snowboard propped up against them, and while she couldn't be sure, she thought she could make out the bold, white print that simply said, "Drink water."

She couldn't contain her smile any more than Paolo could, and she didn't even care to examine why. "Tuck and fly, you said?"

Then without waiting for further instructions, she gave two hard pumps with her poles and crouched low. The final part of the course offered a steep dip, and within seconds wind whistled past her ears. Corey grew bigger and bigger in her vision until the chase abruptly ended. She threw her skis sideways, splashing up a smattering of snow across Corey's jacket and pants. Part of her heart dropped at the realization the thrill hadn't lasted nearly long enough, but another part couldn't give itself over to disappointment with Corey laughing as she shook off the dusting and clapped her gloved hands.

"What are you doing here?" Elise asked.

"I heard a famous skier was sneaking in after-hour workouts, and I thought I'd get a peek at the comeback story of the year before everyone else jumped on the bandwagon."

"As you can see," Elise gestured around the empty flat, "the crowds are pushing in from every side."

"They will be," Corey said. "If that little sprint run is any indication of your progress, I won't be able to get anywhere near you in a few months. I'll be some lowly board bum you used to know."

Elise's heart constricted at the thought of where they'd both be in a few months; then she internally chided herself. In a few months she'd be back on the tour, exactly where she wanted to be. She should find the prospect of competing full-time exhilarating for every reason. Corey's presence now or absence then shouldn't make any difference.

"I like your Spanx," Corey said as she gave her an exaggerated once-over.

"My what?"

"You know, your stretchy, long-john, leotard thingy."

"My downhill racing suit?"

"Aw, don't cheapen the experience for me."

Elise smiled. "Most people aren't as fixated on the suit as what's under it."

"Really?" Corey flipped up her goggles to reveal a little red imprint mark across the bridge of her nose, suggesting she'd exerted herself quite a bit recently. The tell warmed Elise's stomach. Corey hadn't happened by on an off day. The fact that she'd boarded all the way across and up the mountain after a full day of hard work somehow made the visit even more special.

Elise gave herself over to the playfulness in Corey's eyes. "Of all the questions people ask, 'what do you wear under your suit?' comes up more than all the others."

"Ahem," Corey cleared her throat dramatically and grabbed Elise's ski pole. She held the handle like a microphone and talked into it using her best sportscaster voice. "And Ms. Brandeis, will you give us an honest answer to that very important question?"

She held the ski pole handle out to Elise.

She pursed her lips tightly together for a moment, then said, "Well, there is a particular aerodynamics theory called 'skin-to-win.'"

Corey's hazel eyes widened and flicked quickly to Elise's chest, then up again. "And are you saying you're a disciple of this seemingly glorious theory?"

Elise smiled broadly. "A champion never divulges her secrets. Especially to the media."

"Right, right, wouldn't want to lose your edge over other skiers, but," Corey nodded seriously, then put her hand over the top of her "microphone," "off the record, will you tell me what's under the suit?"

Elise thought about letting her off the hook and doing a slow, deliberate unzip from the neck down to reveal a long-sleeve compression shirt and a pair of boring gray yoga pants, but she liked being the one to tease for once. Somehow it leveled the playing field between them more than any joint gym session had.

"I'll make you a deal. You beat me back to the base lodge, and I'll show you."

"Show me?" Corey's grin widened.

"Show you," she confirmed.

"No racing," Paolo said, coming up behind them. "She's not ready to race yet."

"She seemed pretty ready to me a minute ago when she came barreling down on me like her ass had caught fire."

"Thank you," Elise said. "I think."

"Asses on fire or not, she's not ready to race."

"Not even against a lowly snowboarder?" Corey asked. "No need to reach seventy miles per hour. I'll ride fakie."

"No," Elise cut in. "I do not need you to snowboard backwards. We're already halfway down the mountain. It's all blue trails from here, Paolo. We've skied steeper sections this week."

He scratched his chin stubble as he considered the point. "It's a pretty open trail from here down."

"And I'll give her a wide berth," Corey offered. "No cut-offs or bumps. We'll play by your pansy ski rules."

"You're going to pay for that one," Elise said, but she didn't feel any real affront, especially since Paolo wavered. "I have to start competing somewhere, and you don't want it to be on the top of the mountain with the whole team around. Let me start small, with a friend."

"A friend?" Paolo asked with raised eyebrows.

"Yeah, we're friends," she said with a shrug, then added, "I trust her."

"Trust her? She only made the offer to try to get inside your race suit."

Corey laughed. "Right, but other than that, I'm totally trustworthy."

Paolo laughed, too. "I actually believe you, but it's more important to me that Elise wants to share this moment with you."

Her chest constricted again. Did she want to share an important moment with Corey? Did this constitute a milestone for her? For them? She didn't have time to ponder the implications because Paolo finally said, "Okay, fine. Race her down."

Corey handed back her ski pole and quickly snapped into her board bindings before hopping energetically to her feet.

"This trail all the way down," Paolo said. "Corey, stay to the right and out of her way. Elise, no jumps."

They both nodded and pulled down their goggles as they edged right up to the next downhill dip, each angling for a better starting slot.

"If you feel any tightness, you need to pull up. Injury invalidates the bet. Right, Corey?"

"Of course." Corey answered automatically without even needing to look at the warning in Paolo's eyes. "Gentleman's agreement, safety first."

Elise appreciated the gesture, but she wouldn't pull up unless she had to, and they all knew it.

"I'll count down," Paolo said. "And God help me, if you get hurt, I swear to the Virgin Mother and—"

"Count, Paolo," she shouted.

"Three . . . Two . . . One."

They were off. Elise had the benefit of her poles to push off with while Corey had to rely solely on gravity to get going. She would've felt guilty for the initial advantage, but she wasn't responsible for Corey's inferior life choice to pursue boarding over skiing.

She curled into her deep tuck, her calves and thighs accepting the position like second nature. She'd been here earlier in the week, but she hadn't pushed any harder. She might not even have to push now, but with her short leash snapped, she begged her body to kick into a higher gear.

Rounding the first wide turn, she stayed low and allowed her good leg to slide out on a sharp angle. She kept her ski pinned tightly to the snow and smiled as her injured knee gave no protest at being forced to bear the bulk of her weight.

She straightened her line, drawing her knees and ankles close together once more. The terrain was far from challenging, mostly a wide open plain tilted to a moderate grade. She probably wouldn't have felt as though she were racing at all if not for the scrape of a snowboard growing louder behind her. She curled lower over her knees, eyes focused straight ahead as she tried to milk every ounce of speed she could from the snow. The sun had long ago abandoned this side of the mountain to shadows, allowing the base layer of snow to firm up a bit, but not enough for her tastes.

Evergreen trees flew by to her left as the trail narrowed slightly. Everything she passed blurred together in a whir of hunter and white, but a quick glance over her right shoulder revealed a flash of color as Corey whooshed into view. Within another hundred yards, she'd pulled almost neck and neck. She bent her knees deeply, her balance a thing to behold as her body angled slightly toward the nose of the board. She seemed effortless, like a bird gliding on the wind, with only minor movements of her toes or heels to rock the board left or right, but Elise knew wielding something so bulky at such a high speed took as much strength and coordination as it did grace.

As they approached a small rise, Paolo's warning rang through her ears. "Elise, no jumps." Still her every muscle twitched, eager to take flight. It wouldn't be a large leap. A little pump would send her a few inches into the air, and if she kept her skis perfectly level she'd barely feel her landing.

If she kept her skis level.

Still in her tuck, she had to make the decision too quickly to consider her options fully, and instinct took over. She crested the little rise and lifted her chest, slowing down the fraction needed to keep her skis firmly rooted to the snow.

Corey had neither made the same promise, nor shared the same instinct for self-protection. She rocketed over the ridge and into the lead. She landed with a glorious cloud of fresh powder that even from a distance caught Elise's face with a fine sprinkle. Payback for throwing snow on her earlier, no doubt. Were they not in a fight to the finish, Elise might have appreciated the gesture, but as it was, the only thing that mattered was eliminating Corey's lead.

Thankfully another large banked turn loomed ahead on the last major dip before the base lodge. This time she didn't hesitate to sink fully into her tuck and drive a hard line into the turn. She slid her injured leg out wide and smooth across the snow. Her whole body leaned into a forth-five degree angle, and the g-forces grabbed hold, both pinning her down and slingshotting her forward. Corey's board made a whooshing sound ahead, and Elise's eyes narrowed like a laser zooming in on a target. She instantly imprinted her path on her mind; then as she cleared the turn, she drew her leg back. The muscles in her upper thigh and hip flexors gave a brief shout of protest, but she gritted her teeth and the knee held.

She now had a clear sight line to the finish. She sank another inch into her tuck, newly tested knee tight to her chest, and imprinted her path on her mind's eye before lowering her head. She kept her gaze too low and focused to see Corey's face as she pulled ahead. This wasn't about Corey anymore. She could relish in the victory over her once she'd secured it, but for the next three hundred yards, she had one goal, and one goal only: maintaining max speed.

She didn't break form, she didn't smile, she didn't even exhale until she came within yards of the ski center's back deck and heard the hard-grinding scrape of Corey throwing her board sideways behind her.

"You win. You win," Corey shouted. "Slow down."

With a flick of her heels, she shot her skis into a hockey stop position and rode on a wave of her own making for several feet while metal fought to bite ground, but she had enough space.

She had enough speed. She had enough control. She had enough to ride her edge from here on out.

"Holy shit, you're a crazy woman," Corey called, slowing to a more tempered stop next to her.

She merely smiled and tipped her goggles up onto her helmet. "Crazy is a relative term coming from you."

"I thought I had you off the jump," Corey said, but showed no disappointment. She still wore her trademark grin, and her eyes danced with laughter.

"Paolo's no jumps rule put me at a disadvantage there," she admitted, "but sheer competitive drive goes a long way."

"Hey, now." Corey puffed up her chest. "Are you suggesting you're more competitive than I am? Because I'd be happy to go again right now."

"We've given poor Paolo's heart enough stress for one day," Elise said, watching him take a more conservative line down behind them. "Besides, I only meant to imply I had more at stake going into the last turn than you did."

"Because of our bet?"

"Right. The bet." She'd all but forgotten about that, but it offered a convenient cover for the other insecurities chasing her down the moun-tain. "Sorry you had to end the day on a loss. See you tomorrow?"

"You're seriously going to walk away without telling me what's under those super-sexy ski Spanx?"

Elise smiled coyly. "I guess you'll never know."

"Never?" Corey frowned. "That seems a little rash. I mean there's always tomorrow, or next Tuesday. I'm open then, or any other day before hell freezes over."

Elise laughed and bumped her shoulder before sauntering off. "Good night, Corey."

"Yeah, don't rush to a decision," Corey called after her. "You can sleep on it."

Elise shook her head as she walked into the lodge, but she did have to admit, never was an awfully long time to commit to.

❄ ❄ ❄

"You win, Nate," Tigger said, laying down her cards. "I only have a flush."

Everyone at the table groaned.

"What?" Nikki asked innocently.

Corey deferred to Nate. She wouldn't have minded him fleecing the kid a time or two. Maybe when he did she'd learn not to be so gullible. Better to teach that lesson here than get schooled by the Russian team later in the year.

"No," Nate said with a heavy sigh. "A flush beats a straight."

"But yours has an ace in it," Nikki said.

"Doesn't matter how high the straight goes, the flush always beats it."

"Even if the numbers aren't in order?"

"If it were in order, it would be a straight flush which beats almost anything." Nate pulled a few cards from the deck and began to lay them out in various orders to illustrate his point.

Corey couldn't stand poker preschool anymore. "Anyone need a drink?"

"Make mine a double," Elise said, rattling the ice in her otherwise empty glass. Corey walked over to the filtered water pitcher and filled the glass to the brim.

"Go ahead and make one for yourself, too," Elise added. "On me."

"What about you guys?" Corey called to Paolo and Holly, who sat close to each other in armchairs across the living area of Elise's suite. They were too engrossed in each other to even notice she'd addressed them. "Earth to the lovebirds."

Still nothing.

Corey tried one more time, this time calling, "Mom, Holly Anne pulled my hair."

Holly startled up out of the chair, then looked around as if remembering where she was before rolling her eyes. "I hate it when you do that. You know I've got post-tattletale-traumatic-stress."

The others laughed.

"Not from me," Corey said. "I never dragged Mom into something when I could exact my own revenge."

"That's why you were always my favorite sister," Holly said, sitting back down. "The older two were such little snits."

"I'll be sure to tell them you said so when we go home for Christmas."

"Then I'll tell Meg you're the one who dented the fender on her first BMW."

"Then I'll tell Jane you slept with Charlie Matthews after she left for college."

"Ladies, ladies," Paolo cut in.

They both whirled on him, and Nate jumped up. "Dude, do not get in the middle of a LaCroix family catfight."

"This happens often?" Paolo asked, wide eyed.

"Not as much as they used to, but they have hot tempers and long memories. You should see the shit fly when you get all four sisters in the same room."

"He's exaggerating," Corey explained to Elise and Tigger.

Nate silently mouthed, "I'm not."

"For the love of all things holy, I wanted to offer everyone a drink," Corey said exasperated.

"Oh." Holly smiled. "We're good, thanks. We've got wine."

"From my father's personal cellar," Paolo said proudly. "Are you sure you don't want some?"

"What's the drinking age in Argentina?" Nikki asked.

"No," everyone else said in unison.

"I'm almost eighteen," she protested.

"You're also trying to earn a spot on the United States snowboarding team," Corey said, in a tone parental enough to make her skin twitch.

"Alcohol isn't a prohibited substance."

"Because it's not performance enhancing," Elise said seriously. "It's the opposite. Alcohol is terrible for reaction times and muscle rehab. Plus it's full of bad calories. Notice not even Corey is having any."

"Yeah," Corey said. "Wait. 'Not even Corey?' What's that supposed to mean? Am I the lowest bar in the room?"

"Nope," Nate said. "I am. I'll have an Antares cream stout, and then it's your deal."

She grabbed Nate a bottle of the local brew from the cooler.

"At the Junior Worlds last year, the Russians were drinking every night."

"The Russians are crazy." Corey shuffled the cards and dealt two to each person at the table. "Don't hang out with them, and whatever you do, do not drink with them. It ends badly every time."

"Every time?" Elise asked over her hand. "How many times did you need to test it before you learned this particular lesson?"

"Too many," Nate said with a shake of his head.

"Google Corey's name plus Vodka rocket," Holly suggested.

"Don't," Corey said, as she discarded one card, then flipped three up in the middle of the table. "Just trust me. Don't drink with the Russian team."

"Don't drink at all while you're training," Elise added.

"Okay," Nikki nodded seriously, then seemingly apropos of nothing added, "I don't have any brothers or sisters."

"Bet's to you," Corey said.

"Oh." She grabbed a few poker chips and tossed them in. Everyone else followed suit.

"What about you, Elise?" Nikki asked. "Do you have siblings?"

Elise shook her head. "Only child."

Corey watched her eyes, less for a hint at her hand than for any sign of emotion. Elise didn't talk about her family. Everyone knew about the LaCroix sisters, and they'd all met Paolo's parents at dinner a few times. And Nikki's mom was okay enough other than rarely letting her out of sight for more than two hours outside of training sessions. It didn't seem coincidental that after nearly three months of regular contact, she hadn't heard a word about Elise's family.

She dealt one more card up. This time she didn't have to remind Nikki to bet. She quickly tossed out the same amount she had on the last round. "I always wanted a sister, but I would've taken a brother, too. It'd be nice to have someone who was there all the time, you know."

"Be careful what you wish for," Holly said. "There were plenty of times I would've given you one of mine."

"Meg," Corey said. "You could still have Meg most holidays."

"See," Nikki said, as Nate and Elise both made the requisite bets to stay in play. "You guys play off each other. You have history and inside jokes."

Corey placed her bet and flipped the last card to each player face up. "But Holly and I have a similar history with Nate. Blood lines don't guarantee a meaningful connection the way friendship does."

"I guess." Nikki frowned, then tossed out another bet. Unhappiness at the cards, or at the topic? Hell, would it even matter? The kid didn't know a good hand from a bad one. You can't read a player who can't read their cards.

"Are you having a hard time adjusting to the split schedule?" Nate asked.

Everyone stopped and turned to Nikki, who blushed before saying, "No. I mean, maybe. I used to be more of a group kind of person. But now the coaches keep pulling me out to work on my own, and since my mom is here, I don't bunk with the other youth racers."

"And you're with us some days but not others," Corey filled in, "which probably doesn't make you popular with some of the more jealous girls."

"Probably makes you a target to beat, more than a teammate," Elise added sympathetically.

"I don't mind," Nikki said quickly. "I'd rather hang out with you guys anyway. You're more fun."

"But we're not with you all the time," Corey said, "and you're seventeen, and you're not fully in one camp or another."

"But you will be when we leave here," Nate said resolutely. "You're going to make the A team this season."

"Everyone says so, but—"

"I'm not everyone," Nate said. "I'm a professional coach and trainer. You're going to be on the big stage this year, unless you start dogging it."

"I won't." She brightened a little. "Honest."

"You've got to keep working hard and stay healthy," Corey added, a wave of responsibility washing over her. "But when we break camp, I think we'll break together."

The kid beamed, her cheeks rosy like some little cherub on a Hallmark card, but it wasn't her grin Corey focused on. She felt a little tug in her chest as she noticed Elise trying to hide a smile of her own behind her cards. What did that expression mean? The ice queen never gave anything away through her stone-cold poker face, so she couldn't imagine she'd reacted to pocket aces.

"I fold," Elise said, confirming Corey's suspicion something else had sparked her happiness.

"Me, too," Corey said. She didn't have the focus or the inclination to keep playing.

Nate doubled down, though, and Nikki called his bet.

"Show 'em if you got 'em," Nate said, grimacing as he likely realized his standard double entendre might not work as well with a seventeen-year-old across the table. "I mean, lay down your cards."

"Full house, twos and Jacks."

"Son of a bitch." Nate threw his cards face down.

"Did I win again?" Nikki asked hopefully.

"The pot's yours."

"All of it?"

Everyone groaned.

Holly and Paolo walked over to the table, and Holly laid one hand on Nate's shoulder and the other one on Corey's. "As much fun as it is to watch you two lose your shirts to the Tiger Beat here, we're going to call it a night."

Nikki checked her Fitbit. "Oh man, I better go, too. My mom wants me in bed by ten o'clock on training nights."

"That's adorable," Holly said. "Think of all the championships you could've won if you'd gone to bed by ten every night, Core."

"And all the heartbreak I could've saved."

"I don't know about heartbreaks, but it would've saved a great many hangovers in the early days."

"And by hangovers, you mean yours."

Holly tousled her hair. "Probably. I've got meetings in the morning, but I'll see you in the gym around two o'clock?"

Corey and Nate nodded.

"Goodnight, all," Paolo said, then held the door open for Holly.

"You're staying a couple buildings over, right?" Nate asked Nikki.

"Yeah, it feels like a mile after a workout."

"I'll walk with you," he offered.

"You don't have to. I might not be old enough to drink, but if I'm going to be on the Olympic team, I should at least learn to find my way through a hotel."

"I know, but I'd feel safer if I went with you," he said, then to soften the blow, added, "I used to do it with Corey and Holly all the time, right Core?"

"Absolutely," she said.

They both rose and said their goodnights, but no sooner had the door closed behind them when Elise said, "Is she safer with him than without him?"

Corey laughed. "Well, I didn't want to mention that when he used to walk us back to our rooms, or more likely to our van, he also happened to be sleeping with Holly on a semi-regular basis."

"Oh Lord, I was only joking until you said that."

"No worries. She's not his type. Maybe fifteen years ago, but we've all grown more discerning over the last decade. I think he's moving into more of a big-brother role with her, which is funny on another level."

"It does seem like she's grown on all of you," Elise said.

"All of us?" Corey asked. "What about you?"

She lifted one shoulder noncommittally. "Maybe a little."

"And what about me? Am I growing on you, too?"

"Maybe."

"Maybe?" Corey pushed. "I'd say we've made considerable progress from the first night when you didn't even want me to sit at your cafeteria table."

"I suppose if you go all the way back to then, I do find you significantly less annoying now."

"Significantly less annoying? I'll take it."

"Honestly." Elise's expression grew more serious, her brow furrowed slightly. "I like how good you all are with Tigger. I think you and I had different upbringings in our respective sports, and given the choice, I'd rather she emulate yours than mine."

"Yeah?" Corey asked, surprised at the rare opening into Elise's personal life. "Why?"

"Don't get me wrong. I wouldn't change anything that made me successful, no matter what the cost."

"Obviously."

"But you managed to be successful while still making good friends and memories along the way."

"You didn't make good memories?"

"Maybe in different ways. I've seen some beautiful places and met some important people."

"But?" Corey tried to push gently, not wanting to overstep her bounds, but also wanting to know more about the enigmatic woman before her.

"I have no tawdry tales to tell. No inside jokes. No one who shared the whole ride." Elise smiled half-heartedly. "I guess none of that matters in the end."

"I've been hoping those things mattered most in the end."

"I didn't mean to imply they were unimportant, but those things don't win medals or set us atop podiums."

"Don't they?" Corey smiled again as she kicked out her legs and folded her hands behind her head. "I always thought the sense of community, the feeling of knowing where I belonged, anchored me. It gave me the freedom and the backing to take the big risks."

"I'd think risk was part of your nature."

"Maybe, on the slopes, but with things like breaking away from the safety of the tours, or telling the sponsors to shove off, or hell, even trying to become number one again after I've breached the big three-oh." Corey shuddered for effect, and to see Elise smile again. "I know I can do those things because I have my team and the memories of all the things we overcame to get where we are."

"You had an amazing rise," Elise admitted.

"From what I hear, you did, too."

"I had a fast rise. It's different. I never had to work my way up in the ways you did. I had a clear path set before me in middle school. Established organizations, governing rules, coaches and trainers—I never had to make a decision on my own, not about my training or the company I kept. I merely had to do what they said faster and better and harder than anyone else."

"And now?"

"Now I have to do what they say I can't."

Corey's chest ached at the little break in Elise's normally steady voice. "I bet that's sort of terrifying."

She nodded solemnly. "I'm a rule follower, and it always served me well. I trusted in the system, and the system rewarded me. Or maybe I trusted in the system because the system rewarded me. I spent my whole life as the front-runner. I've never been the person other people bet against."

"But now that the system isn't stacked in your favor, you have to relearn your ways of moving through the world."

"I always believed I had everything necessary to be a champion, physically and mentally. I only needed to wield those attributes accordingly to see results."

"Believed? As in, you aren't sure anymore?"

"The injury shook my confidence in my body. I've experienced more pain than I knew possible, and even as I start to think I'm fully rehabbed, I can sense those weaknesses below the surface in ways I never did before. I'm hyperaware of every twitch and twinge."

Corey sat forward, resting her elbows on the table and searching Elise's eyes. "Are you having pain in the knee again?"

"No," she said emphatically, "which in some ways makes it

worse. Pain in my knee would make sense. I could convince myself it was productive pain, part of the journey, but the knee's holding up better than anyone predicted. It's only everything else that hurts."

Corey chuckled nervously. "I know the feeling."

"My ankles swell, my thighs ache, tendons tighten, my lower back seizes, I'm aware of my hamstrings every minute of every day, and I keep asking myself if this is normal recovery, or age, or if I've lost what it takes to win?"

"Elise," she said seriously, "you haven't lost your drive to win."

"Not my drive, but what if . . ." She shook her head. "God, I'm sorry. I don't know what came over me. I think I'm more tired than I realized. We've been working on top of the mountain the last few days, and I must have a touch of mental fatigue."

Corey sighed. "It's only us here. We have a no bullshitting rule, remember?"

Elise pushed up from the table with a little wince and began to collect their glasses from the table. "I'm not bullshitting. I'm honestly exhausted."

"I believe you, but you started to say something else."

"Did I?" She put some physical distance between them under the guise of carrying things to the sink, but Corey rose and shook off the stiffness in her own limbs to follow her.

"You said, 'what if . . .'"

Elise made a little hum and turned on the water.

Corey placed a hand lightly on the strong curve of her hip and pressed gently until Elise turned to face her. "'What if' what?"

"What if I don't have what it takes to come from behind?"

Corey watched a multitude of emotions swirl in the icy depth of her eyes.

"I've never had to do this before," Elise said softly. "I never had to mount a comeback. I barely had to struggle the first time around. I've always won, or at least been right on the edge. What if I'm not resilient enough to fight my way up from the back of the pack?"

"Oh, Elise," Corey pulled her close, cradling the back of her head and letting her gorgeous blond hair sift through her fingers.

"I'm facing younger competition, healthier competition, stronger competition."

"But they're facing one of the greatest champions women's skiing has ever seen. Trust me, they're much more scared of you than you are of them."

She scoffed. "No one's scared of me anymore. We're all back at ground zero together. Only this is a normal process for them. They all know what it's like to struggle and fight and jockey for spots in the middle. They know they have that kind of fight in them. I've only ever breathed rarified air."

"And that's your advantage. You know how the air at the top tastes, how it smells, how it feels against your skin. They can only imagine the things you've experienced," Corey said. She couldn't tell yet if the idea hit home for Elise, but she felt a renewed passion stirring in her own chest. Suddenly she wasn't just talking to the champion in her arms, but to the one living inside herself. "We might not be where we want right now, but we've been there before. We're not kids fumbling through the woods at night with a flashlight and no map. We know what our bodies feel like at their peak. We've got something none of the others have yet."

"What?" Elise asked, as if she at least wanted to believe her.

"We've got experience. We'll know the right path when we see it. And since we've already seen both sides of the mountain, we're both going to fight like hell to get back to the summit."

Elise smiled, and Corey became acutely aware of her hands on Elise's hips. "That was a very good pep talk. Did anyone ever mention you're a lot smarter than you like to project?"

Corey slid her hand up Elise's side and over her shoulder until she cupped her cheek in her hand. "Did anyone ever tell you, you're a lot softer than you like people to see?"

Elise tried to shake her head, but instead Corey guided her mouth down to her own.

Elise parted her lips, either in surprise or under the guise of protest, but instead of pulling away, she caught hold of the belt loop on Corey's jeans and pulled her closer until their whole bodies pressed together. Corey ran her thumb along the smooth skin of Elise's cheek as their mouths yielded more fully to one another. She tasted fresh and crisp like an icy stream on a hot day. Neither of them hurried. The softness of this collision offered a direct contrast to the friction of all their others, but lacked nothing in the way of passion. This high carried the pulse of endorphins without the urgency of a fight, all of the pleasure with none of the pressure, as they seemed to both already have the prize in hand.

They broke apart slowly, and Elise blinked open her eyes, like blue skies burning through a morning haze. "Is there anything you're not good at?"

A rush of warmth filled Corey's chest. "If there is, I hope you never find out."

"Me too, actually," Elise laughed.

"You're not freaking out?"

"I probably should be," Elise said. "Could I have a rain check?"

"Absolutely. Best not to rush into things like moral crises or regrets."

"Moral crisis probably on the way," Elise admitted. "Regrets still seem a long away off."

"Would another kiss speed its arrival or slow its progress?"

"Let's find out." Elise pulled her in this time, dipping her head and taking her mouth with a confidence Corey hadn't experienced the first time. Tongues mingled in a delicious give-and-take. Corey moved her hands up to tangle in the silky strands of hair along Elise's elegant neck, while Elise's took a firm hold of her waist. They played, fingers and palms over smooth skin and hard muscles. Their mouths worked them to dizzying heights until something buzzed against Corey's side.

"It's bedtime," Elise murmured.

"Uh, that seems a little forward of you." Corey smiled against her lips. "But okay."

Elise gave her a little shove, breaking the contact between

them, but by no more than a foot. She held up her Fitbit, which was flashing some sort of alarm. "No, it's my bedtime."

"You set a bedtime alarm?" Corey asked. "Did Tigger's mom make your schedule, too?"

Elise did her best impression of indignant, but Corey could still see the hints of color in her complexion from their kiss. "I often get caught up in research or video sessions and lose track of time. Sleep is every bit as important to recovery as ice or stretching."

"And you were worried about not having what it takes."

Elise rolled her eyes, but Corey slipped an arm around her waist, taking a few seconds to marvel at how right the easy contact felt. "Don't worry, champ. I'm not some stage five clinger here to wreck your workout schedule."

"No?" Elise asked, uncertainty in her voice.

"Not tonight anyway," Corey amended, noticing another uptick in her heart rate. "Let's call this our second bout of cardio for the day."

Elise kissed her again quickly before stepping back once more. "Cardio sounds both fitting and appropriate for two athletes in training."

Corey smiled. "Let no one ever say we skimped on any area of our conditioning."

"Sounds like we've got another weapon in the pursuit of fun," Elise said with a smile.

"Indeed." Corey headed for the door, her muscles feeling decidedly lighter and looser than they had in a long time. Maybe there was something to this new workout regimen. "I'll see you when I see you?"

Elise touched her fingers to her lips in a way that made Corey suspect she was also seeing the benefits of their shared cardio program. "Probably sooner rather than later."

With that she closed the door behind her and gave a little hop. She landed lightly on the well-worn carpet of the hallway and fought the urge to dance her way back to her room.

Chapter Ten

"They're in the gate," Paolo called, and Elise stepped into the tech tent to see the screen more clearly. "Corey's in the red bib. Tigger's in the blue."

"Who are the other two on the outside?" she asked.

"Two Canadians, a rookie and the silver medalist from Sochi," one of the techs explained.

The TV didn't have any sound, but she could tell the racers had been given some sort of cue because they got low like coiled springs. Then the metal gates holding their boards back fell, and they all shot down a steep bank. Corey and Tigger held firm over a small lip and into a first turn while both the Canadians fell in behind them.

"Switch to the rollers," the tech said, and someone pushed a button, sending their view to a different camera in time to see all the racers fly into a section of the course consisting of one large bump followed by six smaller ones. Both Corey and Tigger used the air they got from the first jump to launch themselves over the first two of the smaller ones, but the young Canadian didn't make the leap and wiped out, leaving the field at three as they fell into another steep drop.

All three of them went into a low stance with Corey and Tigger neck and neck. The view switched again to show back-to-back banked turns. Elise's shoulders tightened as she watched Corey and Tigger edge in on each other as they both battled for the inside. Corey won this time if you could call it a win with Tigger right on top of her. Their boards knocked each other and their elbows flew up in defense of body blows.

"Can they do that?" Elise asked.

"Sure," the tech said. "No sucker punching, though."

"Good to know you draw the line somewhere," Elise mumbled, as they traded places into the second turn with Tigger to the inside and Corey pressing down from the back above her. She didn't know how they managed not to get pushed off course—probably through the g-forces generated by their speed and body mass. They rocketed out of the turn and the bottom immediately dropped out below. Both Corey and Tigger held their position, racing forward with perfect form as if they hadn't dropped off a solid ten-foot cliff, but the remaining Canadian actually used the leverage to land almost on top of them. Forced to give way or get squashed, Corey and Tigger split, and the dynamic of the race changed.

They went three wide into the next jump. The steady incline slowed them down only a fraction before they all took flight once more. The huge air caused each racer to rise out of their tuck, and for a moment Corey windmilled her arms once around before righting her line and landing with a soft cloud of power behind her. The minuscule lapse had cost her, though, as she came up a couple of feet short of where Tigger and the Canadian hit the course.

"Oh, she messed up," Elise said to no one in particular.

"Did she?" the tech asked.

Before Elise could answer, Corey ducked low and inside as they headed for the next turn, a tight hairpin that quickly doubled back on itself. The other two racers had already landed too high on the track to dip into the middle and had to ride an upper line around. Corey slid past underneath them both and came out the other side with a slight lead.

"She slowed down on purpose," Elise said, her chest expanding with pride and admiration.

"Here they come." Paolo stepped out of the tent and looked up mountain.

Elise followed, her gaze easily picking up the mass of bodies and the trail of snow as they hit another steep jump. They all three rose and fell in quick succession, but Corey maintained her half-board lead into the last high-sided s-turn. Once again they were all on top of one another. First Corey was on the bottom, then in the middle of the sandwich as they wrestled and bumped and knocked into one another.

"God, she's taking a beating," she whispered.

"Aren't you glad skiers race one at a time?" Paolo asked.

She hadn't even thought about herself in such a position. She hadn't processed far enough to wonder how Corey managed to walk after such a bruising workout, much less lift weights.

They came out of the turn and tucked into the final slope with Corey in the lead and Tigger still right on top of her. From the downhill angle, it actually looked as though their boards might overlap. The Canadian swung wide, obviously trying to pick up speed by removing herself from the friction. The move, however, pulled her away from the most direct line to the bottom.

Elise pressed up on her tiptoes trying to see who had the lead, but they flew past in such a blur she couldn't be sure until they hit the finish line a hundred yards below them. "Who won?" she shouted excitedly. "Who won?"

"Corey," the tech said confidently.

"How could you tell?"

"I watch a lot of these, but also they wear sensors on their ankles to track them, and I can already see she had the best time down. In a competition we'd use the video camera at the finish line to check, but we don't have to in a practice heat."

Elise repeated the only thing that mattered as the rest of the info blurred together: "Corey won."

Paolo laughed. "You seem more excited about the fact than she does."

Elise glanced down the slope. Corey was doubled over, breathing hard.

"Is she okay?" she asked, already moving toward her.

"I'm sure she's fine. I'm going to head up and talk to Nate."

"Go on. I want to talk to Corey."

She didn't defend herself against the accusation in his raised eyebrow. She'd deal with his suspicions later. She'd probably dodged them long enough anyway, but her concern now focused solely on Corey.

The two of them had seen each other several times in the week since their kiss or, more accurately, the first of many kisses, but they'd both been studiously casual, never letting on that anything had changed in front of the others. They worked out. They played cards. Occasionally their whole group would share a meal. No one else noticed anything had changed, and honestly nothing *had* changed, outside of the fact that the minute they were alone together they couldn't keep their mouths apart.

Corey was by far the best kisser Elise had ever paired with. Skilled and attentive without any pressure or pushing for more. She never rushed or overreached, even in the moments Elise would've let her, or might have even begged her to. She made every minute almost magical in the way she owned it. The times when they were kissing offered Elise only a glimpse of what true abandon might be like.

Maybe those hints of true abandon took hold now as she jogged along the blue snow fence to the finish line where all the racers were taking off their boards.

Tigger noticed her first. "What are you doing here, Elise?"

At the mention of her name, Corey smiled one of her broad smiles, the kind so warm it melted the ice in Elise's chest. "I had a meeting with my tech team at the base lodge and finished earlier than expected."

"So you came over to watch us?" Nikki filled in. "That's cool!"

"Yeah, well." Elise didn't want to give too much away. "It was Paolo's idea."

Corey rose slowly and tucked her board under her arm. "Paolo's idea?"

"All his," Elise confirmed.

155

"Did he have to drag you kicking and screaming?"

"I didn't exactly kick." She tried to hide her own smile. "I may have felt a mild curiosity."

"And?" Corey asked, standing on the other side of the fence now. "Did we satisfy you?"

She bit her tongue for a moment, trying to keep herself from spiraling into Corey's whirlpool of innuendo, but the mischief in her hazel eyes was either entrancing or addicting. "I'm not a woman who's easy to satisfy."

"Corey only beat me by like a half a board," Nikki said in her usual obliviousness.

"If that," Corey admitted. "You almost had me."

"Next time," Tigger warned playfully.

"Don't get cocky, kid," Corey warned. "Next time I might put you in the fence."

"Yeah?" Nikki's eyes lit up as if she considered the threat a thrilling prospect. "Let's go then."

"Go where?" Corey and Elise both asked.

"Back up," Tigger said, as it were the only logical answer. "I want to go again."

Corey grimaced quickly before plastering her smile back on, but Elise caught the unguarded response. "I'm done for the day."

"What?" Tigger asked. "That was so much fun. Aren't you amped up?"

"Totally," Corey said, "but I've got a schedule to keep."

"What's more important than a do-over on that heat?"

"She promised to hit the weight room with me."

"Oh," Nikki's shoulders fell. "Are you sure you don't have time for one more? I mean, you guys aren't dressed for weights."

"Be careful," Corey warned. "Elise doesn't like it when you make fun of her Spanx."

"They're not Spanx," Elise said, glancing down. "It's a racing suit and if either of you were wearing one, you might have blown the Canadian clear off the mountain."

Both of them wrinkled their nose in matching distaste.

"Anywho," Corey said with a thinly veiled weariness. "You'll have to wait for another day to get your butt kicked again, kiddo. Silly outfits or not, we have to bolt."

"Okay," Nikki relented. "Should I go with you guys?"

"No," they both said in unison; then Corey laughed. "Go beat someone else. I want to hear tales of glory when I see you tomorrow morning. The more reps the better, the more competitors the better."

"Got it." Nikki gave her a salute and grabbed her board. "And we're all going out to dinner on Saturday?"

"Absolutely," Elise said. "One last hurrah."

"Sweet." With that Nikki hurried off to catch the lift back up.

"You earned the break out there. I couldn't believe how much you guys were on top of each other."

"We're not always so rough, but that was a contentious heat. The Canadians have obviously picked the kid and me as the ones to beat."

"And the kid wants nothing more than to beat her teen idol," Elise added. "You've got a big target on your back."

She grinned. "Maybe."

"Be honest," Elise prodded. "You love it."

"I do. I had the time of my life on the last run. Mixing it up has always been one of my favorite things about the sport. I get bored on the wide-open plains. I love being in the thick of it all, then pulling ahead."

"And you did. You impressed me. I thought you guys were all slackers, but I can't imagine the core strength you need to execute turns that steep while someone presses their body weight on you."

"Feels like a fighter pilot banking a steep maneuver under enemy fire."

"And you're top gun," Elise finished. The image fit. It more than fit. It turned her on.

"I felt like a million bucks when I came across the line first. Like I still had it, you know?"

"And you do."

"I did. I was every bit as good as I've ever been for one run, but

I left it all out there." Corey's voice sounded drained to the point of collapse. "I'm spent."

"You should be. You gave everything you had. You're a champion. We don't leave anything in the tank."

"The kid has more runs in her." Corey sounded haunted. "Endless amounts of runs. It burned every ounce of my energy to beat her, and she's barely breathing hard. How long before she learns to channel her reserves?"

Elise didn't offer some weak platitudes or cheap advice. She didn't have the answers for sure, and she suspected if she did, neither one would like to hear them. She understood how Corey felt to give her best and still feel it wasn't enough, like it might not be enough when it really mattered. She had no happy words to soothe those fears. She wasn't nearly as adept at pep talks as Corey. Still, Elise couldn't live with the thought of leaving her to the doubts Corey often rescued her from.

"Hey." She wrapped her knuckles on Corey's helmet. "Come on. We've got a weight room date."

"We do not," Corey said. "You lied to get the kid out of our hair."

"What? We can't be spontaneous? I thought your type was always banging on about living in the moment."

"My type?" Corey laughed. "Even if I did believe in your stereotypes, I already told you. I'm shot. I don't have a weight regimen left in me."

"What if we forgo the weights and focus on some cardio?"

"Cardio, huh?" Corey lifted her goggles atop her helmet, revealing the little indent across the bridge of her nose, and Elise's core temp rose.

"Maybe. I mean I'd have to go change out of my *racing suit*."

Corey eyes grew even wider. "Well, in that case, I should probably come along. I wouldn't want you to feel lonely."

"You're such a giver." Elise laughed, relieved to see some of Corey's usual humor returning.

Sure, that was it. She was merely hoping to help Corey feel a little better. Isn't that what friends did? Friends who also made out, and may or may not be moving toward something involving less clothing? Friends did those things, right? Because friendship was all she had to offer. Friendship actually constituted a pretty big step for her. Friendship took time and energy and emotions, none of which she had in spades. Anything beyond friendship ran into a dangerous area, one that could prove distracting or draining. God, why hadn't she thought this through before? Corey was also so mellow she'd followed her lead and chosen not to overanalyze, but what if Corey led her right off track?

"You ready?" Corey asked.

"I'm not sure," she answered, before realizing Corey had heard none of her inner conflict and only meant to ask if she wanted to head back to the lodge. "I'm sorry. I mean, yes. I'm ready to go work out. On work. For our jobs."

"And cardio." Corey's smile sent Elise's heart rate up another few notches.

"Yes." She sighed, partly out of exasperation and partly out of dreaminess. "Probably a good bit of cardio, too."

"Cuddle duds?" Corey asked, torn between laughter and disappointment. "All this time I've spent dreaming of peeling that tight little racing number off you only to find cuddle duds underneath? Whatever happened to 'skin to win'?"

Elise threw back her head and laughed so hard her blond hair shook out in waves along her back. "You're never going to recover, are you?"

"I'm mortally wounded."

"And you still managed a healthy dose of cardio."

"Yeah, well. Let no one accuse me of skimping there, but back to this 'skin to win' concept. Are you now telling me you've never wanted to win badly enough to test the theory?"

"I never said 'never,'" Elise replied coyly as she dropped her bag inside her hotel suite door.

"You have raced commando?"

Elise smiled. "Can I get you a drink before the others arrive?"

"I'd rather have an answer to my question."

"How do I know you won't sell the story to a tabloid?"

Corey froze. "What's that supposed to mean?"

Elise turned, the smile fading from her face. "Just a joke."

"Really?"

"Yes," Elise said, "though I get the sense you didn't find it humorous."

"The tabloids aren't funny. They hurt people."

"And by people you mean you?"

"Or you, or other competitors." Corey tried to sound casual.

"Yes, but do you have personal experience?"

"A time or two. I thought maybe you knew."

"I didn't."

"I thought maybe you didn't trust me because of things you'd heard, or read."

"What? Ms. I-Turn-Down-Extravagant-Contracts-Because-Water might sell a story to make a buck?"

"Yeah, well, I didn't mean to paint myself as a Girl Scout," Corey said, not wanting to go into any more detail but feeling the weight of obligation to let Elise know what she was getting into. Not that she knew what they'd gotten into, but the kissing obviously wasn't a one-time thing. She didn't want Elise to look back on their time together and think of herself as one in a long line of one-night stands. The distinction mattered. "When I was younger, I didn't care about anyone's opinion of me, not my competitors, not the press, not even the women I spent time with. Some of those women ended up in grainy photos on websites or magazine covers after the Vancouver Olympics. Don't google it."

"So, I shouldn't google you ever, should I?"

"No." Corey shook her head. "I mean you can, but I'm a different person now. I learned some things the hard way. I want you to know I respect you, and I'd never hurt you that way. I never set out to hurt anyone, but I didn't understand then what I do now."

"I have no idea what you're talking about."

"I'm glad." She laughed nervously. "But I need you to know

that no matter what happens with us, and I have no plans, no need to label, but wherever we go from here, whatever life or the tours or the media throws our way, I won't betray you, or us, or anything we share. I promise."

Elise cupped Corey's face in her hand. "I trust you. You're one of the people I trust most in this business. You wouldn't be in my room if I didn't." She kissed her gently on the mouth, and the tension faded from Corey's shoulders.

"I find it sexy you let me into your room."

"I find it surprising but not unpleasant."

"You sure are good at the sweet-talking."

Elise rolled her eyes and tried to give her a little shove, but Corey caught her wrists and pulled her close once more. "I also find it sexy when you get feisty."

Elise started to protest, but Corey captured her mouth once more. This time they deepened the kiss with a hint of competitiveness. Corey liked the little edge that came from both of them jockeying for top position, but she wanted more than a tongue wrestling match this time. Slipping her arm around Elise's back, she walked her across the room to the faux leather loveseat. She refused to loosen her grip on Elise's waist until she landed on her lap.

Elise tried to scoot off of her. "I'm going to squash you like a little snowboard bug."

Corey laughed. "I might be shorter, but I'm strong enough to withstand your powerful thighs."

"Powerful thighs?" Elise rolled her eyes. "They're enormous."

"They're muscular and firm, and I may have fanaticized a time or ten about being trapped between them."

"You have an active imagination."

She smiled. "I really do. You wouldn't believe the things I've dreamed about doing with you."

"Why has it taken you so long to get around to mentioning them to me?"

"Honestly, for the first few months I held back out of sheer terror of your temper."

"I'm not that bad."

"I think Paolo mentioned something once about not poking the bear," Corey reminded her, then rushed ahead. "But even when I realized you weren't as scary as you wanted everyone to believe, I also figured you must be putting on that show to protect yourself. I'm not the only one who's gun-shy about these sorts of things. You've been burned, too, huh?"

Elise nodded. "From what it sounds like, not in the same way, but yes. You may have noticed I come across as a little standoffish at times."

Corey snorted. "A little?"

"Do you mind? I'm baring my soul here."

"Sorry, proceed."

"I haven't had a lot of relationships. Or maybe even real friendships." Elise's brow creased in consternation. "You can blame my family or my schooling or my competitiveness, but the reason hardly matters when the result is the same. People are drawn to my success. Or I guess I should say they *were* drawn to my success."

"Even your exes?"

"I don't really have exes."

"Are you saying you're a virgin, or is this another one of your 'skin to win' style redirects?"

"Neither. Both." She kissed her again, but only for a second before saying. "Somewhere in the middle."

"I think I've forgotten the question," Corey admitted. She wanted to focus, but Elise's fantastic ass grinding into her made all the blood leave her brain for destinations southward.

"I've never had a serious relationship," Elise explained.

"Oh well, I haven't had anything overly serious either."

"But I've never had a true one-night stand, either."

"Well." Corey drew out the word. "We were right on par until that point."

"I went to school with some driven women."

"This was some high-end, ivy-prep boarding school, wasn't it?"

"Absolutely."

"Do I even want to know what kind of family money you have?"

"Probably not." Elise sounded mildly embarrassed. "But the point is, expectations were high, all around. We found ways to make do."

"Oh my God," Corey said, her smile stretching so far her cheeks ached. "Is there a secret ring of discreet, high-powered, boarding school hook-up buddies?"

"Don't make everything sound scandalous. I have friends who understand the pressure of my life. When our paths cross, we connect. When they don't, we don't."

Corey's face burned at the thought of someone else connecting with Elise the way she was now. She didn't want anyone else to feel her relax as the tension of a race or workout melted from her tight muscles. She didn't want anyone else to feel her flex or contract under their fingers. She hated the idea of another woman brushing their lips against hers, or tasting remnants of salt on her skin. She had no right to say so, though. Instead, she said, "I understand the pressure of your life."

Elise's expression softened. "You do."

"So, maybe when our schedules connect this season, we could, too."

She nodded slowly. "I'd like that, probably more than I should, but I've been afraid to check and see if our schedules connect at all."

"Holly mentioned they don't much," Corey admitted. "But they might sometimes, not that we even have to look ahead."

"Right," Elise agreed. "We both have to focus on having our fun, right?"

Corey's grin wasn't quite as exuberant now. "We also have this moment. We're in the same place. At the same time. With all the fun for the day behind us."

"Maybe not all the fun," Elise said, leaning down and nipping at Corey's bottom lip. "I'm feeling an urgency for more cardio."

"The season is fast approaching. If you think another workout is in order, I wouldn't stand in your way."

"No," Elise agreed. "We're always supportive of joint workouts, but I think your hoodie is restrictive."

Corey shed it without further comment. "I hadn't wanted to bring it up, but your cuddle duds aren't as supportive of our training as they could be, either."

Elise reached between them and grabbed the hem of her long-sleeve gray shirt. Then, beginning a little shimmy that sent a thrill to the point where their bodies connected, she slowly started to raise up the garment over her beautiful torso.

"Knock, knock," someone called as she rapped her knuckles on the door to the suite. "Elise, are you in there?"

"Tigger," Corey groaned as if someone had dunked her who-ha into another ice bath.

"If we ignore her, will she go away?" Elise whispered.

She knocked again. "Hey, Paolo and Holly said to meet them here."

Elise hung her head. "It's like we've adopted an overgrown three-year-old, and all her friends invited themselves for a play date."

"Be right there," Corey called, then kissed Elise one more time. "You go ahead and get changed. I'll handle first shift with the baby."

"Thanks." Elise smiled tightly as she extracted herself from Corey's embrace. "Please tell me we'll get back to whatever we were about to do here."

Corey nodded and tried to use her most nonchalant voice even though every nerve ending in her body screamed, raw from the need for release. "Sure, it'll happen when it's meant to."

"To the future!" Tigger raised her glass of sparkling water.

Nate clinked it with his beer bottle. "To the season ahead."

"To the next step." Holly added her wine glass.

"To living the life," Paolo contributed.

"To comebacks," Corey said confidently.

They all turned to Elise, and she raised her glass, knowing she had to offer up something more than a simple toast, a wish, a hope, not only for herself but something to hold them all over until they found each other again. She opened her mouth, not sure what she'd say until the words spilled out. "To real friends."

They all paused with every glass raised, each making eye contact, memorizing one another's smiles, and imprinting the warmth of the moment to hold them over on the long, cold stretches of work and competition ahead.

Tigger broke first, likely because she didn't yet understand how rare these moments were. Elise envied her naiveté.

"How much longer will you stay down here?"

"We'll stay another few weeks, then head back to Park City for a November first check-in," Elise said, as casually as she could muster. One more hurdle, one more hoop to jump through. One more medical check to clear her to compete. On one hand, three more weeks felt like an eternity when all her friends were already so far ahead, but on the other hand, three weeks didn't seem like nearly enough time to get to where she wanted to be before that check-in.

Corey moved her hand under the table to let it rest lightly on Elise's thigh, before saying, "Then where do you start your season?"

"We'll train the last two weeks in Lake Louise, Canada, before the season opens there December first."

"Hey, we're in Lake Louise in December, too," Tigger exclaimed, but before anyone else at the table had a chance to feel much excitement, Holly said, "Not until the twentieth."

"We'll be in France by then," Paolo said, making it clear the two of them had already compared calendars.

"Oh," Tigger said, with a frown. "We leave for Austria in the middle of November and don't come back until the middle of December. I don't even get a full week off until Christmas, and even then my mom wants to travel to some place fancy in France ahead of our January races."

"Welcome to the big leagues," Nate said dryly. "They ain't what they used to be."

"Even I'm going to the team camp in Austria these days," Corey said.

"You're not going home?" Elise asked.

"I'll be there for a few weeks, but it doesn't make sense to stay in Lake Henry waiting for snow when I can be on the glaciers right next door to where we'll be racing when the season opens," Corey explained, not going into any of the details about her fear that with extra practice the kid and God knows who else might pass her up this year. "I'll head home for two weeks at Christmas, though. What about you?"

"I usually stay in Europe—"

"Usually," Paolo said. "But I've been meaning to mention it might be a good idea to go back to Lake Henry this year."

"Why would a trip back to the states make sense between a mid-December race in France and a January race in Austria?"

"Because all the trainers, coaches, and USSA officials will be there for meetings the week after the holiday. They'll no doubt discuss Olympic team slots, and if you're there, they can see you work out."

"And you can try to browbeat them if I haven't had great results on the tour."

Paolo raised his hands in defense. "I didn't say that."

"You didn't have to. We'll have had two races before then, and if I do well, there won't be any question as to my place on the team."

Corey tightened her grip on her thigh, causing Elise to glance over at her. She saw none of her own tension reflected in her expression.

"Also," Corey said with a smile, "bonus: Your favorite workout partner will be in town."

"So will Paolo's favorite person in the whole world," Holly added with a smile much more suggestive than Corey's.

"A much happier bonus," Paolo said.

"I see." She pretended to pout even in the face of Paolo's love-struck grin. "The LaCroix sisters are the reason you want to add thousands of miles to our already hectic season."

"They are two of many reasons," Paolo said, with as much seriousness as he could muster, but she felt certain he and Holly were
playing footsie under the table. Then again, they weren't the only
ones. Corey ran her fingertips along the seam of Elise's jeans from
her knee to mid-thigh, not quite high enough to be scandalous,
but enough to distract her from her frustration.

"I suppose two races isn't very many for the powers-that-be to
see before they all get together at the new year," she finally said.
"A few publicly supervised workouts wouldn't hurt."

Everyone smiled but Tigger, who'd either missed the subtext
of the discussion or felt sad at being the only member of the
group not going home for the holidays. Elise would've felt sorry
for her if she wasn't also partially relishing the thought of a few
days with Corey, even if they were two months from now. Would
that be their lives from now on? A few days every few months?
She'd never had anything more with any of her other lovers, and
the idea had never bothered her. Why did the concern weigh on
her mind now, with so many other events and challenges between
now and then?

She was still pondering the question half an hour later as they
all headed back to the hotel.

"Nightcap, anyone?" Nate asked as they reached the lobby.

"I can't," Tigger said with a sigh. "My mom already let me stay
out later than usual tonight. I bet she's sitting watching the clock
and checking our flight schedule for tomorrow."

He laughed, then turned to Paolo and Holly. "I know you
two are out, must go shack up one more time before the big
departure."

"Shack up?" Paolo asked. "Is that what we're doing?"

Holly wrapped her arms around his waist and kissed him on
the cheek. "That and so much more, honey."

"Adios," Paolo said, and led her quickly away.

"I'm going to call it a night, too," Elise said, making eye contact
with Corey in a way she hoped made it clear she didn't intend to
go alone.

She must've gotten the message, because she gave a big stage yawn and said, "Me too. I'm beat. Why don't you go ahead and make sure the kid gets home? I'll see you both in the morning."

Nate shrugged. "Okay. It's me and you on the long walk home again."

"Night, guys," Tigger called as they walked away. Corey and Elise stood in the lobby for several long seconds until they were out of view.

"I'm not that tired," Elise finally said.

"Yeah, not even a little bit," Corey said.

"Your room or mine?"

"Mine's closer," Elise said.

"And bigger," Corey added.

"And nicer."

"What are we waiting for?"

The elevator doors barely closed behind them before their lips locked. The ride up five floors had never been so short or warm, and they almost missed the little bell signaling their arrival. Wrenching themselves apart only at the last second, they both did a poor job of acting natural as they speed-walked down the hallway.

They stumbled, groping and fumbling across the room to the couch, and Corey started to ease her down, but Elise held them both up. She needed more space to do what she'd spent all evening thinking about doing. They would need every inch of the glorious, king-size bed.

"Easy, snowboarder," she teased, pulling away from the kiss only enough to keep breathing hot and fast against Corey's neck. "No hard landings tonight. Let's go to the bedroom."

Corey nodded and kissed her throat, nipping and sucking the sensitive skin in a way that sent the most delicious chills down her spine. Elise stepped slowly backward, leading her along with little kisses across her cheek, and tantalizingly brushed her fingers under the bottom of Corey's shirt. She wasn't sure who enjoyed the touching more, because as she traced the line of Corey's amazing lower abs, she had visions of running her tongue along the same path.

Then all contact between them broke as Corey wrenched away.

Elise's eyes flew open as she struggled to process the withdrawal and the screaming need it sent through every nerve ending.

"I can't," Corey panted.

"What?"

"We have to stop."

Elise couldn't make the answer compute. "Why?"

"I can't, um, I can't do it." She exhaled and ran her hands through her hair.

"Like physically can't? You only had one glass of wine at dinner."

"What?" Corey blinked a few times, then shook her head. "No, no, no, trust me. Performance issues aren't a problem here, now or, I mean, ever when you're around, but it's already late. I have a five a.m. flight tomorrow morning. I have to leave here before four."

Elise caught her by the waistband of her jeans and tugged her forward once more. "You can sleep on the plane."

"No. Sweet Jesus, this isn't about sleep."

"What's it about then?"

"You," Corey said softly. "I have to leave you in five hours, and that'll be hard enough as it is. Harder than it should be, and I don't want to do it knowing I left something half done."

"Half done?" Elise asked.

"When I finally get you into bed, I'm going to want more than one go at it. I don't want to rush like some teenagers in the back-seat of a car. Or maybe we will the first time, but not the second or the third."

"Second or third?" Elise repeated as she sank onto the couch, or at least she thought she said the words aloud, but she couldn't hear them over the rush of blood in her own ears. "Are you saying you don't want to sleep with me once because you won't get to do it again?"

"Yeah. When you say it like that, it sounds epically dumb, but I actually meant I don't want to sleep with you *yet*, because I want to wait for a time when we have time to take our time."

"You have to give me a second, because you caught me off guard."

169

"Me too," Corey admitted. "I didn't plan this, and if me-from-three-months-ago could hear me tonight, she'd kick my ass, but after all the talk at dinner of going our separate ways, it doesn't feel right. You deserve better, and maybe for the first time in my life, I want better for myself, too."

Elise hung her head and tried to roll out the tension. What could she say? She didn't think they deserved better? Of course they did, but better wasn't an option for them. They had no guarantees. What happened to living in the moment?

Corey sat down beside her and took her hand. "We'll be home for a week at Christmas."

"Christmas?" Elise asked. "You think we're going to feel this way at Christmas?"

Corey grimaced. "I suppose I was presumptuous to assume you'd still want me two months from now."

"No." Elise shook her head. "That sounded bad. I didn't mean I wouldn't want you, but it'll be mid-season. The pressure will be so strong. Everyone will be watching me. I won't be on vacation. It'll be a training holiday. I'm going there to work. That's the only reason I agreed to travel."

"The only reason?" Corey asked, her eyes searching Elise's. "Christmas in the Adirondacks with the LaCroix clan didn't factor into the decision at all?"

She pursed her lips. "I suppose there's one LaCroix sister I considered in the deal."

"It's Meg, right? You want to meet Meg?"

Elise laughed, once again impressed with Corey's ability to lighten her mood even under the most frustrating circumstances.

"I won't pressure you," Corey said, placing a sweet kiss on her forehead. "I'll try not to make assumptions, but I'm going to ask Santa for you in my bed on Christmas morning."

"What if he can't deliver?"

"I know I'm supposed to say I'll understand, but honestly I will probably regret this moment for the rest of my life. Like I said, 'no pressure.'"

Elise shook her head. Of all the surprises she'd experienced with Corey over the last few months, this one had to take the cake. She wanted to be mad. No woman had ever turned her down. Not ever. She liked to be the one to set the terms, and everyone else gladly accepted them. Then again, that's a big part of what drew her to Corey. She wasn't like anyone else in her life. Why should she expect sex with her to be any different? And if Corey could back up her promise for many hours and multiple times with the passion they brought to every other interaction they'd shared . . . the frustration overwhelmed her again, burning up her chest, but it went only surface deep and stemmed partly from having to admit Corey was probably right, again.

"You're not who I thought you were the first day in the cafeteria," she finally said.

"Maybe I'm not who I thought I was then, either."

"I'm not sure I like you acting as the reflective, logical one in this friendship."

"I know, right?" Corey asked. "I hate responsible Corey. She's a buzzkill."

"I don't know," Elise said, running her fingers through Corey's thick, soft mane of golden hair. "She's frustrating, but also kind of endearing. Everyone's always wanted whatever they can get from me, whenever they can get it. I can't think of a single person in my life, with the exception of maybe Paolo, who cared enough to invest long-term."

Corey leaned in until their foreheads touched and closed her eyes. "Okay," she murmured. "Maybe responsible Corey isn't such an asshole after all."

Elise smiled and inhaled the deep, rich scent of her, cotton and pine, so comfortable, probably too comfortable. She'd made peace with them as friends, and then as friends with the potential for some pleasurable benefits, but the sensation stirring in her chest now hinted at something much deeper, something she feared would linger long after the feel of Corey pressed against her had faded.

Chapter Eleven

December 6, 2017
Montafon, Austria

Corey's vision flashed red as sweat poured down her back in rivulets. She engaged every stabilizer muscle in her body to hold her form under the onslaught of g-forces, and the Russian snowboarder leaned heavily into her path as they cleared the final turn.

She tightened her jaw, bent her knees, flattened her board, and lowered her head. Gravity would be her friend here, or it wouldn't; there were no more technical maneuvers to make. Her stocky build offered her a genetic blessing in the race to the finish. Heavy and compact might not make the most of big air, but it never hurt when someone tried to push her off-track on a downhill run. She felt solid and steady, as if the finish line were racing toward her instead of the other way around, but she took nothing for granted, and refused to so much as glance over her shoulder until the tip of her board crossed the line.

One advantage to having someone practically on top of her at the very end was that she could easily see she'd been the one to get there first. The officials could check the cameras or the sensors, but as soon as she threw her board sideways and rocked back on her heels, the relief washed over her. All the adrenaline and endorphins instantly transitioned from her fight-or-flight instincts to pure biochemical jubilation.

Raising one fist in the air, she gave a shout of joy and searched the crowd for Holly. She came pushing up to the snow fence, and they fell together, cheering and laughing.

The announcer came over the loudspeaker to confirm what Corey had already known. She'd taken first place. The Russian had come in second, and a Swede had come in third.

"One race. One win." Holly shouted to be heard over the raucous crowd echoing through the Alps. Corey turned to shake hands with her fellow finishers when she noticed Tigger getting slowly to her feet.

"Shit." She'd forgotten about her the minute they'd left the gate. They'd been on opposite poles of the starting line, and she hadn't seen her once since she broke out. Tigger must've been behind the pack for the entire race.

She walked over as casually as possible and gave her a high five. "Good race."

Tigger shook her head. "I did terrible. They boxed me out on the first turn. I almost went down. I didn't have the speed to get up the second jump. I had to hop over it, like little baby bunny, or a tiny kangaroo, or—"

"Whoa," Corey said. "It happens. You're fine."

"I looked like I didn't belong out here with you guys. God, what if I don't?" Her pink cheeks turned ashen, and her eyes shimmered with tears.

"No," Corey snapped. "Not here. Geez, what's wrong with you? Don't you dare let them see you shake. Turn your back to the cameras and pull your shit together."

"What?" Her jaw went slack. "Why are you being mean?"

"I'm not. I'm saving you. These people will eat you alive. The racers, the media, they can see you. People all over the world will watch these videos to prepare for upcoming events. You're still competing right now. Everything you do in this moment will come back to you in the next race. You need to act like a badass. You can go cry in a bubble bath later."

She sniffed and nodded. "Okay."

"You're a badass," Corey repeated in her most convincing voice, even though Tigger actually seemed incredibly young, scared, and small amid the crowd and noise. "You're a professional snow-boarder. Start acting like it, even if you have to fake it."

"Okay." She straightened her shoulders and lifted her chin. "I'll walk out of here like I'm not upset."

"No. You're going to stay right here with me and sign autographs until your hand cramps."

"No one will want my autograph. I came in last."

"No, you didn't," Corey snapped again. "You finished fourth out of a field of twenty. You finaled. You did better than the majority of the field. To the girls in the crowd, you're a hero and a role model. It took me too long to understand that. I'm not going to let you make the same mistake."

"Oh, okay." She nodded. "How did you learn all this stuff?"

"The hard way." Corey laughed, feeling better as the color returned to Tigger's complexion. "Come on, let's go meet our adoring public. Holly always has pens because I never do."

They strode like rock stars over to Holly, who held out a Sharpie to Corey.

"The kid needs one, too."

"Sure. Holly fished through her bag and grabbed a red marker. "Use something bright. Make a statement."

"Thanks." Tigger grinned as if the marker were a trophy.

"Start on one side, and I'll hit the other. We'll meet in the middle."

She bounded off like her usual bouncy self, but as Corey turned to head in the opposite direction, Holly caught her by the sleeve.

"What was that?"

"The kid was upset about losing. I told her to buck up."

"Did you also tell her anything that might help her beat you the next time around?"

The question knocked the wind out of her. "What?"

"She's a nice kid," Holly said more quietly. "I'm glad she got to work out with us, but Nate says she has real potential."

"She does," Corey said slowly, not sure she liked the direction the conversation was headed. "She's got the talent."

"And you've got the experience. You're the smartest, most mentally tough rider on the mountain. You each have your own strengths, but she can't give you hers. Maybe you should think twice about giving her yours."

"Where's this coming from?"

Holly sighed. "I love you. You know this, right? I abso-freaking-lutley adore you."

"Well, I am adorable," Corey admitted, but the joke did little to settle the tightness in her stomach.

"And I'm proud of what a good heart you have. I've watched you grow from this impetuous kid into an amazing mentor, and someday I know you're going to take everything you've learned and hand the playbook to the next generation." Holly clasped a hand on her shoulder. "I just want to make sure you're using all the info before you pass it along to the competition."

"Excuse me, Corey," a young man with a microphone called. "Can we get a quick interview?"

"Go on," Holly said, nodding toward the camera that was likely already rolling.

"Sure," Corey turned around and then turned on her trade-mark smile.

"All right. Stand with the finish line in the background." He grabbed her arm and steered her around how he wanted her. The cameraman adjusted quickly, then flashed a thumbs ups. "I'm here live with today's winner, Corey LaCroix. Great race today, Corey."

"Thanks. We came down to the wire, but it's always nice to have the first one of the year in the bag."

"A lot of people picked you to finish in the lower half this year. How's it feel to make a statement early on?"

"I'm not concerned with what other people think." She tried not to look too pointedly at Holly. "I only care about racing my race. I can't change who I am because of other people or my competition or anything else."

"It never concerned you when you got into those gates that you're the oldest person on the course by five years?"

She blew out a heavy exhale. What the hell was everyone's problem today? "You want the honest answer, Chad?"

He laughed nervously. "I'm Jeremy."

"Right. Well, Jeremy, I seriously hadn't considered anyone's age, including my own, until you mentioned it. Thanks for that, by the way."

His big, toothy grinned faltered only for a second. "Well, I guess it's true what they say, age is more in your mind than your legs."

"Maybe," she said with forced cheerfulness, because since he'd mentioned it, her legs felt like Jell-O on a muggy summer day.

"Well, we wish you the best. And while we've got you here, can I ask a real quick question?"

"Shoot."

"Nikki Prince made the finals in her first professional race. Do you think she's everything she's been promised to be?"

"I don't know about any promises anyone has made, but she's the real deal." This time she didn't shy away from meeting Holly's eyes. "We worked together in the off-season, and I'm impressed with the progress she's made, but also with the progress she's inspired in me, too."

Elise approached the third turn, wide, flat, smooth, easy to gain speed, easy to slide too wide. She needed balance here. She needed perfection. At top speed, the turn could make or break her race, her comeback, her career. One inch too wide and she might not have the strength to pull herself back in. One inch too close to the gate and she'd replay the disaster she might never recover from.

"You got a text," Paolo said from right beside her.

She opened her eyes. "Are you serious?"

He shrugged and grinned.

"I'm four racers from the start of my first race back in over a year."

"You told me to watch your phone."

"As in 'make sure no one steals it or runs over it.' Not as in 'play social secretary.' I'm trying to run through the course in my mind. I need to be fully present here. I need to be in my zone, and you, of all people, should understand that."

"Okay, okay." He held up his hands. "I understand, but I also know you've been over this course a million times. I bet you dreamt about your line the last two nights."

She folded her arms across her chest. No need to confirm his suspicions.

"You're pressing, Elise. You didn't look serene. You looked terrified. I don't want you so far in your head you're not here in the moment."

"So you decided to interrupt me with trivial distractions?"

"I only mentioned the message because I thought it might be the right kind of distraction."

"Is it from the president or something?"

"It's from Corey."

"Oh." She glanced at the phone in his hand. It shouldn't have made a difference. She was minutes from the start of a major race. She couldn't afford any interruptions now, not from anyone, but at this point not reading the text would be as distracting as reading it.

"You want me to read it?"

"Yeah. I mean, no." She sighed and extended her hand. "Damn it, give it here."

He handed her the phone with a silly I-told-you-so grin.

She swiped at the screen and read the simple message. "Have fun out there."

She handed it back to Paolo without a word, but she didn't quite manage to hide her smile. Of course Corey'd said the perfect thing. She always did. Even if she'd sounded juvenile or reductive at first glance, she'd always managed to be on point. No major speech. No silly platitudes or false assurances. Just a reminder that winning is fun, so she should do that.

Paolo got the message too, or at least understood she'd gotten the right message, because he didn't press her anymore. He'd been great about respecting the shift in her around Corey. He didn't tease or ask for details she couldn't provide. She didn't have a label for their relationship. They weren't lovers, at least not yet. They were friends, but not like any other friendship she'd ever had before. Corey soothed her and challenged her and made her ache for things she couldn't name, but she also gave her space and the freedom to figure things out for herself. They'd only talked on the phone once since she'd left Argentina, and even that had mostly been innuendo-laden conversation about various workouts. Mostly they contented themselves with text messages ranging from the mundane to the mildly suggestive.

A few months ago, the idea of breaking camp with someone like Corey still in her life would feel suffocating or disruptive. She'd always considered long-term relationships too labor intensive and the people who sought them needy. She couldn't imagine making that kind of time in her schedule, but Corey presented none of those problems. She offered the perfect mix of peace and motivation to keep doing better. As much as she hated to admit it, Elise found herself wanting more, not less.

"Two more to go," Paolo said.

"Two more racers?" Her heart rate increased. So much for Corey not being a distraction. She'd spent God knows how long daydreaming about her when she should've done nothing but visualize the course.

"You're fine," Paolo said, as if he'd read her mind. "Don't tense up again."

"I'm not tense. I'm focused."

He massaged her shoulders. "Your muscles are in knots. You're putting too much pressure on yourself. Don't go back there."

She didn't have to ask where. He'd never once mentioned the fact that she'd gotten hurt by going against his advice. Not in the hospital, not during the long training sessions—he didn't even fully allude to it now.

The skier in front of her slid into the gate. Her heart no longer pounded in her chest. Now it beat in her throat, in her ears, the sound of it reverberating off her skull.

Paolo stepped in front of Elise and placed a hand on each

shoulder, forcing her to meet his dark eyes. "You're a more better skier when you're running on instinct."

She nodded, but the words only bounced off her brain. Nothing could penetrate the rising sense of panic.

"Trust your body. Don't fight it."

Her stomach lurched as the skier ahead of her sped off. She didn't know who it was. She barely knew who she was. As she slid into position, she only knew there was a distinct possibility of her throwing up. God, what was wrong with her? She'd never felt this way in a starting gate before. Her cheeks flushed. Where had all the ice in her veins gone?

Heat where there should have been cold. Panic where she should've felt calm. Distraction where she should've had focus.

The shrill beep of her countdown cut through her ears, and she wrestled her body into a position that should've been automatic.

And she was off. Pump, push, bend, tuck. The trees blurred as she flew by. Fast—too fast, and yet not fast enough. She couldn't see the course coming up in her mind's eye. She was reacting to obstacles instead of acting on instinct. One turn barreled down on her, then another. She wasn't having fun, not on any level. The idea of winning fell below the more pressing desire to simply stay upright. She was out of her tuck and then over a jump. Her right ski landed a half-second ahead of her left. Normally the minor discrepancy would mean a lost second. Now it represented the deeper fear of losing everything once more.

She bore down with every muscle, frantically trying to regain her form, but as she tightened into her tuck, a jagged knife sliced through the back of her calf. The pain, sharp and sudden, drew her up short, and she slid out of bounds with more relief than she cared to admit even to herself.

Corey watched the replay again as she dialed the number she'd tried not to memorize over the last few months. She paused the video from the point where Elise stood doubled over, panting on the sidelines, and tried to read her facial expression. She'd watched the race at least fifty times over the last three days and still couldn't make sense of what she saw.

The phone rang, and she rewound once more. The early parts of the track weren't hard to decipher. It didn't require a deep knowledge of skiing to see Elise didn't seem comfortable. Her lines were off and her form shaky, but she hadn't lost control. She could have finished, albeit not strongly. Still, a rating of Did Not Finish in the first race of the downhill season created an uphill battle for making the Olympic team.

Corey tried to count the rings instead of rehearing the conversation she'd eavesdropped on back at Lake Henry. One ring. Two rings. Three rings. And . . .

"Hello." Elise sounded über professional, as if she hadn't already seen Corey's name on her caller ID screen. Well fine, if she wanted to pretend, then Corey would, too.

"Hello, Ms. Brandeis?" Corey said, in her most telemarketer-esque voice.

"This is she."

"Good evening, Ms. Brandeis, I'm Michelle Amanda Tiffany Jones-Smith calling from the National American Foundation for the Preservation of the Southern Woodland Beaver. May I have a few moments of your time to discuss the dire state of affairs we're facing due to beaver neglect and misuse?"

Elise sighed. "Actually I'm very busy right now. Can I send a check to your organization?"

"While I appreciate the gesture, and you can certainly text your credit card information to this number, the Southern Woodland Beavers need more than your donations. They need attention, care, and regular exercise."

Elise snorted. "Exercise?"

"Yes, regularly and under the supervision of a trained beaver caregiver. The position, if you want to call it that, though the term is reductive because it actually takes multiple positions to do the job right—"

"Hi Corey," Elise said. All the distance was gone from her voice, but the exhaustion had grown as the formality faded.

"I actually prefer to go by Michelle Amanda Tiffany, but for you I'll make an exception."

"Generous of you."

"Yeah, well what's new with you?"

"Corey," Elise said solemnly, "can we skip the chit-chat? I've got a lot on my mind."

"Well, I was going to stick to chit-chat, but since you brought it up, you kind of shit the bed last weekend."

"Excuse me?"

"I'm not judging."

"You said I 'shit the bed.' I don't even know what that means exactly in this context, but it sounds pretty judgmental."

"Nah, happens to the best of us."

"Bed shitting?" she asked. "Please tell Santa to cross me off your Christmas list."

Corey laughed heartily, perhaps even more than the comment warranted, but she'd desperately needed to hear the fire come back into Elise's voice.

"I got a cramp," Elise finally said.

"Right now?"

"No, during the race. I overcorrected on the turn, and I wrenched a small muscle. It felt like someone shanked me in the back of the leg. I felt like . . . like—"

"Like you'd reinjured yourself," Corey finished.

"Yeah. I mean, not exactly. Not my knee, but I, I pulled up."

"Better safe than sorry?" Corey asked.

"I don't think I made a conscious thought. I didn't have time," Elise released a jagged exhale that came through the phone and clawed at Corey's heart. "I panicked."

"We've all been there."

"I haven't," Elise said. "I've never felt so out of place in my life. I completely disconnected, like I'd had someone else's brain dropped into my body."

"What did Paolo say?"

"He said I was too tense. My body went into a fight-or-flight

181

mode and overloaded my senses. My movements became less about the slope and more about survival."

"And when it ended?" Corey tiptoed right up to her main reason for calling.

"I don't know. I was breathing heavy, and the needles in my calf, and I couldn't hear the crowd or even see straight. Later I freaked out about the DNF rating. My Olympic chances. Corey, I don't know if they'll let me on the team."

"Right." Corey waved off those concerns. The team would come or not. Elise's psyche presented the more pressing concern. "But when you pulled up, you were relieved?"

"I'm pissed!" Elise exploded.

"Now you're pissed, but you weren't in the moment. You wanted out more than anything right then. And your body gave you the out."

"You think I threw the race on purpose? How dare—"

"Elise," Corey snapped. "Stop and listen to me. You're a champion. You're the most badass woman I've ever met. You bend the world to your will. I've seen you. If you'd wanted to finish the race more than anything, you would have."

"I did want to. I've worked for over a year. The pain, the sweat, the tears. Every minute had built up to that moment."

"No. Every minute had built up to getting *through* that moment," Corey said. "You viewed the race as an obstacle to be overcome. Another chance for you to hurt or fail or suffer a setback."

Elise didn't respond, but Corey could hear her breathe, so at least she hadn't hung up on her. Did she see her point or was she quietly seething?

"You have to stop seeing your place as precarious," Corey pleaded softly. "You have to stop focusing on 'what if' and what could go wrong or what you stand to lose. You can't think about losing at all. You have to believe it's your race to win."

"I don't believe that," Elise finally said.

"Then you don't belong there," Corey said. The words hurt to deliver, but not as much as it would hurt if Elise accepted them. In this case, poking the bear was a calculated risk.

"I might not belong there yet, but—"

"But nothing. If you don't belong on the top of the mountain, then you don't belong on the tour. Only professionals skiers belong on those courses."

"Stop interrupting me."

"Stop being a baby."

"I'm not being a baby. I'm a grown woman and world champion, damn it. Don't tell me about professional skiers. You don't know half of what I know. This sport has been my whole life since I was prepubescent. I could run these courses in my sleep. I can feel a fall line at seventy miles an hour with my eyes closed. No one on this tour has more knowledge or a better mental makeup than I do."

Corey was glad Elise couldn't see the massive smile spreading across her face, or it might have brought her up short on her little tirade, but Corey couldn't hide her pleasure at the steely set of Elise's voice. She could almost envision the glint of her glacial eyes as they narrowed with her don't-fuck-with-me focus. Watch out skiing world, the ice woman cometh.

"I'm healthy. I'm fit. I'm the person to beat this season."

"Damn right," Corey said. "There's your mantra, baby."

"My mantra?" Elise asked.

"Say it again."

"I'm healthy, I'm fit. I'm the person to beat this season."

"Yes!" Corey shouted.

"I've never had a mantra before," Elise said, her voice tinted with a bit of wonder.

"Now you do. And it's a good one for kicking ass."

"First you give me secret code words, now a mantra. What's next?"

"Hopefully, you'll let me give you a really nice Christmas present."

Elise sighed. "We'll see."

"As in, we'll see each other at Lake Henry in seventeen days."

"I can't make any promises," Elise said stoically. "A lot can happen in seventeen days."

"Yeah," Corey said, hope rising like a balloon in her chest. "A lot of awesome."

Chapter Twelve

December 19, 2017
Val d'Isere, France

Elise tightened her glutes, her calves, her core, and flattened her chest against her thighs, rocketing down the final stretch of the course at Val d'Isere. The French crowd went wild as she crossed the finish line, and part of her wanted to share in their jubilation. She'd finished her first race. She'd made it down safely with a technically sound run, but even before she kicked her skis sideways and skidded to stop, she knew she hadn't done enough to put herself in contention.

"Elise, Elise." A woman rushed toward her with a microphone in hand.

She peeled off her goggles and unhooked the straps of her poles from her wrists, trying to gather herself before the cameraman caught up to the reporter. She met them with what she hoped to be at least a politely neutral expression.

"Elise, how does it feel to be back across a finish line?" the petite, Asian woman asked, craning her neck and holding the microphone up so Elise could effectively use it.

"I wish I'd gotten here faster, but I'm getting better with each run."

"You weren't even supposed to be here this year," the reporter reminded her. "Most of the people who follow the sport said you wouldn't be back this season, or maybe not at all."

"Those people don't know me very well, now do they?" She tried to flash a smile to soften the defiance in the comment, but the reporter's raised eyebrows suggested she might not have pulled it off. She added, "My time here today wasn't what I wanted, but my time in the super G on Sunday will be stronger, and I'm going to keep going up in the standings from here on out."

"What do you say to the people who think you'll never regain your top form?"

"I guess I'd ask if those are the same people who said I wouldn't be on skis this year, because they have a track record of being wrong about these things, while I have a track record of winning ski races."

The reporter turned to face the camera with an amused expression. "There you have it. Elise Brandeis is back, and if her interviews are any indication, so is her edge."

The cameraman nodded and lowered the lens. "Got it."

"Thank you, Elise," the reporter said, extending a hand. "I'm Julie Chen, by the way."

"Nice to meet you, Julie." Elise scanned the crowd for Paolo, who would no doubt be making his way down to her with a myriad of notes.

"We actually met several years ago." Julie continued walking beside her. "I went to your *alma mater*, Experius Academy. You came back to speak to our ski team after you'd been an alternate at the Vancouver Olympics."

Elise stopped. "You went to Experius?"

"I did. I was several years behind you, but we know a few of the same women. You know the alumni network has its backchannels, especially among those of us with more high-profile careers."

Elise searched her dark eyes to confirm the hint of innuendo. Julie was attractive. Small, slender, with gorgeous dark hair clipped up at the back of her neck. Even though she wore gray slacks and a heavy black sweater, the touch of femininity couldn't be hidden even under the bulky clothes. "Then it's nice to meet

185

you again. I'll be sure to offer you my first interviews in the future if you're going to be around more this year."

"I'll be following the tour all season," Julie said, fishing a business card out of her pocket. "If you ever want to leak something to the press or need a way to release some tension, we can get together for a glass of wine or anything else you'd like. Give me a call."

"Elise," Paolo called from the opposite sideline. "More better, much more better this time."

She smiled and shrugged before explaining to Julie. "That's my coach."

"Of course. I know. Go." Then with a wink, she added, "Keep the card for when you need it."

"I will," Elise said, but as she walked away, a twinge of guilt stuck under her ribs. Julie hadn't exactly propositioned her, but the undertones were clear. She should have said she was seeing someone. Was she seeing someone? She and Corey hadn't had the talk. In fact, they'd both worked hard to avoid the talk. She'd assumed that was because they both understood the need to focus on their careers, but what if it also implied an understood freedom. Was Corey exercising her right to roam? The little prick of guilt grew into a hot spot of anger at the thought of other women flirting with Corey the way Julie had flirted with her. The heat continued to spread as she considered the possibility of Corey returning the attention.

"Come on," Paolo said, throwing an arm around her shoulder. "Don't scowl. You finished a race."

"I could've done better," she said absently, still thinking of Julie. Only, in her mind, Julie represented every woman wanting to get their hands on Corey. Would she give them the same speech about respecting them and not wanting to leave them all alone in the morning? Or would she use a little fling to hold her over until Christmas? God, she hadn't said she wasn't going to have sex until then. She'd only said she wasn't going to have sex with *her*. The sentiment didn't seem nearly as sweet when inspected under the harsh light of suspicion.

"Your time was respectable," Paolo said. "With a little tweak, you're in the top ten tomorrow in the Super-G."

"Yeah. I know."

"Then why the pouty face?"

She opened her mouth to tell him about Julie and Corey, but as another skier whizzed across the finish line, the crowd let out a massive cheer and drew her from her dark daydreams. She was still at a race. She'd finished her first run of the season. She'd worked hard for this moment, only to have it completely overshadowed by thoughts of Corey.

Who the hell had she become?

"What is it?" Paolo asked. "What's wrong?"

"Nothing," she said, quickly wrenching her focus to where it belonged. "Nothing but my time. I want to reconceptualize my start for the Super G. I think I noticed a steeper angle out there today, but I'm going to need some video to double check."

"Okay, I can get some various shots lined up. Let's go out to dinner and celebrate first though."

She shook her head. She didn't need quiet conversation in a fancy restaurant to distract her or give her mind time to wander. "No, order in. We've still got a lot of work to do."

Holly's phone dinged, and Corey looked up from her snowboard bindings. She watched her sister's face light up and knew the message had come from Paolo. Did it say something mushy? Were they sexting? Or did the text bring news of Elise's race? Thanks to the time difference between Canada and France, Elise should be wrapping up her day even as Corey prepared for her quarterfinal heat.

"Okay. I'm heading to the finish line," Holly said.

"Cool," Corey said, casually. "See you at the bottom."

Holly gave her a hug and kissed her on the cheek. "Kick some ass."

"That's the plan."

"See you later," Nate called, then turned to Corey. "I want to check your wax real quick."

"Sure, um, just a minute," Corey said as she watched Holly pick her way through the crowd.

"What's wrong?" Nate asked.

"Nothing, I wanted . . . oh fuck it," she muttered before calling out. "Holly, wait."

Holly turned, worry filling her dark eyes. "What? What's the matter?"

"Nothing. Geez, it's no big deal. I was only wondering if Paolo mentioned how Elise did today."

Holly and Nate exchanged a look she couldn't decipher, part smug, part amusement, part concern. "You broke your pre-race concentration for Elise?"

"I was only wondering. Not a big deal. Didn't break concentration."

"She placed eighteenth in the Super-G," Holly said.

"Oh," Corey's shoulder sank.

"She broke the top twenty, Core," Nate said kindly. "It's not like here where there're only twenty racers to begin with. There're like sixty ski racers per event. She made the top third."

"She's not going to be happy with top third. She wants to win every race."

"So does every other racer out there," Holly said. "It's going to take time to get back to the top."

"She doesn't have much time to make the Olympic team. She'll get only one more shot before they announce the teams."

"And you have only five minutes to get your head in today's race."

She sighed. "Can you please stop worrying about my head? I'm not superstitious. I don't have tics or triggers. When I get into the gate, I'll be there one hundred percent."

"I hope so," Holly said.

"I know so," Nate added emphatically. "Beast mode, top to bottom, right?"

Corey smiled. "Hell yeah."

"Okay. Kill it," Holly said, with more enthusiasm, then turned and left.

"You drew the top slot," Nate said. "Beneath you is a rookie Russian you haven't faced yet, the big Finn, and Tigger."

"She's got the inside going into the first turn?"

"Yup," he said, with forced nonchalance. She didn't know why he felt the need to pretend this wasn't a concern. The kid continued to improve daily, and with the start being the most technical part of the course, having the opportunity to punch through it ahead of the pack would play to her strengths.

"Top two advance," he reminded her.

She didn't have to win outright, but she'd never been one to shoot for the qualifying spot. Still, she got the message. If it came down to her and Tigger at the finish line, she could conserve her energy for the next heat.

"The track is fast this morning," Nate said.

Corey squared her shoulders. "Good, 'cause so am I."

He laughed and slapped her on the back. "Go get you some."

She pulled down her goggles and slid into position.

"See you at the bottom, Core," Tigger called as she scooted past her to the far gate.

"Not if I see you first, kiddo," Corey said before she crouched down. She assumed her position naturally. She didn't have to think about it or tick anything off a to-do list, which allowed her to focus on the line she wanted out of the first drop. Tigger had something close to a straight shot, while she'd have to pull the snowboarding equivalent of cutting across three lanes of rush-hour traffic without using her blinker. She wished she had some of Elise's ski speeds, or perhaps her poles.

Elise.

The speed and poles might be a boon here, but they hadn't been enough to get the job done in France this weekend. Finishing twentieth in the downhill and eighteenth in the Super-G might be enough to get her name back in the conversation, but those results were far from the head-turning dominance she was used to, and when averaged with her DNF from the first race, the combination probably didn't offer enough to earn her a spot on the Olympic team. She'd have more pressure than ever going into the next race.

"Racers ready."

She went tightly into her start position, head low, back flat, arms tight and tense against the bars. Then, with a clatter, the metal gates dropped, and off they went. Corey tipped her board over the edge, holding a flat line long enough to pick up the speed she needed to push in on the Russian. The rookie gave way quickly after not having gotten a good starting jump, but the big Finn on the other side of her presented herself as a snowboarding brick wall. She held her line with ramrod form and tucked herself tight for the turn before Corey even got a chance to veer into her space.

To the other side of the Finn, Tigger must not have gotten as good a start as possible, because instead of having the edge, she set up along the higher line into the curve. She and the Finn could run two across if they had enough inertia to pull them through, but there was no way for Corey to push the pack three wide. She had to give way or get pushed out, so she settled for third place right behind the Finn, hoping to catch a little bit of a draft through the turn. They would break hard to the right and double immediately back to the left. If she could hold speed on the switch, she might be able to trade places with Tigger.

She rode out the curve, with her board as flat as possible for as long as possible, attempting to hold or even gain speed before having to switch to her heel edge, but as she set up to make the transition, she saw Tigger out of the corner on her vision. She hadn't maintained the speed she'd needed, and veered lower as the Finn pulled ahead. Corey had to make a quick decision to either try to punch through the open hole and steal second place or hang back and let the kid fall in between them. She chose the former and bent low, trying to ride over the top of the first place rider.

By the time she realized Tigger had lost control of her line, their boards had already collided. The scrape of metal edges jarring into each other grated her nerves like nails on a chalkboard, and the pressure of the friction pinned her down. Elbows rose to defensive heights, and shoulders brushed heavily. Competitive instincts took hold, and Corey bore down, fighting desperately to maintain her position, but she'd set herself up too far inside. Tigger used her higher line to run down over the top of Corey's board and into the lead. The pressure from the downward push on the nose of her board caused her tail to kick up slightly. She could've stabilized anywhere else on the course, but in a tight turn she had nowhere to regain her speed.

The rookie Russian blew past on the now-clear upper line and dropped in immediately in front of her. Corey had no choice but to veer even farther out of her line or t-bone her. She ended up off course and at a full stop.

"Fuck," she shouted, not even concerned one of the nearby cameras could offer viewers a little exercise in R-rated lip reading. She had to hop over a small ridge in the snow to get back on course, then pumped her legs like a fish trying to flop from a shore back into a pool of water. She slowly regained her speed and rode out the rest of the course as best she could. There was always a chance two racers could collide down-track, but when she heard the cheers go up from the crowd below, she knew her fate had been sealed.

Crossing the finish line with as much grace as she could muster, she gritted her teeth and gave a little wave to the medical staff to let them know she hadn't hurt anything but her pride. Then kicking off her board, she trudged over to Holly.

"You okay?" she asked in full big-sister tone.

"Yeah, mostly. A little sore, but I guess I'll have plenty of time to sit in the hot tub tonight since we're going home early."

"Silver linings, I suppose," Holly said.

"Hey Corey." Tigger approached timidly and stood at a distance.

She forced a smile. "Congrats."

"Thanks." The kid nodded. "I didn't get a good start."

"You made up for it in turn two," Holly said, with a hint of judgment in her voice.

"Which was perfectly legal," Corey added.

"I didn't box you out on purpose."

"Why?" Corey asked. "You could have."

"I know, but I didn't want to."

Corey snorted. "Then you're doing it wrong, kid. I had a choice to grab second or fall in behind you. I went for the lead."

"You would've put me into the wall?"

"That's never my goal. If I had the choice, it'd be me and you fighting for first and second every time, but if only one of us could win the second-place spot, I need you to know I'm going to do everything in my power to make damn sure it's me. And next time, it will be me."

Tigger nodded, her eyes a little wide and frightened under her goggles.

"Go get ready for your next heat."

"Okay. I wanted to make sure you weren't mad at me."

"It shouldn't matter whether I am or not."

"Okay." She picked up her board and lifted her chin.

Corey caught her arm and pulled her so close their helmets knocked together. "This isn't a team sport. Unless you're a total dick out there and try to knock someone's teeth out for sport, all you need to worry about is winning your race. Anyone who doesn't understand that doesn't need to be here. Got it?"

Tigger's mouth curled up slightly. "Got it."

Corey slapped her on the back. "Good luck in the semifinals."

"Thanks." The kid started to go, then glanced over her shoulder. "You going to stay and watch?"

She looked to Holly, who clenched her jaw and shook her head.

Corey shrugged, then smiled. "I'm going to hang around and sign autographs. I may look up from my adoring fans long enough to see how you do."

"Cool," she said, and bounded off, the usual bounce back in her step.

They watched her go, before Corey turned back to Holly. "I need a pen."

Holly dug one out of her bag but held it out of Corey's reach. "You're going to kill me with this good-natured mentor routine."

"What?" Corey asked. "You'd rather I act like a spoiled prick and throw a tantrum for losing? I've never been that dude."

"No, but you've never been one to throw your arm around the person who ran you off the course, either."

"If I'd been in her boots, I'd have done the same damn thing. Hell, I was *trying* to do the same thing. I went in with the intent of cutting her off."

"Did you?" Holly asked seriously.

"Yes. Go back and watch the replay. I did my best to cut her off. She beat me to the punch."

They stared at each other as the words sank in. Holly had been so afraid she'd gone easy on Tigger, and Corey had been so focused on defending herself against the charge, neither one of them had seriously considered the implications of the other option.

Tigger had beaten her for the first time.

Chapter Thirteen

December 24, 2017
Lake Henry, New York

"I'm heading over to Holly's now," Paolo said from the doorway of her dorm room. "Are you sure you don't want me to drop you anywhere on the way?"

"No. Thanks. I'm going to do another light workout. Maybe a swim."

His eyes grew sad. "It's Christmas Eve."

"No." She sighed. "'Eve' means 'night.' It's only two o'clock in the afternoon. Besides, I'm Jewish."

"You're half Jewish. You've always celebrated Christmas in the past."

"I sat on a plane all night and in a car all morning. I don't want my muscles to seize up."

"I'm sorry the flight was delayed. You know I wouldn't have scheduled it like that."

"Yeah, well." She almost said something snotty but caught herself. Left to her own, she would've stayed in France over the holiday, but he felt guilty enough already, and if she were truly honest, he'd wanted to leave a day earlier. She'd insisted on getting back out on the mountain at Val d'Isere one more time to try to atone for her disappointing finishes. If she hadn't, they would've missed the snowstorm that delayed air traffic into Montreal the day before. "We're here now. No use rehashing everything, but I do want to at least heat up my muscles a bit."

He rubbed his cleanly shaved chin, a nod to Holly's comfort no doubt, and frowned. "I should stay with you then."

"No," she practically shouted. "Go. I can handle a treadmill and a pool without supervision. You deserve a couple days off, Paolo. It's Christmas Eve."

He laughed. "'Eve' means 'night.'"

"Get out of my room and tell Holly I said 'hi.'"

"We'll see you tomorrow, right?"

"Probably," she admitted, though she'd yet to make her formal decision on the invitation she'd received to the LaCroix family celebration.

"Okay, I won't pressure you, except to say if you aren't there, I'll come find you."

"Yeah, that's not pressuring me at all."

He smiled. "Merry Christmas, Elise."

She shook her head. "Merry Christmas, Paolo."

He closed the door, and she changed her clothes. She'd already hung up her racing suits and one actual suit in the closet and put her more casual clothes away in the dresser drawers. She'd be in town only a week, but she hated living out of a suitcase. Any time she planned to spend more than one night in a hotel, she always put the clothes exactly where she would've if she were at home.

Home.

She didn't even know where that was anymore. She'd sublet her Manhattan apartment after getting hurt. She'd spent months in hospitals, first in Europe, then in Denver, followed by a rehab facility in Park City before coming to Lake Henry the first time. Since then, she'd experienced a string of long-term hotel stays before landing back at the Olympic Training Center dorms. She'd have to go back years to find a place she'd stayed for more than four months, and even that was another dorm back at school.

She pulled on a pair of yoga pants and a neon blue, racerback tank top, then reached for her cross trainers. Maybe she liked having everything in its proper place because she didn't have a proper place for herself.

She shook her head. Where had that thought come from? Jet lag? Not likely. She'd grown pretty immune to the trials of trans-Atlantic travel at a young age. Had her mediocre performance in the season thus far caused her to become more introspective? She didn't think so, but she supposed she'd choose that option over the other one she didn't want to face.

She grabbed her key card and a water bottle and bolted from the room. She didn't have to sit there and dwell on Corey's invitation to her family holiday celebration. Somehow it had seemed fine, simple, even fun to consider an invitation to join her in bed. She'd certainly been prepared to do so before they'd left Argentina, but the whole home-and-hearth component to the holiday schedule felt much less like the ripping each other's clothes off she'd envisioned.

Maybe she needed to step back and consider what she truly wanted here. Was she looking for a quick roll in the hay? A week-long fling? A friendship with benefits? Or something more?

She had time to figure it out. A good workout always cleared her head, and if the ghost-town status of the dorms and lobby areas told her anything, she'd likely have the gym to herself. Apparently not many Olympic athletes, other than her, chose to spend their Christmas at training camp. She hoped that said a good deal about her competitive drive and not her social acumen or lack thereof. Either way, she'd get some much needed peace, quiet, and exercise in service of the mental clarity she needed before facing a potentially big decision tonight. She rounded the corner to the main gym and slid her card through the lock, but as soon as she swung open the lock, she stopped short.

There in all her golden, sweaty, smiling glory stood Corey LaCroix.

They stared at each other for a long time—seconds, minutes, or hours, she didn't know. Long enough for a fire to spread from her chest through her core and down her limbs as every nerve ending burned with desire.

"Hi," Corey finally said.

"I didn't expect to see you here." Elise blurted out the only truth she could verbalize.

Corey laughed, "Clearly. I'm not going to lie. I sort of enjoy knowing I can still catch you off guard."

"I'm not sure I do."

Corey stepped forward and boldly slipped her arm around her waist. "Let me try to tip the scales in my favor."

"You're sweaty." Elise tried to protest, but the comment only came out sounding aroused.

"Don't worry. You'll catch up."

Her face flushed hot, but before she could say anything else, Corey claimed her mouth with her own. The kiss was everything she'd tried to ignore in the long months apart, and her body swallowed her mind as they melted together. They made out right there in the middle of the empty weight room, like kids who had only seven minutes in heaven and didn't want to waste even a fraction of one.

"I missed this," Corey said, fingers tightening on her hips.

"Me, too," Elise mumbled against the corner of her mouth.

Corey rested her forehead against Elise's. "I missed you."

Elise nodded. The words stuck in her throat. She'd missed her too, much more than she'd let herself realize, so much it scared her, even now.

"Come home with me," Corey whispered, then kissed her deeply again. "Please."

Why had she even pretended for a second that she wouldn't go with her? That she wouldn't melt? That she could be so close to her and keep from feeling all the need and passion and desire swirling in her now? She'd sealed her fate the moment she'd boarded the plane to come back here, and she'd known it even then. She only had to say the one word she'd denied herself for too long, and now with the wonder of Corey's body pressed hard and firm against her, the word came easier than she'd ever imagined.

"Yes."

❊ ❊ ❊

"Corey." Elise said her name with both joy and awe as she tilted her head back and stared heavenward.

She grinned with pride. She'd spent months looking forward to inspiring such a reaction, but she never dreamed she'd do so before they even got into the house.

"When you said you had a cabin in the woods, I never expected this."

She surveyed her little piece of mountain paradise, seeing it for the first time through Elise's eyes. A large wraparound deck led to a two-story wall of windows framed in dark logs and bisected by the gray stone of her chimney. The perfect mountain getaway, it offered privacy, comfort, and serenity with a breathtaking view. "It's not a mansion in the Hamptons or a Manhattan penthouse, but—"

"It's better." Elise took her hand and pulled her up toward the front steps. "Show me around."

Corey grabbed Elise's duffle bag from the back of her snowmobile and happily allowed herself to be led up the stairs. When she swung open the front door, Elise stopped again, her blue eyes surveying the large, open space. The living area was outfitted with rough-hewn wood and leather furnishings. Natural light streamed in from three sides, casting patterns of sunset and shade across a thick, blue rug spread out before a massive fireplace. Farther back, a large bar separated the living room from a chef's kitchen, done all in cast iron and granite.

"It's not formal," Corey said, "but it's functional."

"No doubt," Elise said. "When you said we were driving a snowmobile to get here, I expected some sort of rundown miners' shack."

Corey laughed. "No, we not only have running water and electricity, there's a twenty-seat theater downstairs, also a rec room with a bar and a pool table. On the side deck, there's a wood-fire pizza oven and a hot tub."

"Of course there is." Elise placed a sweet kiss on her cheek. "It's so perfectly you."

198

"Yeah. When I designed it, I had grand parties in mind for the lower two levels."

"What about the upper level?"

Corey's grin widened, and she nodded to a natural wood staircase. "I'll show you."

They kicked off their snow boots and the outer layer of winter gear they'd changed into before leaving the training center, then ascended the stairs hand in hand. Moving down a hallway adorned with pictures of mountain scenes and old family photos, they passed a few guest rooms until Corey swung open a wide set of double doors to a large master suite. The room housed a king-sized bed with lush carpet and another stone fireplace. Elise made a slow tour around the room, running her fingers along smooth walnut and stained oak. She peeked her head into the open bathroom door and let out a groan at the sight of a deep soaking tub and a cedar-lined sauna. The sounds stirred something low in Corey's stomach, but she wanted to enjoy this moment before moving to the next. She wandered over to the massive picture window offering an infinite view of pine forests and snowcapped mountains. Waiting until she felt Elise's shoulder brush up against her own, she finally asked. "So, do you think you could bring yourself to wake up here on Christmas morning?"

Elise turned toward her once more, and this time instead of a kiss gave her a sizable shove. "Are you freaking kidding me?"

Corey stumbled a few steps. "You're so much stronger than you look, and I take hits for a living."

"And a good living it must be. This place is amazing. I can't believe you kept this to yourself all summer while I slept in a skinny dorm bed."

"If you'd wanted it then, you could've had it."

"I had no idea. Maybe I would've been a little nicer earlier on if I had."

"No, you wouldn't," Corey said.

"I don't know."

"I do. Plenty of other women played that game with me, and I let them. At first I didn't recognize the sport, but even for a while after I did, I still let them. I actually got to know the type pretty early on, and you're not one of them."

Elise held Corey's face in her hand, running a thumb across her lips before kissing her lightly. "You're right. Seeing this place would've impressed me, but it wouldn't have made a difference back then. What's magnificent about your home is that it's yours. It has your touches, your quiet attention to detail. It shows the way you see the world, places to gather, places to retreat, and places to reflect on the wonder of it all. I wouldn't have understood that fully until I got to know you."

Corey's chest tightened with a new mix of emotions, ones running much deeper than the initial, crushing urge to rip Elise's clothes off. Those desires hadn't faded. They'd merely expanded.

Corey couldn't be certain Elise felt the same, but she certainly moved toward a similar goal as she lowered her head and kissed Corey once more, her long, taut body softening against the area where their hips and chests molded together. Elise ran her fingers under Corey's waffle-weave sweater and the T-shirt beneath it. Raking her fingernails down her stomach, she let loose a low growl in the back of her throat. "Do you know I've been obsessed with your abs ever since we first worked out together?"

"No," Corey said, kissing her temple and breathing the sweet, fresh scent of snow and citrus. "Add that to the long list of things one of us might have mentioned earlier."

"What? And give you a big head?" Elise asked, tugging both shirts over Corey's head at once. The arousal in Elise's eyes as they swept over her body only magnified Corey's.

"For me it was your eyes. Always your eyes."

"My eyes usually turn people off," Elise said, placing kisses around Corey's now-bare shoulders.

"Not me," Corey said as she unfastened the braid of Elise's silken blond hair, then ran her fingers through the lush strands, freeing them in glorious waves. "Your eyes are intense, but that only drew me in. I had to get closer. I couldn't stop myself. Even when you gave me all the other signals, your eyes kept pulling me back."

"You were maddeningly good-natured." Elise punctuated the remark with a little nip to her neck. "And persistent. Tenacious even."

"I've been called those things before," Corey admitted playfully, "but they've never sounded as sexy as when you say them."

"Really? I've actually found you sexy for much longer than I care to admit."

"What took you so long to come around?"

"Well." Elise stepped back and pulled her sweatshirt and tank over her head, leaving only a sports bra between Corey and the full realization of months' worth of imagination. "Someone suggested we needed to wait until the time was right."

"Someone sounds like a real idiot," Corey mumbled.

"I didn't want to mention it, but yes." Elise's grin turned teasing, and she hooked her thumbs under the waistband of her snow pants, then, popping the button, pushed them down over her full hips and thighs.

Corey let out a little whimper at the sight of navy blue boy shorts against alabaster skin.

"Sorry they're not lacier," Elise said, though she didn't seem particularly sorry. "I thought I was going to the gym."

"Nothing to apologize for," Corey managed to say through the need tightening her throat. She resisted the urge to fall to her knees in front of her. "You're stunning."

Elise's smile turned almost shy, but her movements were far from tentative as she eliminated the space between them once more. She flicked open the top of Corey's jeans and let them fall to the floor, evening the clothing score between them. Then, locked in a kiss once more, they tumbled onto the bed. For a moment they were all skin and flexing muscles as they groped and gripped one another in all the ways they'd longed to do for months. Corey sucked on Elise's neck while she cupped her bare breasts in both hands. Reaching for more, Corey tried to sneak a hand around Elise's back and under the straps of her bra, but Elise had other plans. She captured Corey's hands and tried to pin them above her head.

"That's not going to happen," Corey said, and freeing one arm caught Elise's hip, then tried to spin her onto her back. They both wrestled, giving and taking what they wanted, a blur of hands and mouths as they rolled over, trading places several times before Elise established herself on top, straddling Corey's waist.

"I think we've got a little misunderstanding here," Elise said, placing a hand flat against Corey's chest. "I'm used to being in charge."

"Oh no, I understand perfectly. But I'm not one of your school chums. I'm a competitor."

"Oh, a competitor?" Elise asked, her smile becoming almost predatory. "Do we want to make this about our drive to win, because I fear you might be outmatched."

Corey's mouth went dry at the sight of Elise so gloriously cocky above her. If she'd been commanding on the slopes, she was captivating now. It was almost a shame to have to prove her wrong, but that little "outmatched" comment had to be dealt with, and the time for negotiation had long passed.

Sitting up with Elise still astride her lap, Corey cupped two handfuls of her firm ass and massaged while her mouth found a hard nipple straining beneath the tight-stretched lycra of her sports bra. Elise threw her head back and arched into her mouth, her long, blond hair dipping low enough to brush the tops of Corey's core in the most scintillating tease of things to come.

She used Elise's momentary distraction to rid them of the barrier the bra provided and immediately went back to lavishing attention on her full breasts. Then, bringing her hands between them, Corey worked one of them downward until it slipped beneath the band of Elise's boy shorts. Firm abs gave way to a soft swell, and Corey's breath caught as she got closer to the place she'd dreamed of more than she should have. Elise's hips rocked forward at the touch, and the heat radiating from her athletic form ratcheted up another notch.

Sinking lower, Corey's fingers brushed against sensitive skin. Elise gasped, letting her know she'd found what they both needed, and the tension faded from the hard muscles trembling against her.

Elise melted into the palm of her hand, and Corey eased her slowly back onto the bed. Refusing to break the precious contact for even a second, she worked and stroked and teased while she extracted her legs from under Elise's long form. Elise made no protest this time as Corey cupped one breast in her hand and used the other to peel off the final barrier between them. Then she settled her own hips between the meticulously sculpted thighs she'd long admired.

Corey sought the blue eyes that had held her captive so many days and nights. She found them darker and heavy-lidded. Corey wasn't even sure if Elise had the wherewithal to answer the unspoken question as arousal clouded all of their senses, but this wouldn't be an act of conquest.

"Elise," she managed, "I want you."

"Yes." The word came out on in rush of breath, and the long wait ended as Corey pushed inside her.

Elise's chest rose and fell with increasingly shallow breaths. She hooked a long, talented leg over Corey's hip and pulled her harder against her center, while her body coaxed her fingers deeper inside. Corey sought their natural rhythm the way she might seek a fall line, graceful and instinctively as they crested and fell together. The earlier clash and struggle had long since subsided. Now they moved with athletic precision. Elise closed her eyes as her head sank into the thick, down comforter, but Corey couldn't look away, not even long enough to kiss her again. She touched and rocked and stroked, but she couldn't break the hypnotic spell of the woman beneath her. She wanted to watch her writhe, to memorize the sight of her beautiful body arched in pleasure, to see her always as she was right now, and yet continue to see her fully in every other minute from here on out.

The full impact of that thought hit her squarely in the chest, as Elise tightened around her and shuddered. Corey rode out the release to the soundtrack of her own pulse as the images of Elise burned into her mind's eye. The glares, the reluctant smiles, the ferocity of her hard-set jaw and the supple arc of her body bent to their shared will. Even as she remained fully inside of her, she couldn't help feeling as if their reality was the other way around.

※ ※ ※

"God," Elise exclaimed, as she stared up at the ceiling of Corey's bedroom. "That was so much better than I expected."

Corey sat back on her heels, her features especially golden in light streaming low through the windows. "Um, thanks?"

She laughed. "That's not how I meant. You turned my brain to mush."

"Just your brain?"

Elise rolled her head from side to side, then flexed the muscles in her arms and legs. "Yes, only the brain is mush. My biceps are pudding, and my thighs are more like Jell-O. I expected some wrestling, but I wasn't prepared for a complete meltdown."

"I know you think we boarders crash into each other all the time, but I never take by brute strength what I can earn with finesse."

A low hum of contentment escaped her throat, "Finesse. Yes, that's an apt description."

Corey straightened her shoulders, her grin taking on the cocky little twist that always drove Elise crazy.

"Don't look so pleased with yourself."

"Why not? I turned the ice princess into a puddle. How many people can say that truthfully?"

"Not many," Elise admitted reluctantly, then silently added, *not any*. The realization caused that disconcerting little twinge in her chest she'd come to associate with Corey. Normally she'd start searching for an excuse to distance herself from the emotions building in her, but with such a beautiful body nearly naked in front of her, she had other ideas about how she might reassert her own interests.

Sitting up, she kissed Corey, their tongues intertwining as she raked her fingernails up her ribcage before tracing along the soft curve of her breasts. Finally she flattened both hands across her chest and pushed hard. Corey tumbled over backward until her head hit the lush pillows, her hair and tan skin standing out beautifully against the pure white sheets. Corey started to prop herself up on her elbows, but Elise shook her head. "Not this time. I've got your game plan now."

"What makes you think I've only got one game plan?" Corey asked cheekily. "I promised you multiple times and all the things. You didn't think I'd bring any reruns, did you?"

"I honestly didn't think about this much at all."

Corey raised her eyebrows. "You have such a way of making your lovers feel special."

"Oy." She shook her head. "That didn't sound how I meant it at all. I only meant I hadn't let myself fixate on this moment. I couldn't. If I did, I'd have to admit how much I wanted you. No, that's not it. I knew I wanted you, physically at least, but I could easily brush physical attraction off as stupid hormones or a momentary lapse in judgment."

"When you put it that way . . ." Corey grimaced.

"I'm not good at all the emotional stuff. You said yourself, I've got an ice princess reputation. I haven't exactly met many people who wanted to get past that, and even fewer who actually had the skills to do so, especially at a time when I had other things I should've been focusing on. If I let myself daydream about how good you are at kissing or what it might feel like have your hard body pressed against mine . . . ." Her eyes flicked over Corey's torso once more, and her train of thought derailed. "Or run my tongue over those amazing ridges in your abs . . ."

"Yeah. I see what you mean." Corey's hazel eyes danced with mischief once again. "Doesn't sound like you let yourself think about me at all."

"Fine, maybe I let myself go there a time or two, but I couldn't dwell on the possibilities. You have the potential to be distracting."

"I really do," Corey admitted with another big smile. "But it's me and you now. No one to interrupt. Nowhere else to be. You can let your mind or your hands or any other body parts wander wherever they want."

"Except you keep getting grabby." Elise tried to sound stern, but suspected she failed. The prospect of having Corey all to herself, to do with what she pleased, made it hard for her to stay firm about anything.

"I promise to try harder to behave, for a solid ten minutes at least."

"Oh." Elise bent forward, letting their bare chests brush against each other lightly as she lowered her mouth to Corey's ear. "Ten minutes will barely be enough to get started."

"I thought skiers were faster than snowboarders."

"We are, but we also run longer courses." She ran her tongue along Corey's neck and across her shoulder. "Don't worry, though. I'm sure you'll be able to keep up."

Corey opened her mouth, undoubtedly to make some smart retort, but Elise quickly kissed her, deep and hard, her tongue sweeping across Corey's and using more than words to let her know playtime had ended.

They made out for several minutes, mouths and hands growing bolder. She loved the way Corey's muscles tightened under her fingertips, and took her time trying different types of touches on different areas. A gentle caress on her bicep, the flat press of her palm against her stomach, the little dig of fingernails into her back. Corey's magnificent body responded to them all. She could play her like a fine instrument all night, if not for the mouth-watering temptation to taste her.

Dragging her lips across Corey's neck, she paused only long enough to feel the flutter of the pulse point above her collarbone, then ran her tongue along the defined ridge before moving south again. She circled her mouth along Corey's breasts and did nothing to hide her smile as Corey arched her chest up to deepen the contact. She might talk a good game about giving, but the little signs from her body betrayed her desire to receive what Elise had to offer. Gratified by the confirmation of their shared need, Elise bowed her head to the unspoken request giving Corey's chest the attention it deserved. She got a thrill from the hum of pleasure that escaped Corey's throat, enough to keep her in place a moment longer, but she couldn't focus there for long with the abs that had distracted her for months mere inches away.

Edging lower on the bed, she slid her mouth down Corey's sternum to her upper abdomen. She ran her lips over the defined ridge, then placed a kiss on either side before tracing the dividing line the length of her stomach. As she neared the waistband of the dark boxers, Corey's core tightened in anticipation, making her six-pack pop, and Elise groaned in pleasure. Easing back up, she traced the new definition with her tongue, tasting the first hints of salt across the toned torso.

She explored every inch, every ridge, dipping into each crease of her obliques and teasing the individual sections of her abs. Whenever she'd dip low enough, Corey's hips would lift off the bed only for Elise to reverse course, until finally Corey barely managed to strangle a growl. The noise twisted something inside of Elise, and she smiled both at their shared understanding that she could carry out this exquisite torture for as long as Corey could, and the realization she didn't want to. Corey had been patient long enough, and while she envisioned coming back to this spot again sometime soon, it wasn't the only place on the map of her body worth exploring.

Sitting up on her knees between Corey's legs once more, she hooked her fingers in the elastic waist of her boxers and slowly pulled them down. Corey eagerly lifted her hips to help the process along, then kicked the shorts to the floor with a heavy sigh of relief. Elise felt something more complex, equal parts arousal, awe, and honor. Corey's body was sheer perfection, but the idea that she'd let down her playful guard and her competitive instincts to lay herself bare made Elise feel somehow unworthy. She had the unreasonable urge to stop and apologize for every snide remark, for every time she'd underestimated her or taken her company for granted. Thankfully, the need to touch her, to taste her, to make up for lost time rushed hot and heavy through her as well.

Coming to rest between her strong legs, Elise breathed deeply, memorizing this view of Corey, open and anticipatory, one hand cocked behind her golden head, the other tangled in the sheets between them, her lids low over cat-like eyes, and her bottom lip caught between her teeth in an admirable show of restraint. Elise lowered her head and ran her tongue in delicate circles. Corey's hips rocked in time to the rhythm she'd set, and together they molded in unison. The dance was beautifully natural, so intuitively right, Elise had a hard time imagining any time in the past when they hadn't felt close or any moment in the future when they would be apart.

Corey's hand settled on the back of her head, but without even the slightest pressure as she sifted her fingers through Elise's hair. She never groped or pushed, but neither did she shy away from showing her need. Her hips moved in ways to direct Elise toward their mutual goal, her fingers stroked and twitched their encouragement, her breath grew shallow amid little cues, of "Yes, right there." She loved the way Corey brought her good-natured, self-assured characteristics even to this moment, but she wouldn't mind testing those limits a little bit.

Using her shoulders to urge Corey's legs farther apart, Elise eased inside with one steady push. Corey arched almost fully off the bed. She tightened around her almost immediately, and Elise could sense the impending release. Pulling out slowly, she timed her next thrust with some increased pressure from her tongue, and Corey's hips lost all semblance of a rhythm. Her own heart hammered in her chest, nearly as erratic as the ragged breath escaping Corey, her gentle words now reduced to incoherent groans and grunts. The only thing she could verbalize by the next press forward was her name, said in both praise and plea.

"Elise." Corey rose, fell, and called out once more, "Elise."

Then her thighs quaked and her core trembled as Elise did everything she could to stay focused on giving—or was it taking?— every last bit of pleasure she could before they both collapsed to the bed in winded, spent heaps.

As their breathing returned to normal, Elise hesitated to join her back at the head of the bed. The feelings she experienced needed to be sorted out, compartmentalized. The attraction wasn't new. She knew where it belonged. The fondness, the desire to feel close to Corey wasn't disconcerting at this point, either.

She cared for her, convenient or not, and she'd at least made her peace in that area. But the wonder, the awe, the desire to make up for lost time and project into the future didn't mesh with either of their needs to live in this moment. Then again, worrying about future consequences didn't do much for the moment, either.

Pushing herself up, she noticed the last hints of orange had faded from the jagged mountain horizon. Dusk had fallen, and as she glanced back at the beautiful body beside her, she realized she might be falling, too. She'd hoped having her would sate the need, but she now suspected, in the case of Corey LaCroix, that there may be no delineating between the conflict and the cure.

"Come here," Corey said, her voice rich and deep with the remnants of her arousal, or maybe a resurgence of it. Corey opened one arm wide, and Elise settled with her head on her shoulder. Corey pulled the sheet over them both, but from the rapid beat of her heart and the way she worked her skilled fingers down along the curve of Elise's hip, it became clear they'd only entered phase two.

As Corey slid her palm over her stomach and back up to cup her breast, Elise gave a little hum of contentment. With those hands on her once more, there was no future to contend with, as least not one far enough away to be worried about now. Any problems they'd created would still be there tomorrow, but tomorrow felt a long way off as she pondered all the prospects of one gloriously long night with Corey.

Chapter Fourteen

Dreams of Elise had filled the few hours between their collapse and the morning sun streaming between the Adirondacks. The scent of Elise's shampoo filled her senses even before she opened her eyes, bringing with it the slow realization that her Christmas wish had been answered. She smiled, still in the semi-slumber stage before fully waking.

"How do you do that?" Elise whispered.

"Do what?" Corey rolled onto her side and let her eyes flutter open.

"Start smiling before you're even awake?" Elise asked, her blue eyes paler and brighter than ever in the early morning light.

"I'm not sure I do every morning, but it's Christmas, and Santa gave me what I wanted."

Elise's mouth quirked up. "Are you sure Santa gave you what you wanted? Because I think I may have had something to do with filling those requests."

Corey pushed up onto her elbow to view the full line of Elise's long body under the thin, white sheet. "You're a lot better to wake up to than Santa."

"I should hope so," Elise said, her tone light and playful. "I probably spend more time in the gym than he does."

"Probably." Corey closed the gap between them and kissed her, slowly easing Elise onto her back and climbing on top of her. A few sore muscles protested, but her libido egged her on. Pressing up on fully extended arms, she stared down at the stunning woman beneath her. "Have I mentioned lately how awesome that whole gym thing is working out for you? 'Cause, wow."

Elise placed her hands on Corey's hips and pulled her down more fully on top of her. "You're doing pretty well in the wow department yourself."

They kissed again, rolling back onto their sides, legs intertwined, but as they got going, Corey's stomach gave a low growl.

Elise pulled back. "Are you hungry?"

Corey considered her answer. Her hunger existed on multiple levels, and she couldn't yet decide which one she most wanted to fill.

"Please say you're hungry," Elise said.

"Why?" Corey laughed. "Are you?"

"Famished," Elise said dramatically. "You held me captive since like three o'clock yesterday without anything to eat."

"Oh, I'm a terrible hostess."

"I wouldn't go that far. You made up for the lack of food in other ways."

"And to be fair," Corey added, "your mouth was busy for a great many of those hours."

Elise rolled her eyes, but she smiled. "Fair point."

"Still, I'll never let it be said a stay at Chateau LeCroix can't meet all your needs." Corey sat up against the will of every nerve ending begging her to stay pressed against Elise's naked form. "Let's venture to the kitchen, where I happen to have an assortment of pastries, fruit, juices, and maybe even a bottle of champagne to start the holiday right."

"Am I to assume you keep all those things on hand at all times?" Elise asked, extracting herself from the bed with much more grace. "Or did I lead you to believe this breakfast was a foregone conclusion?"

"No, you're never that," Corey pulled on a pair of sweatpants and grabbed a worn T-shirt from her dresser drawer. "Let's say I'm ever the optimist."

"That you are." Elise pulled on her yoga pants from the day before, then took the T-shirt out of Corey's hand. "Thanks for that, by the way."

"Hey, one of us has to be the believer here." Corey grabbed another shirt and tried not to feel inordinately pleased at the sight of Elise wearing her clothes.

"I don't know," Elise said. "You believed from the beginning, but after last night, I might start calling myself a convert."

"It was sort of a religious experience, right?"

"Have I mentioned you're also super modest?"

Corey laughed. "Nothing like a little blasphemy to celebrate the birth of our Lord and Savior."

"Your Lord and Savior," Elise said. "I'm Jewish."

Corey stopped midway to the door. "Really?"

"Well, half Jewish."

"When did that happen?"

"Well, if you believe the hype, God made a covenant with the people of Israel through Sarah and Abraham."

Corey laughed. "Not that. I meant how did I not know this about you?"

Elise shrugged. "It never came up."

Corey's stomach gave another twist that had nothing to do with hunger. How did she know so little about Elise? On some levels she knew her better than any other woman she'd ever woken up with. She understood what made her tick, what annoyed her, what motivated her. They understood the day-to-day stressors, the pressure, the joy of triumph on the big stages of the world. And yet, she didn't know where she grew up, what her parents did for a living, or even her middle name. As she padded down the stairs to the kitchen, she fought a little fear rising within her, suggesting maybe Elise wanted to keep it that way.

"You got awfully quiet, awfully fast," Elise said, leaning against the bar dividing the kitchen from the living room.

"Hmm?" Corey hummed while popping a couple of large cinnamon rolls into the oven.

"You were all playful and cocky until I said I was half Jewish; then you went silent and frowny," Elise said, with a deep crease in her brow. "I hope Jews are still invited to Christmas dinner."

"What?" Corey shook her head. "Oh God, yes of course. We set a big table. All are welcome. I'm sorry if I let you think otherwise. I was thinking about how little I know about you. I mean, I thought I had a pretty good handle on who you were, or who you are now anyway, but I don't know anything about you before July."

"Why would you need to?" Elise asked.

"Because friends talk about things like that. Because I like you, more than a friend."

"I don't see how my upbringing is relevant to you in any way."

Corey's chest tightened. "Because I'm not going to be part of your life much longer?"

"Core," Elise hopped off the stool and came around to cup Corey's face in her hands. "Where did that come from?"

"I don't know. I feel like you're holding me at arms' length, and maybe it's because you don't want me to get too attached."

"We're well past the point of getting attached," Elise said, though Corey couldn't tell how she felt about that fact. "I'm not used to tell-all sessions. I've worked hard to keep my personal life personal. Besides, I'm not close with my family the way you are with yours. I mean, I assume you're close with yours, but I only know there are multiple sisters in the area. It's not like you've handed me your autobiography to read."

"No," Corey admitted, "but you've met Holly, and you're going to meet pretty much everyone else in a few hours. I probably should've given you more warning about this. There's kind of a lot of us."

"Four sisters, right?"

"Four sisters, two brothers-in-law, three nieces, four nephews, two parents, one set of grandparents, two aunts, one uncle, a handful of cousins, and at least four dogs."

"No cats?" Elise asked, her smile returning.

"Yeah, a few, but you won't see them because with everyone home it gets loud and hectic and crowded. And loud. There will be tons of food and probably live music at some point. And yelling, not necessarily at anyone in particular, just yelling, because did I mention we're loud? By the end of the day, you might wish I'd uninvited you for being Jewish."

"It sounds wonderful."

"You might want to reserve judgment," Corey said, a hint of insecurity creeping in. "We're not formal people. None of our Christmas traditions will be as fancy as anything you're probably used to."

"I don't have any Christmas traditions," Elise said flatly. "My dad is Jewish. My mother is completely secular."

"But even secular people have things they lift up at holidays."

"Even before they divorced, the only thing my parents worshipped jointly was success. They sacrificed a great many things on that altar."

Corey blew out a low whistle. "Tell me how you really feel."

Elise sighed and went back to her stool. "You wanted to know more about my family."

"And I still do," Corey said, opening a small wine fridge under the bar and pulling out a bottle of Moët & Chandon champagne. "I'm getting the feeling this conversation might be best served with a mimosa."

"We're still training," Elise said quickly, then rethought her answer. "Maybe one mimosa, heavy on the OJ, wouldn't be a terrible idea."

Corey poured a little bit of bubbly into two flutes, and then topped it off with the juice before handing one to Elise. "Now back up a bit. What is it your parents are so successful at?"

"Well, my father is in print journalism."

"Like, he writes for newspapers?"

"Mostly he owns them."

"Multiples?" Corey asked. "Anything I've read?"

"He's part of an ownership group that has a hand in virtually every English-speaking newspaper worth reading."

"Well then." She sipped from her drink. "I can see how some would deem him rather successful."

"Not as much as my mother."

"Your mother's more accomplished than the guy who owns our news? What does she do?"

"She's heiress to a chain of high-end, home-good stores catering to people with expendable income and time for hobbies."

"What, like Pottery Barn or Williams-Sonoma, or what's the other one with all the exotic lamps and paperweights?"

"Yes," Elise said coolly.

"Yes to which?"

"Yes to all of the above. She's the CEO of the parent company that owns all of them. I'm sure many of the pieces in this room are made by one of her subsidiaries."

Corey hopped up to sit on the counter, not sure she could trust her legs anymore, but still trying desperately to appear chill in the face of the new information. "When you said you went to private school, that was the tip of the iceberg, wasn't it?"

"An elite boarding school that cost more per year than Harvard."

"Wow." So much for chill. She'd lost all her words.

"And now you can see why I don't go into it much."

"I imagine a lot of people have a hard time relating," Corey said thoughtfully. "Did you get a lot of pressure to go into one of the family businesses?"

"No. Thankfully I always had more freedom than that. Both my parents put a lot of emphasis on not being a trust-fund baby. They wanted me to have the drive to accomplish something of my own."

"Well, that's good." Corey hopped down and pulled the cinnamon rolls out of the oven. "I imagine a lot of people you knew had their whole lives planned out for them."

"Yes, you're probably right. Everyone I knew growing up had high expectations and demanding parents. My parents were probably on the more relaxed side of the spectrum. They didn't have a plan for me. All that mattered to them was that I become the best in the world at something. They didn't care so much at what."

She raised her eyebrows. "The best in the world?"

"A CEO of a multinational corporation, a Pulitzer Prize winner, a Nobel Prize winner, president of the United States, lots of valid options. The venue didn't matter, only the mastery of it."

"Magnanimous of them," Corey said, trying to keep the edge out of her voice. No wonder Elise put so much pressure on herself. It's all she'd ever known. "And out of all those choices, you chose world-champion skier?"

"I didn't start skiing with any goal in mind. My father skied a little. My mother liked the spa. On weekends when they wanted to get away from the city, we'd fly up to Vermont for these little family getaways."

"Sounds nice." She began to ice the cinnamon rolls, enjoying the idea of a little Elise zipping around Killington or Stratton with her parents laughing and trying to keep up.

"The slopes were nice, but back in the lodge they fought mercilessly. Not yelling, mind you, but constant sparring. They're both smart enough to know all the words, and calculating enough to choose the ones that stung the other most. They must've been in love at some point, but by the time I was old enough to remember, their relationship had devolved into a war of words."

"I'm sorry. That must've made home pretty tense."

"Not home. When we were in Manhattan, they never had to be in the same room. My mother worked days, my father nights, and they both worked at least every other weekend. The only time they saw each other without colleagues around was on those ski trips."

Corey slathered on another thick layer of icing. Their training regimens would kill tomorrow, but if Christmas morning didn't call for extra sugar, the conversation certainly did. "I'm surprised you didn't grow up hating skiing."

"The skiing offered my only escape. I learned to stay on the slopes from sunup to sundown, and when the trails had lights, I'd ski even later. When I was out there, I didn't have to listen to them bicker, and when I went fast enough, I didn't even hear the echoes of their fights anymore. As I got older and the fights got louder or

216

harsher, I simply had to ski faster until the wind whistling in my ears drowned out everything."

Corey wordlessly slid the cinnamon roll across the counter to her. She wanted to offer comfort, but she didn't want to interrupt. Elise obviously didn't tell these stories lightly, and she felt honored, even while the subject made her uncomfortable.

"They divorced when I was in seventh grade, and I went to boarding school the next year. Things got better, but I'd already become shockingly fast on the slopes. The school ski coach didn't need long to figure that out. And once my parents heard the words 'Olympic potential,' they both poured every ounce of money and influence they had into my training."

"Finally something they could agree on," Corey said dryly.

Elise laughed. "Exactly. I suspect they sold it to themselves that way. If I went on to become a success, they wouldn't have to think of their marriage as a total failure."

"That's a lot of pressure for a kid."

"I suppose so, but I didn't know any other way. Like you said, everyone I grew up with carried some crushing weight of responsibility." Elise shrugged. "The pressure defined us all. Without it I would've probably given up after my injury, or at least taken more time to come back. Maybe if my life had been different, I would've given in to self-pity or taken the easy excuses, but I don't know. Everyone has something that drives them. I have to win. There's never been another option."

Corey couldn't imagine Elise ever giving into self-pity or taking the easy way out. She imagined Elise probably had a good deal of her drive written onto her DNA, and Corey suspected that with the right support and nurturing, she would've achieved every bit as much as she had now without the unhealthy dose of pressure, but she couldn't be certain. What's more, she didn't think saying so now would be helpful in the midst of her comeback.

"Are they still hounding you now that you're grown up?"

"Not since the accident. I guess that's the only real silver lining. Once I wasn't winning anymore, they lost interest in my career. If

I can't be the best, they don't see any reason to bother. They are both shrewd investors, and I'm not a solid bet right now."

"I don't even know what to say," Corey finally admitted. "I wish you'd had a happier childhood, but I'm also impressed with how you turned all that into something productive. You're amazing, and I wouldn't change a thing about the woman you've become, so I guess I have to accept the forces that molded you, but I still really want to hold you right now."

Elise's mouth curled up. "Well, I guess if you need to be comforted, a hug would be acceptable."

Corey came around the bar and wrapped Elise in her arms. She immediately felt the tight muscles in Elise's shoulders and back loosen as she rested her head on Corey's chest. She wasn't the only one soothed by the contact, and she hoped she wasn't the only one reluctant to let go, but she understood now better than before that Elise wasn't someone who would let herself be held for long.

Elise clapped along as Uncle Harry played a wild jig on his violin. Or maybe that was Uncle Mark and he had a son named Harry, but if so, he also had a son named Mark, because one of the boys running in and out from the sledding hill also appeared to be named Mark or Markie to distinguish the two.

She'd spent more than five hours in Corey's parents' house and still hadn't learned everyone's name, much less figured out their relation to one another. She'd made a point to learn Corey's parents and sisters first. Though, to be fair, once she figured out the parents, it would be impossible not to know which women belonged to them. The LaCroixs had an even pair of mini-me's each. Jane and Holly were both lithe and sultry like their mother, while Meg and Corey favored their father from his eyes to his build all the way down to his nose and chin. It would've been easy to split the children into his-and-hers sets based on looks alone if their personalities didn't come spilling out every time they opened their mouths.

"Hey, Markie," Corey called the next time the little boy tromped through the house, snow still dripping from his boots. "You want another cookie?"

"Mom said I can't have any more."

Corey grabbed a little peanut-butter blossom and tossed it to him. "But Aunt Corey says you can."

The boy's eyes widened. "Thanks!"

"Marcus," Meg called from the doorway to the kitchen. "What did she give you?"

Corey made a quick eating motion and pointed to her mouth. He got the message and stuffed the cookie all the way in.

"Nothing," Corey answered for him.

Meg tossed the dishtowel she'd been holding over her shoulder and stepped closer. Corey stage-whispered, "Run, Markie."

The kid bolted back out the door.

"Corey," Meg said, exasperated, her eyes and mouth exactly like Corey's and yet formed in an expression of exasperation the level of which Elise doubted the younger sister had ever experienced. "It's bad enough I have to deal with Dad bending the rules for him. I don't need you doing it, too."

"Come on, Meg. It's Christmas. Beside I only get to seem him a couple times a year. If I don't spoil him hard, how will he know I'm his favorite aunt?"

"A child can develop love and affection through consistency and boundaries," Meg lectured. "Regular letters or phone calls, and age-appropriate educational toys—"

Corey rolled her head back and made a loud, fake snoring noise.

Meg threw the dishtowel at her. "Just because Mom and Dad got tired of enforcing the rules by the time you came along doesn't mean I have to do the same with Markie."

"Why? I turned out fine."

"You gave my six-year-old a sled shaped like a motorcycle."

"I think that proves my point. I'm winning at this aunt thing."

Meg shook her head, clearly realizing she wouldn't win this one. "The least you can do is go supervise him on it for a bit so Holly and Paolo can come inside and get warm."

"Fine," Corey said, standing up with a big stretch. "I'll go supervise my nephew."

"Good." Meg nodded and turned back toward the kitchen, mumbling. "I'm surprised you even know the meaning of the word."

Corey turned to Elise with a smile. "I do know the meaning of 'supervise.' It means 'go teach Markie how to build a ramp out of snow.'"

Elise laughed and shook her head. "She's going to kill you when she finds out."

"Meg? Nah, she's all bluster and no bite. She didn't inherit the killer instinct, unless you consider her ability to nag you to death." Corey pulled on her snow coat as she stepped out onto her parents' back deck. "Jane's the one who will shank you in the back if you cross the line."

"That's the God's honest truth," Holly called from her perch on the railing. "It's always the quiet ones you gotta watch out for."

"Elise knows this lesson already," Paolo said. "She lives it."

She rolled her eyes but couldn't argue the point.

"Aunt Corey," one of the girls called, "come play."

Corey turned to Elise and lifted a shoulder in a silent question of permission, her eyes as hopeful as Markie's had been moments earlier.

"Go on. Show them how you build a snow ramp," Elise said with a smile. "Don't break any of the sleds, though."

"Or any of your bones," Holly called after her.

"Right, none of those, either," Elise said.

They watched in silence for several minutes as Corey marked a spot for the ramp and a safe landing, then began to pack snow onto both areas. Even the older kids got into the mix, piling on and patting down.

"She's going to overdo it," Holly said.

"How do you know?" Paolo asked.

"She always does." Holly's voice was full with love and admiration, such a contrast to Meg's frustration.

"Sounds like someone else I know," Paolo said.

"Was it someone who arrived with her this morning?" Holly teased. "Someone who looks like she spent more time awake than sleeping?"

"I'm standing right here," Elise said.

"You were probably up late waiting for Santa to come," Paolo said. "We were, too."

Elise briefly considered making a joke about him doing something wrong because she and Corey never had to wait long for someone to come, but instead her face flushed. Comments like that rarely even occurred to her. Corey's twelve-year-old-boy mentality must've worn off on her. Besides, he looked too happy to make any jokes at his expense. He'd clearly shaved that morning, and his smile stretched his whole face as he stood behind Holly, his arms around her waist and his hands in her front coat pockets as they both faced the children playing in the snow down below. How long would it be before they added their own kids to the mix?

The thought hit her chest like the cold air coming down the mountain. Paolo and Holly would last. There were no pros and cons to consider, no questions about how, only the easy assumption they'd spend many more Christmases like this. They belonged together, and they would be. Life worked that way sometimes, for some people, and yet the concept still felt foreign. Maybe because she'd never seen it play out in real life, at least not in any life close to her own. She'd always believed her job, or her drive, or her competitiveness ruled out similar possibilities. And yet, didn't Paolo and Holly share her same work-life constraints? Holly was good at her job, and Paolo was certainly every bit as driven as any competitor Elise had ever faced. And yet they would be here again next year, and she likely would not.

"Are you having a nice Christmas?" Paolo asked, pulling her out of her reflection.

"I am," she answered sincerely. "The best one I've had in . . . a long time." *Or ever.*

"You seem more relaxed than I've seen you in a long time."

"Relaxed," she repeated, then turned once more to face Corey and the kids who'd almost completed their launch pad. Was the feeling that had taken hold of her the moment she saw Corey yesterday relaxation or something more? It certainly wasn't anything she felt often, and yet something she remembered, something she'd hoped to get back to, at least subconsciously, something she now associated with this place, these people, and something just over the horizon.

"Hey, Elise," Corey called. "Want be the first one to try our jump? You can show the kids all your mad speed skills."

She laughed and shook her head. "It wouldn't be polite for me to show you up on your own turf. Besides, I don't want to make anyone feel inferior after everyone's been so welcoming to me today."

Corey stared at her for a few seconds, her smile wide and her cheeks rosy from the cold Elise no longer felt through the warmth her amber gaze sent spreading through her core. "Are you sure?"

"Positive," Elise said, as she found a name for the feeling she'd been trying to put her finger on. "I'm happy right here."

"What time do you want me to pick you up tomorrow morning?" Paolo asked as he gathered the coats he and Holly'd brought with them.

"I guess we'd better be on the road by seven."

Holly and Corey gave a little groan, but he nodded. "Do you need to go back to the dorms?"

"No, I was there yesterday, and Corey and I packed up all my stuff to leave from here."

They'd also made use of the dorm bed and then the shower, but Corey didn't feel the need to advertise that fact. What happened at the training center could stay at the training center, but sometimes the best way to wind down after an intense workout was with another workout.

"Did you go to the gym today?" Paolo asked, with forced casualness.

Elise shook her head, the long, blond locks of hair falling down in waves over her shoulders and back. "No, just the slope-side session on Mount Hank. Why?"

"No reason," he said, but even Corey could tell the answer sounded a little strangled. "That was a good workout. You're turning more evenly on your rehabbed knee. Did I tell you one of the coaches even asked me which knee had been hurt because he couldn't tell a difference in the way you moved?"

Nice redirect, Corey thought, but he'd have to think faster if he wanted to outrun Elise's mind.

"Yes. You mentioned it at the time, but what aren't you telling me? Why does it matter if I went to the gym today?"

"I wondered if you'd talked to any of the team officials."

"I would've told you if I did," she said, then let out a heavy sigh. "Like you would tell me if you talked to them."

Paolo glanced at Holly, who shook her head. "Don't look at me. I can't help you here. I'm only glad to know you're terrible at keeping secrets."

"What secret?" Elise asked, her voice so icy even Corey got a chill, or maybe the chill came from a sense of foreboding of what he'd say next. They'd had such a glorious week together, living, training, making love as if almost in a dream state where nothing bad could touch them. Now she feared they were about to face a rude awakening.

"I didn't get an official meeting," Paolo said slowly. "I don't have anything to tell you on the record."

"What about off the record?"

He rubbed his face and sighed. "The good news is the fourth Olympic slot is still open in both the downhill and Super-G."

"Why is that good news?" Elise asked slowly.

"Because it means you still have a chance to win it."

"A chance?" Elise exploded as she whirled around as if searching for something to smash.

Corey felt torn between the urge to soothe her and to get the fuck out of her way. Thankfully, Paolo tried to throw himself on the grenade first.

"It could be worse. After your DNF at the first race, some people wanted to write you off completely."

"Are you trying to make me feel better?"

"Elise, please," he pleaded. "Your doctors said you wouldn't make it back in time, the coaches said you wouldn't make it back, and then when you said you'd made it back, you didn't finish the race. Two weeks ago they all looked right past you, but your top-twenty finish made them stop and think more harder. They could've made the decision this week. They expected to, but they didn't. This is a good sign."

Corey saw his point, but now that she understood Elise's absolutist relationship with success she found it harder to appreciate Paolo's baby steps approach. She'd hoped Elise would win a reprieve from the pressure for a while before the Olympics, but instead it had multiplied.

"You have one more race before they announce the teams," Paolo said resolutely.

"I have to win."

"No, you have to have a top-ten finish," Paolo said as if resigned to laying everything on the table now. "Top ten and you are on the team. More lower, maybe you get the spot or maybe someone else does more better and they get the spot."

"I can't control what anyone else does," Elise snapped. "I have to control my results."

"We'll do everything we can," Paolo said. "But we can't do anything more tonight. Rest, relax, enjoy your time with Corey. We'll have a ten-hour flight tomorrow to discuss our training regimen and game plan."

"Fine," Elise said in the way a woman says 'fine' when she's absolutely not fine. "I'll see you tomorrow."

The chill in her voice was almost palpable, and Paolo had clearly heard the tone enough times to respect the dismissal. Holly wasn't much help either, as she only mouthed a quick and silent "I'm sorry" to Corey before closing the door behind her.

Once they'd gone, the silence reigned heavy and super awkward over her living room. She could try to crack a joke, but as Elise stood before the big wall of windows staring into the darkness, Corey couldn't bring herself to make light of the panic reflected in her eyes.

She walked up behind her and carefully slipped her arms around Elise's waist. She didn't melt this time. The muscles in her back and shoulders remained rock hard even when Corey kissed her lightly on the cheek.

"Come on up to bed," Corey whispered.

Elise shook her head. "I'm not ready."

"We don't have to sleep," Corey said, then worried the comment sounded like a cheap come-on. "We don't have to do anything you're not in the mood for. I want to hold you tonight."

"I won't be able to relax," she said flatly, her tone worrying Corey on a whole new level. Before she'd feared her pulling away, and losing her attention to distraction. While she still hated the idea of spending their final hours together obsessing over a race, now she feared she might actually lose her to something deeper and darker than work.

"Tell me what you need."

"I need to ski faster."

She didn't deliver the line with her usual determined chill, or even the heat of anger. She sounded tired and yet still frantic. The combination haunted Corey as their Christmas morning conversation came rushing back.

Corey turned her around so they faced one another. "You made a good point earlier. You can't control the other skiers, but you know you can't control the past, either."

"I don't know what you mean."

"You can't outrun the pain or fear or doubt. You can't outrun some doctor or coach who said you can't make it."

"I can. I have to." She tried to pull away, but Corey caught her arms and held her tightly.

"You can't will yourself to a win, or a spot on the team."

"Yes I can."

"No," Corey said firmly. "You can only will yourself to *your* best race."

"My best race puts me on the team."

"Maybe it does, maybe it doesn't," Corey said, then, seeing the flash of anger in Elise's eyes added, "On any given day, it probably does."

"It always has before."

"Yes, but you can't count on anything being like before, and you can't count on anything that may happen in the future. You can run the same course three days in a row and get completely different results. The snow is different, the wind is different, hell you're different, even day to day."

Elise didn't respond, at least not verbally. She only stared at her with wounded eyes.

"What is it?"

"I can't do this again," she whispered.

"Again?" Corey asked.

She shoulders sagged. "Two-tenths of a second."

"What?"

"I was two-tenths of a second from being done with all of it."

"All of what?"

"All of the pressure, the killing myself to be perfect, the doubt and the insecurity and the pressure. Did I already say 'the pressure'?" She shook her head. "Two-tenths of a second from being an Olympic medalist."

"Oh." Corey finally understood. "You missed the podium in Sochi by two-tenths of a second."

"Twice." Elise sagged against her. "Four more years. I've already put in four more years. Four years of work and pain and rehab. Now I have one race standing between me and another four years."

Corey wanted to pull her close, to put Elise's head on her chest, to stroke her hair and rub her back. She wanted to soothe her like a child who'd had a bad dream, but Corey knew the demons chasing her now were very much real. She couldn't protect her from them anymore than Elise would be able to outrun them, but the way Elise had said "four more years," as if it were a prison sentence and not a thriving career, had to be addressed.

"You know you don't have to do this, right?"

"Do what?" Elise asked.

"Anything. You don't owe anyone anything. Not the sport, not the fans, not your parents. You could walk away right now, and no one would have a right to say a damn thing."

"Walk away? Are you fucking insane?"

"Probably." Corey laughed. "Probably. But quitting is a valid option for anyone at any time. You aren't a medical courrier or a surgeon. No one will die if you throw in the towel mid-season."

"But I don't want to."

"Really?" Corey asked. "'Cause it doesn't sound like it."

"I don't want to lose. I don't want to fail—"

"But do you want to ski?"

"I want to win."

"But do you want *to ski?* Because that's all that matters. You're so wrapped up in other things that don't matter, you've lost track of everything that does."

"You think winning doesn't matter?" Elise asked.

"Not if you don't want to ski. If you don't go out there every time because you're chomping at the bit to tear down the mountain, to carve it up and make it your own, nothing else matters. If you're more worried about what happened before, or what will happen next that you lose track of where you are in the moment, then you've already lost. The moment is all you have. You can deal with the next moment if you get to it, but you can't live there. All you can do is rip the shit out of the chance you have right now."

Elise stared at her, eyes still wide but now darker and more focused. Her jaw set and her fists clenched at her side, but she no longer looked like a flight risk. Her chest rose and fell steadily while Corey waited for a response. Finally, Elise opened her mouth, and Corey braced for the argument, but instead Elise caught her by the back of the neck and pulled her forward until their mouths met in a crushing kiss.

Corey's head swam with conflicting emotions. Was Elise deflecting? Was she avoiding the argument? She should probably have had those questions answered before responding appropriately, but as Elise pulled her shirt over her head, her ability to reason waivered. Elise then slowly peeled off her own yoga pants, and all capacity for logic went south on the rush of blood headed in the same direction.

In one last-ditch grip for civility and tenderness, Corey managed to whisper, "Are you sure?"

"I want this moment," Elise said in a low, sultry voice and kissed her deeply, then, putting a hand on each of Corey's shoulders, pushed her down to her knees on the plush rug in front of the fireplace.

Corey got the message rather clearly, and who was she to deny a woman what she needed, especially a woman with killer thighs and the know-how to use them in a variety of sexy situations. Corey kissed Elise's legs lightly, plotting a slow trip back up to the beautiful place where they met. Elise, however, had other ideas. Cupping the back of Corey's head in her hand, she sank her fingers into thick hair, massaging as she guided her forward until they both reached the spot she wanted.

Corey understood this wasn't the time for playing around or gentle teasing. Perhaps Elise had taken that live-in-the-moment speech quite literally, because at this rate a minute was all either of them would last, and yet if speed was their game, Corey had more than enough skill to hold her own. Grabbing two handfuls of Elise's tight ass, she once again gave a passing thought to trying to bounce quarters off those glutes before refocusing and tilting her hips forward. The moment her tongue touched Elise's clit, they both groaned. Elise tightened her grip on Corey's hair and used the leverage to both steady herself and set the pace of her mouth.

Normally Corey wouldn't be the type to allow someone else to do the driving, but Elise wasn't like any of the other women she'd been with. Of course she was strong and beautiful and powerful, but Corey suspected the real difference lay in a more personal realm. She'd wanted to please all her lovers. She took great pride in satisfying them, but with Elise the need to please didn't stem from her own sense of accomplishment or some misplaced quest for bragging rights. Corey wanted to give Elise everything she wanted simply because she wanted it.

Giving in to the desire to give in, she used her hands and her mouth to meet Elise's need. If she couldn't dissolve every fear and insecurity, she could at least overcome them or overshadow them for this moment. Taking her own advice, she resolved to make the best of the time they had by making it their own. As Elise started to waver, Corey held her fast, wrapping her arms around her waist and helping support her as she rode through the waves of pleasure causing her to tremble. Then, even after easing her down to the rug, Corey refused to let go.

She clutched Elise tightly to her chest, kissing her hair, her forehead, the bridge of her nose. When she reached the corners of her eyes, she thought she tasted a hint of tears, but it could've been the sweat of exertion.

"Are you okay?" she finally whispered as she settled back to watch the shadows from the fireplace dance along the ceiling.

"Yes," Elise said softly. "Are you?"

"Yes."

"I didn't mean to attack you."

"You surprised me, but I can't say I minded." Corey snuggled closer.

"You're very good at those pep talks, you know?"

"Maybe I should consider a career in motivational speaking."

"Or you should save all your best material for me," Elise said quickly. "I don't like the idea of you giving a live-in-the-moment speech to someone else."

"Hmm." Corey couldn't articulate any response as her heart hammered loudly in her chest.

"Did I say that out loud?" Elise asked.

"You did," Corey said slowly. "Do you want to retract it?"

"Do you want me to?"

Corey thought for a few seconds, waiting for some flight instinct to kick in, but when it didn't, she shook her head. "No."

"What about living in the moment? Asking for exclusive rights to you as we head for different continents tomorrow doesn't seem spontaneous."

"No, but I want you, even when you're far away. I think of you even in moments when we're not together. My moments can still be yours no matter where we happen to spend them."

Elise nipped at her ear and gave a little growl. "I've never considered myself a possessive person, but I like the idea of owning your moments."

Corey laughed. "You know you only get mine if I get yours."

Elise pushed up onto an elbow and ran her gaze over Corey's bare chest and stomach. "I suppose that's a fair trade."

"Yeah?" Corey asked, as giddiness washed over her.

"Yeah." Elise repeated, rolling over until she hovered above Corey, arms extended, legs intertwined. "You have yourself a deal. Think we should seal it with a kiss?"

Corey grinned before lifting her head to meet Elise's mouth. She couldn't think of a better way to spend that moment.

Chapter Fifteen

January 12, 2018
Altenmark
Zauchensee, Austria

"You're good?" Paolo asked.

"Good." Elise nodded.

"Good," he parroted. She should probably give him more to work with, but she couldn't find a better word. She simply felt good, from the bottom of her legs all the way up to her brain. She didn't have a single complaint, physical or emotional. And she knew today's course well. She'd had back-to-back top three finishes here before she'd wrecked, and she'd had top of the pack times in practice all week.

"Do you want to know the standings?" Paolo asked as she slid into line.

She shook her head and pulled down her goggles. "I'm going to ski the best race I can. It doesn't matter what anyone else is doing."

He put his hand on her forehead the best he could with her helmet on, and she shook him off. She supposed his concern was warranted. She hadn't felt much like her old self since leaving Lake Henry two weeks earlier, but she'd certainly seen the old results returning. Two days earlier, she'd finished in tenth place in the downhill race on this mountain, her best result of the season, and one to put her right on the bubble for the team. Now she had her chance to better even that in the Super-G. More impressively, though, she hadn't fixated on those results or the team. "I can't control the other racers' results, and I can't control the committee."

"And this makes you . . . happy?" Paolo asked, sounding confused.

She laughed, a bright, genuine shot of laughter that caused several heads around her to turn. Most of her colleagues had probably never heard that sound from her, especially this close to her starting time. "Yes, I guess it does make me happy, which is funny, right? Normally not being in control makes me angry."

"And yet you're more relaxed than usual ever since Christmas," he said with a slow smile. "You're in love with her?"

"What? God. Why would you say something like that to me right before a race?"

His eyes went wide and his tan complexion turned gray. "What? I thought you were happy, and she made you relax and helped you feel better. And you trust her if you take her advice. Plus, I think you had a lot of sex."

"Why would you say anything about love?"

"I don't know, maybe because happiness and trust and being your best and physical attraction all with the same person—"

"Stop," Elise said, suddenly tense in ways she hadn't been for weeks. "I cannot have this conversation right now. I'm about to start one of the most high-stakes races of my career."

"I'm sorry," Paolo said gravely. "I didn't mean to upset you. I thought you knew."

"There's nothing to know," she snapped.

"Okay." He held up his palms. "We can talk about something else."

She shook her head. "I don't want to talk about anything."

"Fine. I'll stand here quietly."

"No, go on down. Meet me at the finish line."

"What? I stay with you at the top. You can't fire me now."

More people inclined their ears toward them while working hard to appear studiously disinterested. Elise dropped her voice. "You're not fired. I need to clear my head, and I can't do so with you hovering over me. I'd rather have you down-mountain to cheer me on."

"I'm not a fan. I'm your coach. I've been here day and night for almost two years. I didn't let you push me away then. I'm not going to let you push me away now."

Elise took two slow, deep breaths, then clasped him on the shoulders and looked him straight in the eyes. "Paolo, thank you. I know I haven't said it enough, but I mean it. I wouldn't be here without you, but this moment is mine. There's no more coaching you can do."

He opened his mouth to protest, but she cut him off.

"You're an amazing coach, but you're so much more. You're my best friend. When I cross the finish line this time, for better or worse, I want a friend there to greet me."

His smile once again returned, and his eyes glistened in the Austrian sun, but instead of saying anything, he simply pulled her into a big bear hug. His long, strong arms held her so tight she felt a little pop in one of the tight spots in her back. Then standing back, he blinked away a few tears and laughed. "Okay, you win. I'll go. I better hurry, though, because I think you will ski fast today."

She smiled and shook her head as he jogged off as best he could in the snow and crowd of ski equipment. She watched him go as the realization that she was alone now slowly sank in. God, what had she been thinking? Who starts a race without a coach? Who decides to change a routine right before a big race? Who gives up on everything that got them to the top in the moments before trying to secure her position there?

In the moment. She'd acted in the moment. A few deep breaths helped her heart rate return to normal. She made a slow turn to take in the scenery. A beautiful, sunny day in the Alps spread out like a postcard photo before her. Jagged peaks cut in gray and capped in white spread as far as she could see, and the hustle and bustle of a crowd stirred brightly below. The air smelled crisp and clean, and the sound of conversations whirred all around her amid clicks of boots and the swoosh of skis over thickly packed snow. Every sense heightened as she inched closer to her turn in the starting gate. She felt more present than she had in years.

She closed her eyes to picture her path down the course, but all she saw was Corey's face smiling up at her, her eyes dancing with mischief, her skin and hair golden against the fresh sheet of snow.

God, was she in love with her?

No, they simply shared a mutual attraction, perhaps one bordering on infatuation. She couldn't deny their tremendous chemistry in the bedroom. And yet she did miss her in more areas than the physical realm. She thought of her a lot, and not just at night or during down time. She remembered her words on the slopes, in the gym, and apparently even at her most important moments. And what had Paolo said about trusting her? Elise had told her everything about her childhood, her fears, and her insecurities. She also couldn't deny Paolo's point about Corey making her better, both on and off the slopes. Was that the point he'd tried to make all the way back in Argentina? Had he seen her falling even then?

Her chest tightened and her stomach felt jittery, as if she'd made an unexpected drop on a thrilling slope only to land perfectly safe on the other side. Is that what love felt like? Thrilling and unexpected and yet fluid? Instinctual?

She slid into the starting position almost on autopilot, her form as natural as the emotions swelling in her now.

Beep

Beep

Beep

The countdown came like a heart rate on a hospital monitor. Then she was off, falling, flying, whirling around corners and rocketing over jumps. There were times her skis didn't touch the ground, and others when it merely felt that way due to the lightness in her chest. She moved with the mountain, her whole body surrendering to the racing of her heart as it begged to soar higher and faster. She curled in on herself, wanting to form a perfect little ball, to pull even her limbs into the exuberance radiating from her core. Turn after turn raced by, but instead of pinning her down, each one only drew her forward as if even the fall line recognized it had nothing on the fall occurring inside of her.

She crossed the finish in what seemed like seconds, and even through the rush of blood in her ears and the spray of snow she threw up as she stopped, she felt the crowd vibrating around her.

Tossing off her goggles, she searched for Paolo's face in the crowd and heard his voice above all the others.

"Fifth place," he screamed, "top five!"

She needed a few seconds to process his comment through the haze, but she turned to check the leader board. Sure enough, she'd taken over the fifth slot, and what's more, no other American skier had turned in a faster time.

She kicked off her skis and pushed through the crowd of fans and reporters until she and Paolo fell together in another hug, one that made the hug they'd shared up top feel tame. They squeezed and rocked. He picked up her long frame and twirled her around as if she were no bigger than a child, and when he finally set her down, he cried. "You're an Olympian again. You did it! I know you are on the team now."

"I do, too, but I might actually know something even more shocking."

"What?" he called.

She smiled so widely her cheeks hurt. "I'm in love with Corey."

January 14, 2018 - Vallnord-Arcalis Andorra

Corey threw her helmet across the hotel room and got such a sense of satisfaction at the loud crack when it hit the wall, she grabbed a three-ring binder and hurled it, too. It hit the door to the bathroom with a hollow thud, then clattered to the floor, a few papers fluttering behind it. She then reached for the next item on the table, but Holly caught her hand so tightly her nails bit into Corey's skin and cut through her red-tinged rage.

"Not my laptop, Core."

She clenched her teeth and tried to jerk away, but Holly held tight, so Corey kicked the desk chair.

"Whoa," Nate called and grabbed her around the waist. "No kicking."

"I need to blow off steam," Corey shouted, but the anger had already started to ebb.

"Then go to the gym or punch some pillows," Nate said, "but your legs are not expendable mid-season."

"Why? They aren't doing me any good lately."

"At least you made the semifinals," Tigger said, flopping onto the couch. "That's better than you did on Friday."

"Not helpful," Holly said to the kid. "Don't you have a race to get ready for?"

"No, I've got three hours before the finals. The coaches told me to get off my feet, so I came to check on Corey. Glad I did, too."

Both Nate and Holly loosened their grip on Corey to stare at her in disbelief. Corey used the opportunity to send the TV remote careening across the room until it bounced off the bed and smacked into the end table on the other side.

"Damn it, Corey," Holly said.

She sighed and straightened her shoulders. "I'm done now."

"Do you always throw things after a loss?" Nikki asked as if she intended to take notes.

"No," Corey said, "but after two losses in three days . . . still no, actually. I'm frustrated. And tired. I'm sleeping like shit, and I'm sick of getting boxed out."

"Sorry," Tigger looked at the floor.

"Don't fucking apologize. It wasn't even you the last two times." Not that it couldn't have been. Tigger had been on fire all weekend, with a second-place finish in the first race and a prime chance to win later that day. Added to her second-place finish right before Christmas, she'd blown past Corey in the overall tour standings. Corey's only solace was she hadn't had to face her on the course yet, thanks to being seeded in different heats all week. "Simple math. You're racing well. I'm not. I'm fucking depleted."

"Hey, Tigger," Holly cut in. "I know you're supposed to be resting, but would you mind running down to your room and getting Corey some of the blue Gatorade you guys had in there? That always helps her recharge, and blue is her favorite."

"Sure." She hopped up and headed for the door. "I'll be back in, like, five minutes. I'll get some ice, too. Then you can relax because we've got, like, three weeks off before the Olympics."

The older three exchanged a quick look. Nate finally shook his head. "We fly out tomorrow for a quick stop at Lake Henry before the X-Games."

"I thought everyone was skipping the X-Games because it's between when they announce the Olympic team and the actual Olympics. Why risk an injury?"

"Because it's the X-Games," Nate said. "Those are our people."

Nikki cocked her head to the side as if trying to consider the logic.

"Never mind the schedule right now," Holly said. "We need the Gatorade, STAT."

"Right," Nikki said.

"Wait." Corey stopped her again. "If you're not going to the X-Games, where are you headed?"

"Northern Italy. They're having training camp, and the ski team will be nearby so we can get all of our Olympic stuff together, passports and physicals and uniforms. I hope they're nice. Do you think we'll have berets this year?"

They all stared at her. Corey understood the other two were probably annoyed, but the comments triggered something different in her. Hope? Envy? Time off and time with the ski team, the two things she wanted most, given to someone who wouldn't properly appreciate them.

"Right. Gatorade. I'm on it." And off she went.

When the door closed behind her, Holly sighed and turned to Corey. "I like the kid, I do. Most of the time. But can you stop telling her you're depleted?"

"Why?" Corey asked. "It's true. I haven't been able to get my legs right for weeks. Nate, you know I'm right."

"Yeah," he admitted, sinking into the chair she'd recently kicked. "You're getting boxed out because you're getting beat through the first two-hundred yards every time."

"You'll do better at the X-Games," Holly said. "It's your second home."

"Maybe." Corey tried to muster some excitement she didn't feel.

"Maybe what?"

"Maybe I'll do better or maybe I won't. Maybe it'll be nice to be stateside, or maybe I'll be so freaking jet-lagged I won't enjoy myself. And what if I do win? Will it bolster my confidence when I know I've only beaten the B-team, because all the legit Olympians are getting ready for the big show?"

"Whoa," Nate said. "Slow down. Are you saying you don't want to go to the X-games? That's your jam, dude."

"It's been my jam for fifteen years," Corey admitted. "I have enough X-game medals to pave my driveway. What more do I have to prove there? Especially against the scrubs?"

"You want to go to Italy and train for the Olympics? That's never been your bag. Those people aren't even snowboard people. I'm not calling bullshit. I'm just saying it doesn't sound like you, Core."

"No, it sounds like Elise," Holly cut in, her voice cold. "Don't think I didn't do the math there, too. She'll be in Italy, so you want to be in Italy. I had the same instinct about wanting to see Paolo. I get it, but I never thought you'd let a hot date keep you from the X-Games. Would she make the same choice for you?"

She rolled her head from side to side, trying to ease the tension building in her neck and shoulders. Elise had factored in, of course she had, and of course Holly had called her out. That's one of the many reasons she kept Holly around. Sisters could say the things coaches and even friends didn't dare to.

"I doubt it," Corey finally said. She wanted to believe otherwise, but she knew more about Elise than ever now, and she understood what kind of toll a sacrifice like that would take on her. "With the progress she's making right now, I don't imagine anything would pull her off course."

Holly didn't look smug at her victory. Her eyes grew sad. "Then I think you have your answer."

"No. I don't, because she and I are in two difference places right now. She's in the middle of a comeback. I'm in the middle of a tailspin. Asking her to leave a race right now would kill the momentum she's built, but I feel like I'm on a demonic carnival ride and maybe hopping off is the only way to save this season."

"Your season started off fine. It only got out of control when you started caring more about getting back to her than winning races."

"You were there, Holly," Corey said. "The season started well because I was happy and rested and in good shape. It went well before the travel and the daily beatings took their toll. I know no one wants to admit this, least of all me, but I'm 30 years old now."

"And what?" Nate inserted himself back into the discussion. He might not have wanted to touch the relationship talk, but he clearly intended to reassert his role now that they'd moved on to coachable topics. "You reached some age where reporters start asking you about retirement and you roll over?"

"You know I don't care about the reporters. I care about getting beat out of the gate. I care about not having the power in my knees to double-jump rollers. I care about needing twice the recovery time as the kid."

"Your first race of the year you were every bit as strong and sharp as you've ever been."

"I was also as rested as I've ever been, and more rested than any race since. Listen to what I'm saying here. I'm not throwing in the towel. I'm as good once as I've ever been, but I can't go on benders anymore and expect to magically pull out wins at the end of them. We had two races in three days. Now you want me to fly to New York for two days, then fly another three time zones to compete for three days, then back to New York for intense workouts for a week, then go to the Olympics. For what? Another X-Games medal to match the ones I've had since I turned eighteen? To try to prove myself against people I should already know I can beat? To make the political statement, or to try to delude people into thinking I haven't slowed down when everyone can see that I have? To pretend I'm not frustrated, or in pain, or—"

"Hey." Holly put a hand on her shoulder. "Are you hurting?"

"Nothing feels like a knife in my knee, but yeah. Every muscle in my body aches every morning. I'm sore from my scalp to my little toe. I'm tired in a way I've never felt tired before. And I'm sorry if hearing that disappoints you."

"Shut up," Holly said with a shove. "You don't disappointment me, dummy. When I thought you were selling yourself short for Elise, I got pissed because you're every bit as important as she is. I didn't want you to give up something you love as much as the X-Games to please her."

"I have loved the X-Games, but not because I win there, because I have fun there. But I'm not having fun anymore. I want to sleep and eat right. I want to train without all the pressure. I want to surround myself with people who challenge me. And yes, Elise is one of those people, but so is Tigger, God love her bubbly little elf self."

Holly and Nate both smiled.

"I'm not giving in or giving up," Corey said, as much for her benefit as for theirs. "I want to ride. I want to win. I want to feel good again. I think going to Italy is the best way to get me into a position to do so."

Nate cracked first. "I'm in, dude. Hell, I'm geeked out to see you still care enough to shake shit up. I was starting to worry I wanted the win more than you did. If you hadn't thrown Holly's laptop, I might have."

She snorted. "What do you say, Holly? Should we go to Italy, or should I let Nate throw your laptop?"

She grabbed the MacBook off the table and folded it into her arms. "Don't even think about it. I'm going to need this to rearrange our reservations."

"Really?" Corey asked. "You don't mind?"

Holly smiled. "I wanted to go to Italy all along, but I needed to make sure we were doing it for the right reason."

Corey nodded, so glad to have the matter settled she didn't even point out she probably should have said 'reasons, plural.' She did need the rest, and she did need to train with the right people, but she also needed to see Elise, and while the last point probably didn't rank high on Holly's list of "right" reasons, Corey suspected it might end up being the one to make the biggest difference in the long run.

January 26, 2018 - Cortina d' Ampezzo, Italy

Corey raised her glass of sparking water. "To another top-five finish."

"To steady improvement." Elise clinked Corey's glass with her own. She didn't normally brag until she'd made first place, but with a fourth-place finish in the downhill and a bronze medal in the Super-G, she could at least say she'd gotten better with every single race of the season.

"To the three Olympians," Paolo said, nodding to Corey, Elise, and Tigger.

"We celebrated that last week," Holly said, but she raised her glass anyway.

"I want to celebrate that one for the rest of my life." He choked up again, and everyone laughed. He'd started crying when the Olympic announcements were made and had hardly stopped since. At least tonight they were in the back room of the hotel restaurant without the crowd of spectators and reporters to snap pictures. He'd been strong and stoic through a year of adversity, but now the pride and joy seemed almost too much for him to bear. Elise, for her part, had felt only a modicum of relief. One more hurdle cleared. A big one, but not the last. Still, she liked that he felt his efforts had been rewarded, because it lifted the burden of at least one responsibility off her shoulders

Nate patted him on the back as he lifted his bottle of beer. "To having so much to celebrate."

Tigger jumped up with gusto. "Here's to us all spending so much time together."

241

They all laughed again, but this time no one seemed to mind her hanging around. She'd become one of them more and more over the last two weeks. While she hadn't lost her tendency toward obliviousness and still bounded in and out of conversations at weird times, she carried herself well on and off the slopes. She had a good work ethic and a desire to win, but she never took herself so seriously in social situations that she couldn't handle their gentle ribbing from time to time. Plus, if the story she'd heard from Paolo held true, Tigger had been the one to provide Corey with an excuse to spend more time with her, and for that Elise felt endlessly grateful.

As they all lowered their glasses and returned to normal conversations, Elise held Corey's hand under the table and gave a gentle squeeze. Having her there the last two weeks had been nothing short of amazing. She'd surprised her the first day of training and tried to claim Italy was on the way between Andorra and Aspen, Colorado. With her history of geography fails, she got several minutes of teasing in before Elise figured out she was kidding and had come to stay.

She'd had some initial misgivings about Corey sacrificing her own races to support her. She didn't want to be the reason Corey cut herself short, but with every passing day, Corey grew stronger, happier, more productive, and she couldn't deny the same trend in herself or try to pretend the two weren't connected. She was happier than she'd ever been in a training camp, and not only because of her steadily improving position in the world-cup rankings. Her whole mindset was different with Corey working out nearby.

Elise would occasionally stop by the snowboarders' camp at the end of her day to find Corey practically running the show. She practiced jumps and cut moves, laughing as the younger racers fell behind time and time again. She held informal clinics on technique and form. Tigger wasn't her only follower, either. Many of the junior tour members had taken to hanging around her after their official heat times, and the coaches seemed either bemused by or resigned to her new role.

Elise suspected Corey's mentality had rubbed off on her a little, too. She'd yet to laugh her way over a jump or crash into another skier, but lately her own workouts were met with more smiles and less grumbling, which also made Paolo happy. Maybe that's what felt different about this set of moments they'd all shared. For the first time in perhaps her entire life, everyone she cared about was undeniably happy.

Her phone buzzed in her lap, and she looked down to see Julie Chen's number on the screen. This was the second time she'd tried to call tonight. She made a mental note to get back to her soon. She really did owe her an interview, and she intended to make good on the promise, but she hadn't hung around long after her last race since she'd had so many friends there.

"Is that your parents again?" Corey asked quietly.

"No, just a reporter, thankfully." Who would've thought she'd ever be happier to hear from a reporter than the people who were supposed to love her. Her come-from-behind appointment to the Olympic team had suddenly renewed their interest in supporting her career. She'd barely had the stomach for their congratulations and thin shows of support, much less their near-constant attempts to re-establish regular contact.

"Hey," Corey whispered, intertwining their fingers. "You ready to go?"

Immediately the fire ignited in her chest, incinerating all the stressful topics that had occupied her thoughts moments before, and she worried everyone else could tell. They'd made a valiant attempt to be discreet in front of coaches and officials, never offering public displays of affection in the name of professionalism, but anyone who paid attention to how they looked at each other by the end of the day could easily discern their nightly ritual of ripping each other's clothes off. "Yes, let's go."

They smiled the smiles of two people who knew what came next and couldn't wait to get there, then rose and began to say their goodnights.

"Are you guys seriously going to bed this early again?" Tigger asked, disappointment tinging her voice.

"Yep," Corey said.

"Why?"

Nate snickered and said, "I'll explain it to you when you're older."

Her cheeks flushed. "I know they're a couple."

Elise's breath caught at the easy way Tigger made the declaration. Everyone else stopped short as well. No one laughed or offered a quick comeback. Instead, they all deferred to her and Corey.

"What?" Tigger finally asked. "Are we not supposed to talk about it?"

"No," Elise said gently. "It's just not something we've talked about before."

"You haven't talked about it with each other?"

"We have," Elise said, as least they sort of had. They'd had the exclusivity talk, and she'd used the L-word with Paolo, though she hadn't exactly gotten around to dropping that bomb on Corey yet. Neither of them had yet to put a formal title on what they meant to each other, and she didn't know if she liked Tigger being the one to set the label. "But we haven't made any public declarations about being a couple."

"But everyone here knows." Tigger sounded confused. "Right?"

"Um, well"—Corey ran her hand through her golden hair and shrugged—"I suppose."

Elise glanced around the table as everyone nodded their confirmation.

"So, if everybody knows . . ."

Corey looked to Elise, either uncertain about how to answer or unwilling to make the leap alone. Either way, she'd clearly deferred to her. Elise waited for either panic or some natural instinct for self-preservation to rise. She'd always kept her personal life locked in a vault. She didn't want the media attention to distract her or give anyone fuel to damage her image with sponsors. But as she scanned the faces around her now, she couldn't summon any feeling of threat. Maybe she'd never shared these parts of her life because she'd never had friends like these before. When her eyes fell on Corey's once more, she realized something else had also changed. She'd never had someone so worthy of being shared before.

"Yeah," she finally said, surrendering to the moment. "I guess you're right. We're a couple. We know it, you know it, hopefully we're all happy about it, and now we're going to bed."

"To have sex," Corey added.

Everyone laughed.

"Core," Elise said, "do you always have to push things one step too far?"

"Yes." Corey wrapped an arm around her waist. "It's part of my charm."

Elise cracked a smile and shook her head. She couldn't argue, nor could she stand to drag this out anymore. "Come on, Prince Charming, let's go."

As they left the restaurant and headed down the long hallway to the suite they'd basically shared since Corey's arrival, Elise reached for her hand.

Corey accepted the touch with the same easygoing closeness she brought to every situation, but when they reached the room, she didn't immediately move in for more. Instead, she used their intertwined fingers to pull Elise toward the couch instead of the bed. "How you feeling about that little declaration?"

Elise sucked in a deep breath and released it slowly, wanting to give an honest, well-thought-out answer, but all she could come up with was, "Good."

"Good?" Corey asked, clearly waiting for her to elaborate.

"Yes. Undeniably good. My body, my head, my heart, I can't find a single problem, and I guess that's the only issue still hanging over me. I keep waiting for the other shoe to drop. I'm not used to everything working out. I know in some ways I've lived a charmed life, wealth, education, opportunity, success—"

"And don't forget your stunning beauty."

"Of course," she said playfully, "but, there's always been the sense of something chasing me, or me chasing something. Some-

245

thing just out of reach. And if I let myself relax for one moment it would fade away completely."

"And now?"

"I guess the feeling hasn't evaporated, but it's not nearly as strong. Maybe I should worry more, because I know I could still lose everything I've worked for tomorrow. All the dreams can shatter around the next turn or in the next few weeks, but tonight, with our friends, with you? It's hard to summon those fears."

Corey's smile was radiant. "That may be the best compliment anyone has ever given me. And also the best description of what I've felt since arriving here. I know judgment day is coming, and if I don't perform, everyone will scrutinize everything about me and my future and my motivation, not to mention the hell I'll catch from both sides for skipping the X-Games. But, right now, I don't care."

"Really?" Elise asked seriously. "You don't have any regrets about not being in Aspen? I kind of got the sense the event meant a lot to you."

"It has in the past, both on a personal level and as part of my yearly routine, but now it seems like a part of my past. A great part, and maybe it can be part of my future, but this is the best I've felt in months. I want to spend this moment right here with you. I wouldn't trade that for any amount of former glory or to avoid future arguments, no matter how hot the spotlight might get."

Elise rested her head on Corey's shoulder. She didn't have anything else to add. She wasn't naïve enough to believe problems wouldn't arise eventually, but they belonged to tomorrow. Everything she felt for Corey belonged to tonight.

Chapter Sixteen

February 9, 2018
XXIII Olympic Games

"This is the best night of my whole life," Tigger exclaimed, as they finally filed out the of massive PyeongChang Olympic Stadium.

For once Corey agreed with every ounce of her enthusiasm. The night had been amazing. Despite the hours of standing around and being herded like cattle from one staging area to another, while all the athletes in red, white, and blue waited for the announcers to get all the way through the international alphabet, once they all flooded into the arena with the flash of cameras and the screaming crowd, even she got choked up. She'd done all of this before, but somehow sharing the experience with Elise heightened every sense. The fireworks shone brighter, the music boomed louder, the energy coursing through every person made her nerve endings vibrate, and the occasional brush of Elise's hand anchored her to the perfection not only around them, but also between them.

They took pictures with each other, with spectators, with athletes from other countries. They danced, they sang, and when the Olympic flame ignited overhead, Corey watched the fire dance in the glistening reflection of Elise's eyes. Edging so close their shoulders touched, she fought to imprint the image so deep into her memory, she'd never in a million years or a million lifetimes forget the way she looked right then.

"Elise, have you ever seen anything like this?" Tigger bounced in circles around them.

"I've gone to other opening ceremonies," Elise mused, "but tonight's is certainly the most special."

"'Cause the show was better?" Tigger asked.

"No," Elise said, "because the company's better."

Corey blushed uncharacteristically. She'd never been bashful, but she was inordinately pleased to know Elise felt the way she did.

"You guys are so mushy for each other," Tigger said.

"I wasn't only talking about Corey." Elise threw her arm around the kid's shoulder and then caught Corey around the waist so they sandwiched her. "I meant both of you."

"But mostly Corey," Tigger said.

"Maybe she's got the edge over you in a few areas," Elise admitted, "but I've never had friends at something like this before. I always treated the other skiers as my competition, and they probably didn't appreciate that."

"See, skiers and snowboarders should be friends. No jockeying for position against each other," Corey said. "Just living in the moment."

"And it's a first Olympic moment for you," Elise said to Tigger. "I got to see it all again for the first time through your eyes."

"What about you, Corey?" Tigger said. "Did it feel like the first time all over?"

The question hit her in the chest and she stopped walking, pulling both of them up short with her. As she reflected on the evening, the thrills, the emotions, the desire to imprint every-thing on her heart and mind, she hadn't been able to put those feelings into words yet, but now she understood the contrast between her savoring and Tigger's exuberance. The evening hadn't felt like her first time. It'd felt like her last.

"Elise," a woman called from behind a metal barricade. "Elise Brandeis."

They all three turned to face her, and Elise immediately untangled herself from the hold they'd had on each other and made a beeline for her.

"Hi, Julie."

"Do you mind if I ask a few questions for a piece I'm working on? I'll be quick. I know it's a big night for you and your . . . friends."

"I'm sorry, how rude of me. This is Corey LaCroix and Nikki Prince. They're both snowboard-X racers who train at the Lake Henry Olympic center with me," Elise explained. "Corey, Tigger, meet Julie Chen. She's a reporter who went to my *alma mater*."

Corey examined the woman's press pass, her high boots, her waif-like build, and her beautiful, dark eyes. Quite a combination: access, power, a personal connection, and a pretty face. She did her best to put on her polite smile.

"I've actually done a lot of reading on you all this week. It's nice to connect in person."

"You've been reading about me?" Tigger asked, seemingly pleased with the idea, but the hair on the back of Corey's neck stood on end. Something about Julie's smile didn't sit right. She didn't look at Elise like a school chum, and she eyed her like an heiress might regard the hired help.

"I asked for you when the ski team picked up their USA uniforms last week in Munich and was told you'd already come through with the snowboarding team."

"The time slot worked better with my schedule," Elise said breezily. "Sorry I missed you, though. I tried to find you after my last race in Italy. I wanted to give you the podium interview I promised."

Julie didn't seem impressed. "I noticed Corey attended that race."

"So did I," Tigger jumped in. "Team USA all the way."

Corey couldn't tell if the kid noticed the shift in the tone of the interview or if she merely wanted to be included, but Corey could've kissed her for the response.

"And none of you are staying in the athletes' village?" Julie pressed.

"No, the athletes' village is in the center of town. I wanted to be away from the distractions and closer to the mountains."

"And you, Corey?" Julie asked coolly.

"The same. I travel with my coaching staff and my sister, while Tigger has both her parents on the trip. We wanted a more family-friendly set up."

"And by we, you mean you and Elise are sharing the same house?"

Corey shot Elise a WTF expression, which Julie clearly caught.

"So you rearrange your competition schedule to train with Elise and attend her races, while Elise breaks with ski team tradition and rents a house with you during the highest profile race of her career?"

"What kind of story are you working on, Julie?" Elise asked, ice in her voice.

"I'm a ski reporter, not a gossip columnist," Julie said, but the way she clipped her words didn't ease the tension tightening Corey's back and neck. "But your comeback is the big story of the games. People will want the human interest angle."

"Even when it's irrelevant to my performance on the slopes?"

"I guess it's for the readers to decide what's relevant information."

"I expected a high-caliber journalist to show more restraint than an all-out info dump."

"I expected a woman of your caliber to show more restraint in the company she keeps. I guess we've both fallen a little short of our school-day ambitions."

"All right," Corey snapped. "We've all had a big night. The kid has a curfew, and we've all got races to prepare for. This interview is over."

"I agree," Elise said sadly.

Julie didn't seem gleeful either, but certainly resolved. "Yes. I've got everything I need. Best of luck to all of you in the days ahead."

Corey turned to go, catching Tigger by the shoulder and wheeling her around as Elise closed in on the other side.

"No one look back," Corey whispered. "Not another word until we're in the van. In the meantime, smile and wave."

They all raised their chins, plastered celebratory grins on their faces, and strode on through the crowd toward the pick-up area where Paolo would be waiting. To the outside observer, they probably looked like three women ready to take on the world. Any opponents they happened to pass along the way would likely shake in their brightly colored jackets and matching boots, but competition was the farthest thing from Corey's mind. She suspected she and Elise were about to have their mettle tested on a much bigger stage than any mountain they'd ever faced.

"*Another One Bites the Dust, Olympic Skier Falls Hard for Bad Girl of the Mountain.*" Elise read the headline and tossed the paper aside before grabbing another and flipping to the sports section. "*Olympic Score: Snowboarder Lands Top Prize on Opening Night.*"

"At least they're clever," Paolo said.

"Not this one." Holly picked up a paper with the headline *LaCroix Adds Skier to Her Olympic Collection.* "They didn't even try to make a pun."

"I don't think this is helping anything," Corey said, setting another cup of coffee in front of her. She'd been so calm and steady over the last 72 hours. Julie's story broke early the morning after the opening ceremonies, and to her credit she'd managed to land her blow discreetly in a larger piece about how various ski competitors celebrated the start of the Olympics. She'd talked at length about how some skiers were sharing dorm rooms in the Olympic village, while others had rented a slope-side house together so they could focus on all skiing all the time. Then almost as an afterthought she'd slipped in that Elise was "the only American skier to have broken from the pack, choosing instead to share a private rental with her girlfriend, snowboarder Corey LaCroix and another snowboard racer."

Tigger had seemed a little torqued off to not even be named, but Elise had initially hoped such a small line buried deep in a mid-level piece from a mid-level reporter might go unnoticed amid all the other excitement. Corey's grim smile and sad eyes when she'd said it could've been worse told Elise she didn't share her optimism. And Corey's unspoken fears had come to fruition as the story caught like a fire to paper.

At first it spread slowly, little references online, followed by a brief mention on another bigger piece about athlete housing at the Olympics, but then the Austrians got ahold of it, and when the Austrian press got ahold of ski news there was no stopping the fire. By nighttime, the celebrity sites all ran stories on them as part of their attempt to "cover the Olympic games," though they didn't mention a single competitive result. The next morning every major LGBT outlet carried features on them, and by noon Holly had fielded interview requests from the *Today* show and ESPN. Elise's head swam with all the interest in not only an Olympic couple, but a gay Olympic couple. She could hardly fathom why anyone should care so much, but at least the initial inquiries were pleasant. Corey, however, remained steadfast in her insistence that they stay in the moment and focus on what mattered, which meant no personal interviews. Elise soon found out why.

By the next morning, everything had changed. The stories were no longer sweet little fluff pieces about a budding romance. They weren't romantic at all, or flattering. The tabloids had taken off, and the pictures they painted were tawdry. Every one of them suggested Corey led Elise astray. They treated her like some sort of cavalier Casanova who often wooed women and left them. Elise had been uniformly constructed as a good girl gone wrong, a woman in a weakened condition who'd fallen prey to Corey's good looks and charm to the point she'd put her own recovery at risk. All the reporters spun elaborate webs out of mere kernels of truth and fabricated tales of how Corey had blown off the X-games so the two of them could have an X-rated adventure in the Alps.

"Shouldn't we release some sort of statement?" she asked.

"No," Corey and Holly answered in unison.

"They're printing lies."

"And they'll keep printing them until a bigger story comes along," Corey said softly. "We need to ride this out. It's not important. Eyes on the prize."

Paolo's phone rang, and he glanced at the screen. "It's the publicist for the ski team."

"Again?" she asked, dropping her head into her hands. "How is it I don't hear from her for eighteen months, and now it's three calls in two days?"

"Good question," Holly said, pushing up from the table and taking Paolo's phone out of his hand. "One I intend to ask her right now."

"You?" Paolo asked hopefully.

"Yes, honey, but step outside with me so I can show you how it's done."

She then lifted the phone to her ear and headed for the door. "This is Holly LaCroix. I'm currently acting as the publicist for Ms. Brandeis. Any inquiries you have may be directed to me."

Paolo turned to Elise. "Is this okay? She knows more than I do."

She shrugged. "Yeah, fine. I should've hired her three days ago, but go with her in case they actually have some questions pertaining to skiing."

Corey snorted, but waited until Paolo left the room before putting an arm around her shoulder. "It's going to be okay."

"How do you know?" she asked, leaning into the comfort Corey's body offered.

"Because it always is."

"Always?" For some reason the word struck her.

"Yeah, every time something like this flares up, it seems terrible for a few days, and I freak out, and Holly springs into action . . ." Corey's voice trailed off as she must've noticed a change in Elise's expression. "What?"

"You've been through this before," she said flatly, wondering why the idea hadn't occurred to her sooner.

Corey's face flushed. "Not exactly this."

Elise grabbed the papers and sifted through them once more. All the allusions to *another* one, or going there *again*, or being added to a *collection*. They all implied a pattern of behavior, but since they'd blown everything else so wildly out of proportion,

Elise hadn't stopped to consider whether their previous knowledge of Corey's escapades had legitimately colored the lens through which they viewed her current situation. "You've had other scandals with other women, other athletes."

"This is hardly a scandal."

"Corey," she pleaded, "have you slept with other Olympians? Never mind. I know you have. The goalies, the bobsled team."

"I didn't sleep with the whole bobsled team."

"When, Corey?"

"Not since I've been dating you," Corey said, her tone shifting from sweet to defensive. "Not even since I've known you."

"During the last Olympics?"

A muscle in her jaw twitched. "Yes."

"And in Vancouver?"

"Yes."

"What about Turin?"

Corey sighed. "I understand you're upset, but you're being unfair right now. I never judged you for your illicit prep-school liaisons."

"My what?"

"You know, your little friends-with-benefits, trust-fund club where you trade sex like stocks and bonds with members only."

"Well, that sounded awfully judgey to me." Elise pushed away from the table.

"Only because you opened the door. At least the women I've been with were friends, or colleagues who I had a good time hanging out with. Not just people who happened to wear the same class ring."

"And I chose to surround myself with people who shared my background and an understanding of the pressure inherent in it. Women who were discreet and stayed above the fray, at least far enough to keep my personal life from being splashed across every trashy supermarket magazine in America."

"Really? Because, unless I'm mistaken, one of those blue-bloods did exactly that."

Elise froze. Corey was right. Julie had been her contact. Without her, none of this would even be an issue right now. And yet, the sense of betrayal at having one of her last bastions of respect and safety compromised didn't even rank compared with the thought of Corey sleeping her way through the Olympic village.

She sank back into her chair. "What are we doing?"

Corey sighed. "I don't want to fight. I don't want to go through this again, but more than anything, I don't want to put you through this. I'm so sorry."

Elise reached out and cupped her face in her hands. "It's not your fault. You're right. Julie did this. My contact. My fellow alum. I can't even imagine what would cause her to stoop so low."

Corey scoffed and pulled away. "I've got a few ideas, mostly having to do with her inability to accept someone of your stature slumming with someone like me."

"I'm not slumming with you."

"The rest of the world thinks you are. No, only half of them do. The other half think I'm some lesbian predator who seduces nice girls and gets them in trouble." Corey shook her head. "Maybe I am, or maybe I used to be. I never saw myself as predatory, but I used to think it was all a party. God, Elise, I won so young. When someone puts an Olympic medal around your neck at eighteen, you can't possibly understand what that means. Maybe you would have, but I didn't."

"No," Elise admitted. "I can't imagine you in that situation."

"Oh, I enjoyed myself, and everyone else around me enjoyed themselves, too. I went from being a boarder bum most people didn't want on their mountains to a household name. Then when it happened again four years later, this time with the gold, my world exploded." Corey paced now as she talked, her gestures growing more animated as she went. "I couldn't go anywhere without women throwing themselves at me, and I didn't say no nearly as often as I should have. I liked being liked. And I had more money and fame than I could figure out what to do with, so I threw it all around. Parties, women, some of whom ended up in my bed, some of whom ended up on my payroll. I had an entourage the size of a marching band."

"But Nate and Holly? You keep such a close circle now."

"I wasn't always like that. I was stupid. I got swept up in the circus. I kept making the big top even bigger. Then in Sochi, everything came crashing down."

"Fucking Sochi," Elise said under her breath. "Two-tenths of a second."

"I didn't even get that close," Corey admitted. "I washed out in the quarterfinals. The boarder in front of me bit it hard, and I hit her, and we both went down. Done. Over. Not even my fault. And I didn't even care. That's the bullshit. Nothing about me changed because all I only ever cared about was the next race. But suddenly the spotlight focused on someone else."

Elise reached for her hand, but Corey kept pacing in circles around the table. She'd never seen her like this, so wrapped up in the past, so full of regret and pain and perhaps something more fresh.

"The press turned on me. All the reporters who'd found me cute and endearing before labeled me reckless. While they used to see me as suave, they now painted me as a womanizer. Never mind those women all got a lot more out of me than I ever asked for in return." She shook her head. "Doesn't matter. It was never real. None of it. Nothing but the racing, anyway."

"How did it end?" Elise asked. She had to know, and not just for her own fear of being swept up into a similar cycle. She needed to know how the Corey in these stories grew into the woman before her now.

"My results went down with each passing season, and so did the interview requests. The whole 'drink water' thing pissed off the sponsors. I went from being a celebrity to a counter-culture hero to a washed-up has-been who now apparently spends her time preying on younger, brighter stars."

"Corey," Elise said softly. "You know that's not true, right?"

"Which part?"

"Any of it."

"Really?" she asked, clearly rhetorically, because she plowed right on. "You're on the rise. These stories in the papers should be about your comeback. They should talk about your triumphant return, the way you stormed back into the top of the pack."

"And they should talk about your results, too."

"My results have been shit. All reporters have asked me all season is when I plan to retire. They all see these Olympics as my swan song. I was stupid to believe I could escape all that, but this is your time."

"What about your time?"

"They all think my time is past. My story is set. They don't care about who I've become. I'm always going to be who I was at eighteen, but you didn't have to get sucked into that."

"I don't intend to. I'm not dating eighteen-year-old Corey. I wouldn't have liked her much. I didn't sign on for your past. I got invested in the idea of your future."

"You can't," Corey said quickly. "You can't go there anymore than I can go back and undo what I did. You have to stay in this moment. We have to live right here, right now."

"We have to think about the future at some point."

"No." Corey's voice sounded strangled and raw. "Haven't you learned anything from what I told you? Nothing's guaranteed. We have no idea what's coming next for us. It'll be what it'll be."

Something twisted her stomach again. Corey didn't see a future for them. She wasn't thinking about what came next. Her own trauma or fears held her back, or maybe she didn't want to go forward. Maybe that's why she insisted on answering every story with "no comment." If they did interviews together, she'd have to answer questions about the nature of their relationship, where they were headed as a couple, and she couldn't or wouldn't let herself go down that path.

"This story will be old news in two days," Corey finally said. "No one will even remember us rooming together in three months."

The sentiment did little to calm the doubt swirling in her. Where would they be in three months? What did her unwillingness to plan for their future mean? And perhaps more importantly, what did it say about Elise that she'd spent the first three days of the Olympics she'd worked so hard to reach dodging questions about a relationship Corey didn't even want to talk about?

"Hey," Holly said, looking up from her computer screen. "You're home early."

"I don't have anywhere else to go," Corey said, tossing her coat over the back of the couch and then crashing into it herself. "The men are on the boarder cross course today, so we can't get out there. I managed to get a quick workout in the athletes' village, but I can't eat down there or go for a walk without the press hounding me, and God forbid I try to go watch an event. I'm under fucking house arrest."

Holly closed her laptop and came to sit beside her.

"What?" Corey asked, scooting up until the back of her head rested on Holly's legs.

"I thought you might be ready to talk."

"Talk about what?"

Holly rolled her eyes. "Okay, maybe not."

"There's nothing to talk about." Corey folded her arms across her chest like a pouting child. "The press is acting like a pack of ripe assholes, like they do."

"And?" Holly pushed.

"And it sucks, but I can't stop them."

"You could make a statement."

"I shouldn't have to make a statement about my personal life. I'm sick and tired of having to defend myself to people who don't know me, who have never known me. I've only ever been some cartoon character to them. No matter how much I win, all they want to talk about is who I partied with afterward, and maybe I earned that early on, but I've worked hard to become better on and off the course. They don't care."

"Do you think you're really different now?" Holly asked.

"Of course I do," Corey fought off a little pang of hurt that

Holly would question her, too. "I'm training harder than ever. I'm surrounding myself with good people and serious athletes, not playgirls or party boys. And I've tried to do right by Elise, to honor her schedule and respect her dreams. I haven't even looked at another woman for seven months, and I haven't touched anyone else since long before that. I'm not the person the press keeps painting me as, and I'm tired of trying to convince other people of that. Fuck it, maybe I'm tired of everything."

"Have you told Elise any of what you just told me?"

"No," Corey said quickly. "I have to stay upbeat for her. She's already juggling so much. Did you know her dad actually threatened to come down here and handle things? Like she's fourteen or something."

"Yeah, at least Mom and Dad learned their lesson about traveling with us the first time they watched you sleep your way through the athletes' village."

Corey grimaced, another thing she couldn't take back no matter how much she wanted to. "I've made my mistakes. That's why we're in this mess, but this is Elise's big moment. She doesn't need me piling all my stress on top of hers."

"What about your big moment? In case you've forgotten, you're competing at these Olympics, too."

"It's not the same situation."

Holly flicked her ear, hard.

"Ouch, what was that for?"

"Because it's *exactly* the same situation. You and Elise are both Olympic athletes. You've both worked extremely hard to get here. You both have events this week. You're both under the same pressure on your respective courses, and you're both getting grilled by the press. Why are you the only one bending over backwards to make sure she gets what she needs?"

"I want to take care of her," Corey said, the familiar tightness returning to her chest at the thought of Elise hurt or under attack. "I wish I could protect her from everything, physically and emotionally. I want her to have everything she wants, everything she cares about."

"But does she want the same thing for you?"

"I'm sure she does," Corey said quickly, too quickly to let herself consider the question.

"Are you, Core? Don't get me wrong. I think she likes you a lot, but if she sees your career and feelings as important as hers, why are you the one making all the concessions?" Holly pressed, a steely glint firing in her eyes. "Why have you always been the one to change your plans for her? Why do you have to bite your tongue or dodge the topics that make her uncomfortable? Why do her stress levels matter more than yours? Why—?"

"Okay, okay. I get the point."

"I'm not sure you do," Holly said. "Your name's taking a beating in the press, and it's killing me, because I do know how much you've changed. But they act like you seduced her, when I know for a fact you never pushed her. Why's she letting you take the fall?"

"She offered to make a statement," Corey said weakly. "I told her no."

"Why?"

"It's different for her. You don't understand. She has to win. She has to be the best."

"That's all well and good on the slopes, but it's not how relationships work." Holly's voice softened, and she stroked Corey's hair. "It can't be about what one person needs. Everyone has needs, all the time, and for someone as driven as Elise, it's always going to be something, a gold medal, a world championship, a world record. You can't keep taking a backseat to her dreams. Even if you're willing to, she shouldn't let you."

"But, but I think . . . I'm in . . ." Corey's emotions welled up, making it hard to get the word out. "In love with her."

"Oh, Core." Holly laughed, then dropped a kiss on her forehead. "Of all the women in all the world at all the times, you had to pick this one? Right now?"

"I didn't mean to. I can't help it."

"I know," Holly whispered. "You've never done anything the easy way, and I admire that about you. I wish I knew for sure she was worthy of you."

Corey groaned. "All the newspapers make it clear she's out of my league."

"No. You said so yourself, those so-called reporters don't know you. You're strong and kind and loyal to a fault, which scares me, because I'm not sure Elise shares that quality."

"I'm sure she does."

"I hope so. I hope I'm wrong, but I think you're afraid she won't stand by you when things get rough. You're worried if it comes down to you or taking the gold medal, she'll choose the race. And you deserve better, Core. You can't give your everything to a woman who only wants you when she's winning."

She stared at the smooth, white ceiling of the rented cabin until she couldn't focus on even that anymore, then she closed her eyes, wishing she could close her brain for a while, too. She needed to slow down. She needed to back up. She needed time and space to deal with all the questions Holly'd asked and the emotions they stirred in her, but time was not her ally, and it hadn't been for a long time. Maybe of all the different stresses and pressures pushing down on her now, that one bothered her the most. No matter what she did or how fast she went, she couldn't manage to shake the feeling she was running out of time.

Chapter Seventeen

"Elise, Elise, Ms. Brandeis." The reporters mobbed her as they approached the athletes-only area of the downhill course.

"How long have you been with Corey LaCroix?"

"Are you monogamous?"

"How do you feel about Corey's past Olympic record with women?"

Thankfully they'd been prepared for the barrage and braced themselves before even leaving the house. Elise flipped up the collar to her heavy, down coat as security parted the crowd to let her through the competitors' gate. The constant assault of cameras and questions had followed them both to practice for the past few days. Elise's nerves were fried, but she hoped she could turn all that frustration into focus.

She flashed her credentials and pushed through the final security checkpoint with Paolo by her side.

"You okay?" he asked.

"Fine," she lied, and cut the most direct path to the tent where the equipment had been delivered.

"If you want to talk about anything, now's the time to do it."

"No, now's the time to focus on my race."

"Right," he agreed. "You can't drag any baggage onto the course with you. Time to check them, right here."

"I checked them before I left the house," she said, and for the most part she had. She'd kissed Corey goodbye and smiled when she'd told her to have fun out there. They'd kept the tone studiously light, like every other conversation they'd had for the past few days. They didn't mention the press, or the phone calls from sponsors, or emails from team USA officials. They didn't talk about what would happen after the race or after the Olympics. Everyone gave them a wide berth and seemed happy to join in their charade as they both play-acted at normalcy.

And yet, nothing had been normal. Nikki and her family had made themselves scarce, as they probably regretted the decision to share space by now. Nate worked extra hours under the guise of studying tape and course specs. Holly answered phone calls only outside, even with the temperature well below freezing. And Corey's jokes grew flat, her eyes distant, and her touch tentative. Even their kiss before parting ways this morning had felt uncertain. More than once Elise had noticed her staring off into space or pacing the back patio like a caged lion. Was she afraid of the future? Did they even have one?

"You need to get ready," Paolo finally said.

She blinked a few times and glanced around, reminding herself of where she was.

The Olympics.

Everything she'd worked for. Every bead of sweat, every tear shed in pain or frustration, every extra workout, every ice bath, every nightmare she'd wrestled into a dream led her to this moment. Why was she standing atop the most important course she'd ever run fixating on whether or not Corey wanted to be with her three months from now?

She roughly pulled on her racing suit and fastened her helmet. She couldn't afford any distractions. Her whole life had built up to today's race. Her body was as fit as ever, and she'd worked this course repeatedly, running it during the day, watching film in the evenings, and dreaming about it at night until she could've skied it in the dark. She picked up her skis from the tech and ran her fingertips over the bindings before visually inspecting the wax job. Everything met her standards, so she stepped into her boots and tightened them to her minute specifications. Then she stomped into the bindings and slid a few feet to confirm what she'd already known. She had everything she needed to succeed. The only things standing between her and victory existed in her own mind.

"Okay," Paolo said, coming closer again. "Turn three—"

"Banks away from the fall line, I know."

"And the flats—"

"Are getting softer as the sun hits them."

He nodded. "You've got this."

She stared at him, seeing her own fear reflected in his big, brown eyes. She snapped down her goggles to shield them both.

His phone buzzed, and he checked the screen, probably as eager as she to break the eye contact.

"Did they get through?" she asked, her heart rate ticking up a notch.

He nodded. "They got a seat near the officials' tent. The press can't get to them there, but they'll be able to see the big screen and the finish line."

Having Corey and the rest of the crew waiting at the bottom for her should've been the final piece in the puzzle for today's race. Instead it only ratcheted up the pressure. What if she let them down? What if she failed again? What if all the training and the press problems and the stress she'd put everyone through all added up to nothing in the end?

"You have to go," Paolo said.

She nodded grimly. "See you at the bottom."

He opened his mouth as if he wanted to say something, but either didn't know what or changed his mind. She got the message. No one else could save her now. The support, the training, the posse at the bottom of the hill, none of them existed for the next two and a half minutes. This was her mountain, and she needed to face it alone.

And yet, as she slid into the gate, she couldn't quite shake the weight of the world from her back. Everyone's hopes and dreams and futures hung on what she did now. How could she be alone and crowded at the same time? Had she come to rely on the others too much? Had she let their hopes get too intertwined with her own?

Beep.

Or worse, had she let her wishes for a future with Corey dilute the dreams she carried with her for decades?

Beep.

What if she ended up losing both?

Beep.

"She's got everything going right for her," Holly said, squeezing her right hand as Elise exploded out of the gate.

"Does she?" Tigger asked, clinging tightly to her left as Elise tucked into the first turn.

Corey didn't know, and she couldn't have spoken even if she did. Hell, she could barely breath while she watched Elise rocket down the course. God, she was going fast, but they all went damned fast. Who could tell the difference between seventy miles per hours and seventy-two? Her form looked good to Corey, but what did she know?

Elise blew through more turns at terrifying speed and whizzed past the halfway mark. The big screen overhead showed her as being a one-hundredth of a second off the leader's pace.

"She's close," Nate said. "She can make up time."

"But the flats are slow," Nikki said. "Come on, Elise, come on."

Corey wanted to turn away. She'd never been so nervous during her own races, but she'd never felt so helpless either. She thought her heart might beat through her rib cage for the desire to take Elise's place. Sweat pricked her skin and her muscles screamed from the tension. Did she put Holly and Nate through this kind of hell at every race? Surely not. Holly and Nate had never had anything like this invested in one of her races. So much of her life hung on that little clock ticking away as Elise roared down the mountain.

"Here she comes," Nate called, pointing to the place where the course bent into view from their spot in the stands. The location seemed so far away, and Elise looked tiny from the distance, but she also seemed even faster in real time. She flew over the last jump and somehow managed to tuck herself even tighter as she sped down the final drop toward the finish line.

The crowd went wild. All around her people screamed and cheered, but Corey couldn't even manage a squeak as her eyes locked on the same place Elise's sought with her own gaze. As the cloud of snow she'd kicked up wafted away, her final time flashed across the score board, and Corey's heart seized in her chest.

Elise's shoulders dropped, and she jammed her pole into the ground.

"Fourth," Nate said as the crowd around them let out a low groan.

"Well," Tigger said with false cheerfulness, "fourth out of sixty racers is still good."

"Not good enough for her," Corey said, her stomach roiling. "Will you guys excuse me?"

"Of course," Nate said. "We're going to kick around the mountain for a while. Maybe we'll even grab dinner out somewhere tonight."

"Probably a good idea."

"You guys could meet up with us later," Nikki offered.

Corey practiced her fake smile. "We'll see."

Holly gave her hand one more squeeze. "Love you."

"Love you, too," Corey said, then flashed her athletes' badge to get out of the stands at the exit farthest from the press corps, and headed back toward the house.

The walk wasn't nearly as long as she would've liked. They'd chosen the place because of its proximity to the ski course. They could occasionally hear a cheer go up from the crowd while standing on their back deck. Earlier in the week, she'd hoped the sound would inspire them both. Now she worried the echo would haunt her.

She had to stop a few times to wait for more security clearance, and then used a pass to get into the gated, slope-side community they called their home away from home. By the time she reached the front steps, a dark SUV pulled into the driveway behind her. Elise got out, slamming the door in her wake.

"Hey," Corey said softly.

Elise lifted her blue eyes, and looked right through her.

Corey's heart froze, and the frost spread quickly to her limbs. All the warmth was gone out of both of them.

"Come on inside," she managed to mumble. "I'll get a fire going."

"No," Elise said, her voice hollow and flat.

"No, you won't come inside, or no, you don't want a fire?"

"No, I can't do this anymore."

Corey's heart dropped into her stomach. "Can you please come in long enough to define 'this'?"

Elise nodded and followed her through the door but stopped in the foyer.

"I know you're disappointed," Corey said. "I know how hard you worked, and to come up short again has to feel terrible."

"It does," Elise said, "but it's not just today's race. I feel disoriented, like I don't know which way is up anymore. I can't focus on anything. The racing pulls me away from what's happening between you and me, while you take me away from the racing."

"You had a bad day," Corey said slowly. "Please don't set fire to any bridges because of one dark moment."

"This isn't the dark moment. This is the first time I've seen clearly in months. The dark moment came at the top of the mountain today when I couldn't see a future."

"You don't need to be thinking about the future right now."

"That's not true," she snapped, and Corey's temperature rose again, thankful for the spark of life she'd heard there. "This is exactly the time for me to think about my future. I've worked my whole life to get where I stood today. I should've felt like I was teetering on the precipice of greatness. I should've thought of the finish line as the culmination of the pain and the doubt and the pressure. I shouldn't have felt anything but anticipation of gold around my neck. But do you know what I thought about as the countdown ran out?"

Corey was pretty sure she didn't want to hear the answer, but she needed to know as much as Elise needed to say it. "What?"

"Losing, and not just the race. I thought about losing you."

The words hit her chest like a lance, but before she could even formulate a response, Elise pushed on.

"My dreams, my goals, all my work faded, and I worried about *you*. I worried about letting you down. I worried about the press's reaction. I worried about your complete unwillingness to look ahead with me."

"I begged you not to do that," Corey said, anguish creeping into her voice. All the effort she'd put into protecting her added up to nothing in the end. The frustration and exhaustion she'd fought to hold at bay seeped into her senses now. "I begged you to experience the race without obsessing about what comes next, but you can't do it, can you?"

"No." Elise exploded. "And I don't want to. I'm working toward a goal. I want to win, I want sponsors, I want my name etched in the record books. I haven't worked every day since middle school to shrug my shoulders and say 'oh well, those dreams didn't matter.' I want to chase them with everything I have in me for as long as it takes."

It's always going to be something. Holly's voice echoed through her ears. "What about what I want?"

"What?"

"You're upset, and I get that. You're venting, and I'm here to listen, to hold you, to bend the world to your will if I can, but it's unfair to blame me for derailing the dreams of your youth. I've gone through everything you have, the training, the press, the competition, and I've managed to stay in the moment. I haven't asked you to give me anything else. I haven't ever asked you to commit to me beyond right now. All I've ever asked of you is to be here beside me in this moment."

Elise shook her head sadly. "Maybe that's because this is the only moment you have left."

Corey winced and stepped back, all the air in her lungs sharp and jagged. "You're hurt, and you're lashing out. I'm going to give you that blow because you're scared."

"No. You're scared." Elise lashed out again. "Do you think I don't see it? Do you think the world doesn't see it? All your talk about living in the moment and shaking things up, the skipping events, the one-race-at-a-time mentality? You're grasping at straws. You don't let yourself think about the future because you don't have one."

Corey clenched her fists and set her jaw, but the anger that usually accompanied those gestures didn't come. Elise had landed a decisive blow, one she couldn't shake off. Elise didn't think she had a future. There was no coming back from a comment like that.

"You keep saying you want to stay in this moment, but every moment becomes the past eventually. At some point you have the face the future," Elise said sadly. "You're done, Core. You had a great career. You're an inspiration to so many people. You could be so many things if only you'd realize this part is over for you."

"And it's not for you," Corey finally managed to say through the pain. "That's the point, right? You still have another race. Another shot at glory. Hell, you've got other Olympics ahead of you. No matter what happens, you'll keep chasing your dreams. And you can't do that with me on your coattails."

"You think I'm upset about your riding my coattails? Do you really think so little of me?" Elise sounded hurt now, too, as if she was nearing tears. "You think I'm shallow and self-serving and snobby, just like everyone else. You never really had any intention of this lasting."

"I didn't say any of that."

"You didn't deny it either. Not to the press, and not to me." She shook her head. "You don't get it, do you?"

"Get what?"

"I love you, Corey. More than you'll probably ever understand."

"But it's not enough, right?" Corey finished the statement before Elise had the chance to. She could see where this was going. "You can't just be happy with me in the moment. You want more."

Tears glistened in Elise's blue eyes, but they refused to fall. "Yes. I do. I want more than this moment, Corey. I deserve that. I won't give up my future for someone who can't go there with me."

Corey hung her head and let her shoulders sag, the weight of everything she'd propped up finally crashing down around her. That was the end. She couldn't give Elise the future she wanted. She couldn't be enough for her no matter how much she tried. She couldn't will Elise's happiness. No amount of hope or humor or good nature could overcome the fact that Elise was alwaying going to be chasing something more. "Well, I guess that tells me everything I need to know then."

"Does it?" Elise's voice echoed the pain Corey felt ripping her apart from the inside. "You don't disagree? You aren't going to argue or put up a fight?"

"No, I have to let go," Corey said sadly. What was the point in arguing? Elise had already told her being in love wasn't enough for her. What more could either of them say? "I can't keep chasing you while you're chasing the gold medal. We both deserve better."

They stood there searching each other's eyes for a long time before Elise finally said, "I'll send Paolo over later to collect my things. I'll stay at the ski team house."

Corey swallowed the lump of emotions in her throat. "I guess it'll be easier for you to focus over there."

"I guess so." She didn't sound convinced, but Corey stifled the urge to reassure her. That wasn't her job anymore. Perhaps it never had been. And still, even in this moment amid the hurt and insecurity, she couldn't summon any malice toward her, because, deep down, she knew Elise was right. She was destined for bigger things than Corey could offer. The sooner they faced that, the better off they'd both be. "I hope you get everything you've ever dreamed of."

"Thank you," Elise said, then blinked a few times before

turning toward the door. On her way out, she managed to say, "I hope you can find something to make you happy in the long run."

Corey stood stock still and let her go, then pushing the door softly closed behind her, whispered, "I thought I had."

Chapter Eighteen

"Where do you want me to be?" Paolo asked, his eyes tired but sympathetic.

"Stay here," Elise said, as she pulled her goggles into place. "Stay the course."

That had been her motto over the past three days since she'd lost the downhill race. And that's how she insisted on thinking of it, as the day she'd lost the downhill, not the day she'd lost Corey. She'd never really had Corey. She'd have some fun with Corey and had mistaken it for something more, but it couldn't have been love, not if she was the only one feeling anything. She'd been ready to rearrange her future for a woman who'd only wanted some fun in the moment. The thought made her heart hurt all over again. She'd been ready to promise forever to someone who wouldn't even promise to be there two weeks from now. Even when she'd said she loved her, and waited, her heart twisting, practically begging her to return the statement, Corey's response had been that it wasn't enough to overcome their differences. The woman known for taking risks on a snowboard couldn't bring herself to take a risk on them as a long-term investment. Well, at least now she knew. No more doubts to drown in or to distract her from her goals. She had nothing left to do but win.

She'd trained obsessively, both in the gym and on the slopes. She'd met with ski techs and put in time with trainers and studied meteorology reports by the hour. She'd even removed an under-layer of clothing, despite the subzero wind chill. She hadn't quite gone skin-to-win, but close. Too bad Corey wouldn't be around to enjoy the results.

"No," she whispered, and checked the straps on her gloves one more time.

"No what?" Paolo asked.

"No distractions."

"Were you thinking about her again?"

"No."

"Right." He sounded as tired as she felt. She hadn't meant to put him in the middle of everything, but her moving out of the house had made it harder for them to train together, and her focus on video and statistics kept him out late and woke him up early. If the schedule had made things harder, or if the emotional turmoil between her and Corey had affected him and Holly, he hadn't let on. Honestly, she wouldn't have minded a short update on how Corey was faring, but what would be better, knowing she was miserable, or hearing she'd held up fine?

"No," she said again, then added, "sorry. I know I'm a bit intense right now."

"It's expected," he said.

"Because of a breakup? Because Corey's not waiting in the stands? Because she didn't think I was worth building a future with?"

He clasped a hand on her shoulder. "Because you're about to compete in an Olympic race that you've worked eighteens months to get to."

"Oh." She didn't point out she'd actually worked a lot longer than that.

He met her eyes. "You made your choice, Elise."

"Corey made my options clear—"

"No," he said firmly. "You made your choice. You could've made different decisions. There's always something else. You could've chosen journalism. You could've chosen business. You could've chosen to be a socialite or a trophy wife."

She rolled her eyes.

"You could have chosen to stay in the hospital bed a little longer. You could have chosen Corey, but you chose this. Over and over again, you picked *this* race. You can't have any of those choices back, not right now. You're out of choices. The only way to vindicate yourself now is to win."

She nodded solemnly. "At least I'm familiar with that kind of pressure."

"I don't know if that's more better or more worser, but I know you're a winner, at any cost, at all the costs." He stated the fact without a hint of pride or ounce of doubt. "Go do what you were born to do."

She hugged him quickly, then slid into position.

Rocking back and forth in the ruts, she couldn't help but see the connection to her life. Back in the groove, back to the familiar, back to a path that had been cut by someone else.

The gate judge motioned her forward, and she slid her skis between the starting posts. Only a thick, yellow wire separated her from her dreams. She stood mere minutes from ending the pressure. Ending the pain. Ending the crushing sense of doubt and inadequacy. Placing her poles carefully over the line, she fixed her grip. A sense of destiny settled over her. She knew the ending before she even pushed off. The race was once again hers to lose.

But she wouldn't lose. Not this time. Not in this way. The familiar demons were nowhere to be found, but a new chorus rose up in the back of her mind. Paolo was right. At every turn in her life, she'd chosen this path. She'd forgone a normal childhood. She'd let go of friends and relationships with colleagues. She'd sacrificed her body and riddled her brain with competition. And now she'd surrendered her heart, all for the next two minutes of her life.

God, what had she done?

Beep.

She couldn't think. She had to go. She always outran the voices in her head.

Beep.

Only this time the voice was her own. Could she possibly out-run even herself?

Beep.

Explode.

"Go, go, go," Nate shouted at the TV, and Tigger's voice devolved into a high-pitched squeal as Elise passed the final split marker. The line across the bottom of the screen flashed green.

"She's not losing time." Nate stated the obvious. "She's getting better."

Now even the announcers were shouting as she tightened her tuck and bolted toward the finish line. "She's ahead by a huge margin, folks. She might break the course record here."

"She's got this, dude. She's got it," Nate yelled, throwing his hands in the air. Nikki, too, began to jump and dance, but Corey couldn't even breathe until Elise blew across the finish line. She was going so fast she continued to travel at breakneck speed even after kicking her skis sideways, and she nearly broke all the way through the fence separating her from the crowd. Several of the reporters and bystanders had to reach across and prop her up.

Still Corey waited, heart beating painfully in her throat until the official time flashed across the leaderboard, confirming what everyone else had already begun celebrating. Elise had won. She'd blown the competition away. She'd set a new course record. The announcers chattered excitedly about how this would go down as one of the most dominant performances in Olympic ski history.

"She did it," Corey finally whispered. Then with a heavy exhale, she let go of all the tension she'd carried with her for days. Elise was an Olympic gold medalist, and she even had a world record to go with her win. Her name would forever be etched in the history books. At least Corey hadn't cost her that dream. Now she could move forward without some of the guilt that had plagued her for days. Of course, without the fear that she'd wrecked Elise's life, she now had more time and energy to focus on the fact that Elise had likely been right. Corey had been holding her back. Without the distraction of their ill-fated relationship, Elise had the freedom and the focus she needed to achieve everything she wanted in life.

Her stomach churned, and the room grew stiflingly hot. "I need some air," she mumbled to no one in particular and stepped out the sliding glass door to the back deck.

"Okay?" Holly called after her.

"Yeah," she lied. "I'm good."

Holly would listen. She'd hug her, tell her she'd made the right decision, and she deserved someone who would put her first. She'd done so several times over the last few days, but it'd never helped. She'd tried desperately to focus on the end of their conversation, to hang onto Elise saying she didn't want to risk her future on Corey, but she couldn't quite shake the reminder that the assessment had come only after she'd stated Corey didn't have a future of her own.

Watching her cross the finish line moments ago made Corey wonder for about the hundredth time if she'd been right. It certainly felt as if Elise had made the right choice at the moment. She'd be able to write her own ticket to anywhere she wanted to go from here. Corey would likely leave these Olympics in the same fashion in which she'd arrived. Even if she won, and lately she'd even begun to doubt her ability to do that, what would she gain? Mostly a win would buy her more time to keep doing the same things she'd always done.

Six months ago that would've been enough. When had that changed? When she'd started to lose? When the kid had left her in the dust? When Elise had come onto the scene? Or maybe when she'd left. There sure was a lot of losing and getting left behind over the past few months, and in a lot of areas of her life. Maybe that's where her discontent stemmed from. Nothing in the world bothered a racer more than being left behind. How had she let it become her way of life?

She glanced over her shoulder as her friends continued to

laugh and smile about Elise's win. Holly was on the phone and gesturing wildly, no doubt talking to Paolo. This win would secure his career for a long time, too. He'd no doubt get a handsome bonus and plenty of job offers, but she suspected if he had his way, all of those things would take a backseat to his quest to win Holly's hand in marriage. She didn't expect Holly to put up much of a fight, either. Her sister was ready to settle down, and Corey didn't want to think about life on the road without her, but she couldn't ask her to spend months away from Paolo, either. And what if kids came into the picture?

Kids. The term barely fit Tigger anymore. She was still every bit as bouncy as she'd been back in July, but she'd held her own, not only on racetrack, but also on the press circuit. No thanks to Corey, she'd been bombarded with questions and even a few nasty insinuations about her own sexuality, but she'd never taken the bait. She'd remained steadfast, both as a friend and as an athlete. Corey attributed part of her composure to her natural good nature, and the other part to Nate's guiding influence. He'd become a big brother to her as well as a coach and mentor. Corey always thought he'd fallen into his line of work because of their friendship. Only after watching him work with Tigger did she realize his experience, his values, and his ability to get the most from boarders while still respecting their dude culture would make him an asset on any team. Still, if given the choice, she suspected he'd rather work with Team Tigger than anyone else, maybe even her.

They all had futures. They all had their next steps lined up and waiting for them. The only reason they hadn't jumped yet was because of her. She rested her forehead on the cold wood of the deck railing and took a deep breath of the frozen air, but no amount of ice could cool the flames licking her cheeks now.

She was holding everyone back.

They would stay, of course. She didn't doubt their loyalty to her, but what about her responsibility to them? If she had some amazing plan waiting to be unfurled, some awesome adventure around the next bend, she wouldn't hesitate to sweep them up and carry them along with her, but how much longer could she ask them to hang around for the same old stale pattern even she had begun to grow weary of? Hell, how much longer could she ask that of even herself?

She didn't have the answers. She barely even had the energy to keep asking the questions.

The opening strains of "The Star-Spangled Banner" struck up loudly from the giant speakers over Elise's head, and the crowd went wild. An Olympic official unfurled a ribbon strung through the clasp of a gold medal. She watched it dangle, glinting in the white heat of the spotlight before she bowed her head solemnly and the official slipped the silky ribbon over her neck. A teenage girl with big, dark eyes handed her a bouquet of flowers and mumbled what she assumed was congratulations, but between the language barrier and the decibel level of the music, she couldn't be sure.

She couldn't be sure of much as people around her began to sing, "Oh say can you see . . ."

Nothing felt real. It was as if she were watching herself or even someone else on TV. She'd seen this sort of ceremony so many times, both in real life and in her dreams. She'd imagined herself on this podium, felt the weight of her worries replaced by the weight of gold hanging from her neck. She heard the crowd scream her name and saw the American flags wave throughout the crowd. She straightened and glanced behind her to see the Stars and Stripes rising high into the night sky. Everything about those dreams had come true, and she felt all the relief she'd hoped for. As they hailed the "twilight's last gleaming," her chest grew lighter, her head more clear, the tension gone from her shoulders, and yet that's where the change ended.

She acutely felt the absence of everything that had driven her, and yet nothing rushed in to replace it. She'd felt relief before. The first time she'd won a major race, the first time she'd walked after her accident, the moment she'd made the Olympic team, but the emotion had always been tempered by the understanding of the next fight. Now she stood at the pinnacle of the podium, and her heart no longer beat with that sense of challenge or purpose. It barely beat at all. Her whole core felt empty and void.

By "the rocket's red glare," she realized she'd never stopped to consider what might come in after the rush of accomplishment. She'd always assumed there would be something more, something better. Peace? Joy? Contentedness? Happiness? Where were they? Would they come in time? Maybe after all the newness wore off? Would she even recognize those feelings after living without them for so long? Then again, she hadn't lived without them completely. She'd experienced all those emotions on some level lately. She'd known peace with Corey and her family on Christmas day. She'd felt joy skiing across the finish line to find her waiting. She'd known contentedness in those nights when she'd fallen asleep in her arms after a full day of work and play. And she'd felt happiness, even in the little moments, an unexpected touch, the flash of her bright smile, the connection of their eyes across a crowded room.

Elise looked out across the crowd now as they tried in vain to hit the high note accompanying "the land of free." Between the bright lights of the stage and the constant motion of swaying, bundled bodies and waving flags, she couldn't make out any faces. Not that it mattered. The only face she wanted to see wasn't there to be found. Her empty chest seized. She hadn't gotten everything she wanted. Not really. She might have achieved all of the goals she'd admitted to having, the dreams she'd chased in the open, but deep down, she desired something more. She wanted someone to share it all with. Hadn't that been the point all along? She'd only ever skied to escape the pain, the division and strife. When had she let the race become the cause of the things she'd most feared?

Tears stung her eyes as the music faded, and this time instead of fighting them she gave in. No one would think less of her. They all expected her to be overcome with the emotions of the moment. Everyone watching in person and on television would suspect she'd been overwhelmed with pride and jubilation. None of them would believe she'd finally cracked under the burden of knowing, once and for all, that no amount of work or speed or accolades could change the fact that she was truly alone.

She waved to the crowd one time out of a sense of obligation, and allowed herself to be ushered off the stage. Everywhere, people offered praise and congratulations. Camera bulbs flashed, and she hoped she'd managed a facial expression resembling a smile, but she doubted it.

"Go to her," someone whispered close by, and she turned to see Tigger standing beside her.

Her eyes went wide, and a sea of emotions rushed in where moments earlier she'd felt only emptiness. "Where did you—? How did you—? Why?" She couldn't even form a complete question. Instead, she threw her arms around the girl and crushed her close.

They stayed there for a long moment as the kid made no move to pull away. She only patted Elise's back with one hand and squeezed her waist with the other.

"I can't believe you're here," Elise finally managed.

"I didn't want to miss it," Tigger said, standing back. "It was hard enough watching the race on TV."

"You watched the race?"

"We all did," Tigger said. "You should have heard us screaming. I thought Nate was going to have a heart attack. He's never that crazy during the snowboarding."

"Wait," Elise said, as the implications of the story sunk in. "All of you?"

Tigger's smile softened, making her seem older. "All of us."

Her heart beat faster again. She didn't know if she felt better or worse, though. She certainly hadn't earned that kind of loyalty. Not after the awful things she'd said.

"She looked like she was going to throw up until you crossed the finish line. And then—" She caught herself, her own allegiance to Corey likely stopping her from revealing too

280

much. It didn't matter, though. She didn't have to say Corey was being ripped apart. She'd seen the hurt in her eyes, watched her reel from the impact of the knife Elise had stuck in her chest. And yet she'd taken it. She'd been ready to forgive her, to give her a free pass, because she cared so much she was willing to take the pain for her, and still Elise had treated her like she wasn't good enough.

"It's not as fun without you in the house, you know?"

She shook her head, trying to stay with the conversation around her as the walls caved inside. "I was never the fun one. You snowboarders always had a better handle on good times."

"Yeah, well you're part of our family, no matter what. You belong with us. So, I thought now that you're done with the race and all, maybe you would come home."

Home. Family. Belonging.

She'd never had those words directed at her before, and she didn't feel worthy of them now. How could she go back after telling Corey she had no future? How could she ever make up for the choice she'd made? She wouldn't be a returning hero. She would always be the one who sold them out when times got rough. Wouldn't Corey forever feel like she'd taken second place to a cold hunk of medal? She couldn't undo the damage she'd done anymore than she could ski backwards up the mountain. She'd said herself, every moment becomes the past. She'd missed her moment.

"I can't," she finally said. "I can't go back."

Tigger hung her head. "I guess I sort of expected that, but I had to try. I better go now, though. I have a race tomorrow."

"Nikki," Elise scolded, sounding much more like a mom to the kid again. "It'll be after ten by the time you get back. I didn't even think about your race. God, what's come over you? How did your parents or even Nate let you out tonight?"

"I might not have told them I was coming all the way down here." She did a poor job of looking chagrined.

"You really are a snowboarder, aren't you? Always breaking the rules."

"Bending them," Tigger corrected with a grin so much like one of Corey's that Elise's heart hurt.

"Do you need a ride?"

"No, stay down here and enjoy your moment." She pointed to the gold medal. "I bet you can write your own ticket to anywhere you want to go tonight."

She doubted that. Where she wanted to go most wasn't available to her, and the medal wouldn't gain her access. It may forever be a symbol of the day that door closed. Still, the idea of access and tickets sparked an idea. "Actually, there's one ticket I'd like to have."

"Yeah? Which one?"

"Could you get me into the Snowboard-X finals tomorrow?"

Tigger's smile grew wide once more. "Sure. I mean, I could call Holly right now."

"No," Elise said quickly. "I'd rather she and Corey not know I'm there. I got to have my moment, for better or for worse. I don't want to intrude on Corey's."

"I think she'd be happy to see you."

Elise didn't want to disagree with her, but she couldn't take the risk. "I've caused enough turmoil for now. I'd rather not risk taking away from her day. I just want to be there."

"Sure," Tigger said. "I'll get them to Paolo in the morning."

"Thanks," Elise pulled her close and squeezed her tightly once more. "Now get out of here, and good luck tomorrow."

Elise watched her go with a slight smile on her face. Who would've thought the kid would end up being the one to say the right thing at the right moment? She hadn't exactly offered an answer, but a little bit of her hope and faith must've rubbed off, because Elise now had the chance to see Corey again. She wouldn't get to hold her or kiss her, or even try to offer any apology, but she would see her. She could cheer for her. She could begin to show her one ounce of the support Corey had lavished on her, and maybe, just maybe, she could do so without pressuring either of them to be anything other than exactly what they were in the moment.

It wasn't the kind of dream that had powered and sustained her for years. She wouldn't be a hero. If all went well, she'd be only an anonymous face in the crowd. She'd set the bar lower than ever and still had doubts about her ability to clear it, but damned if it didn't already feel better than standing on the podium all alone.

Chapter Nineteen

"She's still third," Nate said as the camera view switched from a high-banked turn to the flat section before a massive jump. "She's not going to pick up speed over the table top."

"She's got to get them on the turn," Corey said.

"She's got to set up better."

"She's got to go lower, off the jump."

"She's too amped up to kill speed."

"No." Corey slapped him on the back. "We worked on this with her."

"But will she be able to pull it off out there on the big stage?"

Tigger hit the jump a second behind the leaders and lifted her chest as both of the riders ahead of her curled into a tuck.

"There she goes," Corey shouted.

"Inside, inside," Nate called as if she could hear him down the course or through the TV screen.

The camera angle switched again, showing Tigger in the middle of the pack, rubbing elbows and edges as no one wanted to give way, but as they broke out of the turn and into the final stretch, she edged the nose of her board into second place and managed to hold on for dear life as they all broke the plane of the finish line.

"She did it." Corey stepped outside the tent and fell exhausted to the snow.

"Are you sure? Nate asked, still staring at the screen "They're going to replay it."

"No need," Corey said. "I know. I always know."

He didn't argue the point. Instead he followed her outside and sat down more gingerly. "She cut that too close for my liking."

"Yeah, but she did the right thing. Top two advance to the finals. There was no need to pull out the big guns yet."

"She raced a good race, technically, but she's going to have to do better in the final."

"Is that what you told her about me?" Corey asked, staring up at the bright blue sky.

Nate didn't answer right away, which told her everything she needed to know.

"It's okay," she finally said. "I know I haven't given anyone much cause to celebrate lately."

"Hey, you're in an Olympic final."

"Only because the two riders ahead of me crashed in the semi."

"You might have caught them anyway."

She rolled over to stare at him. "Why you blowing smoke, Nato?"

"I don't know." He shrugged. "They burned you out of the gate. You lost in the first three hundred yards."

"Does it hurt you to watch something like that?" she asked, honestly interested.

"It's a helpless sort of feeling."

"I never thought about it before, but watching Elise, and then the kid out there, it's hard work in a different kind of way."

He nodded. "It makes me feel like a parent sometimes. You can hold their hand for a while and teach them to look both ways, but you know someday they're going to have to cross a street without you, and you can't make them see the cars."

She stared at him, shocked at the amount of insight and emotion behind the comment. "Did you think I jumped out in front of a bus this morning?"

He grinned. "It felt a little bit like that, yeah, but you came out unscathed."

"Did I?" she asked, leaning back again. The cold of the snow seeping through her ski pants did little to cool the nerves burning up her insides. "What good does it do to earn a spot you didn't deserve?"

"What?"

"I didn't race well. I got in on a technicality."

"Bullshit." His tone changed from exhausted to angry. "The mountain giveth and the mountain taketh away, dude. When did 'deserving' ever come into play? You have to make the most of the chances you're given."

"Yeah, I guess."

"No." He kicked her boot lightly with his own. "You *know*. You fight back harder than anyone else out there, or at least you used to."

"Yeah, I used to fight. I have been great. I was—"

"Oh, fuck that." He swatted a handful of snow in her face. "I've stayed out of the whole Elise thing, because romance and women and not my business, but don't bring that weak shit onto my course."

Corey sat up and wiped the snow from her cheeks. "I didn't even mention Elise."

"You didn't have to. You've been moping around since she walked out on you."

"It's not that simple."

"It never is," he shot back. "Maybe you were an ass, maybe she was, maybe you guys suck as a couple, I don't know. But I do know the Olympics are a freaking pressure cooker."

She didn't argue with him there. "She and I have been in a pressure cooker from day one, and it's not going to change anytime soon."

"So?"

"Maybe I'm tired. Maybe I'm over it. Maybe it's not worth it anymore, but the thought of being under that kind of stress for the rest of my life isn't appealing."

"Who said anything about the rest of your life?"

"She kept talking about the future and all her plans and

286

dreams. Where does someone like me fit into that? I'm barely hanging on race by race here."

"Nothing lasts forever," he said matter-of-factly. "When you won junior worlds all those years ago, did you honestly think we'd still be doing this when we were thirty?"

"You're thirty-two."

He laughed. "Exactly. We've been living on borrowed time for over a decade."

"And what? Now it's over?"

"I didn't say that," he answered quickly. "I didn't even mean to imply it, but at some point we started thinking of this lifestyle as normal instead of always looking forward to the next adventure."

She didn't reply. When had the next race become some foregone conclusion? When had she started fearing what came next instead of charging forward to greet it with open arms? Why all the talk of endings and not anticipation of new challenges?

"Elise said I was scared of the future."

"Let me guess. She mentioned that while asking for some sort of commitment?"

Corey replayed the conversation. "No, she said she couldn't give up her future for someone who didn't want to go there with her."

"And then you said you did want to go there with her?" Nate asked as if it were the most obvious thing in the world.

"No, she said I didn't have a future. She said I was washed up."

"Ouch."

"Yeah, that one still burns."

"Did you argue with her?"

Corey shook her head sadly. "How do you argue with that? I honestly don't know what my future looks like, but it's clearly not as bright as hers. I couldn't ask her to put her life on hold while I figure my shit out. And now the difference between us is even bigger. She's got her medal now. She's going to be busier and more popular than ever, while I'm still a risky investment with no real future in sight."

"No future?" Nate asked. "You really got nothing after this?"

She rolled over onto her stomach, barely resisting the urge to bury her head in the snow. That was the million-dollar question she kept kicking farther down the line, but what did it matter? Corey hadn't been able to give Elise the assurance she'd needed when she'd needed it most. Maybe she'd been a coward in the moment, but that moment had certainly become the past now and she'd moved on.

"Dude, are you okay?"

She nodded slowly.

"Seriously? Because it looks like you might lose your lunch."

She sort of felt that way, too, but before she could answer, Tigger hopped off a snowmobile and made a beeline for them.

"The kid's back," she said, jumping up and jogging over to meet her. Nate followed close behind, and they both pulled her into a huge hug that involved a little bouncing and a lot of laughing.

"That was a hell of race," Nate finally said.

Nikki blushed and smiled. "I learned the little pull-back move from you guys."

"Damn right you did," Corey said proudly.

"But I didn't get the position I wanted into turn three. My line's not right," she said, then her eyes widened. "Not that I'm asking for help."

Corey and Nate exchanged a confused look.

"We're both in the same final," Tigger said.

"Oh," Corey said. She was right. They probably shouldn't talk about the course. In less than an hour they'd have to battle each other for the biggest prize in the sport, quite possibly Corey's last shot at that prize.

"I know you two have to make a game plan, and I'm not part of that," Tigger continued. "I can go now. I just wanted to say good luck."

Corey searched the emotions rattling around her chest. What did it all mean? Especially in the new light of endings, or the prospect for different beginnings. For the first time in her life, she let herself think about the end result, about a legacy, about the doors that would once again swing open for her with a fresh hunk of gold around her neck, and she wanted to win more than she ever had.

But at what cost? What price would she pay to cross the finish line first? Would she be willing to hoard Nate? Would she be willing to set herself not next to Tigger, but against her? What would something like that feel like long-term? Her chest tightened at the thought of turning another friend into an adversary, and she shook her head.

"Fuck that."

"What?" Nate and Tigger both asked.

"Once we hit the course, we're both going to ride our asses off, but until we get into the gate, we're friends first. Hell, we're family."

"Aww." Nate laughed. "You're getting mushy in your old age."

"Maybe I'm following your advice and thinking about what's going to make me happy in the long run. I already lost one person this week because I was afraid of the bigger picture. I won't do it again." Corey threw an arm around each of their shoulders and tried not to picture the tears in Elise's eyes as she asked if Corey intended to fight for her. "If I'm going out, I'm not going out scared. I'm going out on my terms."

Chapter Twenty

Elise flipped up the hood of her coat, a regular one, not the official team USA jacket. She also used the bright, clear day as an excuse to wear her sunglasses. She'd chosen jeans and a boring, everyday pair of snow boots. She didn't want to do anything to draw attention away from Corey or the main event. She even split up with Paolo long before arriving at the spectator section near the finish line, both out of fear he'd be recognized, or that he'd rather be with Holly than her right now. Lord knows, he'd earned some time off after the week she'd put him through.

Still, she felt alone and out of place as she scooted across the cold metal bleachers. She hadn't been able to shake the sense of isolation since her race the day before. Instead of getting better, the excitement all around only magnified her disconnect. Everyone had someone to share the thrill of the moment with but her.

"Elise," called a friendly voice, and without thinking she lifted her head. As soon as she did, she cursed herself and her damned, lonely impulses, because a young woman wearing a press badge holding a cordless microphone caught her eye.

The woman smiled broadly and practically used people's shoulders as stepstools to climb up through the crowd. "I knew you'd be here."

"Really?" Elise asked drolly, trying to remind herself she'd been pouting about being alone a moment earlier. In the future, she'd be more careful about the wishes she sent to the universe.

"Of course." The woman settled beside her, angling her body to face Elise instead of the course. "Do you mind if I ask you a few questions."

"I'd rather you not. I'm here as a spectator today."

The reporter either didn't hear her, or simply didn't care, because she nodded to a camera operator standing at the end of the row and pressed hard on her earpiece before leaning into the microphone and saying, "I've got Elise Brandeis here minutes before the women's Snowboard-X finals. Or I guess I should say, Olympic Gold medalist Elise Brandeis, right?"

She fought the urge to roll her eyes. She'd waited her whole life for the title only to have the phrase grate on her nerves. "No, I'm just Elise right now. I'm here as a fan."

"A fan of one finalist in particular, right?" The reported waggled her finely sculpted eyebrows.

"Actually, I'm friends with two of the finalists. I've trained with both Nikki Prince and Corey LaCroix."

"But rumor has it you're also dating Corey."

Her face flamed. She'd never had to answer questions about her personal life, and she certainly didn't want to start now, but she also couldn't bring herself to deny Corey publicly, not after all the other horrible things she'd already said. She shifted awkwardly in her seat. "Corey's a very special friend."

"Just a friend?" The reporter pushed.

"I wouldn't say *just* a friend, because that implies there's something lacking in her friendship. It's reductive, and anyone who's ever taken the time to get to know Corey realizes she can't be reduced to one term or another. She's an amazing athlete, a great training partner, a caring, kind, and thoughtful person who also has one of the strongest competitive drives I've witnessed."

"Stronger than yours?"

Elise shook her head. "Purer than mine. When she pushes herself or the people around her, it's because she loves what she does. She gives everything to the moment. She doesn't lose track of what's important. She doesn't let winning get in the way of who she is. She never asks what she has to gain or what she has to lose. She does what needs to be done, and she does it with a smile."

"Sounds like she's made quite an impression on you."

Elise sighed. "She has. I wish I were more like her. I let my priorities get way out of line."

"Obviously not too far out of line." The reporter laughed. "You have a shiny new gold medal to show for your efforts."

"A medal I wouldn't have won without Corey. I wouldn't have even made the team without her support, and it doesn't matter anyway."

"The medal doesn't matter," the reporter repeated slowly, her eyes wide in shock, as the camera operator made a hand motion for her to keep going. "If you could say anything to Corey right now as she gets ready to race, what bits of winning advice would you impart?"

She shook her head. "There's nothing I can tell Corey about winning that she doesn't already know. She doesn't need my advice. She doesn't need anything from me. She's out of my league. I hope she knows that, and I hope she knows *I* know that."

"Wow," said the reporter. "Quite a statement of *friendship* there. What's next for you after these Olympic Games?"

"I'm not focused on the future right now. I've already wasted too much time looking too far ahead," Elise said. "I want to make the most of the moment and try to show Corey one-tenth of the support she's given me."

"There you go, folks," she said, turning to face the camera, "Elise Brandeis living in the moment and cheering on Corey LaCroix in the Snowboard-X finals, as soon as we come back."

The camera operator lowered the lens to signal they were no longer live.

"Thanks, Elise," the reported said, hopping up. "I've got to get down to the finish line, but you were fantastic. The people back home will love it. You're made for prime time."

"Prime time?" she asked absently.

"Yeah. NBC, prime-time Olympic coverage."

Her stomach churned. What had she done? She dropped her head into her hands as the reporter crawled over several people to get away. She'd all but recited a love poem for Corey on international television. Corey, who didn't want to make a statement. Corey, who hated the press. Corey, who needed to focus on her race. God, why couldn't she do anything right? Every time she opened her mouth, she made things worse. Her only solace was Corey wouldn't see the interview until after her race ended.

Corey stared at the television screen in the tent long after the coverage had gone to commercial. She couldn't believe what she'd seen. The woman on the screen couldn't have been more different from the woman who'd walked out on her days earlier.

The gold medal didn't matter? Had she actually said that on national TV? She was here. She was in the stands. Corey's heart raced and her head spun to the point that her vision blurred. Elise hadn't given up on her. She told the whole world she had her priorities out of line. And yet she had her gold medal. Was it easier to come back for Corey after she already had everything else she wanted? Now that her future was secure on its own, she didn't have to worry about Corey getting in the way. And yet, an interview like the one she'd just given could certainly get in the way of endorsements and ad deals. She'd publicly tied herself irrevocably to someone the press saw as a hotshot, philandering, reckless playgirl. They would paint Elise as an airhead or a victim all over again, and after all the work she'd put in to change the story away from Corey and back onto her accomplishments.

She tried to run her hands through her hair, but she'd forgotten she had her helmet on. She'd forgotten where she was and what she had to do. None of this made any sense. She needed more information. She needed answers. She needed to get to Elise.

Turning around, fully prepared to make a break for it, she took only three steps before she ran into Nate and Tigger.

"Whoa." Nate grabbed both her shoulders while Tigger hooked an arm around her waist.

"Riders to your gates," an official called.

"It's time, dude," Nate said.

She blinked a few times, hoping to clear the haze from her head. "Time for what?"

"Your race," Nate shouted.

A wave of nausea surged through her. "I can't race right now."

"You have to."

"I have to talk to Elise," she said, as if stating her need for air.

"You can talk to her after."

"No. I have to go now. She's there. She's saying all these things. I don't know. Did you hear?"

"Yeah. She all but told the world she loves you and wants to have your little snowboarding babies. I hope you name them all 'Nate,' but right now you need to get into your gate."

"I'm sorry. I know what you're saying is right, but I can't process anything. None of this makes sense. She has her medal. She has everything she wanted. I have nothing. What if I'm like some Olympic parting gift and the next time things get hard she's going to dump me again?"

Nate opened his mouth to argue, but Tigger beat him to the punch, literally. She slugged Corey hard across her shoulder. "Pull yourself together, you idiot."

The comment was so uncharacteristically forceful it cut through Corey's rising doubts and panic.

"She's at the finish line, dummy. The quickest way there is straight down," she said, then spelled it out even more clearly. "Get. In. The. Gate."

Nate nodded vigorously. "She's right. Go, go go."

Corey nodded. Yes, the course. That was the best way down. She quickly ratcheted the board straps across her boots and hopped into place. She didn't think about her form or her position. Her body knew what to do, even as her mind fixated on the sole goal of getting to Elise.

A countdown must've occurred, but she didn't hear it. She didn't even see the other riders as the gates dropped. She sprang into action like an arrow from a bow, straight on a line to her target.

She must've made a great start, because she rocketed into the first turns with no one blocking her view. She took the lowest line around a giant s-turn and then leaned in to pick up speed toward a steep incline to a table top. Instead of tapping down onto the flat, she soared over the entire feature and curled low to regain her momentum before the next turn. She occasionally heard the scrape of boards as the other riders wrestled for position, but their presence was only relevant in the ways it might affect her line toward the finish.

She reached the rollers and effortlessly hopped the first two, then pumped her legs through the rest, feeling no pain, only purpose. Her muscles and joints felt years younger as she roared into the next set of turns. Only when she came out the other side did she catch the flash of a red-bibbed rider beside her. She didn't care about being passed, but if someone had made up ground on her, it meant she could milk more speed out of her run, so that's what she'd do. No one would beat her to Elise.

The wind whistled through her ear and bit at her face, but she bit back with everything she had, digging her edge in to break hard right as they passed the midway point. She established herself inside once more as she cleared another massive jump. Clutching her board in the air for stability, she wrenched her body into position to land, already leaning into the final series of turns. Weight on her back foot, she dropped down with a little thud, then immediately crouched low, both hands in front of her lead foot.

The crowd flew by in a blur as the noise from the finish line grew louder. She banked hard around the last bend, but not even the g-forces could pin her down. She felt weightless as the stands came into view. For a second she envisioned herself veering off-course, trying to flip up and over the grandstand railing like she used to do on the skateboard back home. The only thing stopping her was that she'd have to surrender speed to take that angle. Instead, she leaned forward once more, her eyes flicking quickly to the right, trying to find Elise, but the only thing she could make out through the wiz of the sidelines flying by was the front tip of Tigger's board.

She smiled broadly. Of course the kid kept up. She wouldn't want to miss out on an adventure. It was just the two of them flying toward a reunion, slicing through all the things that had come between them like their edges cut through the snow. If Elise could outrun her problems, Corey would outride their separation.

The finish line loomed large as they barreled toward the end, but she couldn't summon any sense of tension pertaining to the race. She wasn't in competition with anyone else in this moment. No grind, no press, no pressure. Everything was beautiful and purposeful and full of promise. She glanced down to see her board cross the red line in the snow, and laughed almost hysterically as the sense of peace washed over her.

She skidded to a stop and threw off her goggles as the joy poured out of her, laughter, tears, shaking muscles, heaving chest. She couldn't get out of her bindings fast enough, but when she did, she kicked the board aside and ran to the snow fence, then skidded to a stop at the edge of the grandstand, searched the excited, screaming faces until she found the one that had driven her down the mountain.

"Elise," she called when her eyes met the piercing blues she sought. She began to climb the safety railing like a ladder until she heard Holly shouting.

"Corey, get down. Don't kill yourself before you get the medal."

"Fuck the medal," Corey said and kept climbing. "I need to talk to Elise."

"She's going to get fined for saying 'fuck' on TV." Paolo laughed.

"She's going to break her neck," Holly said.

"Corey," Elise finally yelled, causing Corey to freeze and lift her head. "Stay there. I'll come down to you."

She watched as Elise worked her way down the bleachers with the help of fans parting ways and offering her a hand, or sometimes even a lift. She reached the walkway as Corey grabbed the top rung of the railing.

Elise caught her face in her hands and stared into her eyes. "You're insane."

Corey grinned. "You didn't mention that to the reporter."

Elise shook her head. "How do you know?"

"I saw your interview."

"Where?"

"Up top, in the tent, there was a TV."

"You were watching TV before a race?"

"I heard your voice."

"You should've focused on your moment."

Corey laughed. "I came all the way down here to see you, and I think I might've won a gold medal in the process. Are you scolding me right now?"

Elise's face turned a delightful shade of pink. "I'm sorry."

"It's okay." The width of Corey's smile hurt her cheeks. "You can scold me if you need to."

"No." Elise's expression turned serious. "I mean, I'm sorry for everything. All the awful things I said to you. Walking out the way I did. Instead of admitting how scared I was, I let you accept all the blame."

"Well, you were pretty harsh," Corey admitted even though she couldn't stop smiling.

"Worse than harsh. I was horrendous, and more importantly, I was wrong. Totally, one hundred percent wrong. What I had with you was worth more than a medal. I don't know if I can ever forgive myself for not seeing that sooner. God, everything I said about you should've been said about me. I was the one who was scared. I was stupid. I'll do anything to make it up to you. If you can trust me again, I promise I can do better."

"Well . . ." Corey drew out the word. "I'm glad to hear you say that, but I can't totally agree with you."

Elise hung her head. "I'm too late. I don't blame you for not being able to forgive me."

Corey shook her head, "That's not what I mean. I mean I can't agree with you being wrong about everything. You were right about at least part of it. I was scared of the future. I've never known a time without snowboarding. I've never had a five-year plan. And I didn't know if I could live up to all your ideals. I worried about dragging you down. Then the press agreed. They reinforced that I was over the hill and out of my league with you."

"The press is full of idiots," Elise snapped.

Corey laughed again. "We agree on that at least, but when you said my living-in-the-moment attitude was a way of not having to deal with my future, you were right."

"You have a bright future," Elise said. "Think about what you just did. You won."

"What I did had nothing to do with winning. I raced to you. I needed to see you and talk to you and touch you, more than I've ever needed anything in my life."

"Why?"

"Because I love you," Corey said seriously. "Because for the first time I want to think about the future so long as it's with you. Because snowboarding has never been about winning or records. It's always been about the thrill of racing toward adventure, and now you're my next big adventure. I don't care if all of this falls apart tomorrow, but I don't want to end up alone and without a purpose."

"You don't have to be," Elise said. "You're so good at so many things. You can do anything you want, and I promise, whatever you choose, you'll never face it alone. I meant what I said in the interview. I want to be there for you. I want to be there *with* you."

"But what about your dreams?"

"You're the best dream I wouldn't even let myself have. I want a future with you, no matter how much it conflicts with my schedule."

"Wow," Corey said. "That's a hell of a compliment. And I'm sorry I didn't hear it sooner."

"I didn't say it sooner."

"I think maybe you tried to, but I couldn't hear it through my fear, or maybe I couldn't believe you."

"But you believe me now?" Elise asked, her blue eyes hopeful even under the shimmer of tears.

"Yeah," Corey said, her chest light and her heart full. "I do."

Elise pulled her close, only the metal railing between them, and kissed her hard on the mouth. The crowd went crazy all around them, but as they pulled apart, Elise clearly said, "I love you."

"I love you," Corey shouted, then kissed her again.

Elise pulled away first this time, and wiping away the tears that spilled onto her cheeks said, "You need to go."

"What?" Corey's heart seized. "Why?"

She laughed. "Because you won an Olympic gold medal. I'm pretty sure some people are going to want to talk to you."

"Oh." Corey grinned sheepishly. "I guess you would know these sorts of things now, right?"

"I may have some newly acquired experience in that department," Elise said, finally giving into a cocky grin of her own. "Go on. I'll be here as long as it takes."

"I like the sound of that," Corey said, and started to climb back down the bleacher railing.

"No," Holly and Paolo both shouted from below.

Two Olympic officials ran toward her, and one of them offered her hand. "Ms. LaCroix, would you mind using the stairs this time?"

Corey nodded and let herself be pulled over the rail onto the metal walkway, then taking Elise's hand, gave her a little tug and said, "Come on. If we're going to do this the easy way, you're coming too."

Chapter Twenty-One

They'd threaded their way through the crowd and back to the finish line before Corey finally had to let go, but even as the ceremonies and celebrations raged on, she never got too far away. There had been hugs from Holly and Paolo. Then she'd picked up Tigger and twirled her around in a happy little dance before a few other competitors offered high fives or handshakes. Official and amateur photographers were everywhere, and Olympic officials scrambled to certify results all while arranging people for photographs.

"Were things this crazy when you won?" Holly said, sliding over to stand next to Elise.

She shook her head slowly. "Not at all."

"Snowboarders do things their own way."

"They do," she admitted, "but it was more than that. As soon as I crossed the line, I knew I'd gotten what I wanted, but it wasn't worth the price I paid."

"Good," Holly said.

Elise cocked her head to look at her. Her stubborn streak might have some family ties, because the set of her jaw and the glint in her eyes seemed eerily familiar.

"You know you hurt her, right?" Holly said.

"I do," Elise sighed. "I also know saying sorry isn't enough to undo that pain."

"It's a start," Holly said. "It also helps that you did well in your TV interview."

"Oh my God, did everyone on the mountain see that damn interview?"

Holly laughed. "No. I didn't see it."

"Then how do you know about it?"

"I'm the one who pointed you out to the reporter."

Elise eyed her again, unsure of what to make of that information.

Holly shrugged. "Corey said you'd been willing to make a statement before and she wouldn't let you because she wanted to protect you. I disagreed with that decision. I wanted to know if you were willing to go to bat for her the way she had for you."

"But how did you know what I'd say?"

"I didn't," Holly admitted. "I had my suspicions, but when push came to shove, I didn't know what you'd do. Honestly, I still don't know exactly what you said to make her come flying down the mountain like her ass was on fire, but it must've been good."

Elise smiled ruefully. "You're good at your jobs, all of them. Any chance you'd accept a new client, full time?"

Holly pursed her lips as if considering the questions as her eyes scanned the people in their immediate vicinity. "That depends."

"On what?"

"On what Corey says next." Holly tapped the young NBC reporter on the shoulder. "Would you like an interview with Corey?"

The woman gave her a "duh" sort of expression and said, "She's not an easy person to pin down."

"Tell me about it," Elise mumbled.

Holly didn't have any problem, though. She put her thumb and forefinger in the corners of her mouth and let out a sharp whistle.

Corey's head immediately lifted, and she jogged right over.

"Interview time, champ."

Corey's eyes fell on the reporter and her smile widened. "For you? Any time."

301

Within seconds Holly had arranged them with Corey's back to the finish line and Elise beside the camera operator's shoulder as she signaled to the reporter they were live.

"I'm here with our women's Snowboard-X gold medalist, Corey LaCroix. Congratulations on your win."

"Thanks, it was a meaningful one for me."

"Why's that?"

"A lot of reasons. Most importantly because I had someone special to share it with," Corey said, flashing one of those grins that drove Elise crazy, but then her smile grew softer and more relaxed as she said, "but also because this is my last season."

A murmur went through the crowd around them, but as Elise quickly turned to Holly, she saw none of her own shock reflected there.

"You're retiring?" the reporter asked.

"Why do you sound surprised?" Corey asked. "Reporters have been asking me about retirement all year."

"But you just won a gold medal." The reporter stated the obvious. "You proved all the naysayers wrong. Doesn't that make you want to keep racing?"

Corey shook her head. "I've never done anything because other people expected me to."

A few people around them laughed at the comment, but Elise's heart beat too rapidly for her to find levity in the situation. She silently prayed Corey wasn't doing this for her. As flattering as a sacrifice of that nature would be on the surface, she couldn't live with herself if she derailed her career or, even worse, if Corey had taken to heart her wretched comments about her not having a future.

"Well, then," the reporter started, but Corey cut her off.

"Sorry," she said, "but I see a frowny face next to your camera person, so I need to elaborate. I'm not throwing in the towel because I don't have anything left to give. I'm moving on to the next adventure because I've gotten everything I could want out of this one. I'm going out on top, on my terms. I'm excited about what comes next."

"Any idea of what the next adventure might include?"

Corey looked over her shoulder. "Hey, Tigger?"

Nikki looked up, and Corey nodded for her to join them, then throwing her arm around the kid's shoulder, she stared right into the camera and said, "America, here's your new silver medalist and the future of boardercross."

Nikki beamed and gave a little wave.

"Now to answer your question." Corey turned back to the reporter. "I honestly don't have any set plans for the future, but I'm going to follow this one's career with great excitement. I'm going to offer my special brand of insight to the youth team if the coaches will let me anywhere near them, and probably I'm going to watch a lot more skiing."

The reporter smiled. "Sounds like a good plan. Congratulations again on your win."

"Thanks," Corey said and flashed one more trademark grin at the camera before they signed off.

"Are you really retiring?" Nikki asked.

"Yeah, but don't sweat it. I'm probably going to drive you nuts with more advice than you want."

The kid shook her head so hard her little braids flopped over her shoulder. "I'll always want your advice."

"Good," Corey said. "Then here's the first piece. Go find Nate and make him a job offer. Do it right now before someone else does."

Her eyes widened. "Oh, yeah, great idea. I'm on it."

She ran off, and Corey watched her go before turning back to Elise, who folded her arms across her chest. "Will someone else offer him a job in the next ten minutes?"

"Maybe. I doubt he'd accept one from anyone but her though," Corey admitted. "But I had to get rid of her somehow so I could see what you thought of my big announcement."

Elise did her best to act aloof. "Which part? The one where you retired without talking to me, or the part where you said you didn't have any set plan?"

"What about the part where I said I'd be watching more skiing?"

The corner of her mouth snuck up of its own accord. "What makes you think the ski team wants a snowboarder hanging around?"

"Oh, I'm sure they don't," Corey said with mock seriousness, then stepping closer, added, "but I have great faith in my ability to win them over."

"I don't know. Skiers can be a standoffish breed."

"And snobby and cold and elitist."

Elise rolled her eyes. "What makes you think you stand a chance with someone like that?"

"I'm very charming," Corey said, then cupped Elise's cheek in her hand.

She sighed and leaned into the touch. "Yes, you are."

Corey kissed her lightly on the lips before giving her another one of those cocky grins. "And I like a challenge."

Acknowledgments

As I sit down to write the acknowledgements for my eleventh full-length novel, I'd like to first and foremost thank my readers, who have given me the opportunity to keep doing the job I love for this long. To everyone who has ever bought one of my books, written a review, or reached out to give feedback, without you none of this would be possible. I hope this book lives up to whatever standards you've come to expect from a Rachel Spangler romance because as the Olympic motto says, "Faster, higher, stronger," and that is what I strive to give you with each new book I write.

Next, to my Bywater team, thank you for doing everything you have to make sure my words are polished, presented, and published in a way we can all be proud of. Salem, MKM, Radar, and Kelly, most readers will never understand all of the work you put into each of our books, but I do, and you have my deepest gratitude. You continue to raise the bar in all aspects of lesbian fiction, and I am proud to be a small part of that process. And speaking of raising the bar, Ann McMan continues to soar over every hurdle I've set in the realm of cover design, and this time I set a few of them.

Toni Whitaker and Barb Dallinger are my beloved

friends and beta readers. I continue to be amazed by their tact and insight as they always ask insightful questions that help me see my characters in a new light. From them I send my baby on to Lynda Sandoval, who is part surgeon, part comic relief, part guru, and 100% the best friend any author could have. Despite nearly giving me a heart attack with this one, in a single porch therapy session she revealed more about precision in conflict than I thought existed. Lastly, my sharp eyes proof readers on this novel were a wonderful mix of friends and colleagues including, Cara Gould, Rebecca Cuthbert, Ann Etter, and Marcie Lukach.

And as always is the case, I am grateful for the daily emotional and professional support of friends and colleagues like Georgia Beers, Melissa Brayden, and Nikki Smalls. I might write faster without our constant chats, but I wouldn't write better, and I wouldn't be happier, so what's the point in that? I'd also like to thank my fellow Bywater Books authors, whose collective energy to learn more and do better has rejuvenated me in ways I didn't know I needed.

With this book I stepped into worlds I could only see the fringes of from my spot high up in the cheap seats. Thankfully I had wonderful guides who shared experiences I wouldn't have dreamed I'd ever have access to. My boardercross expert was none other than Olympian Jacqueline Hernandez. Despite the fact that I basically cold-called her with nothing more than "I'm writing about a snowboarder and I know nothing," she graciously answered a myriad of questions about training, schedules, rules, and diet. I can't thank her enough for taking time out of her extremely busy life to do so. Corey is both stronger and cooler for her influence.

On the skiing side of things, I put out a call for

help on Facebook, and a friend, Heather McEntarfer, put me in touch with legendary ski writer Hank McKee, who happened to be from Fredonia, New York, where I currently live. Hank enthusiastically jumped on board with the project, giving me not only answers to my questions, but an abundance of stories that came from decades of traveling the world with professional alpine skiers. He got to see an early draft of the book, and we spent a morning chatting about the great personalities of the sport. I will always cherish those hours with him, and the insights he shared touched every aspect of this book. Sadly, Hank never got to see the final version of the story, as he passed away November 5, 2016. I like to think he would have been proud of this book, because I am certainly proud of the role he played in it.

And, as usual, no acknowledgment would be complete without thanking the people who make it possible for me to chase my dreams daily. Jackson makes my life fun, grounds me to what matters most, and helps me look at the world with joy and wonder. He also helped me research this book by joining me in a mother/son snowboarding lesson, and not surprisingly, he's way better than me. Susan is more than my favorite ski partner. She is my strength, my fortitude, and my anchor. She lets me fly wherever my imagination takes me, secure in the knowledge I will always have a safe place to land. There's no way I can thank her enough, but I strive to keep trying every day, come what may.

And finally, every blessing I have comes not from my own hand or by my own merit, but from the God who is love incarnate. *Soli deo gloria.*

About the Author

Rachel Spangler is the author of eleven lesbian romance novels and novellas. She has won both the Golden Crown Literary Society Award and the Rainbow Award for her work. She lives with her wife and son in Western New York.

You can find Rachel on Facebook, Twitter, Pinterest, Instagram, and at www.RachelSpangler.com.

Previous Novels by Rachel Spangler

Perfect Pairing
Heart of the Game
Does She Love You
Spanish Heart
LoveLife
Trails Merge
Learning Curve

Darlington Romances:
The Long Way Home
Timeless
Close to Home

Bywater
BOOKS

At Bywater Books we love good books about lesbians just like you do, and we're committed to bringing the best of contemporary lesbian writing to our avid readers. Our editorial team is dedicated to finding and developing outstanding writers who create books you won't want to put down.

We sponsor the Bywater Prize for Fiction to help with this quest. Each prize winner receives $1,000 and publication of their novel. We have already discovered amazing writers like Jill Malone, Sally Bellerose, and Hilary Sloin through the Bywater Prize. Which exciting new writer will we find next?

For more information about Bywater Books and the annual Bywater Prize for Fiction, please visit our website.

www.bywaterbooks.com